# FATE & FURIES

HELEN SCHEUERER

FATE
&
FURIES

AN EPIC ROMANTIC FANTASY

THE LEGENDS OF THEZMARR
BOOK III

*For those full of rage,*
*Beware the fury of a patient ~~Delmirian~~ woman.*

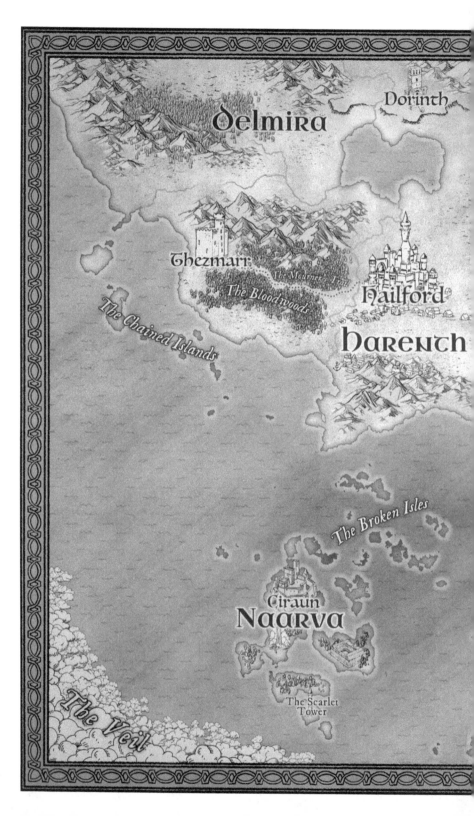

THE MIDREALMS

# PROPHECY OF THE MIDREALMS

*In the shadow of a fallen kingdom, in the eye of the storm*
*A daughter of darkness will wield a blade in one hand*
*And rule death with the other*

*When the skies are blackened, in the end of days*
*The Veil will fall.*
*The tide will turn when her blade is drawn.*

*A dawn of fire and blood.*

# CHAPTER ONE

## THEA

**B**lack blood splattered across the pristine snow, and the Shadow of Death whirled on her feet, carving into the next creature that attacked. In the burnt-gold glow of a freshly broken dawn, darkness leaked from its mouth, as though it was done devouring its host from within and was ready to seek another.

Howlers, they were called. Once men, they had been mutilated by the shadow wraiths, their voices stolen and replaced by blood-curdling howls, their bodies and minds no longer their own. Possessed and incensed as they were, there was no reasoning with them, not as they tried to spread their poison across the midrealms. A gurgling sound escaped the one Thea fought as she thrust her blade into his gut and split him from navel to nose. More black blood flowed.

Thea and her friends were outnumbered a dozen to three.

'Kipp!' she shouted in warning before letting her throwing stars fly.

He ducked just in time as blurs of silver soared through the air and pinned his snarling opponent to the nearby village wall.

With a nod of thanks, Kipp rushed to Cal's side, his sword raised, while Thea swung her own blade, decapitating another howler, his head hitting the ground with a thud, rolling across the snow. On instinct, she reached within for her magic, but it did not answer, not a flicker of the lightning that had once coursed through her veins. She didn't need it, she told herself, twirling her sword, bracing herself for the next attack.

It was not the first time they had come across these cursed men in their year of travel. Darkness had been bleeding into the midrealms since the battle of Notos, poisoning their world with its curse. With it came monsters of every kind. Not six months past, a wave of howlers had come through the various tears in the Veil, plaguing the lands of the midrealms, terrorising the common folk who had little with which to defend themselves. Thea was more than happy to have an outlet for her rage.

*'There are forces at work we do not understand... Things that threaten the peace the three kingdoms have fought so hard for... It creeps across the lands like a poison... A scourge of sorts, breaking through the Veil.'*

It was all because of him.

Wilder Hawthorne.

The fallen Warsword of Thezmarr.

Thea had been hunting him ever since his treachery at Notos, where he had freed the captured half-wraiths and aligned himself with the Daughter of Darkness, who had held Wren hostage in her shadows. Thea had watched Hawthorne spit in the face of everything Thezmarr stood for and flee in a swirling mass of shadow, setting their enemies loose on the midrealms. Because of him, the surge in dark forces breaking through the Veil had increased. Because of him, the wraiths and reapers had humanity at their mercy, their talons digging in deeper by the day. Daylight now only lasted a few hours and spring refused to bloom, even in the warmer parts of the midrealms.

Darkness was a plague on the world.

And it was Hawthorne who had released it from its cage.

'Bring him Thezmarr's justice... Do that, Althea Zoltaire, and his swords are yours,' the Guild Master of Thezmarr had told her, and she had taken his order to heart.

Thea hadn't stopped tracking Hawthorne across the kingdoms. He had fought her at every turn from afar, pulling out all the stops, leading her through swarms of howlers and wraiths. In the quieter moments, she wondered if it was more than him keeping her off his trail – if he was involved in a bigger plan to sow as much chaos and darkness through the lands as possible. He was a fallen Warsword; the depths of their treachery knew no bounds. But Thea slayed every monster he put in her path, and defended the common folk against the evil he spread throughout the midrealms. The calls for help were endless, and she would leave no cry unanswered.

Now, the villagers watched from their windows, their faces horror-stricken as the three Guardians of Thezmarr battled with the cursed men, the snow turning to black sludge beneath their boots, staining the icy hinterlands of Aveum.

Thea rolled, dodging a rusted blade and slicing the tendons behind her opponent's knees, still moving as he fell, dragging her Naarvian steel dagger across the fragile column of his throat. His blood sprayed, hitting her exposed hands in a warm flood before he dropped to the ground like a stone.

A cheer sounded from one of the windows facing the village entrance and Thea glanced up to see the men and women of the tiny town gripping each other in anticipation, shouts of triumph on their lips.

Thea ignored them and turned to the remaining opponents. Cal and Kipp battled a howler each, driving them back from the village, towards the edge of the frozen lake beyond. The cursed men were no wraiths, nor were they trained warriors, but the darkness made them strong and persistent, and Thea had seen that darkness spread like wildfire.

For a fleeting moment, she admired the improvement in Kipp's form. He fought far better than he ever had at Thezmarr, and while he still wasn't a natural, she liked to think her constant drills had helped.

She brought down three more of the enemy herself, before surveying the tainted snow, a bitter taste filling her mouth as she spotted their leader advancing on her. With a twirl of her blade, she readied herself and countered his attack, deflecting a thrust and pivoting, snow crunching, as she delivered a powerful strike to his side. With a beast-like grunt, her opponent blocked messily, only for her dagger to lodge in the soft flesh beneath his chin, driving up into his head. Shadows ripped from his mouth along with a wet, strangled sound. Thea kicked him away with her boot, extricating her blade with a firm tug.

'That's disgusting,' Kipp offered upon approach, wiping the blood from his own sword with a rag.

'Not as bad as that giant spider's web situation we faced a

4

few months back,' Cal countered, his nose wrinkling as he observed Thea's handiwork.

'I'll say. Still, not exactly how I imagined spending my name day,' she admitted with a grimace.

Kipp perked up at that. 'I'm sure the grateful people of this fine village would be more than happy to share their ale with their saviour,' he said hopefully. He'd been trying to convince her to celebrate for the better part of a week.

But Thea was already shaking her head. 'Can't. We've got to keep moving. I don't want to lose his trail in another snowstorm.'

They had tracked Wilder Hawthorne right to the doorstep of the village, right into yet another swarm of gruesome creatures. Thea ground her teeth as she scanned the bodies littering the snow. It was one of countless such instances they'd experienced. The fallen Warsword had led them on a wild goose chase around the midrealms, constantly throwing monsters between them, creating obstacles so he himself didn't have to face them. Ironhelm, Kilgrave, Wilton – Thea had lost count of how many places they'd scoured in their hunt for Hawthorne, but she'd gladly scour a hundred more if it meant vengeance would be hers. It had become her currency, her religion. If she closed her eyes, she could hear the creak of the bow as she drew the string back, aiming for the weak patch in Hawthorne's armour. But he vanished into shadow before she could survey the damage.

Both Cal and Kipp groaned at her determined expression.

'Thea,' Kipp implored. 'Give us one night out of this gods-forsaken cold. One night with a warm bed and a meal that wasn't made by Callahan the Flavourless.'

'How about *you* learn to cook,' Cal muttered.

'Cooking? Is that what you call it —'

But Kipp fell silent as the door to one of the huts opened and a small, frail woman cloaked in furs emerged.

She approached them with a look of reverence. 'Guardians of Thezmarr, how can we repay you?' she asked, her voice gravelly, her eyes bright.

'We were doing our duty,' Thea replied. 'There is no payment required.'

'We wish to show our thanks,' the woman insisted. 'Were it not for you, we might have faced the same cursed fate as those men.' She jutted her chin towards the bodies and black blood staining the snow. 'Might I offer rooms —'

'We're not staying. Though if you're willing, we'll take some rations for the road.' Thea sighed at the crestfallen look on Kipp's face. 'And some ale, if you have any to spare,' she added.

'Of course, of course,' the woman gushed. 'Anything for the Shadow of Death and her right-hand men.'

Kipp's face lit up at that small kindness, but Thea suppressed a flinch.

*The Shadow of Death* was a name that had been thrust upon her as she walked in the footsteps of her former mentor, *the Hand of Death*. There had been an all-too-brief pocket of time where she'd accepted it with pride, but now? Now she loathed it, loathed that despite all she had achieved on her own, she would always be connected to him.

The Great Rite had not called to her yet, but according to the common folk, her reputation preceded her. It didn't sit right with her. Until she captured Wilder Hawthorne and brought him to justice, until she passed the Great Rite, she didn't agree with such a title. It followed her around the midrealms nevertheless. But alongside the reverence came the scrutiny – for why *hadn't* the Shadow of Death captured the traitor? It had been a year since his betrayal in the woodlands of Notos, a year of hunting him down to no avail. Thea had heard the whispers herself.

She addressed the woman again. 'We're looking for someone. A warrior on a black Tverrian stallion. We tracked him to your gates.'

The woman tugged her furs around her against the chill as she nodded. 'Aye, a man like that came through just yesterday.'

Thea's heart rate spiked. 'Did he stop? Did he speak to anyone?'

'No. And we kept well enough away. As you can see, our village hasn't had much luck. We leave strangers alone and hope they're not cursed.'

Flexing her grip around her weapons, Thea fought to keep her voice calm. 'Which way did he go?'

The woman pointed through the ramshackle buildings layered with snow, to a forest that bordered the outskirts. 'He rode straight down this path here and into the woods. We've seen no sign of him since. But those cursed men came soon after...'

Thea nodded, already itching to get back on her horse and run Hawthorne down. She was closer than ever to the treasonous bastard now, and she would not let him slip through her fingers, not this time. Taking a steadying breath, she wiped her blades on the tunics of the dead, sheathing them at her sides.

'You should burn them,' she told the woman, motioning to the corpses.

The villager bowed her head. 'We will. We will light the

pyre in your honour and pray to the Furies that the Moonfire Eclipse brings peace to the midrealms.'

'Much obliged, ma'am,' Cal cut in, clearly sensing Thea's patience wearing thin.

Thea shook her head as the woman went to retrieve their rations. 'That damn eclipse...' she muttered.

The entire midrealms was in a frenzy about the upcoming celestial event, and the trio was yet to meet someone who didn't hold out hope that it would be their salvation against the dark forces lapping at their shores. According to Kipp, the Moonfire Eclipse only happened every century and symbolised a great shift in the magic of their world, wherein light triumphed over darkness. Ever since the battle of Notos, the rulers of the midrealms had bolstered the importance of the event and the people had rallied to their cause. In just a few short weeks, the kings and queens of the remaining kingdoms and their nobles were due to arrive at Vios, the capital of Aveum, to celebrate the occasion in the face of the impending darkness.

Thea shifted on her feet, feeling restless.

'We're close,' Cal reassured her. 'Right on his tail.'

'Exactly,' Thea murmured. 'I don't want to lose the ground we've gained. He's somewhere out there, laughing at us.'

Kipp shrugged. 'He never really struck me as the laughing type.'

'He didn't strike me as the traitorous type, but here we are,' Thea said bitterly.

She should have known he was too good to be true, but she'd let her feelings cloud her judgement. He'd made her believe he'd *loved* her, and for what? To get close to an heir of

Delmira? To collect her secrets and report back to the enemy? She'd been a fool.

'I'm going to get the horses.' Without waiting for a reply, she trudged to the village gates where they'd tethered their mares.

The unrelenting sadness came in those quieter moments, with the scent of leather in the wind, with the sight of Hawthorne's tin of peppermint tea sticking out of her saddlebag. Cursing colourfully, she untied the horses. All the midrealms were in uproar over his betrayal, even twelve months later, and though she wore the same mask of anger day in, day out, the sorrow beneath that surface grew taut. Sorrow for what she had lost, including the flicker of hope she'd had for the future. Sorrow for Malik, who had lost his brother to the very things that had taken his livelihood from him —

'If you want to go, let's go, Thea!' Kipp called loudly, jumping from foot to foot. 'I'm freezing my fucking balls off. Why is it always so damn *cold* here?'

'Frost giants,' Thea replied, before remembering who'd told her that.

'What?'

'Nothing,' she muttered, tugging the horses along, ignoring the whip of wind that swept across the lake behind her, the thick layer of ice creaking and groaning. The frigid air bit at her cheeks and nose as she reached her friends, and she felt a twinge of regret that they wouldn't be lounging before a roaring fire come evening. But there would be time enough for that once the traitor was in chains.

At the thought, Thea gave her pack a quick pull, hearing the metal clink within, feeling instantly reassured. Though she hadn't seen her sister since she'd left Tver, Wren had stayed in touch through a series of letters: updates on the assassin's teapot she'd invented and on Sam and Ida's latest shenanigans, the recipe for Thea's contraceptive tonic, which she still took religiously, and then later, a package that had found Thea and her friends in Kilgrave, Hawthorne's hometown. A set of iron manacles, treated with alchemy that made them unbreakable to a Warsword... Manacles Thea would clamp around Hawthorne's wrists before she dragged him to the rulers of the midrealms to face trial for his crimes.

Thea removed them from her pack now, clipping them to her belt. She'd need them soon enough.

'*Who's going to stop you?*' Hawthorne's words echoed in her mind like a distant song.

'No one,' she muttered to herself. 'Least of all you.'

# CHAPTER TWO

## THEA

Beneath their horses' hooves, snow crunched like broken glass, the only sound to permeate the eerie silence of the forest. The outskirts of the capital, Vios, should have been teeming with wintry woodland life... and yet they were desolate, a graveyard of trees closing in. The centuries-old evergreen pines were dead, and above Thea and her companions, the canopy was barren, naked branches reaching up into the sky like skeletal fingers, more evidence of a cursed and dying world. Cold seeped through every layer of clothing, causing an irrepressible shiver to take hold of Thea.

Early morning light filtered through the treetops, casting a pale blue hue over the frosted landscape before them. The air was so crisp that Thea could taste the ice on her tongue. Frozen streams and icicles hanging from rocks greeted them, and for a moment the midrealms were suspended in time, the stillness of the woods almost hypnotic. But time could not freeze. Thea knew that better than anyone.

Her fate stone warmed against her skin as she rode. She'd

cast the fucking thing into the seas, only to have it find her again hours later. No one could escape fate, or time. She was living proof of that as her name day dawned around them: another year closer to twenty-seven, the age where she'd be wiped from the world.

'Do you know any Warswords who were granted immortality during the Great Rite?' she had asked him once.

'Tell me that's not why you're doing all this? Tell me it's not why you want to become a Warsword? Because you want to live forever?'

'I want to live longer than two and a half more fucking years.'

Thea could have laughed. *Make that one year*, she thought darkly. Hawthorne had told her he'd take her to one of the rare immortal Warswords if she mastered her magic. They'd both failed in that regard. He'd broken his vows, and she'd lost her magic entirely.

In the aftermath of the battle of Notos in Tver, it had ebbed away, despite Wren having removed the suppressant alchemy from her fate stone. For whatever reason, her connection to the storms had severed. Once she had felt them like beacons in the long, dark night, but now... now, there was nothing. Though she hadn't admitted it to the others, she missed the magic sorely, like a piece of herself had vanished and she wasn't entirely whole. She still found herself reaching for it, expecting to feel its spark within, only to remember how empty she was. Even now, thunder rumbled in the distance, and yet she felt nothing.

The Great Rite seemed further away than ever, along with any chance she might have of skirting her fate of death at twenty-seven.

'You're ready, you know.'

'Ready?'

*'For the Great Rite. When you feel its call, you go. Drop everything and go. You will emerge a Warsword. The very best of us.'*

The words had been spoken on the blood-soaked battlefield in Notos, where she'd truly earned the name *Shadow of Death*, so sure she was on the cusp of feeling the Furies' call. For so long she had imagined wielding a Naarvian steel blade of her own and riding a Tverrian stallion across the midrealms. She had pictured accepting the gifts from the rulers of the kingdoms with her head held high: the vial of springwater from Aveum's Pools of Purity, the mysterious vial of poison from Harenth... And though the armoury of Delmira stood no longer, she had the designs for Warsword armour stashed safely in her pack and had sworn to find a master armourer worthy of the task.

Cal and Kipp's voices wrenched her from her thoughts. They were debating something behind her, getting louder and more insistent with each passing moment.

'For Furies' sake,' she muttered, twisting in her saddle. 'What is it now?'

'Nothing,' Cal replied quickly.

'It's not nothing,' Kipp countered with a disbelieving shake of his head. 'That storm ahead got us thinking. We were just talking about your magic.'

Thea's stomach rolled. 'What about it?' she ground out, setting her eyes back on the trail ahead.

'That you haven't used it,' Kipp said. 'Not for a long while now. Not for a year.'

Thea sighed, warring between frustration and weariness. 'I told you, I can't.'

'Can't, or won't?' Kipp pressed.

'Leave it alone, Kristopher,' she warned.

'We have. For months we've kept quiet about it, but now...' Thunder cracked in the near distance again, but he forged on. 'Well, we're almost caught up with Hawthorne. Don't you think you might need to use your magic against him?'

Thea's teeth ached as cold air whistled between them with her sharp intake of breath. 'I'm not talking about this.'

It was a sore subject. Through Wren, Audra had gifted Thea a small box of meditation cards to help her train her magic, but no matter how hard she tried, no matter how many countless hours she spent studying them by the fire, not even a flicker of power had answered her summons. There was one card she carried on her person, one whose words she would chant to herself over and over. The card itself was faded and crumpled from being clutched in her dirty, clammy hands, but the message was seared into her memory: *strong of mind, strong of body, strong of heart.*

Sometimes she suspected she was none of those things, and that was why her magic had left her.

'We're not letting you get away with this anymore, Thea,' Kipp interrupted her thoughts. 'Cal, back me up here.'

Cal sighed. 'Your magic has always manifested when you're angry, right?' he asked her, urging his horse up alongside hers.

Thea shot him a glare. 'I'm always angry.'

'No shit,' he muttered.

'Thea, we've seen what you can do. That kind of power isn't just snuffed out overnight,' Kipp said gently.

Thea clicked her tongue in frustration. 'Well, I'm telling you that mine was. Can we drop it now? We've got a traitor to capture.'

'So you keep saying, but without magic, how in the

realms do you think you'll get those manacles on him?' Kipp argued. 'You may be the Shadow of Death, but Hawthorne is the *Hand of Death*... and traitor or not, he's still got a Warsword's power.'

Cal made a noise of agreement. 'If you tapped into your magic, I think you could cause a thundersnow if you put your mind to it. That'd catch a Warsword, no problem.'

'First, he's no Warsword,' Thea snapped. 'Second, sure – I haven't used magic in a year, but I'll just tap into it and whip up a fucking thundersnow, shall I?'

Kipp snorted a laugh. 'Pfft – even when you and your magic are being more agreeable, I doubt it. There hasn't been one recorded in centuries, not even in the depths of Aveum winters.'

'It's always winter here,' Cal griped.

'Which is exactly why I think we should go to the Singing Hare, just for a —'

'We're not giving up our advantage for you to go get drunk in a tavern,' Thea retorted.

'But... it's your name day.'

'Precisely. So *I* get to choose how I spend this day, and all my limited days to come. And I'll spend them well. Hunting my enemies and bringing them to justice.'

Kipp shook his head. 'You used to be fun,' he muttered.

But Thea had stopped listening. 'Look!' She pointed to the coals of a small campfire a few yards ahead. 'He camped here.'

Kipp's brow furrowed. 'Seems like a stupid spot to camp. We're hardly an hour into the woods.'

'We've been running him ragged. His horse is probably in need of rest – doubt he had much of a choice in the matter.'

Thea jumped down from her saddle and investigated the

nest of now-frozen ashes. There, around the rocks, were deep bootprints in the snow.

'We're gaining on him.'

'Thea...' Kipp said, his voice serious this time. 'We've just ridden through the night and slayed a dozen cursed men. I can't speak for Cal, but my generally useless arse isn't up for a battle with a Warsword. We need to rest. We need to regain our strength before we take him on.'

The truth of his words hit her hard in the chest. She clenched her jaw. 'We make the most of the daylight and ride until nightfall. Then we'll rest. How does that sound?'

'Deeply unpleasant.'

'You can have my share of the ale...' Thea offered.

Kipp gave her a sideways glance. 'Keep talking.'

She laughed. 'That's it. That's my offer. Take it or leave it.'

'You drive a hard bargain, Highness.'

Thea shuddered. It had been a long and hard road to learning her true identity as one of the lost heirs of Delmira, the fallen kingdom. Harder still had been discovering that not only did she and Wren have an older sister, but that this so-called sister was the one they called the Daughter of Darkness, the evil prophesied as the bringer of fire and blood. That she and Wren came from a royal family of power-hungry traitors and shadow-lovers.

*'Beware the fury of a patient Delmirian.'* Malik had spoken those words to her a long time ago now, and when Thea first thought she understood them, she'd assumed they were in reference to her. But she'd been wrong. It wasn't her who Malik had been talking about.

With a start, she realised the others were waiting for her response. 'Piss off,' she quipped, and started forward in earnest once more.

'Not very princess-like!' Cal called after her.

Thea urged her mare to quicken her pace. 'I'm not a fucking princess,' she shouted back.

True to her word, as dusk fell around them, Thea begrudgingly allowed them to stop, handing her flask of ale over to her eager friend. Exhaustion settling deep into her bones, she made her way through the dense forest, searching for a suitable spot to set up camp and finding an alcove that offered a small reprieve from the biting wind. While the others gathered kindling and wood, Thea tried to create a level surface for their tents, her fingers aching in the cold. She knew it would make more sense to share a tent with her friends given the freezing temperatures, but she simply couldn't bring herself to do it. The last tent she'd shared had been with *him* after the battle of Notos.

*'I need you,'* she had whispered.

*'You have me. Every part of me belongs to you...'*

Lies. So many lies. And she'd believed them all. Was he laughing at her out there? At how easily he'd gotten under her skin? At the apprentice he'd fucked and thrown to the wolves?

'Should have stayed in the village,' Cal moaned as he returned and began preparing the fire, holding his blue-tinged fingers over the weak flames and blowing air into the kindling.

'Blame Thea,' Kipp said, cheerfully taking a swig from his flask after tending to the horses.

'Oh, I do,' Cal replied, holding his hand out for the ale.

Thea watched her friends quietly as she finished setting

up her tent, wishing she could find that sense of ease once more. But her mind was troubled by thoughts of the fallen Warsword, of fate stones and daughters of darkness, of a tearing Veil and a world on the brink of destruction. And so she ate her rations in silence and retired to her tent, leaving Cal and Kipp to their ale and bickering.

'Wake me when it's my turn for sentry,' she said, closing the flap behind her and lighting a small lantern.

With more vigour than she intended, she unbuckled and unlaced the outer layers of her armour, hating that *he'd* been the one to give it to her. Every time she put it on, she was plagued with the memory of him kneeling before her, his touch skimming across her body as he strapped her into it. A small part of her had considered getting rid of the set for that reason alone, but it was too fine a make, too good a fit, and she'd never find a decent replacement on the road. So every day, she wore it with resentment, and every time it saved her from bodily harm, she cursed Wilder Hawthorne anew.

Even after she had removed the most cumbersome parts of her armour, Thea feared sleep wouldn't come easily. It rarely did these days. She busied herself with Audra's meditation cards, reading over the mental exercises her former warden expected her to do while she hunted down a traitor. Thea nearly laughed at that. It was exactly the sort of thing Audra would expect. She was a hard-arse, if there ever was one.

She shuffled the cards. Each was the size of her palm, the corners bent, the surfaces smudged with grime and soot, the ink bleeding on some of the ones she'd dropped in the snow. It hardly mattered. She knew most of them by heart now.

Thea closed her eyes and tipped her face towards the

ceiling of her tent, taking a deep breath. *Strong of mind, strong of body, strong of heart,* she told herself. She didn't know why, out of all thirty cards, that one had resonated with her the most. But when those words were echoing in her head, she somehow felt less broken, as though there were some small hope in the world that she might put the pieces of herself back together. It was a brief reprieve from the hollowness inside, where the kernel of her power had once bloomed.

In the privacy of her tent, she sought it out again, night after night, to no avail. She combed through the lessons she'd had with Audra and Wren.

*'What does your lightning and thunder tell you?'* Wren had asked in Notos.

'I am the storm...' Thea muttered now. But with every utterance of those words, that empty space ate away at her, a constant nagging sensation from the deepest part of her soul.

With a quiet curse, Thea stuffed the cards back in her cloak pocket, her fingers brushing against the other item she couldn't seem to leave alone. The sapphire she'd taken from Hawthorne's effects before she'd left Notos.

The brilliant blue gem gleamed in her palm. Of all the things for her to take, she found no rhyme or reason to another woman's jewel making it into her possession.

*Adrienne.* Not that Thea cared, but that had been the name of the lover before her. Apparently, they shared the same bad taste in fallen Warswords. Thea sent her silent commiserations.

With her fingers growing more numb by the second, the cold drove her to her bedroll and blankets. The air was so chilled that the additional layers didn't do much to ease her shivering. But Thea curled up on her side anyway, clutching her fate stone to her chest.

'Remember me.'

The words of the seer came back to her. But Thea could only recall the words alone, nothing of who had whispered them to her in the dark as the piece of jade had been pressed into her palm.

She had tested the fates time and time again. She had tossed the cursed stone into the sea, only for it to find her once more.

'Fate always finds its way,' she muttered to herself bitterly, and prayed to the Furies that sleep found her first.

Gentle fingers grazed her neck, leaving a trail of fire in their wake, followed by a whisper of cold, a pulse of longing in their absence. Naked, Thea arched her back, seeking that intoxicating touch. And she found it as hot lips closed over her nipple, teasing it into a hard point while firm, calloused hands closed around her thighs, spreading them wide.

A familiar weight pressed against her and she moaned in relief. It had been so long. Her whole body was ablaze, every nerve ending alive and ready to be utterly frayed with pleasure. But the pressure of another body was fleeting, and Thea writhed as mouth and tongue moved to her other nipple, teeth scraping gently, causing her to buck in frustration, in demand. She raised her hips, seeking the friction she so desperately wanted between her legs, her core aching with need.

A deep chuckle vibrated against her heated skin, only

driving her closer to the brink of insanity. She needed to be filled, needed to feel every inch of him.

But she wasn't met with the powerful thrust she craved. Hands holding her open all the while, the mouth on her trailed down, in a long, tortuous lick, to the juncture of her thigh and hip, then blew cool air on the most intimate part of her, teasing her, leaving her wet and wanting.

Thea held her breath, waiting for the touch she knew would send her hurtling towards bliss-soaked madness, into oblivion.

At last, his thumb dragged through the slickness at her core before circling her clit, eliciting a shameless moan from her. She was molten with desire, with the feverish need for him —

Thea cried out, her fingers spearing through his soft hair as his mouth closed over her. Her body answered to every stroke of his tongue as he flattened it and licked her from bottom to top, again and again, before sucking on her clit.

Heat swelled between her thighs, tingling and unbearable in the most addictive way. That coil of longing wound tighter and tighter, and she gasped as he slid a thick finger inside her, his tongue still working her.

Arching her hips towards the building pressure, Thea moaned again through the haze of lust as a second finger joined the first, hitting a spot deep inside her as he lavished her.

Her climax hit in a blinding wave of white, barrelling through her like an unyielding storm. As she shuddered through the final spirals, she opened her eyes to see broad, sculpted shoulders and a muscular back... Whorls of black ink covering golden skin and ancient words tattooed down his spine.

*Glory in death, immortality in legend.*

She knew then that she was dreaming. But beneath the warmth of him, she didn't want to wake up. Not yet. She dreamt of the man Wilder Hawthorne had once been to her, his powerful presence, his deep, melodic voice whispering secrets to her in the night.

*'This thing between us is endless. Nothing will stop me loving you.'*

She dreamt of his fingers, his tongue and his cock, of all the wicked ways he could use them. She dreamt of his strong arms guiding her own, the weight of twin swords in her hands as they trained for dual wielding. His gentle touch, soaping her hair as he washed it when it pained her to do so. His laugh, rich and deep, when he finally allowed himself to relax...

*'Because I fucking love you.'*

The words careened into her, and the weight of his body fell upon her own, crushing her to him, his lips finding hers, whispering her name against her skin.

Thea lurched awake with a gasp, the air clouding before her face, her palm pressed to the hammering in her chest. The dreams had been so visceral that she swore she could smell him, traces of rosewood and leather lingering in the tent. For a moment, she breathed in the scent wrapping around her, that deliciously masculine essence she had once known so well.

She swallowed hard, trying to force her heart rate back to normal as the memory of the fallen Warsword faded.

But the scent of him did not abate.

And as she scanned the tent, she saw why.

At the entrance was a small box wrapped in brown paper, a lightning bolt drawn across its surface.

*Hawthorne.* He'd been here.

With a scream of fury, Thea snatched it up and burst from her tent, startling Cal, who was still sitting at the fire.

'Where is he?' she shouted. 'How did he get in my tent?'

Cal blinked at her. 'What are you talking about?'

'Hawthorne! Hawthorne was here!' She waved the small box at him, looking around the campsite wildly. 'Where the fuck is Kipp?'

'On watch…' Cal looked at her as though she were going mad. 'Thea… I think you must have been having a nightmare.'

'Then what the fuck is this?' she exclaimed, shoving the box into his chest, noting that not only was there a lightning bolt sketched across it, but three little words as well:

*Happy name day.*

A taunt.

Rage roiled within Thea, her heart racing once again, beating almost painfully against her ribcage as short, shallow gasps took hold. Her whole body tensed, her fists clenching at her sides.

For a year she had hunted him, had chased him all over the midrealms, had slayed every monster in her path, save for him. Now, here he was, proving that she was as incompetent as the whispers said. He had snuck past Kipp on watch, past Cal at the fire and into her tent to leave this barb at her feet. She hadn't even woken until it was too late. Some would-be Warsword she was.

Cal was turning the object over in his fingers with a frown, and Thea snatched it back to examine it herself.

*Happy name day.*

For the briefest of seconds, her pathetic heart wondered

if it was a true gift, rather than an insult. But it was beyond unfathomable.

With an enraged cry, she threw the box with all her strength into the dark, icy forest, towards the half-frozen river.

'I'm going to kill him.'

# CHAPTER THREE

## WILDER

W ilder Hawthorne slipped back through the frozen
forest like a ghost.

Forcing one foot in front of the other, he left Thea
behind, an ache settling deep in his chest. He hadn't been
able to stop himself from watching her sleep, just for a few
moments. She'd been bundled in layers of furs and blankets
against the icy night, so he had only glimpsed her face. He
had seen her sleeping countless times before, but what had
struck him in the soft glow of her tent was that she looked
different. It had been a year. An entire year since he'd looked
upon her closely. Now, he noticed, the lines of her face
didn't soften in slumber, but somehow seemed sharper, as
though she carried the anger of her waking hours into her
dreams.

There was a time when Wilder would have slept beside
her, held her in his arms until her body melted against his
and her nightmares were kept at bay... but those days were
long gone.

Snow crunched in front of him suddenly. Wilder's hand flew to his sword —

Kipp held his hands up in surrender, his auburn hair flopping into his eyes. 'I know you could kill me before I draw another breath.'

Wilder scanned the Guardian for weapons. Slowly, he removed his hand from the grip of his blade. 'Don't raise the alarm.'

'Wouldn't dream of it,' Kipp replied, his long arms falling to his sides. 'Did Thea see you?'

Wilder stiffened at the sound of her name on the lips of another. 'No.'

'So why the midnight visit?'

'I had something important to give her.'

'A traitor bearing name day gifts, how lovely,' Kipp retorted.

Wilder bit back a growl. 'There's more to this than what you see.'

'I should fucking hope so,' the Guardian said boldly. 'I wouldn't have let you get into camp otherwise.'

Wilder swallowed the lump in his throat. 'How is she?'

'She wouldn't want me talking to you, let alone about her.'

'You're loyal,' Wilder observed. 'Good. I'm glad she has that in her life.'

Kipp crossed his arms. 'No thanks to you.'

'No thanks to me,' Wilder conceded, shoving his hands in his pockets.

Something unreadable flickered across Kipp's face as he seemed to war with himself. Which meant now was the moment.

'Why hasn't she used her magic?' Wilder asked bluntly. There was no way to sugar-coat it.

Kipp glanced back in the direction of the camp. 'Who says she hasn't?'

Wilder hesitated. When they'd been together, he'd been able to feel Thea's power. The hum of it called to him like a song across the seas... but he hadn't felt it for a long while now. At first, he'd assumed it was because their connection had severed over the year of separation. But the lines of worry gracing Kipp's face now confirmed what he'd started to suspect, what he feared...

'It's gone?' he asked.

'Hawthorne, I can't tell you —'

Wilder drew a sharp breath. 'You just did.'

Kipp shook his head, looking lost. 'She won't talk about it, but —' His expression twisted. 'I shouldn't be telling you anything.'

'Why are you?' Wilder asked.

'Because I don't believe everything they say about you... Perhaps that makes me a fool.'

'Perhaps it does.'

Kipp kicked the snow. 'I'm far too clever to be a fool.'

'So I've heard. And your friends?' Wilder pressed.

'Cal's following Torj's orders. Thea's too hurt to see that this is much bigger than you.' His light tone changed to something sharper. '*You* hurt her...'

Wilder didn't respond. Neither man moved, the air growing colder around them by the second. In the near distance, a shout pierced the night. Thea had found his gift, it seemed. He had to get out of there, had to get back to his horse and on the road. News of his findings needed to reach the right people, at the right time.

But Kipp was still staring at him, neither calling out to the others nor moving from his path. 'You're bleeding,' the Guardian told him at last.

'What?'

'Your nose.'

Wilder's brow furrowed as he lifted a hand to his nose, his gloved fingers coming away coated in red.

'Here,' Kipp said, holding out a kerchief.

Wilder accepted the scrap of fabric, blotting the blood from his face and cursing the lone howler that'd managed to get a blow in just before he'd been carved in two. Wilder made to pass the material back to Kipp, but the young man shook his head and finally stepped aside.

'Keep it.'

'A favour from the Son of the Fox?' Wilder raised a brow. 'I'm flattered.'

'So you should be. You'll be needing it before long, Warsword.'

Hearing the increased commotion from the camp, Wilder had no choice but to give Kipp a nod of thanks and push past him. There, he left his hunters to face the frostbitten dawn ahead.

The secret underground tunnels were hardly warmer than the icy climate of Aveum, but at least Wilder was out of the wind. With his stallion, Biscuit, in tow, he travelled far, navigating the twists and turns of the passageways with ease. It certainly wasn't the first time he'd needed to utilise the network beneath the midrealms, and he'd wager it certainly wouldn't be the last. He could do so just as well without the blazing torch he held before him, but after so much darkness, he had hoped the flames might offer a touch of comfort in the deep night.

They didn't.

Thea had lost her magic.

There was no more lightning at her fingertips, no thunder in her heart. Wilder couldn't imagine her without the chaos of magic in her celadon gaze, and yet, he knew it was true. He could sense its absence.

There was one less storm wielder in the wretched world, and it was a loss that would shape the war to come.

The weight that had been sitting on his chest like a boulder intensified at the thought of all the plans in motion, all the moving parts of the rebellion happening in the shadows, and how he was now a part of it. Whether she liked it or not, Thea was too. She had been since the very beginning, which made it all the more vital that he got to his destination.

Wilder kept guiding his horse through the passage. The torchlight flickered, illuminating the rough-hewn walls and ceiling carved from the stone, a path travelled by many fugitives and misfits before him. Around him, the air was damp and musty, an earthy scent permeating the passage. The only sound was the soft nickering from Biscuit as they moved across the uneven terrain. It gave Wilder too much time to think.

He had been content once, slaying monsters across the midrealms and answering to no one. But now he mourned a different taste of life. True happiness had found him for a brief pocket of time.

Flashes of memory assaulted him, snatching the air from his lungs.

In the grand rooms of the Hailford palace, Thea, quaking beneath his touch. *'I've got you,'* he whispered into her hair, holding her tight to his chest as a sob escaped her.

*'And I've got you,'* she said... lowering herself onto the length of him.

The hot springs on the outskirts of Notos, and Thea breathing hard before him. *'A woman can do all of that?'*

*'Not any woman. There is only one. There has only ever been one.'*

Thea tracing the contours of his face, her lips teasing his. *'Remind me that we're alive. Promise me that as long as we're together, and our friends are unharmed, that's all that truly matters.'*

Wilder rubbed at the ache in his chest. It had always been temporary. He'd known that from the start, but the knowledge hadn't made it hurt any less. Fate was fickle like that.

Shaking the thoughts from his head, he turned another corner, willing the journey to be over soon. He wanted to warm his feet by the fire, remove his ill-fitting armour and taste some decent wine, perhaps enough to forget for an hour or so. He might even be spared a moment or two to write to Malik, as he had done every month over the past year. Though, without Thea there to read to him, he wasn't sure if Malik would understand his messages, and he'd had no replies. Probably just as well. The last thing he wanted was to get his older brother caught up in his mess. He'd done enough damage in that department as it was.

Hours passed, and at long last the terrain inclined, eventually leading to the surface, where a small inn and stables waited on the edge of the great frozen lake.

Tethering Biscuit to a post outside, Wilder pulled his hood up around his face and entered the inn, the door swinging closed loudly behind him. Warmth from the roaring hearthfire wrapped around him like a welcome heavy blanket. It was a rundown old place that only travellers and fugitives frequented – a stopover point between real destinations, a location most Aveum folk would happily avoid. It suited Wilder perfectly. But as he entered, he realised it was much busier than usual, with every booth, every table full.

It was the fucking eclipse. People from all over the midrealms were flocking to the winter kingdom to bear witness to its greatness, hoping it would offer a glimpse of the Furies' intentions of fighting against the impending darkness. There was so much excitement and celebration that even the shithole inns in the middle of nowhere were fully booked.

Suddenly wary, Wilder knocked the snow from his boots on the doorframe and entered the bar, keeping his hood up, already on edge. But no one paid him any heed. Here, he was just another patron looking to drink away the fear of darkness and find a warm body for the night. That much was consistent about humanity, at least. Even in the face of death and destruction, they always turned to the same comforts and vices.

Pushing his way to the bar, he signalled to the man behind the counter, just as someone shoved into his side.

'Watch where you're standing,' a ruddy-faced traveller barked at him.

Wilder's nostrils flared at the disrespect, but no one knew him here, and he wore no Warsword totem on his right arm. He was a nobody, and the man was just a drunk.

'What you staring at?' the man slurred, attempting to poke Wilder's chest.

A drunk who didn't know when to shut up.

Wilder snatched his finger in a bone-breaking grip. 'I'm in no mood for horseshit like this tonight,' he growled. 'And it's been a while since I broke a man's nose. I'm feeling that inclination more furiously all of a sudden.' His fingers itched for violence. It would offer an outlet for all that raged within him, and the prick deserved it, his eyes now bulging at Wilder.

'Your drink, sir,' the barkeep called with perfect timing.

Wilder dropped the patron's finger and slid a coin across the countertop, nodding his thanks and turning back to the rest of the inn. Ignoring the spluttering apologies of the man, he glanced around until he spotted who he was looking for, and approached her table at the far end of the bar.

'How long have you been here?' he asked, voice low as he slid into the booth opposite the beautiful woman with long blonde hair.

The general of the fallen kingdom of Naarva's guerrilla forces gave a pointed look to the several empty tankards in front of her. 'A while.'

Wilder huffed a bitter laugh. 'Glad you've been staying out of the cold and drinking your fill.'

'Someone's got to do their part for the midrealms,' she replied, draining the last of her current drink and raising a single brow, amused. 'No wine tonight?'

Wilder gave the filthy, raucous tavern a pointed look. 'Read the room.'

This only seemed to amuse her. 'You're even moodier than I remember, Hawthorne.'

'There's a lot to be moody about these days, Adrienne,' he

retorted, tossing back his drink and reaching for the jug between them.

'A lot to be grateful for as well, I'd say. Reunions with old friends, for one.' She bumped her tankard against his.

'We were hardly friends,' he said flatly.

Adrienne laughed. 'I was being polite, you sour bastard.'

'Don't remember you being that polite, either.'

She sat back and studied him. 'Glad to know some things don't change.'

Wilder shook his head. 'What news do you have?'

'You want the good or the bad?'

'I didn't realise there would be any good,' he said gruffly.

'The good news is that with Notos still rebuilding and recovering after the battle, there has been little to no talk among the rulers or remaining Warswords of hunting down supposed heirs to fallen kingdoms. The common folk have too many mouths to feed and are too busy boarding up their houses against howlers to go bounty hunting. Any talk of heirs that occurred before Tver almost fell to the reapers has died down... for now.'

'And the bad news?'

'Everything else.'

'Care to be more specific?' Wilder growled.

'You've been travelling the same lands as I have, Hawthorne. You've seen the darkening of the midrealms, same as me,' she replied. 'We've lost count of the tears in the Veil now. Monsters of all kinds are creeping through, being found in the most unlikely of places, as though they're being planted there...'

'*When the skies are blackened, in the end of days... The Veil will fall. The tide will turn when her blade is drawn...*' Wilder murmured.

Adrienne passed a hand over her face with a grimace. '*A dawn of fire and blood*,' she finished. 'The prophecy is a fucking plague in itself.'

'Something we agree on,' Wilder replied.

'I'm glad to hear it, because you won't like what I ask next...'

Wilder nearly groaned. 'Then don't ask —'

'How did it go with your storm wielder?'

He tensed, his grip tightening around his tankard. 'She's not mine.'

Adrienne rolled her eyes. 'Could've fooled me, Warsword.'

'I'm not a Warsword either. Not anymore.'

Adrienne simply waited, her arms folded over her chest expectantly. Wilder almost laughed. She hadn't put up with his shit years ago either.

'We've got a problem,' he admitted.

'Oh?'

Wilder glanced around the inn for prying eyes and eager ears. 'It was as I suspected.'

'You know this how?'

'According to her friend, Thea hasn't used her magic, not in a long while.'

Adrienne's brows shot up. 'How long's a while?'

'He didn't say. But he seemed concerned.' He loosed a breath. '*I'm* concerned.'

Adrienne scanned the bar as well before lowering her voice. 'Her magic is important. We're going to need it in the war ahead.'

Wilder suppressed the urge to shift in his seat. The general didn't know the half of it, didn't know about the fate stone that hung between Thea's breasts, her life ticking away before her eyes. But that was her secret, and Wilder would guard it with his life.

'It's not just her magic that's important,' he said instead. 'It's her. All of her.'

Adrienne scrutinised him. 'Wasn't she able to summon storms when she was with you?'

Wilder heaved a sigh and ran his fingers through his hair. 'That was before.'

'Before what?'

'Before I betrayed her.'

Adrienne's expression softened, and she reached across the table, covering his hand with hers. 'That doesn't mean all hope is lost.'

Wilder pulled his hands back sharply, out of her grasp. It had been a long time since anyone had offered him any sort of comfort or empathy. He didn't deserve it.

But the general didn't seem fazed. Instead, she pinned him with a determined gaze. She was relentless. 'Thea needs her magic, Hawthorne. She needs *you*. We all do.' Adrienne sat back once more and topped up his tankard with the last of the ale. 'It's not like you to give up. Anya and the prince wouldn't want —'

'He's not my prince.'

Wilder ran his fingers through his hair and rolled his shoulders, hoping to ease some of the tension that felt like solid stone down his back. There was no relief to be had. He'd left Thea's name day gift by her sleeping form, but upon recalling the sound of her discovering it, he suddenly doubted she would see it for what it truly was... And if that was the case, what then? What else would be at stake? Her call to the Great Rite? *Her life?*

He glanced up to find Adrienne still watching him, always calculating.

'Whatever's going on in that head of yours, you're asking yourself all the wrong questions,' she said bluntly. 'Instead of the only one that matters.'

Wilder's jaw clenched involuntarily. 'And what's that, then?'

'What are you going to do about it?'

Her words found their mark, sinking deep into him and fanning those embers within. He drained the tankard and got to his feet.

'Meet me on the northern side of the mountain,' he said.

'And where are you going?'

Wilder met her gaze, hard and determined. 'To get us a damn storm wielder.'

# CHAPTER FOUR

## THEA

L ivid wasn't a strong enough word to describe the feeling surging through Thea as she tracked the traitor across the icy terrain. With every step of her horse, with every fresh bite of cold into her bones, she raged on. Her fury only intensified as she followed the trail across the woodlands and a half-frozen river, only to see the tracks stop before a blank cliff face.

She bit back an enraged scream.

There was no sign of him. The trail ended at the foot of the rock. As though he had vanished.

'Where the fuck are we?' she asked, whirling around to face Cal and Kipp.

Cal grimaced as he fished the map out of his saddlebag and consulted the landmarks around them. 'By the looks of things, we're still in this forest.' He pointed to the parchment. 'But a fair way further north than we were before. If I had to take a guess, I'd say we're parallel to the halfway point of the lake. Vios is to the north-west.'

Thea pinched the bridge of her nose. 'I can't believe this. Yesterday we were so close —'

Kipp motioned for quiet. Not tearing his eyes away from the cliff base, he jumped down from his horse and traced his gloved fingers across the rock. 'The tracks just end,' he said, more to himself than to Thea and Cal. 'It's like... like he walked straight through it. Fascinating.'

'Impossible, you mean,' Cal corrected from his saddle, still frowning over the map.

'He's working with dark forces,' Thea ventured, fury crackling in her veins. 'Back in Notos I saw him vanish into shadow myself. Nothing is impossible.'

She didn't miss the way Kipp's gaze darted up to Cal as they shared a non-verbal exchange. They were doing that more and more lately, which only served to aggravate her further.

'We'll have to go around,' Cal said. 'If we travel close to the base of this cliff, we'll come upon a road by the lake. It'll take us north, which seems to be where Hawthorne's heading —'

'And how long will that take?' Thea sounded sharper than she'd intended, but time was of the essence. Why did no one understand that?

'As long as it takes,' Cal replied with an equal edge to his voice. 'He can't have gone through solid rock, Thea.'

She didn't miss the strange, fleeting expression that crossed Kipp's face at that, but her friend schooled his features into neutrality and shrugged. 'We'll find him.'

Thea bit back a retort about his failures as a sentry guard, about how, if it weren't for him, Hawthorne might already be in chains. No, assigning blame would do no good here, and she had been hard enough on Kipp earlier.

*Strong of mind, strong of body, strong of heart,* she chanted to herself.

'There's a fishing village not far from here.' Cal pocketed the map and gave Thea a hard look. 'We'll stop there to rest and get dry.'

Thea opened her mouth —

Cal raised a hand. 'No arguments. You might be the Shadow of Death, Thea, you might be a lost princess of Delmira, but Kipp and I are spent. We're no good to you this tired. Especially if we need to subdue a fucking Warsword.'

Kipp cleared his throat and mounted his horse before meeting Thea's gaze. 'In case it wasn't obvious, I'm with the Flaming Arrow on this one.'

Thea's chest tightened. 'You don't understand.'

'Don't we?' Kipp countered. 'We've been on the road with you for a year, Thea. We *do* understand. It's not just about Warsword treason and the enemy in the shadows. It's personal. Trust me, we get it.'

'He —'

'We *know*,' Cal said gently as he guided his horse through the trees. 'He betrayed you. Which means he betrayed us. But us freezing and starving to death in the woods isn't revenge, it's stupid.'

Begrudgingly, Thea urged her mare after her friends. 'I never claimed to be smart,' she muttered.

'Luckily I'm smart enough for all of us,' Kipp replied, offering a grin.

The midday sun offered little warmth throughout the forest, but the light itself seemed to lift their spirits. Though Thea would never admit it, the thought of a hot meal and a cosy armchair by the fire had her listening to her friends with amusement for the first time in weeks.

'Should have seen the way she was looking at me in Notos,' Kipp was saying to Cal, his expression earnest. 'I really think she's starting to warm to me.'

Cal snorted. 'Horseshit.'

Kipp put a hand to his heart. 'I swear it. There's something between Wren and me, you can't deny it.'

A rough laugh bubbled from Thea's lips, some of the tension ebbing away from her shoulders. 'Wren? As in my sister?'

'Is there another Wren we know of?' Kipp asked. 'Intelligent, beautiful? Has a knack for potions and powders? Tell me, Thea, I'm in with a chance, aren't I? She appreciates a strong mind, no doubt.'

'*I* was the one who saved her from the Daughter of Darkness,' Cal said, puffing his chest out. '*I* was the one who took out that winged commander —'

'One flaming arrow through a half-wraith doesn't make you a hero,' Kipp replied.

'It might in Wren's eyes.'

Thea shook her head in disbelief and addressed Kipp. 'Safe to say that you're not still mooning over Milla, then?'

Kipp blinked slowly. 'Who?'

'Milla!' Cal exclaimed. 'The raven-haired beauty from the Laughing Fox? The one you wouldn't shut up about for the first four months we were travelling? The one we saw kissing that other man...'

Kipp scratched his chin before shrugging. 'No idea who you mean.'

Thea found herself smiling. It was moments like these

she missed out on when she was lost in her fury. She had to appreciate them while she could.

'You're ridiculous,' Cal said.

Kipp reached across and attempted to pat his shoulder. 'It's alright to be jealous, Callahan.'

'I'm hardly —'

'You can't teach it,' Kipp continued, sitting up straight in his saddle. 'Some of us are just born this way.'

'And what way is that?'

'Oh, you know, *gifted*.'

Cal's face reddened. 'You're such a —'

'Wren will never have him,' Thea interjected, sharing a pitying look with Cal. 'He's too annoying.'

'That's a nice word for it,' Cal muttered.

The banter made for a quicker ride, and sooner than expected, Thea found herself at the edge of the forest, looking out onto a road that was bustling despite the harsh conditions. Carriages and horse-drawn carts groaned along the worn, icy path, wheels creaking beneath the weight of wares and weary travellers. There were people on foot as well, bundled in cloaks and blankets, shuffling along with packs strapped high on their backs, their breath visible in the frigid air.

'The fuck is this?' Cal blurted, watching the rumbling carts leaving deep ruts in the increasingly muddied slush.

'Maybe they're all here to celebrate Thea's name day,' Kipp declared.

'My name day is well and truly over, Kipp,' Thea said drily, her hand drifting to her fate stone.

'We're here to watch the eclipse in Vios, boy,' an elderly man croaked from the side of the road, cupping his hands before his mouth, attempting to warm himself.

Cal shot Thea an apprehensive look.

'You've been before?' she asked the man.

He shook his head. 'First time going to Vios for it,' he replied. 'But if there was ever a time for it, it's now, eh?'

'You think it'll save the midrealms?' Thea pressed, brows knitted together in scepticism.

'Me? No. I think we're all fucked.'

'That's the spirit,' Kipp retorted from his horse.

The old man shrugged. 'My wife was a spiritual woman. She was always on about how the alignment of the sun, moon and world was a reminder of the interconnectedness of all things. How an eclipse is the lifting of the veil between our world and what's next – how it gives us access to the gods, to the Furies themselves.'

'Right...' Kipp scratched his head awkwardly. 'She somewhere in this chaos, then?' He nodded to the bustling activity on the road.

'She's dead,' the man said.

Kipp baulked. 'Oh, I'm sorry.'

'Wraiths got her. Not five months ago.'

'Our condolences,' Thea offered.

The man gave a stiff nod. 'I don't know about all that stuff she said,' he told them. 'But it was either freeze my arse off in my empty village or go to Vios for her. To see something she cared about, something that symbolises triumph over darkness.'

Cal cleared his throat, looking misty-eyed.

'Does it sound stupid to you, boy?' the man asked.

Thea expected Cal to flinch or shift back from the traveller. Instead, her friend reached down and grasped the stranger's shoulder. 'Not at all, sir. It sounds right.'

The man stared for a moment, taken aback, before he

gave a gruff nod. 'You'll want to get ahead of this lot if you want a room in the village tonight.' He nodded to the crowd winding around the bend in the road. 'You're a long way from home, Guardians of Thezmarr.'

Kipp tugged his cloak tighter around his neck, his lips a deep shade of blue. 'You're right about that, sir.'

The trio bid the man farewell and rode ahead of the travellers. The path before them had been trodden by countless hooves and footsteps and was now a thick layer of brown slush.

'The chances of a warm bed are looking slimmer by the minute,' Kipp groused.

'We'll find you something,' Thea told him, suddenly feeling sorry for her friend. 'Come on – if we pick up the pace, you'll have a pint in your hand by sundown.'

'What sun?' Cal grunted.

But Kipp's expression brightened instantly, and he urged his horse forward. Thea followed suit, eager to put distance between their company and the travellers before someone realised who she was, and who she was hunting.

The icy wind whipped at her face as they cantered, a fresh flurry of snow dancing in the frigid air, veiling much of the road before them in a hazy mist. Thea glanced to her right, where the vast and ancient Great Lake of Aveum stretched, frozen as far as the eye could see. It was like frosted glass, cloaked in an eerie stillness and a haunting silence broken only by the creaks and groans of the ice.

It made her all the more eager to reach the village. She urged her mare into a gallop up the crest in the terrain. She couldn't remember the last time she'd had full feeling in her fingers, or had arisen well-rested. Perhaps she'd made a mistake. Perhaps she should have allowed them to stop for respite in the previous village. Rest or no, Hawthorne had eluded her again regardless.

Thea drew her mare closer to Cal and Kipp, a twinge of guilt sharp in her gut as they slowed, turning to her with open expressions.

'I'm sorry,' she told them breathlessly. 'I'm sorry I've been so —'

Thea stopped short. For over the ridge, along the curve of the shore, was a scene carved from nightmares.

A pile of bodies was burning on the banks of the fishing village, and trails of black and red blood led to the frozen lake's edge.

# CHAPTER FIVE

## THEA

Thea charged down the rise towards the banks, where villagers stood in small huddles on the icy shores, shaking and in shock. Plumes of smoke drifted from the pyre into the wintry afternoon sky. Black stained the snow.

'What happened?' Thea called, drawing her horse up short and leaping from the saddle, her hands already on her weapons.

She heard Cal and Kipp catch up, the snow crunching beneath their boots as they too dismounted and scanned the area.

'What happened here?' Thea demanded again, reaching a group of elders who met her gaze.

A silver-haired woman stepped forward, her lined face wary, grief-stricken. 'The howlers came.'

Thea whirled around, surveying the shores for signs of more danger. 'Where from? How many?'

'From everywhere,' the woman said. 'Pockets of darkness opened up all over like portals, and they came through.'

Frowning, Thea adjusted her grips on her sword and dagger. 'What... Where are they now?'

The woman raised a finger, pointing to the flaming pyre. 'Dead,' she replied, before turning her finger towards the lake's edge, where black smears mixed with red. 'Or dragged back to the darkness.'

Thea glanced at Cal and Kipp, who were both looking baffled.

'You have warriors here? Guardians from Thezmarr stationed nearby?' Thea pressed, still unable to understand how a group of fishermen had fended off the significant attack.

The woman shook her head. 'He came from the forest.'

'Who did?'

'The man. Some said he was a Warsword.'

Thea's stomach bottomed out and she felt her friends tense beside her. 'What Warsword?'

'He slayed the cursed men, protected our village... We would have perished, met the same fate as them if he hadn't.'

Thea wasn't sure she was breathing; wasn't sure she could move. 'Where is he now?'

'It took him. That... thing.' The woman was still pointing a shaking finger towards the lake.

Thea took in the sight of the red blood mixed with the black, so stark against the pristine white of the snow. Something sharp clawed inside her, constricting her airway, clouding her thoughts. She didn't even realise she was walking to the lake until she stood at its frozen edge. There, she crouched in the blood-stained snow, tasting the ash from the pyre on her tongue.

*It took him.*

Thea turned her gaze upon the vast lake. There was not a

single crack in its surface, no sign of a breach but for the mess at its shore. She grasped a fistful of snow, letting the cold seep through her glove as a sense of disbelief settled over her like a heavy mist. It wasn't true. It couldn't be. She hadn't scoured the midrealms for a year to capture Wilder Hawthorne, only for him to be snatched up by a monster beneath a frozen lake.

Every breath felt heavy, threatening to pull her under.

'Thea?' Kipp asked, coming to her side with Cal.

'It can't be him.' She stared at the snow melting between her fingers. Beside her, she sensed rather than saw Cal and Kipp exchanging another one of their looks. Thea's vision blurred, her muscles suddenly going weak. 'He was mine to capture. Mine to —'

A scream pierced the air like an arrow.

Thea shot to her feet, turning in time to see a tentacle of darkness shoot from beneath the lake's surface, shattering the ice and wrapping around the closest villager.

With a shout and no regard for her own safety, Thea surged towards it, brandishing her sword as she tore across the ice. Fighting to keep herself upright as the surface grew slick beneath her boots, she made for the monster and its victim.

A young woman dangled in its grasp, her mouth open in a silent scream as black poison dripped from its suckers, eating at her skin.

'Hold on!' Thea shouted, swinging her blade as she reached the limb protruding from the ice and slicing through its rubbery flesh with a sickening wet sound.

At the contact, something rumbled beneath the surface, the ice creaking loudly. Thea thrust her blade in deep this time, blood spurting from the creature's wound, but it didn't let go – the girl was still flailing in its grasp overhead. She screamed in agony as its poison seeped into her.

'Thea, watch out!' Cal shouted, just as something broke through the ice beneath her and grabbed her ankle. A pale hand, webbed with darkness, a blackened nail at the tip of each clawing finger.

Thea cried out in surprise and severed it at the wrist, sending it skidding across the frozen surface of the lake with a smear of black blood.

'What the fuck…' she panted, starting back towards the festering tentacle. There was no time to think, to feel, only to act. As she ran, another hand, and another, shot up through the ice, sending shards flying like glass, grasping for her feet, her ankles, trying to trip her up, to pull her down. Thea dodged their attempts and palmed her dagger of Naarvian steel as she eyed a second tentacle tearing through the ice, reaching for the poor girl's kicking legs, as though it meant to tear her in half.

With all her might, Thea thrust her dagger into the base of the monster's limb, twisting viciously before bracing her feet on the ice as best she could and swinging her sword overhead, hacking through the skin and muscle, hot blood gushing across her.

A shriek sounded as the young woman held hostage by the creature fell to the snowy banks of the shore. Villagers rushed forward to pull her to her feet. Dazed, Thea watched for a moment; the girl could walk, could move her body fully. She would be battered and bruised, no doubt, but she was mostly unharmed.

Just as a distant sense of relief blossomed in Thea's chest, ice shattered by her boots and another black-veined hand broke through the surface. With a swipe of her blade, she severed its fingers. She kicked it back beneath the ice just before a cry from the lakeside snatched her attention back to her friends.

She inhaled sharply, the cold hitting her lungs anew.

At some point during her battle with the tentacled creature, several cursed men had broken through the ice and breached the shore. There, Cal and Kipp, along with a handful of fishermen, fought them back.

Adjusting her grip on her blades, Thea made for the fray, ready to spill blood, ready to carve the enemy into tiny pieces and add them to the pyre. She would choose violence, for everything she had gained and lost, for everything that had hurt her, for —

Thea became lighter than air, more fluid than water. She felt the world shift around her, felt the kiss of a blade before it struck, saw the decision in a man's eyes before he made it. This, *this* was what she lived for now: the song of steel, the splatter of blood, the final breath a host of darkness stole before she took its life.

With her own blood roaring in her ears, she couldn't feel the bite of the cold, or the blows of her enemy. She felt only the call to fight, and keep fighting. She carved through one howler after another, relishing each demise with a cold smile.

Until the ice groaned.

Burying her dagger in her opponent's gut, Thea turned to the lake, where three creatures had emerged, shadows rippling from their slimy, squid-like bodies.

'What the fuck are they?' she gasped. The monsters were revolting, their bulbous heads looming over flailing arms, giant beady eyes seeming to stare at everything all at once.

'Juvenile reef dwellers,' Kipp managed, shoving a howler

away, allowing Cal to thrust his blade through its side. 'Like kraken from the storybooks. Cursed ones, by the looks of it. Don't know what they're doing here, though. They're supposed to be from the sea. Mind the suckers – they're poisonous.' He panted as he momentarily rested his hands on his knees, not taking his eyes off the monsters that had now reached the snowy shore. 'I'm guessing they're the offspring of the big one that had that girl in its grasp.'

As if in answer, two more massive tentacles shattered the ice, sweeping across the shore, snatching up one of the slower villagers and tossing them aside with a sickening thud. The rest of the common folk began to scream in earnest then, and a good portion of the men who'd been fighting alongside the trio fled.

Thea was already twirling her sword, eyeing up the smaller monsters. 'Any particular way to kill them?'

Kipp seemed to gather his strength. 'Cut off all its arms, shove your blade in its brain and light it on fire for good measure?'

'Suppose that'd do it,' Thea retorted. 'And the big one?'

'How about we deal with one terrifying monster at a time,' Cal said, his eyes widening as the giant tentacles thrashed the banks of the lake again, toppling over the pyre of burning bodies.

Thea charged.

The reef dwellers were each about the size of a horse. Having fought *rheguld reapers* and shadow wraiths, Thea conceded that she'd dealt with worse. But as she battled the first of the water monsters, she realised its *eight arms* were the problem. She severed one, and another already lashing out at her, threatening to swipe her legs out from under her, or worse, wrap itself around her middle and lift her up into the air.

These creatures didn't belong on the banks of a frozen lake. They had been sent here, cursed with darkness just like the howlers and set upon a place in which they had no business being. There was no other explanation.

Thea kept swinging, ignoring the exhaustion that had latched onto her bones. A powerful tentacle hit her in the side, sending her sprawling across the snow, knocking the air from her lungs. On all fours, she gasped for air, winded, only to be struck by another tentacle. A sharp pain blazed through her head as she hit something hard beneath the snow.

Dots swimming in her vision, she staggered to her feet, almost falling over herself. She should have listened to the others. They weren't at full strength. Thea's skin burned through her shirt as another tentacle made contact, but she ducked beneath it, messily dodging its attack in order to get close to its body.

With a cry of disgust, she lunged at what looked to be its head, driving her dagger into its skull, right between its many sets of eyes.

The creature made a last surge to grab her, but as she yanked her dagger from its head, it sagged into the snow, its tentacles twitching.

A blood-curdling shriek echoed across the lake – and the entire frozen surface shattered. More tentacles shot out at them, sending a tidal wave of freezing water raining down on the banks.

And the thing that emerged...

A scream caught in Thea's throat.

The cursed reef dweller surged towards them, Cal and

Kipp still locked in a battle with one of its young, Thea covered in the blood of another.

The monster drew closer, close enough for Thea to see the texture of its skin, and the poison leaking from its suckers —

It wasn't attacking. It was *falling*.

The monster plunged through the air, raining down glacial lake water and poison. Thea bolted out of the way as its body fell, as though time had slowed, before it collapsed in an enormous heap in the snow, black blood and shadows oozing from its corpse.

Ice crunched. A figure landed deftly on the shore, his powerful frame dripping wet, a giant, bloody black mass grasped in his fist.

Thea's knees buckled, but she remained upright as the heart of a cursed reef dweller landed with a splatter at her feet.

She looked from the still-pulsing organ to the silver eyes that met hers, her breath catching.

She hadn't seen him in a year.

But that steely gaze was as fierce as ever; more so – it was utterly ablaze as it latched onto her.

Thea didn't move. Not yet. She didn't know if she could trust her sight.

The man towering before her looked more savage than he ever had, with a new fracture on his nose, his beard longer, his plain armour in tatters. Icicles clung to his thick lashes and dark hair. A tremor ran down the strong column of his throat as he returned her stare, his knuckles paling as he gripped the hilt of his sword. Even in the icy wind, the scent of rosewood and leather enveloped her.

Everything else faded around them.

It was just her and him, and Thea felt herself teetering on the precipice… of what, she didn't know.

He took a step towards her, and another, closing the distance between them.

The memory of him struck her without warning, so visceral she could taste him on her lips, could feel the push of him inside her. The longing that surged through her was intense, uncomfortable. All the while she warred with herself.

Wilder Hawthorne reached for the lone piece of hair that had escaped her braid and tucked it behind her ear. 'Thea…' he murmured, his voice broken and hoarse.

The breath lodged in her lungs loosened and she stepped forward, eliminating that final space between them and looking up at him, at those silver eyes she'd known so well, her heart pounding.

'We need to talk,' he said softly. 'I can explain everything.'

Thea couldn't help it. She leant in close, her body alight with fire despite the cold. 'There'll be plenty of time to talk,' she heard herself say, her clothes growing damp against the press of his wet armour.

A subtle quiver traced his strong jaw. 'Gods, I've missed you.'

'Have you?' she whispered against his lips.

'Every day…' He rested his brow against hers, his chest rising and falling as he inhaled her scent. 'Every fucking day.'

She lingered for a second longer, meeting his gaze. 'You may come to regret that,' she said.

Before she snapped the manacles into place around his wrists.

# CHAPTER SIX

## WILDER

Wilder was fixated on her mouth, wondering if she was about to kiss him, when the click of the chains sounded. The noise hauled him back to reality, the one in which Thea wasn't his, and he was only hers in the sense that he was her enemy. Startled, Wilder stared down at the iron cuffs around his wrists, everything about them feeling *wrong*, feeling *unnatural*. Still dazed, he tested the chain linking his hands and found that it wouldn't yield to his Furies-given strength. Normal irons he could break, but these...

He nearly laughed. *Of course* Thea would have asked Wren to create some sort of power-suppressing substance to capture him. Perhaps it was even the same that had suppressed Thea's magic for all those years before. *Clever.* He wondered if removing the manacles was a matter of simply locating the key, or if there was more complex alchemy at play. He'd put nothing past the Zoltaire sisters.

Wilder couldn't help but peer into Thea's beautiful face, drinking in her features like someone parched and desperate. What he hadn't anticipated was how much it would hurt to look at her, to have her look at him. She stared at him like she didn't know him, like he wore the face of someone else, someone she no longer recognised. Those eyes that had once gazed upon him with love, with admiration, were cold and hard. It was his own doing, he knew, but that didn't make it hurt any less.

In the year they had been apart, he'd tried to convince himself that she'd understand, that she would learn that the important parts had always been true.

But he'd been lying to himself.

'It's been a long time, Apprentice,' he said at last, managing to keep the crack from his voice.

Her eyes narrowed, her hand gripping the chained link between his manacles hard, as though she could somehow stop him if he chose to run, or fight.

'I'm not your apprentice,' she replied, devoid of any emotion. 'I'm not your anything,'

Wilder sucked in a breath. He had yearned to hear her voice for so long, but these words... They were primed to cut. Where was she? The lightning-wielding warrior he'd fought alongside? The woman he'd held in his arms?

Thea's rage was palpable, raw and unbroken, more so than he'd ever experienced before. And yet... he felt not a flicker of magic from her. That, more than anything, made him worry. It made things all the more precarious.

Stupidly, he hadn't decided what role he would play, what mask he would wear when he saw her again. But the way she gripped his manacles snapped something inside him, and curiosity got the better of him. He needed to test her, to push her, to see what still simmered beneath the surface.

He rattled his irons and raised a brow. 'If you wanted me in chains, Princess...' His voice was low and sultry. 'All you had to do was ask.'

Fury flashed in her eyes, but she veered back as though burned. 'Don't presume to know what I want, traitor.'

The anger was there, but there was no sign of her storm powers, no spark of lightning calling out to him to dance with her. *Where are you, Princess?*

Wilder looked from his chains back to Thea, flakes of snow caught in her bronze-and-gold hair. 'And just how do you plan to get me back to Thezmarr? My hands may be bound, but not even the Shadow of Death can force me to walk... Not even with your friends could you overpower me.'

In a blur of movement, Thea had something sharp pressed to his throat. Not the tip of a dagger like he expected; something far finer.

He baulked.

Thea had a pin pressed to his neck. The faint aroma of Naarvian nightshade tickled his nostrils.

'One move and I'll send you into oblivion,' she hissed.

'You're going to drug me?'

'I'll do whatever I have to. I'd actually prefer you unconscious, just to shut that big mouth of yours.'

'Here I was thinking you liked my mouth just fine.'

Wilder heard her sharp intake of breath, felt the needle's point pierce the first few layers of skin.

'You have a death wish? Keep talking,' she warned.

Nearby, Kipp coughed pointedly. 'Seriously, I wouldn't...' he said, eyeing Wilder warily.

Thea eased the poison-tipped pin away from his skin ever so slightly as her friends at last dared to approach. Both young men were shivering, and grimacing at the sight of master and apprentice.

'So we're taking him back to Thezmarr, then?' Cal asked, teeth chattering.

'Over my dead body,' Thea replied. 'We'll take him to Vios. All the rulers will be there for the eclipse. He can face their justice there, before all the people of the midrealms.'

'But we always said —'

Kipp waved Cal into silence. 'Can we have this argument from the comfort of the local tavern? I was promised a pint by sundown, and I intend to collect.'

The adrenaline had started to wear off, and the icy bite of Aveum air had its fangs in them all. Wilder didn't take his eyes off Thea, nor did she take hers off him, the pin still at his neck, her hand still gripping the chain of his manacles.

'Take his swords,' she ordered her friends.

'Uh...' Cal started.

'Just do it.'

Wilder allowed a smirk to tug at the corner of his mouth, still gazing upon his apprentice as Cal fumbled with his weapons. When he was relieved of his belt, scabbards and blades, their weight instantly missed, Wilder raised a brow at Thea in challenge.

She glared at him before addressing her friends. 'Let's get the fuck out of this cold.'

Wilder managed to hide his surprise. He could have sworn Thea would charge ahead with the ride to Vios, wanting him to face his sentence as soon as possible. But judging by the bedraggled state of the trio, they hadn't stopped in weeks. Thea had been relentless in her pursuit of him, and now the smart move was certainly to get warm and dry before continuing —

'Move,' Thea snapped, her dagger – Malik's dagger – pressed to the small of his back. His brother would probably find that amusing. But she wasn't done. She took Wilder's swords from Cal as well. 'These are mine now,' she told him, her words laced with menace.

*All that anger and no magic to light the fire,* he thought, allowing her to guide him towards the edge of the town. A year ago, he'd known he'd be able to disarm her in a heartbeat; now he wasn't so sure. Even without her magic, she had grown stronger than he could have imagined. Even without the Furies-given gifts of the Great Rite, she was a would-be Warsword through and through. Thea had taken everything he had thrown in her path and triumphed, learning from each and every error, forging herself sharper and better than ever before.

But despite her gains, something deeper was broken inside. Which was why Wilder let her lead him to the local inn with his brother's dagger at his back, his swords in her possession. He needed to find out more about her missing magic. He needed to know if she still had a role to play in the war ahead. And maybe, just maybe, he could get her to listen.

After the violence on the shores, the inn of the fishing village was nearly empty, and Wilder guessed that many of the locals had fled. The handful of people who remained stared at him and the trio behind him, eyeing the thick irons around his wrists and the blade at his spine, utterly perturbed. He couldn't blame them for their confusion. Even if they knew him as the fallen Warsword of Thezmarr, he hadn't acted the part when he'd carved through the cursed men on their shores, or when he'd charged into the frigid lake to slay the cursed mother reef dweller. His lungs still burned from the effort.

As Thea directed them all to a booth in the far corner, the locals averted their gazes. No doubt they'd seen enough bloodshed and death for one day. And if Thea's glare was anything to go by, they knew they were best leaving the Thezmarrians well enough alone.

Kipp paused at the head of the table, clapping his hands together suddenly. 'Drinks,' he declared. 'We'll need drinks. *Lots* of drinks.'

'We're not here to get drunk,' Thea muttered.

'Speak for yourself, Highness.' Kipp was already striding towards the counter, signalling to the barkeep.

Wilder met Thea's gaze across the table. 'Now you have me, Apprentice, what exactly do you plan to do with me?'

'I thought I made myself clear enough before,' she said, her tone as cold as the lake's ice. 'You're being taken to Vios for trial. After that, the rulers can do with you what they will.'

Wilder stared at her. She had looked at him as though she didn't recognise him, but now he felt the same way about her... Who was this cruel woman? Where was Thea?

Beside Wilder, Cal shifted in his seat, awkwardly peering over them towards Kipp.

Toying with the chain between his irons, Wilder considered the woman before him. 'If those are your intentions, surely you understand why I'll have to decline.'

'You're not in a position to decline,' she told him. 'I'll drug you and strap you to a damn horse if I have to.'

A tray of foaming tankards slid onto the table. 'Who's going to deal with his hulking mass lumped over their saddle?' Kipp argued, already halfway through a pint.

To Wilder's surprise, Thea reached for a tankard. 'His

horse is around here somewhere. He only needs to whistle, remember?'

'Right.' Kipp nodded. 'Perks of being a Warsword.'

'He's no Warsword,' Thea said coldly.

'Semantics,' Kipp replied.

Cal cleared his throat. 'So, we drug him and take him to Vios. That's settled, then.'

Wilder watched the exchange unfold between the trio, studying Thea for any signs of uncertainty, of hesitation. He saw none. Had he been arrogant enough to think that the mere sight of him would unravel her? That in his presence, upon meeting his gaze, her magic would break through those walls in a tidal wave? He'd been a fool. He had to try to bring it back, bring *Thea* back, before he met up with Adrienne and the others.

He rested his chained hands on the table. 'I have a counteroffer,' he said, looking at only her, only Thea. 'I'll come with you willingly, if you give me a fair hearing.'

'Furies save us,' Cal muttered, downing his tankard and reaching for another.

Thea scoffed. 'It's not up to me to put you on trial. I'll save that for the rulers. They'll decide your fate.'

Wilder swallowed the lump in his throat. 'I don't mean for my crimes against the midrealms.'

A muscle twitched in Thea's jaw. 'What, then?'

'Everything else.'

Thea's hands clenched around her tankard, her knuckles paling.

Kipp, however, knocked his drink against hers. 'Sounds like a fair deal to me.'

She shoved him off. 'We don't make deals with traitors.'

'Of course not,' Kipp continued. 'But I for one don't fancy

lugging the likes of him from here to Vios. Come on, Thea. Listen, don't listen. But for Furies' sake, look at him. He'd be fucking heavy.' He looked to Cal for backup.

Cal studied Wilder, seeming to weigh up their options. 'Make him remove his armour. If he tries to run, if he tries anything at all... I'll shoot him through the heart with a flaming arrow.'

'Fair,' Wilder agreed, offering one of his bound hands.

Kipp leapt to his feet. 'Now that we're all in agreement, I've had baths drawn for us —'

Thea threw her hands up in frustration. 'Kipp, I said one fucking pint —'

Kipp levelled her with a firm stare. 'And *I* said, if you'll recall, nothing of the fucking sort. We haven't washed properly in *weeks*. I'm not going another yard on the road without a bath, a hot meal and a nap. If you don't like it, oh royal one, you can drug me up with your moody friend there and carry me to Vios too.'

Thea's mouth fell open and Wilder fought to keep a straight face as Kipp scooped up as many tankards as he could carry and made for the stairs.

'Three hours, Kristopher!' Thea barked after him. 'I'll give you three hours and no more.'

Kipp made an offensive gesture over his shoulder and didn't look back.

Cal made his excuses, looking relieved to get away from the pair of them. 'See you in three hours, then, Thea. I'll make sure Kipp's ready.'

'Thank you,' she muttered, staring at her drink.

'Just...' He hesitated, long enough that Thea looked up, brow furrowed.

'What?' she demanded.

'Just don't do anything stupid,' he said quickly, before darting towards the stairs.

Wilder raised a brow at Thea. 'What exactly is he worried you might do?'

'Slit your throat in your sleep.'

Despite himself, Wilder chuckled. 'I don't think that was it.'

Thea was on her feet. 'Get up.'

'Going to give me a sponge bath, Princess?'

She grabbed him and shoved him towards the stairs. 'Fuck off, Hawthorne.'

That made him smile, just a little.

An inn worker on the next floor pointed them towards another set of stairs. 'That's the room the other two left for you. It's in the attic.'

'Bastards,' Thea muttered, shaking her head.

Wilder made a mental note to thank them later. He needed to talk to Thea alone. He needed to make her see him as something other than a traitor to the realm, a traitor to her.

The attic room was tiny; Wilder couldn't even stand completely upright inside. But there was a wooden tub, full to the brim with steaming water, and he nearly sighed with relief at the sight. A single chair stood in the corner, fresh towels atop it.

'Ladies first,' Wilder said, motioning to the tub.

'You've got to be fucking kidding me.'

'Wouldn't be the first time we've shared a bath…' he ventured, hoping his audacity would hit that raw nerve of anger that sparked her power back to life.

But Thea simply swiped the towels off the chair and sat

down, crossing her ankles and holding his swords unsheathed across her lap. 'Get on with it, then.'

His brows shot up. 'You're just going to sit there and watch me bathe?'

Her face betrayed nothing, but he could see the flutter of her pulse in her neck as she spoke. 'I don't trust you. If you want to bathe, then bathe. But I'm not going anywhere. One false move and I'll shove your own blade through your heart.'

'You going to take these off, then?' he asked, rattling his irons.

'No.'

'How am I meant to —' He gestured to the armour across his chest.

Thea traced the edge of his Naarvian steel blade with her fingertip, a flush creeping up her neck as she considered him with narrowed eyes.

Time stretched between them, until at last she stood, and dragged his own blade to his throat. 'You don't move a muscle.'

Wilder didn't think she'd appreciate the reminder that some physical reactions were beyond his control. He remained still as stone as she reached for the buckles of his breastplate. She was close enough that he could feel the kiss of her breath on his skin, close enough to make his cock twitch.

Thea undid the first strap, then the second, refusing to look at him as he gazed down at her. Gods, she was beautiful, even more so with fury rippling off her. Lips pursed, she removed the protective plates from his torso, her fingers brushing the bare skin of his collarbone.

He heard her intake of breath at the same time he felt the

fire of her touch, sending him almost feral with the need for her. A year without her had been a lifetime.

But her face was a mask of cold indifference. She dropped the plates onto the floor before removing his gauntlets, which were in pieces anyway.

'There,' she ground out.

Wilder gave his shirt and pants a pointed look. 'You don't want to help me out of the rest of my clothes, Princess? You used to like doing that.'

He was met with a razor-sharp glare. 'Figure it out.'

Wilder shrugged, surveying his tattered clothes. 'Fine.' And then he tore straight down the middle of his shirt, ripping the ruined fabric away completely, the manacles jangling as he did.

He didn't look at Thea as he worked the buttons of his pants, but he could feel her gaze like a brand on his naked skin, could hear her breathing turn shallow as he slid the material down his thighs.

When his trousers were off and he was naked but for his chains, he turned to her, letting her see every inch of him.

Her mouth parted, her cheeks flushed, and he swore that beautiful body of hers tensed as her legs clenched together.

'Nothing to hide from you, Princess,' he told her, before he stepped into the tub and sank beneath the hot water.

# CHAPTER SEVEN

## THEA

I t had been a year. A year since she'd seen that glorious body, sculpted by the Furies themselves. It was every bit as chiselled and powerful as before: golden skin, broad, round shoulders, a torso corded with hard muscle, and a V-shaped dip of sinew that pointed straight to his —

Thea swallowed hard as Hawthorne's impressive frame disappeared beneath the steaming water and his head tipped back to rest on the lip of the tub, his eyes closed. Forgetting herself, she let her gaze follow the dark ink swirling across the warrior's skin, noting the scatter of new scars cutting through the pattern, a sight that made her chest ache involuntarily. She remembered tracing that tattoo with her fingers, with her tongue, the flash of memory sending a ripple of longing through her.

'You're welcome to join me.' Hawthorne didn't even deign to open his eyes. 'If staring's not doing enough for you.'

That wrenched her out of her trance. 'I'd sooner claw my eyes out.'

'That's not the reaction I recall.'

'Enough,' Thea snapped, her face heating.

'I've told you before, it's never enough, Princess. You damn well know it.'

Thea's toes curled in her boots, but she kept her voice flat, betraying nothing of the desire coursing through her traitorous body. 'I thought you wanted to explain yourself? Get a fair hearing, or so you said.'

'You didn't strike me as being in the mood to talk... Something else, perhaps? To ease the tension?'

Thea ground her teeth. 'I know what you're doing,' she told him coldly. 'It won't work.'

'What's that?'

'You want me to lose control —'

A smirk tugged at the corner of his mouth. 'That's one way to describe it.'

'Of my magic, you bastard. You want to report back to your masters about my powers? That ship has sailed. I've got nothing for you.'

'Magic doesn't just vanish.'

'What would you know about it?'

'More than you, Apprentice.'

The arrogant prick still hadn't opened his eyes, hadn't moved from where he lounged in the hot soapy water while she sat in her filthy, damp clothes.

*Strong of mind, strong of body, strong of heart.* She tried to ground herself with the meditation. And failed.

'Fuck this,' she snapped, jumping to her feet. 'You move, I'll kill you.'

At that, Hawthorne opened his eyes and fixed her with his silver stare. 'We both know that if you wanted me dead,

Althea Zoltaire, that arrow would have hit my heart, not my shoulder.'

Thea held back a gasp, her gaze dropping to the thick, raised line of jagged pink skin above his pectoral.

*'Don't say my name... Don't ever say my name again.'* Those were the last words she had said to him in those woods, in the moment before she'd let that arrow fly.

'Next time, I won't miss.'

'You didn't miss, Thea. You hit me exactly where you wanted.'

Thea couldn't stand it anymore. Rage pounded in her ears, and with a scream of fury, she yanked the door open and left the traitor in the tub, slamming the door closed behind her.

She was so enraged that she nearly barged straight into Kipp, the ends of his hair wet.

'It's going well, then?' he asked with a grimace.

'Don't even fucking start, Kristopher,' she ground out. 'Tell me there's more hot water?'

He had the good sense to get out of her way with a flourish. 'Level below, second door on the left.'

'You'll watch the traitor?'

'He's not really my type.'

*'Kipp.'*

Her friend raised his hands in surrender. 'I'll guard the door, but we both know I'm useless. I've got no chance against that behemoth if he wants to get past me.'

'In case you were wondering,' Hawthorne called from behind the door, 'the walls are really thin. But rest assured, I won't be going anywhere until I've said my piece.'

'Oh, I'm so fucking assured,' Thea muttered.

Kipp simply shrugged, as though the word of a known traitor was good enough for him.

'For fuck's sake,' Thea sighed, and headed for her bath.

~

Although it was on her own orders that they were back in their saddles in the freezing cold, Thea mourned the loss of the giant tub she'd submerged herself in, and the perfectly adequate feather bed she'd left untouched in the inn.

'We're not taking the main road,' she said, clenching her teeth to stop them from chattering.

'The main road will get us to Vios faster,' Hawthorne countered from atop his stallion. 'Or do you want to spend more time with me, Princess?'

'A former Warsword will attract attention on the main route. That will delay us more than uneven terrain —'

'Couldn't we have had this discussion by the fire?' Kipp moaned, pulling his hood tighter around his face. 'Rather than in the middle of a fucking thundersnow?'

'This isn't a fucking thundersnow. You said so yourself: there hasn't been one in centuries. And this isn't a discussion. We're going through the forest,' Thea declared, starting her horse towards the icy treeline.

She caught Hawthorne's shrug from the corner of her eye, as though he'd known she'd make that choice all along. Had he only suggested the road so she'd dig her heels in on the idea of the alternative route? Was he playing games with her? Her body tensed at the thought of him humiliating her again. She refused to let that happen.

'Move out,' she ordered, squeezing her mare's sides with her thighs, desperate to put some distance between herself and the fallen Warsword, the image of him in the bath still seared into her mind.

The days were getting shorter, reduced to a few fleeting hours of light hemmed in by the dark. Night had long since fallen, and Cal and Kipp carried torches to illuminate the barren trees and snow falling in earnest around them. Checking her compass, Thea led their small party from the main trade route of Aveum into the frozen forests, taking the less travelled path. They made for the capital, Vios, where the rulers of the midrealms would soon gather for the eclipse, and to decide Wilder Hawthorne's fate.

Thankfully, the forest offered shelter from the howling winds whipping down the main road, but in its place was an eerie quiet, broken only by the rattling of Hawthorne's chains with every step of his horse. Thea told herself to be grateful for the sound, for it served as a reminder that it was Hawthorne the traitor in her midst, not Wilder, her former mentor, former lover... The man whose hands had guided hers across her weapons, teaching her; whose arms she'd slept in without fear of nightmares.

She shook the thoughts from her head and focused on the icicles glistening in the torchlight. Soon, they would arrive in Vios. She could shove her prisoner before the rulers and claim her prize – his swords and her dignity – and leave him to whatever sentence awaited him.

Movement to her left caught her eye and she ground her teeth as the fallen Warsword in question brought his horse up alongside hers. In the flickering light, shadows masked his face. *Fitting*, Thea thought as she tried to pull ahead.

Each time she steered away, he wove through the gnarled, naked trees and found her again.

On his fourth attempt, he leant across and practically growled at her, 'You promised to give me a fair hearing.'

Thea's jaw already ached from clenching it so hard. 'So speak,' she said.

'It's not a fair hearing if the judge refuses to actually listen.'

She glanced across at him. His expression was hard. 'What could you, a traitor, possibly say to sway me? After everything you have done?' Her cheeks burned despite the cold. She knew Cal and Kipp could hear every word, knew exactly what she'd been like in the months after the battle of Notos, after Hawthorne.

The fallen Warsword's gaze followed hers and a flicker of understanding crossed his face before that mask of indifference slid back into place. 'You will hear me, Apprentice, one way or another.'

Thea's grip tightened on her reins, her whole body going rigid with rage. 'Tell me, Hawthorne – were you always a traitor? Right from the beginning? Or did something sway you along the way?'

Hawthorne narrowed his eyes. 'You know nothing about it, Princess. Nothing.' His voice, once melodic and gentle, now resonated with a thunderous timbre that echoed through the air. Each word dripped with venomous scorn.

'And yet you don't deny it,' Thea challenged.

'I don't deny what you saw in Notos with the shadow-touched. But it wasn't what it looked like,' he told her. 'Let me explain, please.'

Thea *hated* that her curiosity was piqued, that she *wanted* to know the reasoning behind his madness. Seeing him free those half-wraiths in Notos had been like a knife to the gut. Time had slowed as she'd felt everything between them unravel. All of it lies. But in her weaker moments since, a tiny part of her had wanted it to make sense, for there to be a logical explanation. She had spent the last year going over those final minutes again and again, trying to work out what she'd missed, trying to understand how it had all ended up the way it had.

'Tell me, then,' she said, fighting to keep her voice even.

Relief flashed in Hawthorne's eyes. 'The shadow-touched I saved – they weren't part of the enemy force. They're not in league with the reapers, or the other monsters plaguing the midrealms.'

'No?' Thea replied. 'You're telling me that the half-wraith creatures who leak shadow and darkness, who bear wings on their backs and talons at their fingertips, are not born of the same evil?'

'They are victims of it, like so many other people in the midrealms. They may not have lost their lives, but they have lost more than you can know – a part of themselves.' Hawthorne paused for a moment, seeming to gather himself. 'A shadow-touched person is the result of a reaper trying to curse a human in the same way it would create a howler or spread its darkness to another monster. It nearly happened to you in the Bloodwoods...'

Not for the first time, that little voice in Thea's head pressed: *What if he's telling the truth?* But she had to be doing the right thing, for what was the alternative? That she'd gone too far down the wrong path? That her choices had led them all here? No. That wasn't an option.

She didn't look at him. She kept her mouth shut, affording him the opportunity to continue his tale, just as she'd promised.

He forged on. 'Only, a shadow-touched person remains

true to themselves. We don't know if it's to do with willpower or strength of character, or something else entirely. But the shadow-touched are those who fight against the curse when a reaper attempts to turn them. The result is a human with special abilities and wraith traits. They are nothing like the monsters themselves. Those people in that cage in Notos were innocent, Thea.'

But it wasn't the prisoners who Thea pictured. It was the winged storm wielder who'd held Wren captive with her shadows, her face a mask of menace, her taunting words laced with cruelty. She pictured the carnage on the battlefield, the mutilated unit of Tverrian soldiers and the terror-etched faces of those forced to live through their nightmares in a relentless cycle.

A derisive laugh broke from Thea's lips then. 'Innocent?' she scoffed. 'I don't know what's worse... If this is the best lie you can come up with, or if you truly believe it yourself.'

Hawthorne's expression twisted with pain. 'Open your eyes for a moment, Thea —'

Her hand flew to the hilt of her dagger. 'Oh, my eyes are wide open, traitor. I see you for exactly what you are.'

Hawthorne stared at her for a moment, as though debating how far to push her.

'You don't,' he said at last, shaking his head and allowing his horse to fall back. 'But you will.'

Thea hated that he'd had the last word, but she hated his presence more. Hated that even after everything she had seen him do, he thought he could change her mind about him. She had seen him with the enemy; she had heard the familiarity with which they spoke to one another. He had freed the monsters the warriors of the midrealms had lost their lives to capture, and she had witnessed him vanishing amid the shadows.

Within the depths of Thea's soul, a tempest brewed, dark and unyielding. Hawthorne's betrayal, not only of the guild, but of her, was like a poisonous viper that had struck the very core of her being. Her rage blazed through her, ready to consume all in its path. And yet... she felt no magic, no storm waiting to break from the confines of her body, no lightning singing through her veins. Though her heart pounded fiercely, its merciless rhythm like the beat of a war drum, she felt not a whisper of otherworldly power at her fingertips. It was as though it had never been there.

*Why?* Anger had been the key many times before, tapping into that symphony of fury that so often simmered beneath her skin. There was no denying she felt that way now. Lately, her body was always coiled in anger, always ready to strike. She yearned to unleash the full force of her wrath, and yet...

Thea inhaled the icy night air, hoping it would smother the inferno within. She had no such luck. Instead she fixed her eyes upon the snow ahead and pushed on, as she had done for the past year.

Hours later, Thea could no longer dismiss the sheen of sweat on her mare's coat and called the others to a halt.

'The horses need to rest,' she said flatly, swinging down from the saddle as she spotted a nearby stream.

'They're not the only ones,' Kipp said, following her lead and bringing his horse to the water's edge. Cal was already starting a fire at the base of a large oak tree.

Gods, she was glad for Kipp and Cal. Anything to avoid being alone with Hawthorne again.

Thea scanned the forest in a sudden panic, but spotted Hawthorne collecting branches despite the irons around his wrists. She loosed a breath and averted her gaze, opting to sift through her saddlebag to distract herself.

But soon, his voice pierced the frigid air. 'There has been no call from the Rite, I take it?'

Kipp was already shaking his head, but Thea flung out a hand.

'Don't tell him anything,' she commanded. 'He's not to be trusted.' Seating herself on a nearby fallen trunk, she unsheathed Malik's dagger and turned it over in her hands. The weapon, once gleaming with a deadly shine, now bore the scars of time, its edge dulled by the countless enemies she'd slain with it.

'I taught you to care for your blades better than that,' Hawthorne's voice sounded again.

Thea ignored him, having already reached for her whetstone. Esyllt, the weapons master of Thezmarr, had given it to her before she'd departed Tver. Its coarse surface was a testament to its years of service to him. Thea dropped her shoulders and unclenched her jaw, trying to remember one of Audra's meditations as her hand closed around the hilt of her dagger and she drew its blade across the unyielding edge of the whetstone.

The sound took her away from the fallen Warsword in their midst, and back into echoes of battles past. It was the seemingly insignificant details that came back to her: the weight of a lifeless body, the trail of dragged feet in the sand, the suspended moment of time between when a gutted opponent realised he was a dead man and when he took his last breath. Her focus narrowed. She was glad to lose herself in the task at hand, her movements fluid as the blade's dulled edge gave way to a renewed sharpness.

'Did you get my gift?' That rich timbre speared through her thoughts.

Tensing, Thea glided the last stroke of the whetstone across the dagger's edge and held the weapon to the flickering campfire. It gleamed with a brightness that seemed to defy the darkness around them, the blade now ready to slice through the heart of a monster, or sever the bond between body and soul.

She pinned her former mentor with a cold, hard stare. 'I threw it into the river,' she told him, sheathing the sharpened dagger.

She waited for some smart-arsed retort from Hawthorne, but he simply looked away, staring into the flames of the campfire. Where she expected the sweet taste of victory, there was only bitterness on her tongue. Suddenly restless, she stood, swiping Cal's bow and quiver from his side and walking off into the night. Thankfully, her friends didn't try to stop her. They had learnt long ago when to give her space.

Thea shouldered the quiver of arrows and clutched the weapon in her gloved hand. They didn't need any game, not when their saddlebags were packed with rations from the grateful villagers. But Thea couldn't think straight. She needed to move, needed to get away from the deceptive lull of the fire and the molten silver eyes across from her.

Without her magic, everything felt so bottled up inside, with no outlet. She desperately wanted to conjure the bolts of lightning she had once mastered, to summon the clouds and thunder that soothed her heart like a healer's balm. But that power did not speak to her any longer.

*I am the storm...*

She scoffed. She was no storm. She didn't know what she was anymore.

Moonlight penetrated the skeletal canopy of the forest. Thea scanned the snow for tracks, glad for the distraction when she found what looked to be the hoofprints of a deer. Snow had been falling since they'd started out from the fishing village, so the tracks couldn't be that old. Relishing the kiss of icy flakes against her face, she followed the prints to the stream. They continued on the other side, and so she leapt across the narrow channel of water with ease and followed on.

Thea's breath clouded before her face as she wove through the barren underbrush, following the imprints in the snowy ground. With each step, the tension in her shoulders eased and the winter air hit her burning lungs, soothing that fire that raged white-hot within.

With a stifled gasp, she stopped short.

In the ethereal silence of the wintry woodlands, a graceful doe lowered its mouth to the ground, seeking roughage beneath the snow. It was a beautiful animal, elegant and regal, its long lashes framing wide, innocent eyes.

Silently, Thea reached for an arrow, nocking it to Cal's bow and drawing the string taut. For a moment, she simply breathed, appreciating that all-too-fragile balance between life and death as it teetered on the edge, frozen at her command —

'You're still dropping your elbow.'

Hawthorne's low voice skittered along her bones.

She nearly jumped, only just managing to master herself.

But the damage was done – the doe's ears pricked and the creature darted away.

Thea relaxed the bowstring and whirled around to face him. 'Happy now?' she ground out.

'Are you?' he countered, eyes aflame.

Thea reminded herself to unclench her jaw, starting towards where the doe had fled.

'Why isn't Callahan the Flaming Arrow doing the hunting?' Hawthorne asked, following.

'I was trying to get away from you,' Thea said through gritted teeth, pausing at the spot where the doe's fresh tracks began. 'You take all the air.'

Hawthorne raked his bound hands through his hair and sighed. 'It's me who can't breathe when I'm around you…'

White-hot fury lanced through Thea and she rounded on him. 'You have no right,' she hissed. 'I don't want to hear it.'

'You don't want to hear anything, it seems.'

Thea stormed deeper into the forest, following the hoof imprints in the snow, the trees becoming denser as they led to a near-vertical rock face. 'No. Not from you. Not after you betrayed the guild, betrayed the midrealms, betrayed —'

'Betrayed *you?*' he finished for her.

A tidal wave of anger crashed against the shores of her composure, threatening to shatter the walls she had built as she took in the warrior before her. 'I owe you *nothing*. Not a moment of my time, not a single —'

'Do you truly believe me to be evil?'

*'Stay away from him, Thee… He's the worst one,'* Wren had warned her once, a long time ago. If only she'd listened.

'You truly think I have fallen to the side of the *wraiths?*' Hawthorne pressed, his gaze intense. 'You think I've aligned myself with the monsters who did that to my brother? To Tal—'

Thea stepped towards him, hand ready at her dagger. 'How did you vanish earlier? Your tracks just stopped. Am I supposed to believe that you're not in league with them? That you didn't use shadow magic to —'

Hawthorne took a step backward and ran his hands along the rock. 'There are tunnels and secret passages all over the midrealms… If you know where to look.'

'There was no passage there,' Thea argued.

'Wasn't there?' Hawthorne said cryptically, starting along the base of the cliff. He cut a striking figure in the moonlight, snow drifting around his powerful frame. Thea had no choice but to follow him.

They walked for a few minutes in silence, Thea stewing in her own rage, her hand still clamped around her dagger. She shouldn't be out here alone with him.

Hawthorne slowed when he got to an overhang in the cliffside, icicles hanging like knives from the mouth of a cave. 'This is part of the network. Leads through to the other side of the mountain.'

'This proves nothing. For all I know, it's just a hole in the rock.'

Hawthorne ducked inside. 'If you don't believe me, see for yourself.'

'I don't think so,' she said coldly, her fingers reaching for the poison-tipped pin Wren had prepared for her.

'You seem a bit too far away to stick your little needle in my neck,' he taunted, shifting deeper into the dark cave.

Thea palmed her dagger and brandished the pin. If she had to tie the traitor up and drag him through the snow with her horse, she'd do it in a heartbeat. Anything to be rid of him, rid of the unending wrath that haunted her every day he escaped his retribution.

She stepped into the cave.

'Think you can bring me down, Princess?' he murmured in the dark.

Thea braced herself for an attack. 'When I've given you over to the rulers,' she said quietly, lacing her words with venom, 'I'll wash my hands of you forever. I'll never have to see you again, will never have to utter your name... It will be as though you never existed.'

'Well...' Hawthorne's voice was like golden honey. 'I can't have that.'

Thea found him in the dark, right by the mouth of the cave. She locked eyes with him, just as he lifted his manacled fists to the wall, striking an all-powerful blow.

She lurched forward, panic spiking.

'You bastard —' she cried, as the whole mountain above rumbled.

'I never claimed to be a gentleman.'

Beneath the blow of his Furies-given strength, snow and debris rained down at the mouth of the cave.

Trapping both Thea and the traitor within.

# CHAPTER EIGHT

## WILDER

In the pitch-black, her dagger was at his throat. In that moment, Wilder knew he must be deeply twisted inside, because his cock twitched at the cold press of her steel.

'What the fuck have you done?' Thea hissed, her body flush with his.

Gods, he'd missed the feel of her, the scent of her – like a kiss from the sea, laced with hints of bergamot. In the dark, it was as though she were wrapped around all his senses.

'Bought myself some time,' he murmured, only just stopping himself from breathing her in.

Her blade drifted from the soft skin of his neck down his chest, to rest above his armour. He couldn't see her, could only feel the press of the dagger as he remained still, awaiting her next move. His heart was there, hers for the taking, so why didn't she claim it?

'Thea!' Kipp's muffled, panicked voice sounded through the debris. 'Thea, are you in there?'

'Thea, can you hear us?' Cal shouted.

'She's safe,' Wilder called back through the wreckage. 'There was a cave-in.'

'Should we move the rocks —'

'No!' Wilder replied, easing back from Thea's blade and feeling along the cave wall for the torch he knew was there somewhere. 'Follow the base of the cliff north with the horses. This is a tunnel, and it comes out on the other side of the mountain. You can meet us there.'

He searched his pockets for his flint. Striking the two pieces together, he lit the torch, light flooding the antechamber, casting a golden glow across Thea.

'You planned this...' she said, her dagger dropping to her side.

'You didn't give me much choice.'

Her gaze was bright with anger. 'If you were attempting to win my trust, you just failed.'

'Uhhh, Thea?' Kipp called out again. 'We probably need confirmation that, you know, you're alive...?'

Wilder didn't look away from her. 'I needed you alone for this conversation,' he told her. 'Needed you somewhere you couldn't run away or cut me off. You will hear everything I have to say. As you promised. We're still heading towards Vios; the meet point is close to where the Wesford Road meets the main trade route of Aveum. And should you still wish it by the end, this detour will not interfere with your quest for vengeance. You have my word.'

'Your word means nothing to me,' Thea said, her eyes deadened. 'Is this a trap? Where you lead me to your shadow masters and hand me over?'

Gods, he hated that he'd made her doubt him so thoroughly, that she truly thought so little of him after all they'd shared. If he could just get her to listen, he could offer to show her the camp, to introduce her to the real shadow-touched folk. He could get her to talk to Anya, to Dratos – and if they couldn't sway her, then perhaps it was a job for the Shadow Prince himself.

'It's not a trap,' Wilder said quietly, trying to strip the hurt from his voice.

Thea stared him down, hard. There was so much anger there, so much grief. But she seemed to realise she had no choice, and slowly, she sheathed her dagger and cupped her hands around her mouth. 'I'm alive, Kipp!' she shouted. 'See you on the other side.'

A wave of relief flooded through Wilder. He had time, time to explain to her and only her what he'd been through, what had happened a year ago...

She was waiting with a flat expression and motioned for him to lead. 'You apparently know the way.'

Wilder started down the passageway, torch held high. They walked in silence, Wilder marvelling all the while that after all this time, he was standing beside her once more. Long after the fever from the arrow she'd shot had left him, he'd dreamt of her, every night. Now... it had been a year without her touch, a year without her kiss, her laugh...

Though she vibrated with fury beside him, he wanted her. He would always want her.

And yet, Althea Zoltaire, Althea *Embervale*, had a bigger role to play in the stage the midrealms had set. It was this that forced the words from his mouth when he knew she didn't want to hear them, knew they caused her pain.

'So, why haven't you used it?' he asked, feigning casualness. 'Your magic?'

'Who says I haven't?' she replied.

Wilder simply raised a brow. He wasn't about to throw Kipp to the wolves.

Thea sighed. 'How do you know I haven't?'

'You don't want to know.' It wasn't until he'd spoken to Kipp that he'd been sure, but he kept that detail to himself.

Thea kept walking, but he sensed her body go rigid beside him. 'All I have ever asked of you is the truth, so don't tell me what I want.'

Wilder took the hit. 'I can feel its absence in the world. Ever since we —'

'Don't,' Thea cut him off.

He tried again. 'We're connected —'

'I said, don't.' But her voice was strained, and where Wilder would once have felt a crackle of magic alongside her warning, there was empty silence.

'Grief can affect —'

Her gaze snapped to his, full of fire. 'You think I grieve for you?'

Wilder swallowed the lump in his throat. 'I think you grieve for a lot of things, Princess.'

'Is this what's meant to save you? Dredging up our shitty history? One that was built on lies?'

'I never lied about how I felt. Not about you, not about us —'

'There is no us. I don't want to hear any more about it.'

The air was knocked out of Wilder's lungs, and he struggled to compose himself, grateful to be the one holding the torch, angling it away from the devastation he knew was clearly written on his face.

'But you'll listen to the rest?' he asked.

'I have nothing better to do.'

It wasn't exactly how he wanted to tell her after all this

time, but as they moved through the tunnel beneath the mountain, Wilder knew he may not get another chance with her alone. He took a deep breath and straightened his shoulders.

'It all starts with Talemir,' he began.

He felt, rather than saw, the shift in Thea at the mention of his former mentor, the legendary Warsword of Thezmarr, the Prince of Hearts.

'The day Malik was hurt in Naarva, something happened to Talemir as well,' he continued, wishing he'd had the foresight to bring a canteen. His mouth was already dry. 'A reaper... A reaper pinned him down, got its talons in his chest. I couldn't get there in time. I tried – gods, I tried. To help Malik, to help Tal, but... it already had him. It lifted him up in the air with its shadows, pierced his heart with its fucking claws. Eventually I managed to bring it down, but Tal... Tal was hurt, and our unit was in pieces. I got him and Mal on their horses and retreated, to get them back to Thezmarr, to Farissa and the healers.'

Wilder paused, fighting to keep his voice even. He'd never told this story aloud before, not like this.

'Malik... Well, you know what fate Malik faced, what he still endures. But Tal... For a while, Tal seemed to heal. He was out of the infirmary in a matter of hours. He was broken up about Malik, same as me. But he was himself. Or so I thought.'

'He was still hurt?' Thea asked, seeming to forget her vow of silence momentarily. Wilder was grateful. Her voice grounded him.

He nodded. 'In a way... It wasn't until months after that battle at Islaton, after he and I got sent to the ruins of Naarva on another mission, that I found out the truth.'

He could see Thea fighting with herself over whether to engage with his tale, wringing her hands before her. In the end, curiosity won. 'Which was?'

'He'd been cursed. In the same way you nearly were in the Bloodwoods after the initiation test. The reaper who attacked him got its darkness in his heart. He's...'

'He's what?' Thea pressed, all pretence of nonchalance forgotten.

Wilder hated saying it, even now, even after all these years. 'He's a half-wraith. Like those people you saw caged in Tver, like the poor creatures you saw imprisoned in Artos' dungeons... Like the one Cal and Torj shot from the sky. If the reaper had succeeded, he'd be something far worse – kin to the howlers, or a full wraith himself.'

Thea blinked at him. 'You're telling me that Talemir Starling, the legendary Warsword, the Prince of Hearts, Thezmarr's undefeated dual wielding champion, is a fucking shadow wraith?'

'Half,' Wilder corrected her. 'Though his kind prefer to be called shadow-touched. Like I told you in the woods, he's still human. But he has shadow power, and wings, and claws when he wants.'

Thea shook her head.

'I swear it,' Wilder implored. 'I know my word means nothing to you now, but this... this is so much bigger than you and me. This is about the midrealms' survival.'

'So I'm supposed to believe that Talemir Starling is leading his half-wraith army, alongside the Daughter of Darkness, in league with the reapers, to bring down the kingdoms?'

'I told you before, the shadow-touched aren't in league with the reapers, or anything that's trying to come through the Veil and destroy the kingdoms. They're on our side, Thea.'

'Side? And what side is that, exactly?'

He wanted to reach out and shake her by the shoulders. She knew him better than this, she had to... But he kept walking. 'The side that wants to see the light triumph over darkness.'

Thea was quiet, and for that he couldn't blame her. Furies knew he hadn't handled it well when he'd finally discovered the truth about Talemir. The brawl they'd had amid the sun orchids in Naarva had been one for the ages.

He slowed his pace ever so slightly, hoping Thea wouldn't notice. He'd do anything to give her more time to process the truth, to give them more time to work through this together.

They walked through the tunnel in silence while Wilder waited for her questions to come. He knew she was turning things over in her mind, putting the pieces of the puzzle together – the messages from Dratos, how he'd corrected her on the cliffs of Thezmarr when she'd called the shadow-touched man caught in the vine blight *it* instead of *he*. How he'd put King Artos' prisoners out of their misery and prevented another from being questioned by Torj. And then the cage of shadow-touched people in Tver... She would see. She had to.

'But it didn't all start with Talemir...' Thea said slowly.

Wilder glanced across at her. 'What do you mean?'

'He wasn't the first half-wraith,' she ventured.

'Well, I don't think we can ever know who was the *first*.'

'But we know there was at least one before him.'

The realisation barrelled into Wilder like a wave. 'Anya.'

A muscle in Thea's jaw tensed. 'Anya.'

'I didn't know...' Wilder heard himself saying. 'I didn't know who she was to you.'

'Who she is to me hardly matters. It's who she is to the midrealms that will count. They were right about the Embervales... Power-hungry, shadow-wielding royals...'

'That's not —'

'Then what is it?' she challenged.

Wilder shook his head. 'The shadow-touched are innocent. And there are forces out there taking them, torturing them... Murdering children.'

'Children?' Thea scoffed. 'The only one I've seen torturing anyone is Anya. I've seen her camps. I've heard the screams. She's the monster.'

'It's not Anya.'

'If not the Daughter of Darkness, then who?'

'It's Artos, Thea.'

A beat of silence pulsed between them before Thea burst into a dark laugh. 'Of course you think the man who has called for your capture is the enemy.'

Wilder had to stop himself throwing his hands up in exasperation. '*Artos* is responsible for the blight upon the midrealms. *He's* the one letting the reapers and monsters through the Veil.'

'What a load of horseshit.'

She charged ahead, as though she couldn't stand his presence a moment longer, and for a minute, Wilder stared after her.

'Where did you go, Thea?' he whispered into the dark.

A cold knot of dread settled in Wilder's gut as he led Thea through the mountain passageway. He had known, deep down, that it would take more than words to sway her. He'd broken something between them, something he wasn't sure he could mend. It was this crack in their foundation that was blinding her to the truth. He would have to find a way to show her, to pull her from the darkness into the light.

The silence between them was festering. She hadn't said a word in – what, an hour? He simply couldn't – wouldn't – bear it any longer. He turned to her, ready to implore her, ready to —

Even in the torchlight he could see that her face was colourless.

Her whole body was wracked with tremors.

He thought he had slowed the pace, but in reality... She was barely shuffling beside him.

'Thea?'

She didn't look at him, her expression unchanged, like she hadn't even heard him.

He reached across, his hand closing over her arm. Her cloak was wet and freezing cold.

'Fuck,' he muttered, drawing her to a stop and scanning her face.

Her lips were blue.

'Furies save me, why didn't you say something?' He patted her clothing, finding it all soaked. Had it been like that since he'd brought down the entrance to the cave? Panic seized his chest in a tight fist as she stared at him with a vacant expression, her teeth barely chattering any more.

'Thea...' He uttered her name in a plea. 'We've got to get you warm.'

Wilder tried to shut down his fear for her as he surveyed

the desolate cave floor for something he could use as fuel for a fire. There was hardly anything. A few twigs and leaves that had been blown in by the wind at some point, and gathering them would be a challenge with his wrists bound in chains. But he wouldn't let her freeze.

Torches. There had to be more torches lining the walls. That was how the tunnels were set up, so that if an entire unit passed through, they could illuminate the whole passageway.

Thea didn't protest as he sat her down on a nearby rock. That fact alone was concerning enough. It spurred Wilder into action. He raced down the tunnel, scouring the walls for sconces and unlit torches, snatching up any he could find. But he couldn't leave Thea alone for too long.

When he returned, she was rocking where she sat, her gaze distant.

'Gods,' Wilder muttered, throwing the torches to the ground and making quick work of layering the kindling he'd gathered. He cursed his manacles for slowing his movements before touching his lit torch to the pile. It wasn't the blazing fire she needed, but it was better than nothing.

Wilder gathered her in his arms and placed her by the flames, holding her hands to the heat for her.

He waited a few moments, but her state remained unchanged.

'It's these fucking clothes,' he said, rubbing the end of one sodden sleeve between his fingers. He ran a hand through his hair, manacles clanking. 'As if you didn't hate me enough already...'

He reached for the buttons of her cloak.

'I have to get these off,' he told her, though he doubted his words even registered at this point. 'We have to get you warm. Now. Tell me this is okay,' he pleaded. If he didn't do this, there was a real chance that she would die. He'd seen it happen countless times before. He knew she'd argue that there was no way she could die, because of the fate stone that hung around her neck, but Wilder refused to risk her life based on some superstitious gem.

She didn't argue, didn't bat his hands away, but that wasn't enough, not for him.

'Thea, tell me you understand. Tell me I have permission to take these wet clothes off. Please. Your life is at stake.'

He waited, growing more panicked by the second.

Until a rattling wheeze sounded. 'I understand,' she croaked, her eyes now closed. 'Take them.'

He had her permission, her consent, but it didn't stop the regret weighing down every movement as he pushed her cloak from her shoulders and started on the laces of her shirt. Of all the ways he'd imagined undressing Thea for the first time after everything… this hadn't been one. He tried to avert his gaze where he could, but there was no missing the weight she'd lost in the last year, how much of her softness had hardened. And scars. So many new scars.

There was a soft thud as a tattered pack of cards tumbled from one of her pockets. Thea didn't play cards. Not that he knew of. He caught a glimpse of the text on one card, which was barely legible: *strong of mind, strong of body, strong of heart.* The words sent a shiver down his spine. There was something strangely familiar about them, something that made the hair at his nape stand on end.

But with Enovius, the god of death, waiting in the wings for Thea, a deck of cards was the least of Wilder's concerns. Finding the key to his manacles in one of her pockets, he undid his irons and spread his cloak down on the cave floor.

Then, he removed his own clothing. Leaving only his undershorts on, he created a bed of insulation with his still-warm layers. Laying Thea down, facing the fire, he settled behind her, wincing as her icy skin pressed against him. But he would give her all his warmth, everything he had in a heartbeat. Ignoring the damp press of her undergarments, he wrapped himself around her and covered them with his cloak, willing the heat of his body to soak into her.

He clung to her, pulling her as close as possible. 'I wish we had stayed in those hot springs in the forest,' he told her, pressing a kiss to her hair. 'I wish that every day.'

Thea didn't reply.

# CHAPTER NINE

## THEA

A solid wall of heat engulfed her. Tremors wracked Thea's body, but someone held her tightly, wrapping her in warmth, and the comforting scent of rosewood and leather.

*Wilder.*

She took a trembling breath, her whole body aching. *What happened?* she wondered sluggishly. *How did I end up here?* She remembered walking, listening to Hawthorne explain about the shadow wraiths, about his mentor, but...

She was almost *naked. He* was almost naked.

'Thea?' he murmured against her bare skin, his grip tightening ever so slightly.

She was still shaking, her mind foggy with what she now realised was delirium, fever. Her breaths became short, shallow gasps, each one burning her lungs.

'You're alright,' the warrior told her, the rich sound of his voice vibrating against her back. 'I've got you.'

Thea couldn't open her eyes, but the colours behind her lids were vivid as they took the shape of memories: finding

Malik's dagger on the Mourner's Trail, spying on the Warswords atop the cliffs, Wilder twirling her dagger between his fingers.

*'Looking for this?'*

Each memory barrelled into her with an intensity to match the fever that had her in its grasp. Kissing Wilder on the doorstep of his cabin, the kiss that had obliterated every other experience before it. That first time in the Bloodwoods, where she'd gripped the arrow as he drove into her. Carving out the reaper's heart after the initiation test. Training with him in the arena, his hands guiding hers. Those same hands strapping on her armour. Every kiss, every intimate moment swam in Thea's spotted vision.

*Because I fucking love you.*

*This thing between us is endless.*

*Every part of me belongs to you.*

A sob shuddered through Thea, at the pain, at the fever, at everything. 'Was any of it real?' she croaked, her voice raw and trembling. 'Did any of it mean anything?'

Her shivering eased as those powerful arms tensed around her. 'How do you think you survived that reaper attack in the Bloodwoods?'

Thea opened her mouth, but the words wouldn't come, a fresh wave of tremors taking her.

'Aveum springwater can only do so much on its own,' the melodic voice replied, sounding suddenly distant.

She remembered the sweet trickle of water, crisp and fresh on her parched tongue, how her whole body had tingled as its magical properties surged through her. She remembered watching in awe as the deepest of her wounds knitted together, leaving only faint pink scars behind. As the network of black veins across her skin retreated, disappearing entirely within mere moments.

'But when it's used on someone you love?' he said. 'There is nothing more powerful.'

Thea clung to those words with all her remaining strength, but it wasn't enough. The visions before her ceased, and she slipped beneath the veil of consciousness.

Thea stirred, nestling into the delicious heat that pressed against her front. Warm, comforting and solid, a heartbeat drumming steadily against her own, the gentle pressure of a broad palm across her bare back.

She inhaled deeply, her breathing free of tremors, free to lose herself in the familiarity of his smell. She could almost taste him.

*Him.*

Thea's eyes flew open, meeting a bare, tattooed chest.

She was naked but for her undergarments, curled up against an equally near-naked Wilder Hawthorne.

They lay on their sides, atop a pile of clothes, beneath his cloak, with Thea tucked under the warrior's bearded chin. One of his muscular legs was draped over her lower half, trapping the warmth around her, the weight of it pressing her to his —

Desire pulsed between her thighs, and Thea fought the urge to move beneath him, so that she might...

What was she thinking? Was a muscled body and a warm embrace all it took for her to forget why she was here in the first place?

Hawthorne stirred, more of his nakedness brushing

against her.

Thea stiffened in his arms.

'It seems we've come full circle, Princess…' His voice was thick with sleep.

He was right. They had been here before, and yet they had not. Not like this, not with him as her enemy.

She scrambled away from him, scanning the floor for her clothes in the light of the dying fire. They were spread out on the opposite side, and she snatched them up, the fabric cool but dry on her warm skin.

Hawthorne rose onto his elbows and blinked sleepily, the cloak dangerously low around his hips. 'Are you alright?'

Thea laced her shirt with more vigour than she intended. 'We need to get moving.'

Realisation dawned on the warrior's face. 'You went into shock,' he said. 'From exposure to the cold. I wasn't trying to take advantage of you. I hope you know that.'

Thea couldn't bring herself to look at him. Regardless of what she believed and didn't believe about the fallen Warsword, she knew in her bones that he would never do that.

'We need to move,' she said again.

No matter how hard Thea tried, she couldn't reconcile the two men she had known. The fierce, hardened warrior who had betrayed his guild, his people, and the man who had told her he was hers, who had fought at her side and chased her nightmares away.

She turned her back as Hawthorne stood, letting the cloak fall as he reached for his clothes.

'Thank you,' she said, facing the jagged cave wall. 'For what you did.'

'Couldn't let you die without your vengeance, Princess.'

Thea tensed at the nickname, hating how it made her toes curl, even now. She distracted herself by picking up the cards Audra had given her from where they'd been left in a neat stack. She ran her thumb over the bleeding words on the top card: *Strong of mind, strong of body, strong of heart...*

'I'm decent,' Hawthorne told her.

But when she turned around, he was still buttoning his shirt, much of his golden skin still on display.

Thea started as his manacles rattled. *How's that possible?* How had he removed his clothing with the irons linking his wrists? Was she imagining things? She tried to remember whether he'd been wearing them when they'd awoken, but her mind was fuzzy. She fumbled in her pocket. The key was exactly where she'd left it. She was still delirious from the fever, she decided. But it was his scar that caught Thea's gaze next. The scar she had given him with her arrow. The satisfaction she expected to feel didn't come.

'Admiring your handiwork?' Hawthorne asked, tugging his shirt in place.

Jaw clenched, Thea scooped his cloak up from the ground and thrust it at him, but he caught her hand at his chest, his fingers gripping her palm firmly.

'It was real,' he breathed. 'All of it.'

It was an echo of something that had passed between them the night before, but the memory was just out of Thea's grasp, lost amid the remaining fog of her fever. She made to pull back, but the warrior held firm, his silver gaze molten as it pierced her own.

'Tell me you don't want me, Thea. I need to hear you to say the words.'

He was close enough that she could feel the heat radiating from him, the same heat he'd offered her in the depths of her cold exposure. Yet despite the furnace of a man standing before her now, she shivered, digging deep for the power of will.

'I don't want you,' she told him, knees buckling.

'I don't believe you.' He closed the small gap between them, still clutching her hand. 'My shirt smells like you,' he murmured, the sound a low rumble in the shell of her ear. 'I still have your marks on my back from our last night together. You claimed me long ago, Thea. You don't get to say I'm not yours now.'

The mere mention of that night in the war camp had her thighs clenching together. She knew better than this by now. She knew he wasn't to be trusted. But her body was a traitor, just like him. Already she was leaning into his touch. Already she imagined the feel of him inside her, filling her and stretching her until everything else fell away.

Hawthorne's gaze darkened, as though he could see straight through her, as though he was picturing the very same thing. Manacles clanking, his hands slid down her sides, gripping her hips, drawing her even closer. The press of hard muscle against her was thrilling, need dampening her undergarments, blurring her senses.

His lips brushed the line of her jaw.

'I...' The words caught in her throat.

Hawthorne stilled at the first sign of her hesitation, his chest rising and falling. 'I didn't have a choice,' he said, voice hoarse.

Thea stepped back. 'Choice? You want to talk to me about not having a choice?' It was as though an icy bucket of reality had been tipped over her head and she scrambled to put more distance between them, horrified at what she'd almost done.

'I can't believe I almost fell for it, for you. Again. Your lies are poison.'

Hawthorne's hand drifted to where the arrow scar marred his skin beneath his shirt, his face falling before he seemed to gather himself, swinging his cloak around his shoulders and fastening it at his collarbone.

'To Vios it is, then.' He picked up one of the still-burning torches and started down the tunnel.

They had been walking in silence for over an hour. The only sounds were the dripping of the cave walls, the rattling of Hawthorne's chains and the crunch of stone beneath their boots. It was still cold enough for Thea's breath to mist before her face, but her clothes were dry and she wasn't shivering.

*Thanks to him*, she thought bitterly.

But with only her anger and resentment for company, the hours stretched on infinitely, and after a time, Thea glanced across at her surly prisoner.

'Let's pick up the pace. I want to get to Vios before this fucking eclipse.'

To her surprise, Hawthorne gave a dark laugh at that. 'We wouldn't want to miss the festivities, would we?'

Thea scoffed. 'Festivities? It's hardly a celebration. More like a final prayer for the Furies to swoop in and save us all.'

'Because the gods are always so benevolent.' Hawthorne examined the torch he was holding, no doubt noticing the flames dimming. 'You didn't think the midrealms would miss this opportunity, did you? Even *I* know there is to be a ball in King Artos' honour.'

Thea frowned. 'What?'

'A thank you gift, from the people of the midrealms, or at least their tax coin, for the way he has taken Tver under his wing – providing resources and housing, helping to rebuild at his kingdom's own expense...'

'That's...'

'Very generous, yes.' Though the way Hawthorne said it between gritted teeth made it clear he was far from impressed.

'You've never liked him – Artos, I mean.'

'Can't say I have. Are you forgetting that he tried to use his empath abilities on you at his last grand affair?'

'No.'

'Glad to hear it. At least you've got your wits about you in that respect.'

Thea's cheeks burned at the jab. 'How much longer?' she asked.

'Not far now.'

'How descriptive.'

'You always used to appreciate my cryptic nature,' he replied, but his tone was heavy with resignation. After a moment, he sighed. 'You don't believe what I told you last night, do you?'

'It's hard to believe the word of a traitor.'

He recoiled at that. 'Where is she?' he demanded. 'The Thea I knew would have questions.'

'The Thea you knew is dead.'

'The Thea I knew had a few more years left, according to that damn stone around her neck.'

It was Thea's turn to flinch.

'Ask me,' Hawthorne implored, stopping abruptly and turning to face her. 'Ask me anything and I'll tell you.'

'Fine,' she snapped, reaching for the question that was never far from the forefront of her mind, the subject he'd refused to share more about in the past. 'How do you become an immortal Warsword?'

He hesitated, just for a second, before he answered. 'When you pass the Great Rite, you ask the Furies.'

'It can't be that simple.'

'You ask and they decide.'

'And they said "no" to you?' Thea asked, incredulous.

'No.'

She spun to face him, a thousand accusations primed and ready to strike. 'What are you saying? That you've been an immortal Warsword this entire time?'

'No, Thea. I'm saying I never asked.'

Suddenly, Thea wasn't sure she was breathing. 'Why?' she croaked.

There was a long silence before Hawthorne spoke again. 'Why would I want to watch the world fester, and the people I care about perish? Almost all of those who were gifted immortal life moved on beyond the Veil long ago, into realms that understood such things. For me... living alone forever in any wretched place was the last thing I wanted.'

Despite herself, a lump formed in Thea's throat at that confession, her heart aching for the man she had once known and the pain he'd faced making that decision. But that was a different person to the one who walked beside her now.

*'Bring him Thezmarr's justice... Do that, Althea Zoltaire, and his swords are yours.'*

'Please, Thea...' Hawthorne murmured. 'Keep talking. Keep asking me whatever you need. I'm an open book.'

'It's a little late for that.' Thea increased her pace. It didn't matter who he had once been. It didn't matter what he'd told her about the shadow wraiths, or *shadow-touched*, as he called them. He had still betrayed his Warsword vows, still betrayed the midrealms, and there was no coming back from that. Not for him, and not for her, not when her sole goal in her limited days was to become the very thing he had spurned.

'Then I'll show you,' he said firmly, catching up. 'I'll show you the truth, and you can decide on which side you fall.'

'I side with the midrealms,' Thea argued. 'As did you, once upon a time.'

'Not all is what it seems —'

'It never is with you,' she snapped, before she noticed the hint of light ahead. 'We're nearly out,' she said, more to herself than to Hawthorne. Even the air felt fresher suddenly.

Hawthorne cleared his throat, slowing unexpectedly, as though he wasn't quite ready to leave the confines of the tunnel.

'What is it?' Thea said, eyes narrowing. His hesitancy only made her increase her pace. If he didn't want to leave here, that was exactly what she should be doing, and fast.

'There might be a travelling companion of mine there,' he managed.

'Ah, another traitor, then?' Thea quipped, her hand going to her sword.

'No,' Hawthorne ground out. 'But there's something you need to know —'

But they had reached the open mouth of the tunnel, the late afternoon light nearly blinding after so much time in the dark. When Thea's eyes adjusted, she saw that right in front of the entrance were Cal and Kipp, a campfire blazing beside them with a goat roasting above the flames. They were both grinning like fools, holding flasks Thea didn't recognise —

A stranger's laugh sounded.

Thea looked to the other side of the fire, where a beautiful woman in fighting leathers stood, raising a flagon of wine to her lips. Her gaze snapped up at Thea and Hawthorne's approach, recognition – relief – flooding her expression as she clapped eyes on the hulking warrior at Thea's back.

Thea glanced at Cal and Kipp, noting with a pang of jealousy that they looked happier in the company of this stranger than they had in the last year with her.

'Thea!' Kipp rushed forward, sweeping her up in a drunken embrace. 'You made it!'

'She almost didn't,' Hawthorne muttered from behind her, but the others didn't hear.

She pierced him with a stare. 'Friend of yours, then?' she asked, nodding in greeting to the newcomer, noting the fine make of her leathers and weapons, a calibre she hadn't seen in some time.

Hawthorne cleared his throat. 'Something like that...'

The woman grinned, offering her hand, and Thea took it without thinking, shaking it firmly.

'Pleased to meet you,' the newcomer told her. 'The name's Adrienne Ashford. Ranger and general to the guerrilla forces of Naarva.'

Thea was still shaking her hand when the thread of recognition drew taut.

*Adrienne.* The name echoed in her mind for a moment before she realised. This was *the* Adrienne. Hawthorne's former lover.

The pained expression on Hawthorne's face confirmed it.

# CHAPTER TEN

## THEA

Abitter taste spread across Thea's tongue. For the past year, she had been hunting the traitor Wilder Hawthorne, and he'd been... What? Shacking up with an old flame?

*'I cared about her a lot. She was good to me.'* Hawthorne had told her of the Naarvian ranger over a year ago amid the ruins of Delmira. And Thea had replied that he deserved someone to be good to him. She had truly believed that, once.

'Glad to meet you at last, Thea,' Adrienne said warmly.

She was beautiful. Her blonde hair framed her pretty face and hung loose past her shoulders. Her features were feminine, not even close to marred by the smudges of dirt across her flawless skin. She smiled with full lips, luscious lips that Thea couldn't help but picture brushing against Hawthorne's mouth. Her mind conjured up the image of them together, a tangle of perfect, naked limbs —

Releasing the woman's hand, Thea chastised herself. None of it mattered. Not a single thing.

'Thea —' There was a pleading note in Hawthorne's voice as it interrupted her thoughts, but he was cut off by a snort of amusement.

Adrienne was surveying the heavy manacles around his wrists. 'Things are going well then, I take it?'

'I've got it under control,' Hawthorne grunted, approaching the fire.

For another second, Thea could see them together, so easily. The Naarvian rebel and the fallen Warsword... The way they spoke to one another was with such familiarity as well. She could imagine the blonde in his arms, beneath his body, in his bed. *It doesn't matter*, Thea chanted to herself.

Adrienne gave another chuckle at Hawthorne's expense. 'Sure looks that way,' she quipped, before she turned her gaze on Thea. 'You look like her, you know...'

The Naarvian didn't need to specify to whom she referred. The prickling on Thea's nape told her all she needed to know. Hawthorne's former lover was telling her that she looked like her long-lost shadow-wielding sister, Anya. The true heir of Delmira.

A flurry of memories came back to her then, shown to her once by a reaper in Delmira. *A field of flowers. Two pairs of small hands braiding them together to form a necklace. The smell of heather. The darkness of being hidden in a wagon, hurtling over uneven terrain, a small body either side of her.*

Thea clenched her fists at her sides. 'If you're in league with the Daughter of Darkness, and you're in league with the traitor here, then you're a traitor too.'

To her surprise, Adrienne grinned, tapping the longsword strapped to her back. 'Oh, I was a traitor long before I met Anya, or Hawthorne's moody arse.'

Hawthorne made a noise of agreement from afar. 'You've never been one for the rules, I'll give you that.'

'Nor has Thea, from what I hear,' Adrienne offered, giving Malik's dagger at her belt a meaningful look.

*Fair point*, Thea thought, but there was no way she'd admit it aloud. Instead, she sought Cal and Kipp, striding to their side of the fire, noting their rosy cheeks and red-tipped noses.

'Why aren't you detaining her?' she hissed, with a glance across at their unwelcome guest.

Kipp's brow furrowed. 'Detaining her? For what?'

'Associating with a known traitor?' Thea bit back.

'You want to arrest everyone he's ever talked to?' Cal hiccuped.

Thea rolled her eyes. Men. Absolutely useless.

But her attention was drawn back across the fire to where Adrienne was speaking with Hawthorne.

'Any luck?' the ranger asked him.

'No,' he replied bluntly.

She clapped him heartily on the shoulder. 'I guess it's plan B, then. I'll let the others know what to expect.'

'You think I'm just going to let you go?' Thea blurted in disbelief.

Adrienne looked amused. 'You sound like Anya too.'

'I'm *nothing* like her,' Thea snapped. 'And you're mad if you think I'm setting you loose on the midrealms when you serve her.'

'You may have your Warsword in chains, storm wielder, but without your magic, I don't see you being able to stop us all.'

Thea's jaw nearly dropped, for more than one reason.

This woman knew who she was. Knew of her power and

her loss of it. Which meant that Hawthorne had done more than betray her – he'd sold her secrets to the enemy as well.

Her hands itched for her dagger, her sword, her throwing stars in her boots. 'I have fought and slain worse than the likes of you.'

'I don't doubt it,' Adrienne allowed. 'But for the record... I don't serve Anya,' the rebel said calmly. 'I serve the Shadow Prince.'

Thea's mouth went dry at the mention of the other enemy leader. Someone worse than the Daughter of Darkness, who united the strange creatures that sprouted wings and talons like their monster counterparts...

'Thea...' Cal interjected. 'Maybe you should eat something? Sit down by the fire for a while?'

Thea's whole body was taut with tension, but Kipp came to her side and nudged her gently with his elbow. 'He's right, you know. No one is going anywhere yet. There's roast goat to be had and wine to be drunk, and it's too fucking cold to leave the fire.'

Thea suppressed a sigh as she scanned the campsite. No one was fleeing the scene; no one was whispering treasonous plans in the dark. In fact, Hawthorne had edged away from the group, and was tending to his stallion as best as his bound hands would allow.

The memory hit her without warning, and the Wesford Road materialised before her, Hawthorne at her side.

*'You never told me what your horse's name is...'*

*Wilder's cheeks flushed and he outwardly grimaced. 'His name is Biscuit.'*

*Thea blinked. 'Biscuit?'*

*Wilder was clearly trying to keep a straight face. 'Malik and Talemir's idea of a joke,' he admitted. 'Bastards were there when I claimed him. They jumped in when it came to finalising the poor creature's name. It stuck.'*

*A laugh bubbled out of her. 'Biscuit. Your warhorse, the gift you received for being one of the most infamous warriors in all the midrealms... is called Biscuit.'*

Not long after, Hawthorne had threatened to follow her to Tver and name her stallion *Pancake*. She'd only laughed.

Now, Thea watched him, the man who'd shed the facade of friendship, of something more, to ally with those who sought to destroy everything she held dear. She tracked his tender yet masculine motions as he brushed the burrs from Biscuit's coat and checked the shoe on each foot for stones. The picture before her was a myriad of contradictions.

'What even is a ranger?' Cal asked Adrienne loudly. 'Are you some sort of spy?'

The newcomer laughed. 'We're more like scouts, I suppose. We guard and protect the remaining lands of Naarva. That can mean spying or conducting raids... Mostly we deal with the blight of the shadow wraiths.'

'But without Naarvian steel, how do you —'

Kipp came to Thea's side. 'You alright?' he asked quietly.

'Fine,' she replied, trying to block out the delicate sound of Adrienne's voice as she chatted to Cal with so much ease. 'Where's this food, then?' Thea couldn't remember the last time she'd eaten properly, and now, as the aroma of roast goat filled the air, her stomach rumbled.

Kipp threw an arm around her. 'Come on, I'll fix you a plate.'

Thea let Kipp lead her to a fallen tree and sit her on one of the saddle blankets. She couldn't help but watch the ranger and Hawthorne, something ugly prickling under her skin as she did.

'Kipp?' she asked, remembering what the Warsword had told her in the cave. 'What do you know of Aveum springwater?'

Kipp's brows furrowed. 'You mean beyond the widely known healing properties? That it comes from the sacred Pools of Purity in the winter kingdom?'

'Yes, besides all that. Is there anything that…' She swallowed the lump in her throat that formed as she watched Hawthorne pass Adrienne a flask. 'Is there anything that makes it more potent?'

'Surely Wren would have told you?' Kipp said casually.

Thea imagined there were many things Wren had told her in their early days of alchemy that she had been too stubborn to learn. She had been too focused on wielding swords and shields to commit much else to memory back then. 'Told me what?'

He followed her gaze to the Warsword and Naarvian. 'That when it's used on someone you love, it's the most powerful healing tonic known to the midrealms.'

Thea blinked.

Kipp nodded across the campsite to Hawthorne. 'He used his vial on you after the initiation test, didn't he?'

Thea ran a hand over her face, fighting down the emotion welling up inside her. 'He did.'

Kipp sighed. 'Don't suppose you fancy a drink?'

At last, Thea tore her gaze away from the duo and glanced up at her friend. 'Actually, Kipp… A drink sounds fucking amazing.'

Dusk settled around them, the hours passing quickly with the chatter between Thea's friends and Adrienne. Thea kept to herself, sipping on the flask of wine Kipp had given her and picking at her plate of meat. It was the most relaxed she'd seen her friends in a long time, and she fought the voice within that told her to force them onwards to Vios. For Adrienne was right: without her magic, there was no way she could detain Hawthorne *and* stop the ranger from leaving.

Hawthorne sat closer to the group, resting his elbows on his knees, contributing to the conversation every now and then in a low, barely audible tone. Whenever he spoke, Adrienne listened intently, sometimes laughing at something he said.

Thea finished her food and wine, passing the empty flask back to Kipp. 'I need to rest,' she told him.

She wasn't sure she liked how his face softened in understanding.

'We set your tent up just over there. I put a heated stone on your bedroll. Hawthorne said...' Kipp cringed, as though he expected her to erupt at any moment. 'Well, he mentioned you had some trouble with cold exposure in the tunnel. That you needed —'

'Thank you,' Thea interjected. 'Thank you, Kipp.'

Her friend seemed taken aback, his look of surprise only serving to wound her. Had she truly been so terrible? She winced inwardly. She knew the answer to that already.

Squeezing his shoulder in thanks and offering a wave to Cal, Thea left the campfire and headed for her tent.

Inside the canvas, she removed her outer layers and weapons one by one, sliding her boots off at the heel, careful of her hidden throwing stars. Along with her meditation cards, she placed these in a neat row at the edge of her tent, imagining each and every way she might stop Adrienne from leaving. There were several creative methods she had in mind.

She pulled the damned sapphire from the folds of her pocket too and vaguely wondered if she should give it back to the ranger. And that was how Thea drifted to sleep.

When she emerged from her tent the next morning, Adrienne had gone. Panicked, Thea scanned the frozen forest for Hawthorne.

'Looking for me, Princess?' he asked, from where he leant against a tree, arms folded over his broad, armoured chest, watching her.

'You didn't run,' she managed, approaching him, noting the manacles still around his wrists.

'I didn't run,' he agreed.

'You didn't want to follow your… friend?'

Hawthorne shook his head, the corner of his mouth quirking upward, showing a hint of that dimple beneath his beard. 'You and I aren't done.'

'I thought I made it clear yesterday, we're *very much* done.'

Her harsh words didn't seem to faze him. In fact… there was a brightness to those silver eyes that hadn't been there the day before.

'What?' she demanded, flicking her braid over her shoulder.

He leant in slowly, deliberately. 'Admit it,' he growled, his gaze dropping to her mouth. 'You were jealous.'

Thea's cheeks flamed and her body tensed instantly, involuntarily, infuriated and heated all at once. 'No.'

Hawthorne's laugh was rich and melodic, sending a pulse of longing straight to her core. 'Gods, you're stubborn,' he said, his lips almost close enough to graze hers.

Thea could feel him everywhere, even though he hadn't so much as touched her. She hated that she wanted him, even now, even amid all this mess, in the shadow of his betrayal. She hadn't dared admit it to herself before, but... she fucking *missed* him. She missed his voice and the ease of their conversations. She missed his mouth on hers, missed his hands and his body, missed the way he could unravel her so thoroughly.

He seemed to watch every subtle change in her expression as the conflict passed over her face. She had never been any good at masking her feelings – Wren had always told her so.

'There's nothing between Adrienne and me.' He reached for her, his fingers hooking into the waistband of her pants and tugging her closer. 'There hasn't been for years.'

'I don't care.'

'Keep telling yourself that, Princess.'

'I don't need to tell myself anything.'

'No? Not even after you've dreamt of me night after night? Not after your hands have somehow found their way into your pants as you thought of me?'

Thea bit her lip to keep herself in check, willing her body to remain rigid. There was no way he could know those things. He was baiting her.

Those silver eyes surveyed her, seeing straight through any notion of a facade. 'I knew from the moment I first kissed you that I'd never think of another woman again.

That you were it for me. Despite everything, that hasn't changed. Nor will it.'

Thea opened her mouth to argue, braced herself to shove his hands away, but a strange sound pierced the air, like something shooting through the forest —

'Flare,' Hawthorne said, his gaze snapping to the canopy, where beyond, a fiery red light carved through the sky.

'What?' Cal stumbled bleary-eyed from his tent, wincing at the cold.

'Red flare,' Hawthorne repeated. 'It's coming from the Wesford Road. A royal signal for help.'

Thea was already moving towards her mare, snatching up Hawthorne's swords of Naarvian steel. 'This had better not be a fucking trap you've set with your friends.' She swung herself up into her saddle, urging her horse towards where the flare had come from. Hawthorne was already up on his stallion, close behind her.

She heard Kipp and Cal rush to hurry after them, but she was already cantering through the forest, to where the Wesford Road met the Aveum trade route, the dreaded scent of burnt hair filling her nostrils.

When she came upon the road, she saw it immediately.

A beautiful carriage in Harenth's royal colours, surrounded by whorls of darkness, and three shadow wraiths clawing at its doors —

Steel sang as Thea unsheathed the former Warsword's blades.

'Thea,' Hawthorne shouted. 'Unchain me! I'm no use like this —'

But there wasn't time, even if she wanted to release him. All the guards were dead and the wraiths had broken through the window. A shriek sounded from within.

'Princess Jasira!' Thea gasped, lunging towards the carriage.

'Thea!' Hawthorne roared. 'Let me loose!'

But she was already surrounded by shadow, cleaving through cords of onyx with Naarvian steel, fighting her way to the source as another of the princess' screams pierced the forest. At her approach, the wraiths' attention snapped up. Tendrils of obsidian lashed out at her, and she answered them with her blades, the wraiths hissing in protest as they stalked towards her, circling her.

Thea didn't think of how she was to fight all three, didn't think of anything except for the princess who was sobbing inside the carriage.

She raised her blades against the monsters born of shadow and malice, just as Hawthorne had taught her, and Talemir Starling had taught him before. With perfect balance and timing, she wielded the two shimmering swords, the blades singing a battle hymn as they carved through the air and then through the arm of the first wraith, its screech utterly blood-curdling.

A talon swiped across the front of her armour, the impact sending her sprawling back, but she maintained her footing, lunging at her attacker, her swords slicing through muscles and tendons, black blood spraying. She parried another deadly strike of shadow, her blade piercing another limb before she was viciously thrown through the air, hitting a tree.

She rasped, the wind knocked out of her as she staggered to her feet, blinking in a daze at the three shadow wraiths still swarming the royal carriage, still eyeing her with brutal intent. The great swords in her hands were heavier than she recalled, for she had wielded them against worse than this and won. What was different now?

'Thea! For Furies' sake.' Hawthorne rushed to her side. 'Set me loose. Let me fight.'

She tasted iron, and felt a trickle of blood escape the corner of her mouth. She wiped it away with the back of her hand.

'No,' she said, throwing herself back at the wraiths. The last time he'd been loose around these creatures, Hawthorne had betrayed the entire midrealms. She'd be damned if that happened on her watch again, not with Princess Jasira so vulnerable amid it all.

The monsters blocked out the morning sun in a wave of shadow.

Thea heard Cal and Kipp's shouts from beyond the darkness, but she narrowed her focus on the wraiths, brandishing her swords, slicing through the lashing power and severing a taloned hand, the limb rolling across the ground with a thud. Undeterred by the onslaught, she countered their attacks with a quick barrage of slashes and parries, her steel carving arcs of what should have been utter devastation through the midnight around her —

But the wraiths evaded her, their shadows whipping at her no matter how fast her footwork, no matter her unwavering focus.

*Something is different*, she realised, panting.

She was losing.

So she did what came naturally to her. She looked inward, to her storm power, clawing at the place it had once been inside her.

It did not come. She had no magic at her fingertips, no lightning to spear them with —

Suddenly, a powerful hand lifted one of the swords from her grasp, the steel glimmering in the broken light.

*Hawthorne.*

Unbound, the alchemy-treated manacles discarded by his feet.

And Kipp, standing by his side, key in hand.

# CHAPTER ELEVEN

## WILDER

There was nothing like the weight of steel in hand to ground a warrior amid unyielding darkness. Gripping his sword, Wilder Hawthorne planted his feet apart, taking his place at Thea's side, where he belonged.

The look of betrayal on her face was fleeting as she flung herself back into the fight. Despite the blows she'd dealt, all three wraiths prevailed, their sinewy bodies twisting, contorting along with their shadows. They hissed viciously in his direction, sniffing through the slits in their faces, scenting the Furies-given power on him.

The first monster lunged and Wilder met its talons with a resounding clash, his Naarvian steel singing through the icy air, cutting through the darkness with swift precision. If he could immobilise them, Thea could carve out their hearts. They had done so before in the woods outside of Tver, as a team.

He shielded his mind against the lashes of onyx power that threatened to bring his worst memories to the surface and delivered a flurry of attacks, slicing through the veil of darkness that enveloped the road and the surrounding forest, ignoring the screams of despair that sounded from the royal carriage.

Amid the symphony of steel and shadow he could feel Thea fighting alongside him, whirling his second blade against the treacherous creatures, fighting back the tendrils, forcing her way to the heart of the fray.

Wilder followed her, as he always would. Their blades swept in radiant arcs of silver against the waves of obsidian, the wraiths hissing and recoiling, only to strike out again. Wilder spun on his heel, pivoting to deliver a powerful overhead swipe that shattered the inky essence around them, creating a window for Thea, who sliced through the outer defences. At last, the opportune moment presented itself and Wilder feinted right, thrusting his blade up in between one of the monster's ribs. Thea was there in an instant, leaping upon the falling body, her dagger already carving through the creature's torso to its heart. Shadows flickered as she wrenched the bloody, still-pulsing mass from the chest cavity.

But Wilder didn't stop. He channelled all his strength into another devastating slash and was rewarded with a cascade of hot, black blood hitting his front. With his free hand, he punched through the wraith's torso and closed his fist around its throbbing heart, tearing it directly from its body.

The beast screamed. High-pitched and ear-piercing.

Wilder tossed its heart to the ground and turned to the final wraith, whose shadows still clawed at the carriage.

Thea advanced, blood leaking from her nose, looking every bit the warrior he'd come to know she was. But something wasn't right. He had seen her take on this many monsters before with less effort, with less of her own blood spilt.

His gaze lingered on her a fraction too long, long enough for a cord of shadow to strike with teeth-rattling intensity, slamming him onto the road, sending him rolling across the gritty surface. The gravel and ice scraped at his exposed flesh and tore at his clothes —

'Wilder!' Thea screamed.

The wraith was upon him, pinning him to the ground, ribbons of darkness lashing at him, drawing his worst fears, his most traumatic experiences to the forefront of his mind, so that they started to take shape before him.

Gods, these wraiths were strong. Stronger than those he'd fought before. They almost held the full power of a reaper. He tried to pull his sword arm back so he could thrust his blade into the monster, but he was beneath the full weight of the creature now, its dark tendrils locking him in place, its shadows creeping closer and closer to his face, and to his heart. He closed his eyes with the force of his effort, trying to hold the attack off with his bloodied hands —

A high-pitched screech pierced the air, an agonised wail that nearly burst Wilder's eardrums and sent an icy shiver down his spine.

His eyes flew open to see the tip of his own sword protruding from the wraith's chest, and Thea standing in its wake.

The grip of the shadows weakened and a flash of silver blurred in his vision. Suddenly he had Malik's dagger in his hand, had caught it by reflex as Thea had thrown it to him.

Without thinking, he palmed the dagger and lunged for the incapacitated creature, piercing flesh, muscle and bone as he sliced through its front, digging deep with the blade to get to its heart.

The overwhelming scent of burnt hair and blood filled his nostrils, but Wilder didn't stop until he tore the wraith's heart from its body and flung it across the blackened snow.

Panting, he watched as the swirling masses of shadow disintegrated, leaving behind mutilated corpses and mangled monster hearts.

'Princess!'

Thea's voice carved through the chaos, and Wilder suddenly remembered why they were there in the first place.

Princess Jasira was in that carriage.

Still clutching Thea's dagger, he sprang to his feet, rushing towards the carriage, where Thea was already breaking the door open.

The young princess fell into her arms, sobbing.

'I thought...' she gasped. 'I thought I was going to die.'

'I would never let that happen,' Thea vowed, holding the princess upright.

For a second, it hit Wilder: a princess of Delmira had saved the Princess of Harenth, but no one would ever know it, except him, and —

He whirled around, scanning the roadside. Where were Cal and Kipp? He remembered their shouts at some point during the battle, but they had never made it past the initial shadows, had they?

At last, he spotted them beneath a towering oak. Cal knelt before Kipp, who was hunched over his knees, head hung to his chest. With Thea occupied by Jasira, Wilder jogged over to them.

'Are you hurt?' he asked the pair.

'He'll live,' Cal replied, with forced lightness, Wilder noted.

He surveyed Kipp. He couldn't see any blood, but that didn't mean there wasn't an internal injury. 'What happened?'

'Our swords do fuck all against those shadowy bastards,' Kipp grumbled. 'The big one got in a swipe at me. I ended up in the damn canopy.' He was holding his ribs.

'Anything broken?' Wilder demanded.

'You mean besides my pride?'

'Didn't know you had any of that,' Wilder quipped, gripping the lad's shoulder gently.

Kipp half laughed before he gasped in pain. 'Didn't know you made jokes.'

'Who said I was joking?'

'Hilarious.'

The tension in Wilder's chest eased. If Kipp was up for verbal sparring, the damage wasn't permanent. He looked to Cal. 'And you?'

'I'm fine,' the archer said, voice strained.

Kipp wheezed. 'Fine... You were practically sobbing when I came to.'

'I thought you were dead,' Cal replied, passing a hand over his face with a grimace.

'It's touching to know you'd weep for me —'

'I was *not* weeping —'

Wilder clapped a hand on Cal's back. 'Sounds like you both have it under control,' he told them, turning back to where Thea was talking softly with Princess Jasira.

'The only time I've seen a wraith before was at Thezmarr,' the princess said between ragged gasps, her face still wet with tears.

'You were at Thezmarr twenty years ago?' Wilder asked, wiping black blood spatters from his face with an equally grimy sleeve. 'You could have only been a child. You remember them? That's —'

The princess looked up in surprise and backed away, horror etched on her face. 'It's you,' she managed, retreating another clumsy step, her slippered feet sliding in the slush as she spun towards Thea. 'He's the fallen Warsword you've been hunting.' She surveyed the carnage around them with wide eyes. 'Was this *his* doing?'

Wilder cringed at that. He could only imagine what he looked like to the princess, covered in wraith blood, holding Thea's dagger as he half limped towards them.

But he couldn't let her believe the worst. 'I —'

'He's my prisoner,' Thea said sharply.

The princess' gaze darted between them. 'He... he doesn't look like a prisoner.'

Thea tensed, her own eyes flicking to the manacles he'd discarded in the snow.

With a heavy weight within pulling him down, Wilder did the only thing he could think of. He went to the irons, scooping them up from the sludge, handing them to Thea.

And then he offered her his wrists.

# CHAPTER TWELVE

## THEA

Thea hesitated, just for a moment, before locking the manacles around the warrior's blood-spattered skin.

'One day you'll trust me again,' he murmured, low enough for only her to hear.

'One good deed does not undo the wrong you've inflicted upon the midrealms,' she replied, striding towards Kipp, who stood with a wince, looking sheepish.

'Key,' she demanded.

He produced the key to the manacles. 'I stand by what I did. We would have died without him.'

Thea said nothing, but threaded the key through the leather string of her fate stone, where the metal came to rest against the gem.

'Fitting, that...' Hawthorne said, nodding to it. 'Both our fates entwined.'

His words stirred something raw in Thea's chest, and she turned her back to him so he couldn't see the conflict in her face. She needed to steel herself against all that roiled within. This wasn't about what she felt or didn't feel anymore. It was about duty and loyalty to the midrealms, to the guild he'd betrayed.

'The purpose of our journey has become twofold,' she addressed the group. 'We'll take the fallen Warsword to Vios for trial as agreed, and we'll escort the princess safely to her father. Her guards have been killed. She needs our protection.'

Cal and Kipp bowed low to Princess Jasira, both looking as exhausted as Thea felt.

The princess was unsteady on her feet, swaying as though she were about to collapse, so Thea moved closer, resting a reassuring hand on her shoulder.

'You're safe now,' she soothed. 'We won't let anything happen to you.'

Tears lined Jasira's gaze, her expression contorting as she tried to hold herself together. 'I...' She fell into Thea, burying her face in the crook of her neck, a sob breaking loose.

Thea held the princess and let her cry. 'It's alright,' she told her. 'You're alright.'

The men backed away quietly as the princess struggled to compose herself, hiccupping against Thea's shoulder. When she at last pulled back and wiped her red-rimmed eyes, Thea was struck by how similar they were to her father's.

Sniffling and patting her face dry with her sleeve, Princess Jasira regained her composure and turned to Cal and Kipp. 'Thank you, Guardians of Thezmarr,' she said, holding a trembling hand to her chest. 'I am in your debt.'

'It's our duty and our honour, Highness,' Cal replied earnestly. 'We'll find your horses at once and you can return to the warmth of your carriage.'

'The horses will be halfway back to Harenth by now,'

Kipp interjected. 'We should harness two of our mares to the carriage for the princess and I'll take the reins. Cal, you can ride the spare horse, and Thea, since you're so determined to watch Hawthorne at all times, you can ride double with him on the stallion. That will get us to Vios sooner. These roads aren't safe for the princess.'

Thea's gaze snapped to Kipp, her eyes narrowing, but her friend avoided her glare of disbelief, busying himself with *her* mare, leading it to the front of the royal carriage along with his own.

It took some time to set the horses up and return to their campsite to hastily pack away the rest of their things. Thea didn't speak as they went about their tasks in the frigid cold, keenly aware that the shadow wraiths could return at any moment with reinforcements – and that the former Warsword was following her every move.

*Strong of mind, strong of body, strong of heart.* She was determined to live by that mantra now. She would not be swayed by his games, by his words or the way he looked at her. The sooner this was over, the sooner she could go back to preparing for the Great Rite, which would hopefully call to her soon enough. She just had to get through these next few days.

Thea cornered Kipp as he finished securing his saddlebags. 'That's twice you've interfered,' she said, keeping her voice quiet.

To her surprise, frustration flashed across Kipp's face. 'That you know of,' he countered. 'And it'll be that many times my interference saves you in one way or another.'

Thea blinked, unease stirring low in her gut. 'I thought you were on my side...'

'I *am* on your side,' he argued. 'But you're too caught up in your own shit to see it.'

'I —'

'You might have accepted your power when you asked Wren to remove the alchemy on your fate stone. But that's not enough. You won't be able to master it until you stop resenting it. Until you —'

'This isn't about magic.'

'The fuck it's not. It's who you are. You need to come to terms —'

'I don't —'

'Horseshit, Thea,' Kipp said calmly. 'You blame it for messing with your plans to become a Warsword, for the burden of the throne, and...'

'Oh? There's more? Do tell.'

Kipp looked hesitant for a moment, but he ploughed on. 'I think you also blame it for what happened with Hawthorne.'

'Don't say his name to me.'

'You can slay a dozen monsters, but the name of a supposed fallen Warsword scares you?'

Thea glanced around, wary of being overheard. 'It doesn't scare me, I —'

'I'm calling horseshit again, Thea.'

Spotting Cal nearby, Thea looked to him for help, but their friend shrugged.

'I'm with Kipp on this one.'

Her friends left her holding her bedroll, staring after them. When had things changed for them? When had they started to doubt their mission? Doubt *her*? Thea tried to swallow down the lump in her throat, but the damn thing kept forming, leaving her with a tightness in her chest that wouldn't abate.

When at last they had finished packing up and the princess was settled in her carriage, Thea couldn't stop her gaze from falling on Hawthorne, who waited by his stallion for her. He stood tall and powerful, despite the irons at his wrists, the irons that he'd *let her* chain him with. Manacles or no, he was still every bit the seasoned warrior: his armour splattered with wraith blood, his muscled body primed for battle.

The sight made her knees weak.

The last thing she needed was to share a saddle with him. If anything, she needed to be as far away from him as possible, before her resolve fractured, before she bowed to the questions that had started brimming at the edges of her mind.

When she reached him, her chest ached at the thought of what came next.

*One last ride together*, she thought, fitting her boot to the stirrup and mounting Biscuit. She hated that she cared, despite how many times she told herself that she didn't, that he was a traitor and deserved whatever fate awaited him.

The saddle rocked as Hawthorne swung himself up behind her. His thick, muscular thighs cradled her sides, the heat of him already tempting her to lean back against him.

'Do you mind...?' he said gruffly, trailing off as his chains rattled.

She twisted to see him gesturing with the manacles, and her stomach dipped. He meant to put the chains over her head and around her front.

'Otherwise my fists will be digging into your back the whole ride,' he explained.

With her heart in her throat, all Thea could manage was a nod.

Hawthorne's arms came up and over her, his bound hands locking around her waist, a broad palm flat against her abdomen.

*Furies save me*, she thought, her gaze lifting to where the sun broke through the canopy before she addressed Cal and Kipp. 'Shall we?'

Cal was atop his own mare, while Kipp was in the driver's seat of the carriage, looking cold and uncomfortable. *Serves him right*, she mused, squeezing Biscuit's sides.

'You take the front, we'll take the rear,' she told Cal before she guided Hawthorne's stallion to the back of the princess' carriage and trained her gaze ahead.

They started down the road, the carriage rattling along, and her friends staring very intensely ahead. There was nothing to focus on but the press of the warrior at her back, and that warm palm spread across her middle.

Thea warred with herself, with everything she had told herself over the last year, with everything she'd thought she had known. She couldn't shake the sinking feeling of dread in her gut, nor could she slow the whirring of her mind. Ignoring the brush of Hawthorne's beard and the heat of his breath against her neck, she thought back to their detour through the mountain pass and what he'd told her along the way.

That the shadow-touched were innocent. That Talemir Starling was one of them. That Anya, the woman touted as the Daughter of Darkness, was on the side of light.

Thea shook the notion from her head. It wasn't possible.

Not after all she had seen of the winged leader. Not after she'd taken Wren.

'I can hear you thinking.'

The rich timbre of Hawthorne's voice sent a shiver down her spine. His grip around her tightened slightly, as though he'd felt the wave rush over her.

'What can I do?' he murmured softly. 'What more can I do to prove myself?'

'You —'

But Hawthorne forged on. 'I have fought beside you. I have saved your life. I have saved a princess of the midrealms. I have killed shadow wraiths and cursed reef dwellers. I have come willingly, submitted to your chains, all for a chance to talk with you...'

'And I have listened,' Thea replied, her knuckles burning with how hard she was clutching the reins.

'And yet...' The warrior's words were sad.

'And yet it's not up to me. I'm a warrior of Thezmarr. You once knew that better than anyone. My loyalty is to the guild, and it demands you face trial.'

'The guild is not all that matters in these realms.'

'No?' Thea snapped, her blood heating. 'What else matters, then?'

'Us,' he said simply.

'There is no us, Hawthorne. You made damn sure of that —'

He tensed behind her, drawing a sharp, impassioned breath. 'You can be angry all you want,' he told her. 'But don't deny this.'

His hand trailed up her middle and he rested his palm against her own racing heart. The warmth of him was utterly feverish, intoxicating.

'Don't you dare deny this,' he said in her ear.

Thea's entire body went taut beneath his touch, at the vibration of his voice against her skin. Were his hand to shift slightly, he'd find her nipples hard beneath her layers. Were it to drift south, he'd find arousal slick between her legs.

*It's a physical reaction to him, that's all*, she told herself, fidgeting in the saddle, trying not to generate any friction that might —

But with the smallest movement, she rubbed against him, and there was no denying the rock-hard length that pressed against her backside.

Hawthorne hissed. 'You keep doing that, Princess, and I won't be held accountable for what happens next.'

'Stop playing these games,' she told him quietly.

'You think this is a game to me?' He yanked her back against him, so she could feel every inch of his cock, even with the layers between them. 'I haven't stopped burning for you,' he growled. 'And I never will.'

Thea's breath caught as something dormant within flickered to life.

Hawthorne's hand trailed up her chest, past her throat, until he gripped her chin and turned her head to the side, so his gaze met hers.

He looked at her as though she were the one thing he'd been starved of his whole life. 'You're still in love with me, Thea.' His voice was like warm honey sliding down her skin, his touch like a brand.

But for all she felt, for all that warred within, Thea couldn't fathom what he'd done, and what he was now asking her to accept. So she dug deep for that anger she'd clung to for the last twelve months, for her sense of duty and for the vows she'd made to the guild.

'No, Hawthorne,' she told him coldly. 'I'm not. I hate you. And when I give you over to the rulers of the midrealms, you'll know just how much.'

She shoved his hand away, and returned her focus to the road ahead, to see the floating domes of Aveum on the snow-capped horizon.

# CHAPTER THIRTEEN

## WILDER

As they rode towards the capital, Wilder couldn't blame Thea. It had taken him years to accept what he now knew about the shadow-touched folk, years to pull the pieces into place about what had been transpiring in the midrealms for all this time. But what he could not accept was that Thea didn't believe *him*. He had thought they were stronger than that, that she understood what he felt for her, that it was more powerful than any darkness descending upon them.

But he also knew the power of the guild, the sense of duty that came with being anointed a Guardian of the midrealms, let alone one who wished to undertake the Great Rite. And that was all she had ever wanted, until him.

He'd broken her trust and then underestimated how hard it would be to forge it anew. He could sense her resolve wavering, could practically hear the questions on the tip of her tongue, and although he wanted to keep talking, keep explaining, he knew that time had passed. Thea needed to see it for herself.

As they rocked in the saddle together, drawing closer and closer to the city, her voice echoed in his mind.

*I hate you.*

Her words had said one thing, but her body had said another.

His Thea was somewhere in there. There was hope yet.

It wasn't long before they were passing through the outer villages of Vios. They always reminded him of his hometown, Kilgrave, with buildings made of stone and timber, their roofs heavy with snow. The streets were narrow and winding, not quite built to accommodate a royal carriage and a Thezmarrian escort, but the company made do. The deeper into the capital they got, the more shops and stalls spilt out into the streets, selling all manner of goods, from warm fur hats and gloves to steaming cups of spiced wine.

The aroma of meat roasting on spits wafted through the crisp air, and the sound of laughter and music drifted from the taverns that lined the side alleys. There was a sense of celebration so poignant it was hard to reconcile that only a few hours ago, the road they were on had been doused in shadow and violence. It was surreal.

In front of him, Thea took it all in, her attention lingering on a quartet of performers juggling flaming torches on the street corner. Though Wilder couldn't see her face, he recognised the tension in her shoulders. She knew it wasn't right to be walking amid such festivities when the midrealms were on the brink of destruction. All the same, she urged Biscuit forward through the crowds.

Who was this woman? Where was the Thea who questioned everything? The young shieldbearer and then Guardian who had challenged him at every turn? Where was she?

As though sensing the source of his anguish, Thea shifted slightly in the saddle, her focus trained all too hard on the heart of the city ahead.

Vios was nestled in a valley on the banks of a glacier-fed river, overlooking the frozen lake. The palace was traditional only in name, consisting of three floating domes that hovered above the ground, bathed in a wintry, ethereal glow. It was Wilder's favourite of the three remaining kingdoms of the midrealms, and as such, he'd spent a lot of time here, particularly in his younger days, always captivated by the magic of the domes. The first was adorned with intricate crystals of ice, housing Aveum's library and renowned university. The second, resplendent in swirling mist, housed the royal family, along with the throne and ballrooms. Wilder had never entered the third, but it was known as the arts centre of the kingdom, housing a famous opera theatre in which the Aveum orchestra often performed. Wilder wondered if it would still be standing at the end of all this.

Before he knew it, their company had reached the official gates to the inner city, halting as a unit of mounted guards approached, dressed in Harenth's colours, not Aveum's.

'Princess Jasira?' Wilder recognised the leader who greeted their party, his brow furrowed in confusion at the sight of Thezmarrians rather than his own men.

The princess pulled back the curtain and peered out. 'I'm glad to see you, Captain Barker,' she said. The relief on her face was plain.

'Trouble on the road, Highness?' Barker asked, looking concerned.

'A conversation for behind closed doors,' Thea interjected, urging the stallion forward to position herself between the guard and the princess.

Wilder wasn't surprised to see the whole unit bow their heads in deference to the woman seated before him, some of them even touching three fingers to their shoulders in respect, as though she were already a Warsword. It wasn't the first time he'd seen soldiers of the midrealms offer Thea such a tribute. She'd saved many lives in Tver.

'Of course, Guardian Zoltaire,' Captain Barker said, before his eyes widened at the sight of Wilder at her back. Wilder noticed the bob of his throat and the paling of his complexion before he cleared his throat. 'We'll escort Princess Jasira to her father right away.' He addressed the princess next. 'His Majesty was worried sick about your delay.'

'He will be put at ease soon enough, Captain. Thanks to Thea and her companions here.' Princess Jasira scanned the three Guardians. 'This debt will not be forgotten. My father shall know of my saviours.'

'There's no need for that,' Cal said. 'You are safe, and that's all that matters to us.'

The princess rewarded him with a warm smile. 'All the same.' Then she turned to Thea. 'I will send for you when everyone is settled.'

'Of course, Your Highness.' Thea bowed her head.

The guards of Harenth surrounded the carriage and escorted the princess through the royal gates. Wilder had the distant realisation that Thea should have been escorted through alongside her, as a fellow royal of the midrealms.

And yet she shared his saddle, covered in wraith blood just as he was, clad in armour and weapons, the echo of violence still singing at her fingertips.

Cal and Kipp looked to her with reproach.

'Let's find somewhere to talk,' Kipp suggested. 'Before we go in...'

To Wilder's surprise, Thea nodded, guiding Biscuit after the two men.

They found themselves at the noblemen's stables and Wilder reluctantly removed his arms from around Thea, letting her dismount, his front suddenly cold without the press of her body against his.

He leapt down from Biscuit's back and eyed the trio warily. But Cal and Kipp pulled Thea aside, into an empty stall. They weren't out of earshot, though. Cal's voice was clear.

'I don't like this. Something doesn't feel right.'

Kipp made a noise of agreement. 'You can't deny it, Thea. He's acted like anything but a fallen Warsword.'

Ah, so they were to decide his fate in the stables, a mere few feet away from the halls of Vios where his judges awaited.

'We know he lied, Thea,' Cal pressed. 'We know he hurt you and betrayed the midrealms during the battle of Tver, but...'

'But what?' Thea bit back. 'We've gotten him this far. Justice awaits beyond those walls —'

'Are you sure?' Cal asked.

Kipp chimed in, 'We have to question what's happening when everything points to something strange beneath the surface. You know what his fate could be.'

Wilder listened intently. It was a conversation he'd had

both with others and himself throughout his years of service to the midrealms. What was blind loyalty? What was duty amid a system of corruption?

'But it's all just words,' Thea murmured. 'This is what he did before...' Her voice wavered. 'He wears many faces, masks that we have all fallen for at one time or another. He made me fall once... I won't do so again. He can't be trusted.'

Wilder's heart ached, but he remained rooted to the ground.

'Is that what you truly believe?' Kipp asked quietly.

'I...' Thea drew a strained breath, and for the first time Wilder heard the fear, the uncertainty in her voice. 'I don't know what to believe anymore.'

All reason left him. All he knew was that were he to face whatever came next, he would not regret one last moment with her. Wilder didn't even realise he was moving, but in an instant he stood at the stall's gate, his heart thundering.

Cal and Kipp startled, before glancing between him and Thea and exchanging a look. Silence stretched between them all. Then, without a word, the Guardians left to tend to their horses, leaving Wilder and Thea alone.

'If you need something to believe,' he said, his blood heating as he closed the gap between them and hauled her body to his, 'then believe this.'

He kissed her.

It was the kiss he'd been dying to give her, the kiss that fractured every doubt between them and reforged the cracks with something golden. She tasted just as he remembered, like hope and salvation, like home and *his*.

Thea's mouth opened for him, her hands closing around the back of his neck as his tongue brushed hers. Her lips were warm and lush against his own, her body melting into his, sending bolts of longing straight to his hard, aching cock.

He devoured her, his urgency dark, frenzied and unchecked as his hands roved across her curves, curves he'd dreamt of worshipping again for so long.

Her body answered his kiss in kind, grinding against him, seeking that all-consuming friction between them. Her palms drifted down across the broad expanse of his chest, and she moaned against his lips, the sound nearly undoing him where he stood.

White-hot need blazed through him and everything else fell away but for the woman growing molten beneath his touch. She met every sweep of his tongue, every scrape of his teeth with her own, only harder and fiercer.

'Thea...' he murmured, unable to stand the feverishness of his own skin, needing to rid them of the layers between them —

She broke their kiss, panting, pulling back from him with one hand clutching the leather string that held both her fate stone and the key to his irons. Her eyes were lined with tears.

'I can't...' Her voice broke then, along with Wilder's heart.

It took all his Furies-given strength not to fall to his knees. 'For whatever it's worth,' he told her hoarsely, 'I'll never stop being yours.'

'Wilder, I —'

But her words were cut off by the distinct rattling of armour, and within moments, the Aveum Kingsguard darkened the doorway of the stall.

'Guardian Zoltaire,' the commander addressed Thea, bowing his head in respect. 'We were informed of your arrival, and your great victory in capturing the fugitive, Wilder Hawthorne.'

He looked momentarily perturbed by the single set of manacles around Wilder's wrists, but he gave a firm nod to his men. Half a dozen guards surged forward, roughly taking Wilder into custody.

Irons were clamped around his ankles. Thick, alchemy-treated chains were fastened around his torso, trapping his arms at his sides. As each link locked in place, Wilder felt more and more of his strength dampening. Wren had shared her concoction with the rulers, it seemed.

Thea watched on, not wiping the expression of horror from her face.

'Worry not, Guardian Zoltaire,' the commander reassured her. 'There's no escaping justice for him this time. We'll take it from here.'

She schooled her features into something that resembled indifference and gave the man a nod.

'You're invited to meet with the rulers in the throne room,' he added, before shoving Wilder towards the door.

Even with his strength diminished, it took all six men to escort him away from Thea. For the first time since they'd found one another again, she looked unsure.

*Good*, he thought. *Then this was all worth it.*

He lifted his chin as they led him not to the rulers of the midrealms, but to the ice dungeons deep below the frozen earth. There was to be no trial, no reckoning today.

As he was forced into a freezing cell and the icy air hit his lungs, Wilder closed his eyes. He had done all he could.

It was up to Thea now.

# CHAPTER FOURTEEN

## THEA

Thea, Cal and Kipp stood before the rulers of the midrealms in the glass throne room of Vios. Crystal-clear floor-to-ceiling windows gave a full view of the mountains behind the floating domes and the great frozen lake.

The entire space was adorned with finery, furs and glimmering light. It was the embodiment of opulence, wealth, power. Beautiful, and yet... lacking. Thea realised she missed the Great Hall of the fortress back in Thezmarr, its simplicity, its unlikely warmth.

Although the cavernous space around her now was enchanted to keep the wintry air at bay, Thea felt cold to her bones. Before her stood King Artos of Harenth, King Leiko of Tver, and King Elkan and Queen Reyna of Aveum. All of them wore cloaks of thick fur, and intricate jewelled crowns atop their heads.

'Welcome to Vios, Althea Zoltaire of Thezmarr,' Queen Reyna declared, opening her arms wide in a grand gesture.

'And of course, welcome to your companions as well.' She dipped her head to Cal and Kipp.

The trio bowed low. It was not their first time before royalty, but Thea didn't think it got any easier.

'Thank you, Your Majesty. Your kingdom is every bit as beautiful as they say,' Thea managed, daring to glance up at the dais. Her training kept her reaction in check, but she nearly baulked at who she saw stationed nearby. One of King Artos' dungeon masters. She wouldn't have recognised him but for the jewellery he wore. Even a year ago she'd found it odd for a man in his position: a gemstone nasal piercing and a dozen bronze bangles on each wrist. He'd been there in the dungeons of Hailford when Hawthorne had interrogated those half-wraiths.

'And as unforgiving, no doubt,' the queen replied with a small smile, wrenching Thea's attention back to the rulers. 'We have you to thank for the capture and imprisonment of the fallen Warsword, Wilder Hawthorne, is that correct?'

Thea had been dreaming of this moment for a solid year. Almost every night she had imagined the warm satisfaction that would pour through her with this victory. Over and over she had fantasised about how all would feel right in the world again, how every hurt, every trial would have been worth it to see justice done. And yet, not a flicker of those emotions came. There was no joy, no sense of achievement, no pride at having fulfilled a duty. Instead, she found herself suppressing the urge to fidget, to look around the hall for any sign of the man himself.

But she nodded. 'Yes, Your Majesty. Along with my fellow Thezmarrians, Callahan Whitlock and Kristopher Snowden.'

'The midrealms owes you a great debt, Guardians.'

'We only did what honour and duty demanded, Your Majesty,' Thea replied.

'You have done us proud, Althea!' King Artos' voice boomed, and he strode down the dais steps and clasped Thea's hands in his, his emerald eyes bright. 'I knew you were destined for greatness the moment you saved my life at the feast all that time ago.'

Hawthorne's words crept to the forefront of her mind. *'It's Artos, Thea...* Artos *is responsible for the blight upon the midrealms.* He's *the one letting the reapers and monsters through the Veil.'*

Thea hadn't believed him, hadn't wanted to. But something oily slid across her skin at Artos' touch, and she resisted the impulse to pull her hands from his. 'Thank you, sire.'

He didn't let go. 'You timed it perfectly. While we celebrate the ultimate triumph over darkness with the Moonfire Eclipse, you have indeed triumphed over shadow and brought a traitor to justice.'

In her periphery, Thea caught a blur of movement. Two towering figures standing by the farthest wall.

Torj Elderbrock, the Bear Slayer, with his war hammer strapped to his back... and Vernich Warner, the Bloodletter. The two remaining Warswords of Thezmarr. The last time she'd seen them, they'd both given her their blessing to hunt their comrade down.

The back of her neck prickled as she felt another pair of eyes settle on her.

Osiris, the Guild Master of Thezmarr.

*'Bring him Thezmarr's justice... Do that, Althea Zoltaire, and his swords are yours.'* His final words to her rang clear as bells in her ears. She had done exactly that. She had both of

Hawthorne's scabbards strapped to her back, the weight of Naarvian steel somehow not as comforting as it had once been. What if she didn't want his swords? What if she wanted her own, as she'd always intended?

'When is the trial?' she asked, only just remembering to tack on, 'Your Majesty?'

King Artos at last dropped her hands and turned to his fellow rulers. 'We had not yet set a date, had we?'

King Leiko of Tver shook his head. 'Let him rot a while, I say.'

It took all of Thea's training to suppress the flinch that followed those words.

'Queen Reyna?' King Artos prompted the Aveum ruler with a respectful nod to her husband as well.

'We shall deal with the details of the trial after the eclipse. The celestial event is far more important than the fate of a fallen Warsword,' the queen answered.

Thea's stomach churned.

'Indeed, my love,' King Elkan agreed. 'We shall hear no more of his treachery until after the festivities. He has darkened our realms enough this past year.'

King Artos gave a nod of approval. 'As our hosts wish it.'

Unease coiled tightly in Thea, but her attention was snatched to where Captain Barker lingered on the outskirts of the hall, not so subtly trying to catch King Artos' attention. The king beckoned him forth, and the captain approached, whispering something inaudible. When he was done, he slipped away without ceremony, leaving King Artos to turn back to Thea.

'My dear Guardian... First, you save my life in Harenth, now you have saved my daughter's as well?' His voice boomed across the hall, full of pride and gratitude, commanding the attention of everyone in attendance. The space radiated with his joy, his warmth. 'Captain Barker has just informed me of your heroics on the road. Jasira has told him that were it not for you, she would be dead... or worse.'

A unified gasp echoed around the room.

King Artos rested a hand over his heart. 'I will forever be in your debt, Althea Zoltaire.'

A smattering of applause followed, awed murmurs breaking out across the gathered crowd.

'To have saved both king and princess? She's a true warrior of Thezmarr!'

'She truly is the Shadow of Death.'

'Wraith slayer! A legend of Thezmarr in our midst...'

The whispers filled the hall, each one coloured with more admiration than the last. Once, Thea had dreamt of such praise and respect, had yearned for this very reputation as one of the midrealms' elite. But an icy shiver raked down her spine, like the scrape of a talon. She glanced across at Cal and Kipp, who, like the rest of the court, were beaming all too brightly. Gratitude and reverence shone in their stares – an unnatural display of feeling, she realised.

While she could no longer wield magic herself, her brief experience with it had made her familiar with such things, and now she recognised the strange emotional fog that had cloaked the room for what it was: empath magic.

But Thea was no fool. She bowed graciously, adding a flourish of enthusiasm. 'We were merely doing our duty, Your Majesty.'

It seemed the line had become the unofficial motto of their quest, its meaning more blurred with every utterance.

King Artos looked pleased. 'You are all to be honoured at tomorrow night's masquerade ball, for your valour and endurance. And Althea, Princess Jasira has requested that you attend as her personal guest.'

'It would be my honour,' Thea said, bowing again before daring to ask: 'And the prisoner? Might I see him? I wish to ensure that he is adequately secured after our efforts.'

King Artos gave a rich laugh. 'Althea, you may rest easy now. He is locked away in Aveum's most fortified dungeon, guarded by the best of all three kingdoms and Thezmarr's own. You have nothing to worry about. There's no need for you to go.'

Thea was quick to nod. 'Thank you, sire. I only wish to serve the midrealms.'

Queen Reyna stood and gazed at Thea, her expression more distant than before. 'And serve the midrealms you have, most valiantly.' She descended the dais, her voice taking on an aloof tone. 'Not long ago, I had a disturbing vision of a betrayal and an attack on our beloved kingdom —'

A wave of shock rippled across the court, and Thea's own skin prickled with the queen's admission.

'But you,' Queen Reyna continued, 'you have saved us from a terrible fate. Darkness was coming for us, and you stopped it in its tracks. You faced the verdant stare of evil and put it in chains. For that, we thank you.'

Thea dipped her head, and when she looked up, Queen Reyna appeared to be herself again.

'Now is the time to rest and recover,' she said. 'Prepare yourself for the celebrations ahead. We have arranged rooms for your stay. Nothing but the best for Thezmarr's champions.'

More bowing and mumbles of thanks ensued before a

flurry of servants came forth to escort Thea, Cal and Kipp away.

'Thank the gods for that,' Kipp muttered as they left the throne room, the thrall of empath magic apparently gone.

Thea agreed. She'd felt considerably more uneasy in that hall than she had fighting the wraiths on the Wesford Road. Her skin hadn't stopped crawling since she'd entered the floating dome.

*Verdant stare of evil...* The queen's words echoed oddly in her mind. The reapers' gazes were ice blue... and Hawthorne? Thea had searched those silver eyes countless times, had peered into them enough to know beyond a shadow of a doubt that there was not a fleck of green in them.

*Green.*

That oily feeling was back, sliding across her flesh. There was only one green stare that came to mind.

She glanced at Cal and Kipp, who were alert enough to catch her eye as she raised a single finger to her lips and peeled away from the group. To their credit, neither Guardian broke their stride, continuing down the glistening corridor.

Thea ducked away, finding a small balcony and closing the curtains behind her. The balcony didn't lead outside, but looked out onto another hall, and Thea made quick work of climbing over the rail and entering the empty room below, unseen by the guards stationed around its perimeter. It was not the first time she had needed to make herself invisible. She was glad for all her years of training in secret – those skills had come in just as handy as any she had learnt as a shieldbearer or Guardian.

For the first time in a long while, Thea followed her

instincts instead of her head, Artos' emerald eyes bright in her mind, his words loud. *'He is locked away in Aveum's most fortified dungeon... There's no need to go.'*

When someone told her not to go somewhere, that was usually *exactly* where she needed to go. She had reasoned and reasoned, churned things over in her mind for far too long.

Now was the time to go with her gut, and it demanded that she see Wilder Hawthorne.

# CHAPTER FIFTEEN

## THEA

The Aveum dungeons were made of ice.

Of course they were.

The first few levels were easy enough to navigate and talk her way into, but the deeper she delved, the harder it became. It wasn't long before she opted to use her remaining stash of the soot root powder Wren had gifted her, creating the perfect cover of darkness for her to slip past the more dedicated guards.

By the time she got to the last level, she was shivering, despite her cloak and hood.

Here, even the bars to the cells themselves were made of thick blocks of ice. She passed several unconscious prisoners, strung up in chains within. Around her, the quiet festered like a disease, pulsating with a keen *wrongness* that set her teeth on edge. For all the pristine glass halls and awe-inspiring views of Aveum above, this horrific place existed beneath the surface.

Then, she saw him.

Through bars of ice, there was no missing Wilder

Hawthorne's powerful body pulled taut between thick chains that came from the ceiling and floor. They'd stripped him of everything but his undershorts. His breath clouded before his face, and the chains rattled with his shivering.

He'd been beaten.

Nothing could have quelled the guilt that lanced through Thea as she surveyed his bloodied and bruised appearance. They had hurt him. Hurt him because of her. She gripped the bars of the cell without thinking, and Hawthorne looked up, strands of dark hair hanging loose in his eyes.

Her horror must have been written all over her face.

'The cold is worse than the scratches, Princess,' he muttered, his voice hoarse.

'I...' But what could she say? He had explained it all to her, the reason for his betrayal, how not all was as it seemed in the midrealms. He'd even told her who was responsible. And she hadn't believed him. Hadn't *wanted* to believe him. She had clung to her own anger so desperately it had blinded her.

He watched her, as though he could sense every thought that passed through her.

The gaze she met was no verdant stare of evil, but one of soft silver. The Warsword before her wasn't the betrayer of whom Queen Reyna's vision spoke.

'I need you to do something for me,' he rasped. 'I'm in no position to bargain, but... go to the end of the cell row.'

Thea's heart stuttered. 'What?'

'The end of the row.'

Her feet moved of their own accord, though she was shaking uncontrollably and her chest tugged painfully as she moved away from Hawthorne, further into the dungeon. She was numb as she put one boot in front of the other and found herself closer and closer to the cell at the end of the corridor.

She nearly choked on her gasp.

Inside the icy cell were several *children*. They were all huddled together, barely conscious.

At their backs were membranous wings.

Some of them had darkened fingertips, some had black veins around their eyes, but there were no wisps of shadow around them, no scent of burnt hair, no malice in their stares.

They were... children. Just children.

None of them looked up at her. They averted their gazes as though they had learnt the hard way not to make eye contact with whomever approached from the other side of the bars. They trembled beneath her gaze, huddling closer together, tugging what little clothing they had tighter around themselves.

Thea backed away in horror, finding herself back at Hawthorne's cell.

'You saw them,' Hawthorne managed, struggling now to lift his head.

'But...'

He met her gaze then. 'I tried to tell you.'

Thea's words were lodged in her throat and she scoured her mind for some sense of logic. She knew that often in times of war, hard decisions needed to be made, that there might be explanations... but this?

She tried to reason with herself, with him, that her actions, the very ones that had led them to this point, had been justified. 'You led me on a wild goose chase...' she forced herself to say. 'You did everything in your power to avoid capture, to hand us over to every monster imaginable.'

Hawthorne shook his head, his battered body heaving in the chains. 'You should have kept your name day gift.'

Thea blinked, glancing back down the end of the prison row. 'What does that have to do with anything?'

'Everything,' he told her. 'It's time to open your eyes, Thea.'

'I —'

'I'll wager Artos didn't want you down here? I wonder why.'

Someone shouted from the stairs above, startling her.

'Go,' Hawthorne said roughly.

Thea's boots were frozen to the spot.

'Get out of here,' he growled. 'Lest you end up in the cell beside me.'

Heart hammering, Thea withdrew. She had disobeyed a direct order from the king to be here; there would be no talking her way out if she were discovered. With the images of Hawthorne and the imprisoned shadow-touched children seared into her mind, she ducked away, slipping past the guards. She made her way to the floating glass dome once more, her skin crawling as enchanted heat enveloped her, the brightness of the winter's day an eerie contrast to the darkness that rotted below.

'Althea!' someone called. 'Althea, wait!'

Princess Jasira was lifting her skirts and hurrying towards her.

'I've had someone looking for you!'

Numb, Thea mustered what little strength she had left to school her face into an apologetic expression. 'I'm sorry, Your Highness. I think I got lost after we left the throne room. With the events of the day, I'm afraid I got turned around.'

The princess' brow crinkled before she nodded in understanding and linked her arm through Thea's, not caring that her pristine, freshly pressed gown was in contact with Thea's filthy armour. 'I can only imagine how exhausted you are,' she said kindly.

'I'll be fine, Highness,' Thea assured her.

'Of that I have no doubt.' Jasira smiled. 'My father told you of my invitation?'

'He did, Your Highness —'

'Please, Thea, as I've told you before, call me Jasi. Surely we are past the formalities now?'

Thea gave a tired smile. 'I suppose if anything strikes out the need for titles, it's surviving a wraith attack on the road.'

'My thoughts exactly.' Jasira started walking, her arm still linked through Thea's. 'You once told me that you'd never been to a ball. Now I get to accompany you to your first, of hopefully many.'

The palace halls were buzzing with activity, banners and floral arrangements being raised to the ceilings, silverware being rushed every which way. It was dizzying.

Jasira patted her arm. 'Let me show you to your quarters.'

'I'm sure one of your attendants could do that —'

'But I *want* to.'

'If you insist.' Thea didn't have the energy to argue. 'I told your father I was honoured by your invitation,' she said.

'So you'll attend?'

'Of course.' What was it Hawthorne had once told her? *If the king invites you to sit at his table, you sit at his table...* She imagined the same could be said for princesses.

'Are you alright, Thea?' Princess Jasira asked, peering into Thea's face with concern.

'A little sore, a little tired, that's all, Your – Jasi.'

The princess gave her a knowing look as they continued down the glass corridor, passing more of the frantic preparations for the masquerade ball. 'I can't imagine how difficult this past year has been for you.'

'I have certainly missed hot baths,' Thea joked weakly, desperate to get to her rooms and think.

'That's not what I meant,' Princess Jasira said. 'Do you want to talk about him?'

'Who?'

'Wilder Hawthorne.' The princess gave a sigh. 'I know the pain of losing someone as you did...'

'Your Highness —'

'Jasi,' the princess corrected firmly. 'There was a man, after my mother passed away,' she offered quietly. 'He helped me through my grief, shared it with me. We... we fell in love.'

Thea trained her gaze ahead, realising that the princess might never have uttered those words aloud to anyone. Judging from her tone, the tale did not end happily, which likely meant the man in question hadn't been an appropriate match for a princess. The irony of these thoughts was not lost on Thea, given the secret heritage she harboured herself.

'But a few months after we'd told each other how we felt, he...' The princess faltered for a moment. 'He confessed there was someone else, that what he'd felt for me had been fleeting.'

Thea baulked. 'I'm so sorry.'

Princess Jasira gave a grim smile. 'Mother always told me I was too open with my heart. That I would learn the hard way before long to guard it closely.' She sniffed. 'There was something similar between you and the fallen Warsword, wasn't there? There were rumours last spring in Harenth. People saw you together at the Laughing Fox.'

The image of Hawthorne chained up in that freezing cell hit her like a fist to the gut. 'He wasn't who I thought he was.'

Jasira squeezed her arm in solidarity. The princess' kindness struck a nerve in Thea. In the past year, she hadn't shared her struggles with a single soul. Cal and Kipp were her friends, her best friends, but... she hadn't shared her heart with them. They weren't Wren, they weren't Sam and Ida from the fortress. Stunned, she realised that it had been over six years since she'd cried with Wren on the clifftops of Thezmarr about Evander, the stable master's apprentice – and that she hadn't shed a single tear for Wilder Hawthorne.

Princess Jasira drew to a stop outside a door covered in gold filigree. She leant in and gave Thea a hug. Thea winced as the fine gown made contact with her grimy clothes.

Jasira pulled back and looked at her. 'You just captured a fallen Warsword,' she said, a note of reproach in her voice. 'You need rest. And then, you're allowed to enjoy yourself. The ball will do you good. Drink sparkling wine. Dance with a handsome stranger... Watch the miracle of the eclipse. Know that you were part of our triumph over the dark.'

# CHAPTER SIXTEEN

## THEA

In a daze, Thea paced the quarters she'd been given. The last time she'd been in rooms this grand had been in Harenth, with Wilder... The opulence of it all was similar to the palace in Hailford – an enormous four-poster bed with elegant drapes, a sitting area before a fireplace and a view of the kingdom to die for.

*'Use your words, Princess... What do you want?'*

His voice came to her in a whisper, tickling the shell of her ear. She felt his phantom caress along her neck, her collarbone, her sternum... Her mind became a tangled web of their moments together; intimate touches and softly spoken promises.

*'Because I fucking love you.'*

Thea barely registered her movements as she entered the bathing chamber, removing her soiled armour and clothing in a trance, recalling how Wilder had washed her hair when she was injured, those long fingers massaging soap into her scalp and tending to her wound.

*Wilder.* When had he become Wilder again? Rather than Hawthorne?

The water in the tub was tepid after her delay, but she didn't care. Her skin was hot from the memory of their kiss in the stables. She had been drunk on the taste of him.

*'I'll never stop being yours.'*

An unexpected sob escaped Thea and she smacked her palms into the water. How had this happened? How had things got so twisted? And how could she bear the thought of him chained up like an animal in the cold?

He had been someone to her. He had been *everything* to her.

Panic inched its way into her body, gripping every muscle painfully, making her head tight with tension. She scrubbed at her skin until it was pink and raw, until the water was cold enough to drive her from it. With her mind still churning through the past year, the last few days in particular, she dressed in a plain pair of pants and a linen shirt. Towelling her hair dry, her stomach roiling with unease, she emerged from the bathing room to find Cal and Kipp waiting for her on the settee by the window.

'You saw him?' Kipp said instantly.

Wordlessly, she nodded.

'It's bad?' he pressed, getting to his feet.

Again, she nodded.

Kipp pushed his auburn hair from his brow and started to pace. 'Am I right in thinking we're all on the same page at last?'

'What do you mean?' Thea asked.

'That we're doubting the nature of Hawthorne's fall... and anything we might have been told regarding the state of the midrealms?'

Thea cast her damp towel aside and sat on the end of her bed, resting her elbows on her knees and hanging her head. 'I think so.'

She looked up in time to see Kipp exchange a look with Cal, who grimaced before he asked, 'What did Hawthorne say?'

Thea wet her cracked lips, trying to summon strength from her bruised body and battered heart. 'He said I should have kept my name day gift.'

Kipp frowned. 'He what?'

'Said —'

'No, I heard you, it's just... You know, a weird thing to say when you're half frozen to death in an ice dungeon.'

His words hit Thea like a blow. Wilder was in there because of her.

'Maybe that's why he said it... Maybe he wasn't quite lucid...' Even as the words left her tongue, she didn't believe them. 'What do you think it was? The gift?' she asked them, not bothering to mask her pained expression.

'Why don't you find out?' Cal replied.

Thea sighed, running her fingers through her damp hair. 'I can't. You saw me throw it away.'

'I did,' Cal allowed. 'But...' He surged for the door and left abruptly.

Thea turned to Kipp in question. But her friend shrugged.

'Don't look at me.'

Moments later, Cal came rushing back, closing the door behind him and approaching Thea with an outstretched hand. 'I saw you throw it away, but you didn't see me go and fish it out of the bushes...'

In his hand was the small box wrapped in brown paper.

The lightning bolt drawn across its surface had faded, as had the words *Happy name day*.

Thea's mouth fell open as she stared at Cal in disbelief. 'You...'

Cal was still holding the box out to her. 'Kept it, yep. Uh... don't be angry, I guess?'

Thea threw her arms around him, hugging him hard. 'Thank you,' she croaked, tears stinging her eyes. 'Thank you for knowing me better than I knew myself.'

After a moment of shock, Cal returned her embrace. 'What are friends for, eh?'

A pointed cough sounded from the other side of the room. 'This is all very touching, but can we open the fucking box now? I feel like it might be a tad important...' Kipp said, arms crossed over his chest, foot tapping impatiently on the marble floor.

Palming a tear from her cheek, Thea took the box from Cal and went to the settee. Cal followed, sitting to her left, and Kipp took his place to her right.

'I'm scared...' she whispered, turning the small parcel over in her fingers.

'I don't think you have anything to fear from him,' Kipp said quietly.

'That's not what I'm scared of.'

'What then?' Cal asked.

'I'm scared that if I open this...' She swallowed. She couldn't finish the sentence.

'If you open it, you'll know the truth. At least about him,' Kipp told her, gently nudging her with his elbow.

Biting her lower lip, Thea nodded. With trembling fingers, she began to peel away the brown paper.

When the wrappings fell to the floor, she was left with a

dainty wooden box. It was plain in design, with a simple sliding lid that she removed easily. Reaching inside, she found a small silver ball within, and slowly, she drew it out to hold it in her palm. It was covered in a flourish of engravings, a language Thea recognised but didn't understand. The same language that graced the length of Wilder's spine in ink, the same language carved into the blade of her dagger.

*Glory in death, immortality in legend.* She knew those words like the back of her hand. And she could just make them out across the ball's surface, amid a web of others.

'What is it?' Cal asked, brow furrowed.

Thea turned the object over, tracing the engravings. 'I don't know...'

But Kipp was staring in awe. 'I didn't think those things were real. If it's what I think it is... it's from realms far beyond the Veil, from other races that have mastered magical objects in a way that we can't even fathom. The name is in a language I can't pronounce, but it's a memory orb. There should be a small divot at the top...'

There was. Kipp's eyes widened as Thea tilted the object to him in confirmation.

'I think Cal and I should go,' he said. 'And then you should press it.'

'But what —'

'Just trust me, Thea,' Kipp said, tugging on Cal's sleeve and pulling him towards the door. 'Trust *him*,' he told her, before he pushed Cal from the room and followed, closing the door with a click behind them.

Alone, Thea gazed at the silver sphere, heart pounding, eyes burning with unshed tears. Whatever magic it held, she knew a reckoning was coming, one she wasn't sure she was ready for.

But Thea had never run from a fight before.

She wasn't going to start now.

Taking a deep breath, she brought her finger to the divot and pressed it. Time stilled for a moment.

And then the room was awash with golden light.

# CHAPTER SEVENTEEN

## WILDER

In all his years of fighting, Wilder had never been taken prisoner. Injured in battle, yes, but never chained up like an animal, never left to freeze and starve belowground. He knew Talemir had never faced such a thing either, but Malik... A long time ago they had suspected that Malik had. A mission beyond the Veil, wherein he hadn't returned for three months and when he had, he wouldn't speak of it. Until now, that had been Wilder's only measure for such things.

His body ached from the constant assault of shivering. They had left him in his undershorts and nothing more. He supposed he should be grateful for that small dignity, especially in this cold. But he was finding gratitude hard to come by with his teeth chattering so violently his head hurt.

Instead, when he closed his eyes, he pictured Thea at the bars of his cell, her celadon gaze horror-stricken, her whole being taut with shock. He hated that it had come to this, that she'd seen him like this, that she'd seen the brutalised innocents who occupied the great ice cells of Aveum. But it had been necessary.

Now he just needed to get out.

Adrienne had known things might go awry, but whether she'd been able to get word to the shadow-touched to call for help was another thing entirely. And Thea... He wasn't sure what she was going to do, whether being down here and seeing the children had been enough to sway her.

He cursed himself silently for leaving the memory orb for her on her name day like that. He had gone to great lengths to obtain such an object. They were nearly unheard of in the midrealms, save for conversations among academics and scholars of the realms beyond the Veil. He should have known Thea would act in anger, that everything he had gathered to show her would end up buried beneath the snow of the forest floor or at the bottom of a now-frozen river.

Wilder took a shallow breath. He needed to regulate his body temperature, he needed to grit his teeth through the pain, and he needed to figure out how to remove the alchemy-treated chains. He had no doubt now that they were indeed Wren's invention – a genius one at that. He only wished she hadn't shared the details with the midrealms just yet.

Shifting in his irons to relieve some of the pressure around his wrists, he peered out through the bars of ice. There was no rotation of guards this far down, for the prisoners were so cold they could barely move. There was no natural light either, and as such, there was no knowing how long he had been down here already, or how long the shadow-touched had been.

He couldn't stand the feeling of being helpless, couldn't

stand the press of tainted iron against his skin, muting that Furies-given strength that had seen him through so many tight spots. He tried to think, but he could feel his mind slowing from exposure to the cold. His fingers and toes were painful blocks of ice, and the frigid air had latched onto his bones. Unconsciousness tempted him, an escape from the pain and discomfort, a reprieve from the mess in his head.

He heard Thea, though, heard her call his name. Not 'Hawthorne', as she'd used for the better part of their recent time together, but *Wilder*. His given name, the name she'd whispered against his lips and said with a softness he hadn't seen from her in a long time. He missed it, missed her.

It was with thoughts of her that he let oblivion lure him under. The ice and pain faded as his eyes closed, and then all he saw was black.

'Don't go,' a much younger Wilder begged, snatching a fistful of his older brother's cloak, trying to stop him from saddling his horse.

Even as a young teenager, Malik was an immovable force, easily the tallest, strongest boy in their village. All the girls blushed when he came near, and the boys warred between hating him and wanting to be his best friend. But Wilder knew he was his brother's *true* best friend. They did everything together. Which was why he didn't understand why Mal was leaving now, why he was giving Wilder a look of resignation, seeming far older and wiser than he had any right to.

'I have to,' Mal said, gently removing Wilder's grip.

Always so gentle, even with hands that had the strength to shatter skulls.

'You don't.' Wilder knew he sounded every bit the child he was, but he was too hot-headed to care.

'Aye, he does,' came their father's voice from the doorway of the barn. 'I'm too old and broken to fight, but Mal... Mal was born to be a Warsword. You can tell just by looking at him.'

Wilder was mortified to find his eyes stinging with unshed tears. 'But...'

'You'll understand soon enough, son,' his father said. 'Delmira's fall was not the end of things, boys. A reckoning is coming. And the midrealms will need all the help it can get when it arrives.'

'Then I'll go too!' Wilder insisted, surging forward again.

His father's hand snatched the back of his cloak, pulling him close. 'You're too young for Thezmarr —'

'There are babies there,' Wilder countered.

'Not babies with swords in their hands and violence in their hearts.' He held out a beautiful braided belt. 'Go on, give Malik his gift. Perhaps if you're lucky, he'll outgrow it and give it to you one day.'

Scowling, Wilder approached his big brother with the intricate leather belt his father had crafted. 'Here,' he said sullenly.

It only annoyed him more when Malik smiled, accepting the gift with a nod of thanks to their father. 'It'll be alright, Wilder.'

'I don't want you to go,' he repeated.

Malik ruffled his hair. 'I know.'

Their father approached and picked Wilder up, and all that fear and frustration that had been building up since his brother announced his plans spilt over. He buried his face in his father's neck and cried.

His brother and father spoke softly, and only when he heard the swing of the stall gate opening did Wilder peer through his tears.

Malik was astride the family's old mare, and he looked so much older, so much fiercer all of a sudden. Wilder realised there was a sword strapped to his back. It was nothing like the great blades he'd heard of in tales and songs, but it was a sword nonetheless, and his brother was to wield it.

Wilder sniffed, his nose running, his hands shaking. He didn't know much, but he knew that those who went to the fortress at Thezmarr rarely came back.

His father held him tightly as Malik guided his horse past them and out of the barn.

Just before he started towards the road, he looked back and caught Wilder's gaze; grey eyes meeting silver, a grin spreading across Malik's young face.

'Come find me at Thezmarr, little brother,' he said. 'We'll be Warswords together.'

A different moment in time unfolded before Wilder, one he remembered all too well.

On the fragile shores of the Broken Isles, just off the coast of Naarva, he was an eager Guardian awaiting orders. Their small party was led by two Warswords: Malik the Shieldbreaker and Talemir Starling, the Prince of Hearts. The two men stood on the sandy bank, overlooking the foaming waves in confusion.

'The report said there was a sea drake here, injured on

the rocks...' Malik said to Talemir, shielding his eyes from the glare of the sun.

Talemir shrugged. 'Reports can be wrong.'

'Big thing to be wrong about,' Malik replied, still frowning, before glancing at Wilder and the half dozen Guardians that stood around him. 'You'd have been better off training,' he told them. 'Don't know why Osiris insisted we bring them.'

Wilder had been more than keen to accompany the Warswords on an official mission of the guild. Talemir's training had been doing his head in and he longed for the opportunity to swing his blade for real.

Talemir snorted. 'Well, now they're trained in the art of disappointment. Job well done, Shieldbreaker.'

Malik rolled his eyes.

'That's it?' asked Torj Elderbrock, another Guardian. 'We've come all this way, only to jump back in the boats and go home?'

Wilder bit back a huff of laughter. Torj might have been favoured to be the next to undergo the Great Rite, but he often opened his mouth without thinking first.

'Had something better planned, did you?' Talemir asked, brows raised. 'Missions from the guild getting in the way of your social life?'

'No, sir. I was just saying —'

Talemir shook his head, and it was enough to shut Torj up, his cheeks aflame.

Malik trudged back across the sand to address them. 'We'll head back shortly. But first I want you to scour the shores for any sign of a drake. Scales, tracks, anything that might suggest one was here. They're powerful creatures.

Thezmarr needs to know if there's one somewhere in our midst.'

'Do you think it came through the Veil?' someone asked.

'Possibly,' Malik allowed. 'Though it's also entirely possible that it's been beneath our seas all this time. They're creatures of the ancient deep, after all. Now go.'

There was a flurry of movement. Wilder went to the shore. Resting his hand on his sword pommel, he surveyed the pale sand glistening in the midday sun. Besides the Warswords' bootprints, it was entirely smooth, not a disturbance in sight —

'Tal,' Malik called from nearby. 'You smell that?'

Wilder whipped around, watching as his brother and his mentor grew suddenly tense.

'I smell it,' Talemir replied, unsheathing his two swords at once. 'Guardians, get in first formation. *Now.*'

The Guardians burst into action, following their orders, and as Wilder joined them, he smelt what their leaders had been talking about.

*Burnt hair.*

The scent of the shadow wraiths.

'Think it was a trap?' Talemir muttered to Malik, who brandished his sword and heaved his shield in place.

'Well, it doesn't look great, does it?' Malik replied, with a meaningful look at Wilder. He was always doing this, ensuring that Wilder heard certain things, but never explaining them.

A screech shattered the quiet of the Broken Isles, and masses of darkness materialised on the dunes before them.

Wilder and his fellow Guardians unsheathed their own blades, sticking to the formation as ordered.

'No one but Malik and I are to engage,' Talemir shouted. 'Do you understand?'

'Yes, sir!' came the unified reply.

'Your blades won't be able to pierce their chest cavities, do you understand?' Talemir reiterated, not taking his eyes off the wraiths that now emerged from the swirling shadows.

'Yes, sir!'

Wilder joined in the chorus, but his knuckles burned from the tight grip around his sword. He had been training every moment of every day since he'd arrived at Thezmarr years ago. He wanted to spill wraith blood, and he wanted to do so alongside Malik the Shieldbreaker and the Prince of Hearts.

'Three against two,' Malik said to Talemir.

'I can count, you giant oaf,' Talemir responded fondly.

Malik took a step towards the wraiths, swinging his sword menacingly. 'I've got several examples where that's debatable.'

'Quit your griping,' Talemir told him. 'Only one of us is called the Prince of Hearts.'

Malik laughed. All the while, the monsters stalked towards them. 'I wasn't under the impression that had anything to do with battle heroics.'

Talemir grinned. 'A gentleman never tells.'

Another screech echoed across the isles, high-pitched enough to make Wilder wince from where they'd been ordered to stand down.

'These wraith attacks are getting a little too common,' Malik said seriously, sizing up the three that approached, ribbons of onyx cutting through the air around them.

'Agreed,' Talemir replied. 'The rulers should be doing more.'

'We'll talk to Osiris upon our return.'

Malik launched himself at the first of the shadow wraiths.

There was a reason the Warswords of Thezmarr had earnt their titles. It was evident from the first strike of their blades. Malik and Talemir moved as a single unit, as though they had been fighting together for centuries, as though they could feel the energy of violence shifting and pivoting around them. They moved like water, like the shadows they were trying to destroy, slicing through the rotten, sinewy flesh of the wraiths like butter.

Wilder gripped his own sword, tense as he watched the skirmish unfold, restless beyond words as he fought with the instinct to throw himself into the battle as well.

The three wraiths surrounded the two warriors, their shadows lashing dangerously close, their hisses and snarls permeating the quiet of the shores. But Talemir and Malik were a force like no other, beating the darkness back with their Naarvian steel and their Furies-given strength.

Sand and blood sprayed while shadows danced around the battle, encircling the Warswords in a swirling mass of obsidian, obscuring them from view.

Wilder heard Malik shout from within, and he took a step forward, poised to run —

'Don't,' Torj told him, a hand on his vambrace. 'We have to follow orders.'

The mass of shadow deepened, roiling outwards, tendrils creeping towards where the Guardians were posted on the dunes.

Wilder shook Torj off and looked to their peers. Some of

their faces had paled, their gazes distant as though they were seeing something far different to what was unfolding before them in real time.

Another shout of pain sounded from within the chaos, and Wilder didn't think. He was running towards the storm of shadow, brandishing his blade. He might not be able to carve out a heart with regular steel, but that didn't mean he couldn't cause some damage along the way.

With a curse, he crossed the threshold of darkness – and blanched at the sight of the battle within.

Malik and Talemir were in the heart of the fray, fighting back lashes of onyx power, blocking swipes of razor-sharp talons. But their usually precise movements were sluggish all of a sudden, and it became clear that neither Warsword was in their right mind, that they were seeing things that weren't there.

Wilder took advantage of the element of surprise, cleaving through the arm of one of the wraiths before dragging his blade from its throat to its navel with all his might. Black blood spurted, hitting his chest. A shout sounded from behind him and he knew that Torj had followed him into the madness. Good – they could prove that Guardians could do more than stand by and idly watch. He relished the song of steel carving through more wraith flesh, seeming to snatch Malik and Talemir from their trances.

He gave a victorious shout —

Pain seared across his back as darkness lashed him harder than any whip.

Wilder staggered with a ragged gasp, suddenly unable to see past the agony that lanced through him. His vision spotted and he stumbled again as he was hit by another, the force of the impact sending him sprawling across the sand, a sea of his darkest moments rising up to greet him.

An ear-piercing screech sounded in the near distance and the shore beneath him vibrated. Wilder staggered to his feet, his grip on his blade weakened, but there. He had to help Malik and Talemir, he had to —

A huge form passed through his vision and he watched in awe as Malik cleaved the head of a wraith clean off its shoulders before taking his dagger of Naarvian steel to its chest, removing the thick mass of its heart with a grunt of disgust.

Then he was moving again. To Wilder.

Wilder watched him, utterly dazed at the warrior his brother had transformed into since he'd first left Kilgrave on the family's old mare.

He felt the kiss of another whip of shadow, but Malik was there, with dagger and sword, fighting back the darkness, blow after mighty blow.

Someone grabbed Wilder under the arm and pulled him upright.

'You and I are going to have words, Apprentice,' Talemir growled, fury in his hazel eyes as he watched Malik finish off the third shadow wraith and toss its heart into the sea.

'I just —'

'You just nothing,' Talemir snapped. 'You disobeyed direct orders. You could have been fucking killed.'

'You were losing —'

'Losing?' Talemir barked, shaking his head in disbelief. 'Furies fucking save me, Hawthorne. I could kill you myself.' He released his bruising grip. 'I'll let Malik deal with you for a change. You're a fucking idiot sometimes, you know that?'

Covered in wraith blood, his twin swords strapped

across his back once more, Talemir Starling stormed off, no doubt to discipline Torj and the others who might have broken formation.

'He's not wrong,' Malik's voice sounded behind Wilder.

He turned to see his brother washing his hands in the shallows and grimacing as he spat blood onto the sand.

'I'm sorry,' Wilder said. 'I thought you were in danger —'

'We're always in danger,' Malik cut him off. 'But your heart was in the right place. I'm guessing it was just you and Torj?'

'I think so.' Wilder loosed a breath. For all his visions of glory, he'd taken a few lashes and failed spectacularly.

'Interesting,' Malik said, not sounding as angry as Wilder expected.

'What is?' he asked, scanning his brother for any outward signs of injury. Malik was always so much larger than life that it was hard to imagine anything getting through him. There was a cut bleeding on his brow, but other than that, he seemed to be in one piece.

'Nothing,' he replied, waving Wilder off. 'You shouldn't have done what you did.'

'I know...'

'Talemir will have you in the armoury with the shieldbearers for a month.'

'I know.'

'He was scared for you,' Malik clarified. 'He feels responsible for you... But he's forgetting one thing.'

Wilder sighed, his face hot with embarrassment. 'What's that?'

'That I've always got your back, little brother.'

Wilder knew Malik was refraining from ruffling his hair like he used to when Wilder was a boy. For they were not boys anymore. They were warriors in a realm of encroaching darkness.

Wilder nudged his older brother, the immovable giant that he was. 'And I've got yours,' he told him.

Malik grinned, his teeth lined with red. 'I have no doubt.'

'You're a fucking fool, Hawthorne.'

The familiar voice startled him awake. His chains rattled as he fought against them, until he remembered where he was and why he was so fucking cold.

Torj Elderbrock looked at him from the other side of the ice bars, shaking his head as he leant on his war hammer.

'Hello to you too,' Wilder rasped.

Torj's expression was unreadable, but Wilder ventured that his reaction to what had occurred in the final hours of the battle of Tver had been similar to Thea's. The betrayal of the guild, of the midrealms, of their brotherhood echoed between them. Perhaps Torj had simply wanted the opportunity to see the bastard of Thezmarr for himself, to make sure that his chains were sturdy and his suffering was great. Wilder would have felt the same if he thought Torj had betrayed him.

'You've seen better days,' the Bear Slayer commented as he surveyed Wilder's almost-naked body, which still bore the blood and grime of the wraith fight on the road, as well as one or two open wounds from the Aveum guards.

'Could say the same for you,' Wilder retorted, trying to suppress a gasp of pain. 'What's your excuse?'

The golden-haired Warsword gave a rough laugh. 'Oh, you know, chasing monsters all over the midrealms, beating back curses from the Veil every other day... Dealing with fucking Vernich breathing down my neck.'

'So the usual.'

'Something like that.'

Wilder sucked in a breath, unable to help his next words. 'You seen Mal?'

Torj dipped his head. 'I have.'

'And?'

'And he's... Malik.'

'What's that supposed to mean?' Wilder growled.

'It means he is unchanged, but he's safe... In fact, a young alchemist we know has been his constant companion.'

'Wren?'

'You didn't hear it from me.'

'Course not.' The relief was short-lived as Wilder steeled himself for what came next. 'Anyone in particular send you to taunt me, then?'

'Is that what I'm doing? Feels a little tame for that, don't you think?'

'You were always slow to warm up, Elderbrock.'

To his surprise, Torj didn't continue the verbal sparring, but instead shook his head again, almost in disbelief.

'What?' Wilder demanded, jerking in his restraints.

'I received a letter...' Torj said slowly, taking in the ice walls around them, glancing towards the frost-covered stairs.

'Oh?' Wilder didn't dare to hope, didn't let the possibility even form in his mind. Torj was here out of morbid curiosity, nothing more.

But the Bear Slayer paced before the cell. 'Marise is here, by the way...'

Wilder was thrown by the change of subject. Why were

they talking of the wine merchant from Harenth? 'Do I get to request my last meal and drink before my execution, then? Being a prisoner is thirsty work. It was thoughtful of him to come.'

Torj snorted. 'He says you've got an unpaid tab.'

'I've been a little busy,' Wilder muttered.

'Albert from the Fox sends his regards, too…'

'How kind. All the traders of the midrealms paying tribute.' Wilder tried to shift his weight again, the ache in his wrists closer to a burn now. 'What are you really doing here, Elderbrock?'

'Why? Got something better to do?' Torj mused. 'I told you, I got a letter.'

'So you said. From who?' In a moment of rashness, Wilder dared to say the names aloud. 'Anya? Adrienne? Dratos?'

Torj's gaze snapped back to his. 'No,' he said. 'From Talemir Starling.'

# CHAPTER EIGHTEEN

## THEA

The grand room around Thea was no longer there. The small silver sphere opened up an entirely different world before her eyes. A world of warriors and monsters, and a glimpse of Great Rites long past. Through a vast projection of light, she saw them – past Warswords of Thezmarr, and the challenges they'd faced.

Whatever the silver ball was, it contained unimaginable power, magic that captured the pasts of Guardians that came before, magic that led her through each recollection as though she were following a thread through a maze.

It showed her a giant reef dweller, surging from the foaming sea towards a warrior of Thezmarr on the shore, poison seeping from its tentacles. The Guardian's blade was drawn and he sliced at the first swipe of the monster, engaging in a deadly battle.

With a flare of light, the silver sphere revealed a lone figure, another Thezmarrian, trekking through a blizzard, the wind whipping snow and debris all around him, enough to draw blood from his exposed cheeks. His lips were black with frostbite, but his face was etched with determination.

The images shifted again, showing Thea a man standing before a vast spider's web, someone trapped within its confines. With a roar, the warrior charged, cleaving through the sticky substance to get to the hostage inside...

The orb showed her as Guardians of Thezmarr were pitted against evil in all forms: cursed men they once knew, wraiths and reapers, howlers, frost giants, arachnes and basilisks... It showed her the might of the Guardians – their mental fortitude, their strength as they battled monster after monster, their blades blurs of silver, blood spilling in their wake. Thea recognised countless manoeuvres as ones she'd been taught by her mentor, as ones she'd used many times during her hunt for vengeance.

And it wasn't just the monsters, but the horrific terrain, the extreme conditions... Each scene was more familiar than the last.

The sphere continued to play them out before her. It was a vision of the previous Guardians' pain, and the deepest nightmares they faced during the sacred ritual of the Furies. The trials they confronted were within and without: mind, body, heart.

And beyond it all was golden light.

Wilder had given her decades – *centuries* of Great Rite experiences wrapped up in that tiny silver sphere.

And then, she saw him.

Thea watched as he travelled the midrealms and beyond, silver orb in hand, visiting those whose recollections she'd just witnessed. Far and wide he trekked, across ice and snow, beyond stretches of desert and firestorms, through ragged ravines and a city among the treetops, all the while bartering with the former Guardians and Warswords of Thezmarr for their memories.

Thea observed each exchange with a lump in her throat as Wilder Hawthorne returned to the world as she knew it, armed with the knowledge to do exactly as he'd promised.

With fresh eyes, she saw him shape the past year – the punishing terrain, the monsters that had been thrown in her path... With every instance that flashed before her, Thea understood exactly what Wilder Hawthorne had been doing for the last twelve months.

He had fulfilled his vow to her.

He had been training her.

Wilder had never wanted to be her mentor, yet he'd spent the past year doing exactly that. He had recreated every Great Rite he knew of, every challenge he had seen in these memories, for her to master, to conquer, so that when her time came... she would be ready.

Wilder Hawthorne, her mentor, her friend, her love, had endured it all for her.

The Great Rites he'd seen poured forth, showing her more and more.

When it was done, Thea was sobbing from the force of it all.

And there was something else. She went to her pile of dirty clothes and pulled Audra's cards from one of the pockets, finding the card she favoured instantly by its tattered edges.

Of the three trials every Warsword faced, there was a challenge for each of these. One to test the mind, one to test the body, one to test the heart.

Audra, too, had known, and prepared her the only way she could.

*Strong of mind, strong of body, strong of heart.*

And Wilder had shown her the rest.

Thea's mind was unyielding, her body was strong, but her heart... It was her heart that needed mending.

When the light faded and Thea once more felt the cool marble beneath her feet, her eyes were wide open.

She told Cal and Kipp everything she had seen, and they listened in tense silence as the words poured out of her. Facing the truth out loud, she could not deny how wrong she'd been all this time. For a year, she had hunted and hated Wilder, and for a year, he'd been showing her how much he cared, how far he was willing to go to keep his promise to her. She had been a fool. Now, he was trapped alongside innocent children in those dungeons, and she could have stopped it. Regret threatened to consume her. But instead, she honed her focus. Instead, she plotted how she'd get him out of Aveum's ice prison.

'I don't expect you to risk yourselves,' she told her friends. 'It's my fault he's in there, my mess to clean up —'

Kipp gave a long-suffering sigh. 'Don't you get it by now?'

Thea looked at him blankly. 'Get what?'

Cal shook his head as though she'd just asked what colour the sky was. 'We're not following the guild, Thea. We haven't been for some time.'

'What do you mean?'

'It's *you* we're following,' Kipp said. 'Though in this moment I have no idea why. You're as thick as Cal's skull.'

Cal rolled his eyes. 'What he's saying is that we're with

you. It's you we're loyal to, not some antiquated horseshit laws of Thezmarr.'

Thea's eyes burned.

'If you say we need to get Hawthorne out of the dungeons, then that's what we do,' Kipp added.

'You know what will happen if you're caught getting involved in this...?' she ventured.

'We'll probably die long and painful deaths,' Kipp offered helpfully.

Cal made a noise at the back of his throat. 'Let's try to avoid that.'

Thea shook her head. 'I'm being serious.'

'As are we, Your Royal Highness. We're just glad you've seen the light,' Kipp replied – then, more gently, 'He loves you. That was never in any doubt. Not to us. I'll wager that everything he does is for you.'

For the first time, Thea didn't argue. She only vowed with that much more ferocity that she'd get him back.

As the sun passed over the mountains and lake beyond the floating domes, the trio strategised late into the day. They were going to get Wilder Hawthorne back, and they were going to use the masquerade ball to do it.

# CHAPTER NINETEEN

## THEA

The next night, on the evening of the eclipse, Thea readied herself for battle. In the privacy of her chambers, she donned a rose-gold gown like armour, and strapped her dagger and throwing stars to her legs beneath her full skirts.

The others had ensured that the rest of her weapons, and Wilder's, were stashed just outside the ballroom, and her pack was hidden away in Cal's quarters. Everything was in place, almost. Steadying her hand, she swept a line of dark kohl across each of her eyelids as Wren had once taught her, and painted her lips a deep blood red. She braided her hair in her usual warrior's style, only to pin it to the crown of her head, exposing the line of her neck. When she was finished, she studied herself in the full-length mirror, hardly recognising the woman before her.

*Good*, she thought, raising her mask to her face and tying it at the back of her head. The woman she had been this past year would be no good to her tonight. She had to rid herself of that person, had to shed her like a second skin. Wilder needed her, and she would see him free of the shackles she'd forced him into.

With a final glance at her glittering appearance and drake-inspired mask, Thea left her rooms and sought Princess Jasira.

In her royal suite, the Princess of Harenth was surrounded by fussing attendants, but when she saw Thea, her face broke into a wide smile.

'Thea, you're here!'

'I wouldn't miss it, Your – Jasi.'

The princess shooed away her assistants and gestured to her gown. 'What do you think?' She was resplendent in deep-sea blue, jewels glistening all over.

'Beautiful,' Thea told her.

'As are you, my friend.'

Thea offered a grateful smile and her arm. 'Shall we?'

Jasira took it and started towards the door. 'Care to make a wager on how many men ask us to dance tonight?'

Thea forced a laugh. Dancing was the last thing on her mind. 'I imagine you have a better idea of these things than I do. It would be a foolish bet on my part.'

'Nonsense.'

The princess' royal guard escorted the two women through the corridors of the floating dome, everything bathed in golden torchlight and garlands of native Aveum flowers. Thea kept her chin up and forced one foot in front of the other, holding the thoughts of Wilder in that ice cell at bay. He was strong. He was the strongest person she knew. Now, she had to be strong for him.

As the entrance to the grand ballroom came into view, she threw a final plea up to the Furies themselves that all would not be in vain before she squared her shoulders and the double doors opened inward.

She stifled the gasp on her lips.

In the heart of the floating dome, surrounded by the snow-capped peaks and evergreen forests beyond the windows, was a ballroom unlike anything she had ever seen. It was as though it had been plucked from a dream, bathed in moonlight, the vaulted ceilings adorned with glimmering chandeliers made from icicles. Everything about it was a testament to the genius of the kingdom: the wintry glow, the enchanted warmth, the illusion of falling snow. Every surface sparkled and shimmered, fashioned almost entirely out of crystal and glass, light refracting and dancing across the space in a myriad of colours. Garlands of blooms wrapped around white stone pillars while thick velvet curtains framed every entrance.

Thea and the princess watched from their private vantage point as at the other entrances, noblemen and warriors were stripped of their weapons. There were to be no blades of any kind amid the celebrations, no temptation for violence and darkness. Thea had been warned of this beforehand. But for the first time in her life, dresses and cosmetics worked in her favour. She and the princess breezed past the palace guards and through the royal entrance without being checked.

'Queen Reyna has outdone herself,' Jasira declared as they stepped inside.

'Princess Jasira of Harenth,' a herald announced. 'And her honoured guest, Guardian Althea Zoltaire of Thezmarr.'

Thea tensed under the scrutiny that was immediately upon them, not failing to notice how the public acknowledgement of her title caused no flutter of pride in her chest. Once, she had dreamt of such a thing, and now, she felt nothing.

'Come, Thea.' Jasira pulled at her arm. 'Let's do a lap of the vendors.'

Thea startled. Lining the walls of the ballroom were countless stalls decorated with frost-kissed wreaths and snowflake ornaments. It was as though Queen Reyna had brought the very best of the midrealms' markets indoors, offering the most premium wares in a vibrant tapestry within her halls.

'It it normal to have merchants like this at a ball?' Thea asked.

'In Aveum it is. Queen Reyna usually invites the most exceptional vendors from all over the midrealms. She prides herself on offering her guests the best of everything – plus, it's good for the kingdom. There are more than usual tonight, though. I think it's because people believe the Moonfire Eclipse will bless their wares and bring good fortune.'

Thea's brows knitted together. 'There seems to be a lot riding on this eclipse...'

With a gentle touch to her arm, Jasira chided her quietly, 'People find hope where they can.'

Thea's cheeks burned, but Jasira didn't let the point linger. Instead, she led them down the first row, where each stall offered a treasure trove of delights. Roasted chestnuts, miniature cakes with thick icing, spiced cider and toffee apples, exotic winter flowers preserved in glass domes, vibrant frosted jewels... Everything was artisan-made and beautifully presented, and the vendors themselves were draped in luxurious winter garments for the occasion, each trying to capture the princess' attention.

The fanfare and beauty felt rotten to Thea. For beneath these opulent rooms was an ice cell full of children, and another containing the most noble of Thezmarr's Warswords. The riches, the smiles, the decadence – it was all a farce, and Thea would see it ended.

Jasira's arm tightened around hers and Thea followed her gaze across the room. What little food she'd eaten curdled in her gut as she saw who the princess was making eyes at.

'He's quite handsome, isn't he?' Jasira's cheeks flushed as Sebastos Barlowe, apprentice to Vernich Warner, offered her a charming smile.

*So, he recovered from Wilder's blows after all... Pity.* Though Thea noted with no small sense of satisfaction that the once-straight line of Seb's nose was now permanently crooked, thanks to the punch she'd landed before the battle of Notos.

Thea struggled to keep her voice even. 'Jasira, I can safely say that he's a festering fucking prick of a —'

She cut herself off, face flaming at the coarse language that had flown from her mouth in the presence of —

'I'm so sorry, Your Highness, I wasn't...'

But Jasira was grinning from ear to ear. 'Is he *really?*'

Thea shuddered, recalling the moments where Seb's existence had threatened her own and that of her friends, where his cruelty and malice had gone beyond reason. She thought of how he'd mistreated Malik and old embers of rage instantly flared to life anew.

'If you catapulted him beyond the Veil, he still wouldn't be far enough away.'

Jasira tilted her head. 'You two... You have a history?'

Thea tore her eyes away from the bastard and realised what the princess was asking. 'Furies, no, not like that. I wouldn't touch him with a ten-foot pole unless it was to beat him senseless with it.' The words flew out of Thea's mouth before she could stop them. 'Sorry,' she mumbled.

Thankfully, the princess simply laughed. 'Don't be. It's good to know not to trust a pretty face.'

Thea bit back another nasty remark about Seb being anything but pretty. He was as much a monster as the wraiths that cursed the midrealms, in her eyes. She could feel his gaze on them still, boring holes in them, likely already scheming about how he could turn the princess against her.

But Jasira's attention on him had been fleeting. She seemed to have a particular stall in mind, and she bypassed several eager tradesfolk and led Thea to the farthest corner of the ballroom.

'Ah, I was hoping he'd be here!' she said, tugging Thea towards her intended stall.

Thea's brow furrowed. She recognised that man.

'Marise!' Princess Jasira waved.

It was the wine merchant from Harenth to whom Wilder had once introduced Thea.

Marise, who was surrounded by a small crowd of people with several bottles of wine open in front of him, beamed at the princess. 'Your Highness! What a sight for sore eyes you are. Everyone, move! You sorry lot of drunks. Make way for the princess.'

Jasira laughed as the crowd parted and she and Thea approached the stall.

Marise's eyes widened at the sight of Thea. 'And another honoured patron! What a delight to see you, Guardian Zoltaire.'

Thea gave him a stiff nod. It was all she could do with thoughts of Wilder flooding her mind. She just had to get through the first hour of the ball, then she'd be back in her armour, seeing him freed.

'At long last you have come for a tasting!' Marise continued, then lowered his voice. 'I expected you some time ago, with a certain Warsword we do not speak of...'

'I've been on the road,' Thea murmured, with an awkward glance at the princess, who seemed not to hear.

'But of course.' He bowed his head before clapping his hands together enthusiastically. 'Today we will taste three of my best wines.'

The merchant busied himself with setting six small glasses on the table before them. All the while, Thea scanned the ballroom, which was growing more crowded by the minute. That was good. The more people in the room, the more chaotic things would become when Cal and Kipp triggered the diversion. Thankfully, she spotted them at the ballroom's edge, both holding goblets but not drinking, not even Kipp. She suppressed a sigh of relief. They were exactly where they were meant to be.

Marise pressed a glass into her hand. 'This first, my intense friend. It's a lighter red from the provinces of Valia, beyond the Veil.'

Thea didn't know which information to absorb first: the fact that Marise had called her *intense* again, just as he had the first time they'd met, or that the wine she now held was from a place beyond the Veil. The same place that was home to the women warriors after whom she styled her hair.

Thea was distracted, so much so that she only heard every few words from the master wine merchant. Something about hints of blackberry and cassis, something else about a barnyard aroma and spice on the nose, whatever that meant. She dutifully sampled the wine, nodding appreciatively at Princess Jasira's observations. The young royal seemed to have an impressive grasp on the niche vocabulary needed for such things.

Before Thea knew it, the third and final drop was being pushed towards her and she sipped it self-consciously, noting that Marise's gaze was fixed on her this time.

The moment the wine hit her tongue, she closed her eyes. *Delicious* didn't cover it. It was otherworldly, elegant and complex all at once.

Marise was looking at her strangely.

'It's lovely,' she admitted.

'Curious that you should like that one the best...' He smiled faintly.

Princess Jasira had been drawn into a conversation with a nearby nobleman, and Thea frowned at the wine merchant. 'Why do you say that?'

He shrugged. 'It's nothing. Perhaps it's just that all you Warswords have the same taste.'

'I'm not a Warsword.'

'No?'

'Not yet.'

'You could have fooled me.'

Thea slid the glass back across the table. 'Thank you for the tasting.'

'May the Moonfire Eclipse bring you all the light you may need.'

Thea hesitated, just for a moment, before allowing the words to tumble from her mouth, the wine having loosened her lips. 'This doesn't seem strange to you, then... All this celebration while darkness creeps towards us?'

Marise offered her a broad smile. 'Let me tell you

something, Althea Zoltaire. A fine wine is just like this event... It's all about the finish.'

Then he winked at her, before turning to a fresh crowd of patrons.

Baffled, Thea left his stall, gesturing to Jasira that she would catch up with her later. She went to Cal and Kipp, who were still stationed on the opposite side of the ballroom. Both men had been fitted with brand new tunics and jackets.

'You two scrub up alright,' she told them, taking her place next to Kipp.

'You're not so bad yourself, Highness,' Kipp replied. 'Everything is in place. We just need to wait for the royals to make their entrance... Then the diversion will be underway, as will we.'

Thea nodded. 'Good... That's good.'

She noted Cal's attention elsewhere, following his stare to a woman in the far corner.

Thea elbowed Kipp and nodded to their friend. 'What's wrong with him?'

Kipp rolled his eyes. 'Lovestruck, apparently.'

Cal sighed. 'She's the most beautiful girl I've ever seen.'

'Really?' Kipp said with interest, craning his neck to get a better look. 'Do you think so?'

'Definitely.'

It was at that moment that the woman in question chose to cross the ballroom, making a beeline not for Cal, but for Kipp.

She draped her arms over his shoulders. 'Kristopher —'

Kipp grimaced.

'I've been waiting to hear from you,' she said, her voice sultry.

Cal looked between them. 'You've got to be kidding.'

Thea nudged him. 'Focus,' she warned. 'There are bigger things at stake here.'

Kipp made a point of untangling himself from the woman, whispering reassurances to her before rejoining them with a sheepish look.

Cal shook his head. 'Do you have a girl in every fucking port or something?'

Kipp scratched the back of his head. 'Uh, not exactly.'

There was a pause before Cal stiffened at the sight of something – someone – across the room. 'Did you see who else is here?' he asked, thrusting his chin opposite them.

Thea's gaze fell upon Seb once again. 'I saw him, alright,' she muttered, fists clenching at her sides.

'Bet you wish you'd let my arrow fly now...' Cal mused as Seb pinned them with a hateful glare.

'A moment of weakness on my part,' Thea said.

'Should have shot him in the dick instead,' Kipp offered. 'I would have paid to see that.'

Cal laughed. 'Too small a target, even for me.'

Seeming to sense that he was the topic of their conversation, Sebastos Barlowe sauntered over, his lip curled into its usual ugly sneer. 'Should have known you three would be here —'

'You mean doing our jobs?' Kipp supplied, eyes narrowed.

Seb looked Thea up and down, gaze lingering on her curves. 'I suppose being the whore of a traitor *is* a job —'

Cal surged forward, fists clenched and raised, but Thea thrust her arm out across his chest. 'Not here,' she said, her voice calm and steady.

Cal was trembling with rage, but he did as she asked.

It only seemed to make Seb smugger. 'You always do what fortress sluts tell you, Whitlock?'

Thea heard Cal's measured exhale as he fought to keep his rage under control.

Kipp stepped in, placing himself in front of Cal, even deigning to rest a patronising hand on Seb's shoulder. 'No friends of your own to play with, Seb?' he said lightly. 'Nothing better to do than sling moronic insults at your betters?'

Seb made a noise of disgust, jerking away from Kipp's touch. 'Get the fuck off me. And *betters*? You?'

'Why else do you constantly seek us out?' Thea mused, eyeing Kipp as he peeled off his gloves and tucked them carefully in the outer pocket of his dark tunic, a fleck of violet shining there.

'Because you're a fucking insult to the institute of Thezmarr,' Seb hissed. 'You're fooling yourself if you think you'll *ever* hear the call of the Great Rite. A woman? Please. You don't have what it takes. You've only got to where you are by flashing your tits and sucking cock —'

Icy anger flooded Thea, and she allowed herself a step forward. 'I have saved your life several times now, Barlowe, and your gratitude has been less than underwhelming. So, I'll remind you of a little vow I made to you once... When we face each other again, I'll have you on the ground. And unlike me, you won't get back up.'

'The watery promise of a woman.' Seb snorted. 'I'm still standing, *stray*.'

'Because I allowed it,' Thea said darkly. 'Walk away, Seb, before I rob you of your ability to do so.'

Seb opened his mouth to respond, but quiet fell across the ballroom, the shift in the atmosphere of the room halting him. The orchestra was taking their seats on the stage, readying to perform. With a glare, Seb backed away, returning to Vernich Warner's side at the opposite end of the ballroom. There, the Bloodletter didn't acknowledge his apprentice, but simply watched the festivities with his usual scowl.

Thea's shoulders sagged.

'Definitely should have let me shoot him,' Cal griped, staring after Seb. 'The things I'd do to see that prick in a world of pain...'

'Well, you might not be there to see it, but I assure you, he'll be in a world of pain,' Kipp said, looking mighty pleased with himself.

Brows raised and suspicion prickling, Thea said, 'What are you talking about?'

Kipp was openly beaming now. 'Before we left Notos, the beautiful Wren supplied me with an *intriguing* substance... Widow's Ash – I believe you know of it?'

Thea gaped at her friend. 'You didn't...'

'Oh, I absolutely did.'

'Did what?' Cal demanded.

A hoarse laugh broke from Thea's lips, and she shook her head in disbelief. 'Let's just say that poor Seb is in for a rough and *itchy* night.'

Cal grinned. 'I like the sound of that.'

But Thea's attention had moved to the orchestra. Now settled, the musicians placed bows to violins, fingers to harps and lips to flutes. 'Where are the rulers?' she whispered. 'Surely they're to be announced before —'

There was an intake of breath as the musicians burst into their first performance of the evening. Suddenly, the ballroom came alive with laughter and melody, couples taking to the grand floor, twirling gracefully, layers of tulle and silk sweeping across the shining surface. Moonlight spilt through the vast windows, casting an ethereal glow upon the nobles.

Thea squinted across the room to the grand entrance, where the guards and heralds all stood to attention, with no sign of the kings and queen of the midrealms. She needed the royals in the midst of the action before they could implement the first stage of their rescue mission.

Poised to throw herself into action, Thea took a step forward as the delicate notes of the orchestra echoed through the chamber, the lavish gowns and regal attire creating a kaleidoscope of sheer opulence. 'Any minute now...'

'Not yet!' Kipp tried to grab her arm.

But she twisted out of his reach, starting towards the exit. She would not leave Wilder to freeze in that cell a moment longer. She would take her chances, she would —

A large hand, covered in grazes, enveloped hers. Another closed around her waist, sweeping her onto the dance floor effortlessly, wrapping her in the scent of leather and rosewood.

With a stifled cry, she looked up.

Behind an intricate mask of black-and-red embellishments, a pair of silver eyes met hers.

'Heard you were looking for me, Princess.'

# CHAPTER TWENTY

## WILDER

Wilder met Thea's gaze and the atmosphere crackled around them as he took her in his arms, guiding them across the ballroom in one fluid motion. He forgot the pain as he felt her chest hitch against his before she melted beneath his touch. He breathed her in, savouring the glancing contact of her skin against his and tracing the exposed elegant curve of her neck with his gaze.

Seemingly pliant with shock, Thea allowed him to take the lead, allowed him to pull her closer, locking them together as the melody took hold. Wilder couldn't tear his eyes away from hers, their bodies moving in perfect sync, as they always had. For a moment, the world around them faded into a distant blur. Every twist and turn, every brush of their legs together whispered of that bond between them. Wilder's steps were measured, but beneath that control, fire simmered, threatening to consume them both.

Resplendent in rose gold, Thea was magnetic, and the way she was looking at him, with her lush mouth slightly parted, was as though she didn't quite believe he was real, as though a million words were on her lips, and she couldn't find the right one.

'No sharp remarks for me today, Princess?' he said quietly, but his voice threatened to fracture beneath the weight of everything it had taken to get to this point.

'You...' Her grip on his shoulder tightened, like she needed to reassure herself he wasn't a figment of her imagination. 'You were training me all along,' she whispered, her eyes lined with tears.

Beneath his mask, his brows shot up. 'You said you threw it away... The gift.'

'I did.' She followed his lead through another series of waltz steps. 'But I got it back.'

The dance was a perilous game, teetering on the precipice of discovery – but it was important, Wilder knew, more than important that they have this moment, for they might not get another.

He swallowed the lump in his throat and pulled her closer, so all he could breathe in was her, and that sea-salt-and-bergamot scent of hers.

'I told myself that it was enough,' he murmured into her hair, his voice hoarse. 'That I should be grateful for the time we had. It was more love than most people get in a lifetime. But the truth is, Thea... A thousand lifetimes with you wouldn't be enough.'

He wanted to kiss her, more than anything, to let everything that had stood between them fall away into nothing.

But Thea's breath caught. 'I'm sorry. I'm sorry for everything —'

'Later,' he said, his hand tightening on her waist.

Her tongue swept her lips as she studied his face, her

gaze growing hooded, and it was all he could do not to kiss her then, to finish what he'd started in the stables before his arrest. He ached at the thought of it, and at how close she was now, how her body hummed in response to his.

But he steeled himself. There was so much they needed to talk about, so much they needed to understand and forgive, and a ballroom was no place for such things.

'We were going to get you out,' she whispered with a note of desperation. 'We had a plan.'

'Later,' Wilder said again, spreading his fingers so they brushed her ribs, slowing them to match the pace of the new piece the orchestra began. 'The eclipse will start soon,' he told her. 'We should get to the balcony.'

'Is this wise?' she asked, as he led them from the heart of the waltz.

'Wiser than continuing this dance. One of us is bound to do something stupid,' he said, his voice low as he withdrew them from the dance floor and slipped into the crowd gathering at the balcony doors.

It had been a risk to enter the ball rather than just escape the floating domes, but Marise had argued that sometimes hiding in plain sight was better. Wilder couldn't deny that, though he was willing to bet they didn't have long before the guards awoke from their supposed drunken stupors and his absence from his cell was noted. There wasn't enough wine in the world to repay Marise and Torj the favour. As for the third party involved... He wasn't ready to think about that yet.

He noticed Thea signal to Cal and Kipp, who were a few yards away in the crowd. There hadn't been time to brief any of them, not without risking his cover. He didn't know which of Torj's friends he had to thank for the formal attire or the mask, but he refused to look a gift horse in the mouth at a time like this.

Wilder brought Thea close to him, sheltering her from the jostling of the crowd as nobles fought to get a decent viewing spot from the balcony of the dome. But his apprentice gave as good as she got, carving a path for them to one of the railings, her face bright and alert beneath her mask. He caught her stealing glances at him as they moved, her stormy gaze clouded with regret, her hand drifting to the fate stone he knew was tucked down her cleavage.

A year had passed.

A year was left.

A reality that was always at the forefront of his mind, even during the most chaotic of times. He hated that fate had Thea racing against an hourglass, that the last twelve months had not been kind to either of them, that he knew nothing of the time ahead.

When Thea next reached for the stone, he took her hand instead, stroking his thumb along the scar-flecked skin there. Thea's lower lip trembled before she clamped it between her teeth and turned her face to the stars.

Wilder didn't know what to expect from the eclipse, but the anticipation in the air around them was palpable. It made him uneasy, as did the crush of bodies around him. The people of Aveum, and the people of the midrealms, had been preparing for this moment for months, praying that this rare celestial event would save them all.

'Welcome one and all,' Queen Reyna's voice projected across the far reaches of the crowd from a secondary balcony above. 'Today is a monumental day in our history... A day wherein we will bear witness to the magic and glory of the Moonfire Eclipse. For too long now, the midrealms have been plagued by the prophecy thrust upon us.'

The winter queen took a deep breath before reciting:
*'In the shadow of a fallen kingdom, in the eye of the storm*
*A daughter of darkness will wield a blade in one hand*
*And rule death with the other*
*When the skies are blackened, in the end of days*
*The Veil will fall.*
*The tide will turn when her blade is drawn.*
*A dawn of fire and blood.'*

An awed silence washed over the revellers.

Queen Reyna gestured to the night sky. 'The Moonfire Eclipse will turn these tides of fate. This is no ordinary eclipse – it lasts only a matter of seconds, and is the first of its kind in a century. And it will ensure that we find peace in our lands again. This celestial event is a blessing sent from the Furies themselves. May it give us strength and power in its triumph over darkness.'

Wilder felt Thea stiffen in front of him.

He leant in to say something – what, he wasn't sure; he just wanted to reassure her, to be closer to her, so that the ice around his heart might thaw.

But gasps sounded, and awed whispers echoed across the crowd.

All eyes were fixed on the sky as the darkness began its slow journey across the face of the moon, casting an eerie shadow over the frozen landscape. As the eclipse progressed, the world around them grew darker and darker. The snow-covered trees became silhouettes against the darkening sky, and the once bright white snow now took on an orange hue. It was as though a spectral hand had cast a veil over the glowing orb of the moon, transforming it from a radiant beacon of white into a globe of blood red, draping the midrealms in obscurity, blanketing the lands with an unsettling stillness.

Wilder inhaled the icy air, pulling Thea to him and holding her close. He had yearned to hold her like this for so long, a year of want, of need unmet. Now, he didn't want to let her go. The stars seemed to dim in deference and a sense of ancient magic permeated the world around them. He wondered if she could feel it too, if the storm within her would wake from its slumber and rise in the presence of otherworldly power.

But there was no hint of a storm, no crackle of lightning in her touch, only her breath clouding before her face in the frigid night air.

Wilder took in the people around them: the warriors ablaze with desperate fervour, the royals and their smug expressions, the people on the streets below, wide-eyed and hopeful... He knew that, whether by the Furies themselves or not, the event occurring before them all was a pivotal moment in the tides of fate. He knew that further out in the villages, despite the cold, the common folk would be standing outside in awe of the spectacle, some whispering prayers to their gods, others simply marvelling at the strange beauty of the eclipse.

Beneath the might of the blood-red orb, the air grew even colder, settling deep into his bones. He, like the rest of Vios, waited with bated breath for those seconds to pass, for the shadow across the moon to recede, for the world to be bathed in light once more.

Only the light didn't come.

Close by, a gasp sounded.

Commotion followed, shock rippling through the crowd.

Thea still in his arms, Wilder craned his neck to see, noting the guards with their hands on their weapons, forcing their way into the throng.

Someone screamed.

Thea whirled towards the sound, her hand inching her dress up to reveal a dagger strapped to her thigh —

Suddenly, all around the silk slippers, tulle skirts and marble floors, darkness surged. It swept in like a tide, lapping at people's feet, flooding the balcony and bleeding into the ballroom inside. It split into vines, crawling up the walls of the domes, wrapping around people's ankles.

Shrieks of terror filled the air.

The royal guard fought through the crowd, ready for battle.

Above, the red moon lingered as darkness descended.

And still, the light did not come.

# CHAPTER TWENTY-ONE

## THEA

A roar ripped through the night and a wind as sharp as daggers whipped through the throngs of people, slamming windows shut, causing the whole dome to rattle. Thea and Wilder were suddenly caught in the wave of desperate people fleeing the chaos, trampling one another to get away, their faces etched with terror and desperation.

Thea's heart was racing as she tried to find the source of that roar. It was no reaper, no shadow wraith, but something else. She saw nothing but the clawing of limbs and the wide-eyed panic of the nobles around her. Wilder tried to brace her against his chest and shield her from the onslaught, but she pulled him with her, ducking into the masses. They stood no chance against the tide of terrified people. They had to move with the throng, if only to stand their ground within it.

The candles inside had been snuffed out, and the unending eclipse beyond the glass walls illuminated no sign of the creature that had caused the mayhem. Thea tightened her grip on Wilder's hand, not willing to be separated yet, not when he had no means of defence, and she had only her throwing stars and her dagger. He seemed to have the same thought, scanning the space around them for a makeshift weapon.

Thea dropped his hand and unsheathed her dagger, holding it out to him.

'Keep it,' Wilder growled, seizing a chair and breaking off two of its legs.

She didn't argue, but reached for her skirts, tearing them from her legs for ease of movement, plucking several throwing stars from the straps around her thighs while she was at it.

Another near-deafening roar sounded from the balcony, spurring him and Thea into action as human screams echoed across the dance floor. Glass shattered as vendors' tables were knocked over like dominoes in the crowd's bid to escape the darkness that now lashed through the open doors.

'What the fuck is that?'

Cal had appeared, holding two candlesticks above his head like clubs.

'No idea. Not a wraith or a reaper,' Thea called. 'Where's Kipp?'

'Went to get our swords,' he replied, scanning the handful of unarmed Guardians around them and the royals cowering behind their guards on the stage amid the orchestra's abandoned instruments.

Thea palmed her dagger as the balcony outside groaned beneath the weight of something monstrous. 'Feels like a set-up.'

'No shit.' Torj appeared at Cal's side, brandishing two

iron pokers from the great hearth. 'Long time no see, Apprentice.'

Cal grinned. 'Good time for a reunion, I'd say.'

Thea looked to Wilder, who still wore his mask, but in such familiar company, there was no hiding who he was.

'You should go,' she hissed, trying to push him subtly towards the door. 'Go while you still can.'

He didn't move an inch. 'There's nothing in the world that can take me from you now,' he said. And then, with a glance at Torj: 'Besides, who'd you think helped me get out?'

Thea wove through the remaining fleeing nobles towards the stage. 'Fuck,' she cursed when she spotted who cowered amid the shattered harps and violins: Princess Jasira, Queen Reyna and King Elkan, with no sign of the other rulers, or their royal guards.

Thea skidded to a halt and crouched at their sides. 'You need to get out of here, Your Majesties. There must be a place to hide? Somewhere secure —'

Queen Reyna's mouth opened in a silent scream and the hair on Thea's nape stood up.

'Run,' she begged the royals, reaching for Jasira and squeezing her hand before she turned to their remaining guard. 'Get them out of here. Do your duty!'

But the icy wind that swept through the broken ballroom told her there was no time left. With a final pleading look, she stood, turning on her heel to face whatever shade of darkness had come with the eclipse.

Thea barely registered the scream that sounded behind her, but she felt it vibrate in her chest as her gaze met the mass of shadow before her, darkness unfurling around it, temporarily obscuring it from view.

But it was no wraith, no reaper... Because it *scuttled*

through the open doors from the balcony, shattering much of the glass wall with it, the cracks splintering into a thousand fractures. It loomed there in the entry, its foreign form shifting and undulating, a sinister silhouette.

'The fuck...?' Thea heard Vernich's gravelly tone nearby, and for once she was glad to be fighting on the side of the Bloodletter, hoping he would live up to his name.

With a spine-chilling clicking noise, the ribbons of onyx mist dissipated around the monster, and a gasp of horror escaped Thea.

It was like nothing she'd ever seen before. Easily twice the size of a Tverrian stallion, with the mangled upper torso, arms and head of a human, it had purplish skin and eight yellow eyes. Fangs gnashed in its mouth, and claws protruded from once-human hands. At its lower half was a massive spiderlike abdomen, and eight giant legs covered in fine hair.

'It's an arachne,' Wilder called, circling, still holding his broken chair legs like they might somehow stand against such a monster. 'Watch out for its web.'

'And its pincers!' Torj added, twirling his iron pokers. 'They're dripping with venom. One drop in an open wound and —'

A web shot out of nowhere, missing Torj by a hair's breadth.

'And?' Thea pressed, her grip tightening on her dagger. It was the only Naarvian steel they had. One dagger against the might of whatever evil this was.

'And there's a fifty-fifty chance it'll kill you. It's slow to activate, so you won't know right away,' the Bear Slayer told them. 'But basically, avoid it at all costs. It'll fuck you up either way.'

'Furies save us...' Cal looked pale. 'Is it cursed?'

The clicking sound intensified and the creature scanned them all with its eight eyes, seeming to consider which of them to kill first.

'Yes. An arachne doesn't usually wield shadow as well as webs,' Torj replied, not taking his eyes off the monster.

'Wonderful,' Cal muttered.

Heart in her throat, with only her dagger in her hand, Thea reached for her magic on instinct, rallying the power of the storm within and without, waiting for that first flicker of lightning to spark at her fingertips, ready to unleash the chaos she craved.

*I am the storm*, she told herself, digging deep.

A shot of web came flying at her. Thea leapt from its path, rolling across the floor and flipping to her feet with a hiss of frustration.

Her magic was gone. She'd have to deal with this beast the old-fashioned way.

'Warswords!' she shouted. 'Three-point formation!'

Thea didn't look to see if they followed her command. She simply threw herself into action, springing off the stage, ducking the first swipe of shadow and dodging the next, running in a zigzag towards the creature's body amid the darkness swirling around it.

Gods, she hoped Kipp would hurry up with the swords. She could hear the shouts of the others, could hear their cries as they rushed the monster in their own attacks, but she focused on her own path. If she could just get the dagger close, she could do some damage. All her dealings with shadow monsters had taught her that nothing was impervious to Naarvian steel —

She skidded to a stop, her blood running cold as several

eyes latched onto her, burning with a bright, otherworldly malevolence.

And the creature scuttled *up the fucking wall.*

Shuddering in disgust, Thea flung several throwing stars. The tiny spiked discs became but blurs of silver as they spun through the air.

The thing screeched, the sound utterly blood-curdling, as two of the stars found their marks in its eyes and it slipped from the wall.

Wilder lunged forward, and with an almighty strike, stabbed the monster through the leg with one of his chair leg spikes, pinning it to the floor.

'Thea, now!' he shouted.

Thea threw herself into action, using the immobilised leg to wrangle her way towards its body, ducking swipes from its other legs, barely dodging a shot of sticky web that came from somewhere she couldn't even see.

'A little help!' she ground out, before putting her dagger between her teeth and continuing her scramble through the rough surface of its legs, grimacing at the spiked hair that met her hands.

An iron poker soared through the air, spearing another of the arachne's legs to the far wall.

The monster's body jerked and Thea held on for dear life, slowly closing the distance between her and the human-like part of the arachne.

Its six remaining eyes latched onto her and Thea jumped, landing on the lower part of its body, palming her dagger. She had killed reapers and wraiths without magic; she could kill this monstrosity too. Surely in that purplish chest cavity there was a beating heart she could carve out —

A shout of pain – Wilder's – caused her to falter, and

suddenly, she was falling.

Thea hit the ground hard, the impact knocking the wind out of her and rattling her teeth.

Someone grabbed her by the arm and hauled her back, just as a wet mass of web slapped against the marble floor where she'd been a second before.

Panting, she looked around madly, seeing it was Kipp at her side.

'Swords?' she gasped, wincing at the pain throbbing through her body.

Kipp pressed the scabbards into her hand, but just as Thea went to unsheathe Wilder's blades, a roar shattered the icicle chandeliers.

The arachne ripped its legs free in a shower of black blood. Darkness flooded the ballroom in a physical assault, sending everyone flying.

Thea's back hit an upturned table, something sharp sticking into her side. But she was on her feet in an instant, swords in hand, the taste of ash in her mouth.

Slowly, the shadows receded.

A silent cry formed on Thea's lips.

For amid the carnage of the ballroom was not only the arachne, free from all restraints and churning with dark power, but Anya, the Daughter of Darkness, her wings flaring behind her, a bloodied scythe in her hand as she stalked towards the rulers of the midrealms.

They were all there now. Even King Artos, who was shoving Princess Jasira behind him, using his body as a shield to protect her.

*Why didn't they flee when I told them to?*

Thea gaped as King Leiko of Tver scrambled back, and Queen Reyna and King Elkan clutched one another close. To

Thea's horror, the leg of King Elkan's pants was ripped and bloodied, a layer of something translucent coating his skin.

'Thea!' Princess Jasira's desperate plea rang out above all else.

Thea surged towards her, blades raised.

Time both slowed and sped up, and Thea saw several things happen at once.

Lashes of darkness whipped through the air. Anya brandished her weapon, the steel gleaming in the remaining watery light. And the arachne shattered an entire glass wall, sending thousands of shards splintering into the night.

Within seconds, Thea was all that stood between the Daughter of Darkness and the royal families of the midrealms, her gaze trained on the woman who shared her celadon eyes, one marred by a brutal scar. The air around them crackled, not with Thea's magic, but with Anya's. Thea could taste it on her tongue, familiar and heady.

Shadows poured around them, and Anya took a step forward. 'Move,' she growled.

Thea's grip tightened on her swords. 'Never.'

Anya's gaze narrowed before it fell to the fate stone that had escaped Thea's gown. The Daughter of Darkness blanched before she whirled her weapon menacingly. 'I won't ask again.'

'Thea...' Wilder's voice sounded distant, but she didn't look at him, not yet.

Instead, she took a deep breath, gathering all her remaining strength, and charged at her sister —

A rush of darkness crept over the balustrade and swept in like a tidal wave, tearing Thea from the ground, whipping the air around her. A warm hand closed over hers.

And then she was falling.

# CHAPTER TWENTY-TWO

## WILDER

Clutching Thea to him, Wilder tried to cushion their fall through shadow and air, through darkness and ice. They hit the ground hard, the woodlands frosted beneath them, far beyond the floating domes of Vios.

In the night sky above, the eclipse was frozen in time, blocking out the moonlight and casting an unending darkness across the realms.

Thea groaned, but he clapped a hand over her mouth, drawing a single finger to his own lips before pointing to what he had spotted beyond the treeline.

Illuminated by torches and campfires was an enemy unit. Shadow wraiths, cursed men and a variety of other creatures who seemed to leak darkness into the night. They were armed, blades gleaming, and though Wilder couldn't make out their words, he knew that violence was on the horizon.

Thea was still trying to catch her breath, but she looked at him in a panic. 'Cal and Kipp...' She struggled against his hold. 'Torj. Everyone – we have to get back. We must fight —'

'They'll be fine. There's a plan. Torj knows where to take them —'

'But Anya, her arachne, they'll —'

'Anya won't hurt them,' Wilder tried to tell her. 'And the arachne is no ally of hers. But she'll see it slain. And Cal and Kipp will be safe.' Though he knew the next part sounded stupid given the past year, he added: 'I promise.'

There were a thousand questions in her eyes, yet somehow the words seemed to calm her, and Thea followed his stare, taking in the ominous sight before them. 'She sent us here to die,' she managed, turning back to him, horror etched on that beautiful face.

'No,' he told her. 'She sent us here to *see*.'

He pointed again, this time to the two figures at the heart of the operation below.

He waited as Thea tensed beside him, her mouth falling open as she processed what was plain as day before them.

'That's the Harenth dungeon master...' she murmured, her breath clouding. 'I recognise the jewellery.'

'I believe he calls himself an inquisitor.' It was hard to miss a gemstone nasal piercing and a dozen bronze bangles on each wrist in a war camp. 'Do you notice anything else?'

Thea scanned the campsite, chewing her lower lip. 'Their sigils... They're... wings. The same as the one I pulled from those enemy forces off the coast of Thezmarr last year.'

'The very same,' Wilder agreed. 'And what about the power radiating around us? Do you feel it?' he said quietly, watching her face for any signs of recognition. Her eyes grew wide with realisation as the familiar warmth of magic hummed out towards them.

'That's...' Thea took a ragged breath. 'That's empath magic I feel, isn't it?'

'You tell me... You've felt it before, haven't you?'

Slowly, Thea nodded, returning her gaze to the enemy force below. 'Artos... It's Artos' magic.'

Wilder dipped his head.

'How can this be?' Thea gaped, her eyes roaming over the Harenth dungeon master as he moved across the campsite. 'I... I don't understand.'

'We think he's been using his empath ability to get others to do his bidding for some time now, and framing Anya for their work.'

Thea whipped around to face him. 'Framing her? You saw what she is.'

'A master of shadow, yes – but *who* was she attacking in that ballroom, Thea?'

Slowly, a crease formed between Thea's brows, her features slackening as she visibly swallowed. 'Artos.'

'Artos,' Wilder agreed, flinching as an elongated shadow was cast across the campsite below. 'Look on the northern side,' he told Thea, not daring to take his eyes off the reaper he saw there.

She let out a muffled cry as she saw it too, watching as its sinewy body stalked towards a pen of prisoners chained together.

'Wilder,' she breathed, gripping his arm and starting forward.

But he held her back. There was no saving these people, not now. Time and time again he had tried himself, but to no avail.

Frozen in horror, Wilder and Thea watched as the king of wraiths reached into a villager's chest, darkness spreading like a disease around them, the smell of burnt hair permeating the air. A lump formed in Wilder's throat as he warred with his instinct to pull Thea away from this nightmare, but she needed to see it for herself, needed to see what Artos was capable of, what he was doing to their world.

In silence, they watched as the reaper wrought its curse upon the innocent prisoner. Ribbons of darkness dancing around the campsite, screams piercing the night.

'Is this how the shadow-touched are made?' Thea whispered, her face pale. 'Is this what you meant?'

'A shadow-touched person is the result of a failed attempt at what they're trying to do here,' Wilder replied slowly, trying to keep his own memories from overwhelming him. 'This is something worse... See the creatures created here? They are not of the same ilk as shadow-touched folk. They are mutilated with shadow from inside, not out... They are cursed experiments, blindly carrying out the will of their master. He has a hold over them.'

'And you're sure it's Artos?' she asked with resignation.

'He's the most powerful empath in history,' Wilder said, clenching his jaw. 'Do you remember that mercenary attack in Harenth? The prices on our heads?' It had been a shameful moment of weakness for Wilder, but a pivotal moment in Thea's warrior education.

'How could I forget that? I killed eleven men that day.'

Wilder remembered it well. 'It was Artos. Artos put out the hit. My sources confirmed it a few weeks ago.'

Thea was quiet for a moment before she spoke again. 'He seemed so outraged...'

'A fine actor, apparently,' Wilder allowed.

'If all this is true... What does he have planned?'

'Artos collects people and power,' Wilder told her quietly,

his skin prickling at the proximity to the horrors below. 'We have no idea who is under his control. We can't know who he's influencing, not when he's so strong.'

'He used his power on me in Harenth...'

'He did.'

Thea's throat bobbed. 'I didn't even know it was happening until you intervened. He used it to comfort me, to make me feel... at ease.'

'Therein lies the danger.'

Thea made to stand, but Wilder yanked her back down to the forest floor.

She shot him a look of disbelief. 'We need to help them,' she said, as though it were the simplest thing in the world.

Regret laced Wilder's words. 'We can't help them on our own...'

'We can, we've beaten worse odds —'

Wilder sighed heavily and placed a gentle hand on her shoulder. She was trembling, whether with cold or rage, he didn't know. 'Sometimes being a Warsword is not only about fighting, but learning when to live to fight another day.'

'Wilder...' she implored.

But he shook his head. 'We need to leave. We need to rejoin the others.'

He thought she was going to argue more, but instead, she gave a stiff nod and reached for the swords in the dirt. *His* swords.

With trembling hands, she offered them to him.

'You won them,' he said. 'You captured me. That was the deal you made with Osiris, wasn't it? They made a point of telling me that in the ice cell.' He tried and failed to keep the note of bitterness from his voice.

Thea pressed the weight of the weapons more firmly into his hands.

'I don't need yours,' she told him, sounding steadier than he expected. 'I'm going to earn my own.'

Wilder stared at her for a moment, taking in the ruined remains of her gown, the scratches and bruises across her exposed skin. *She must be freezing.*

'I have never doubted that for a second,' he told her, and accepted his blades, strapping them to his back, revelling in their weight once more.

She met his gaze. 'I know that now.'

Wilder's hand twitched at his side as he considered lacing his fingers through hers, but something stopped him. Alert as ever, Thea noted his hesitation, but said nothing, her expression unreadable.

Wilder steeled himself, squaring his shoulders and starting away from the horrors unfolding in the campsite below. 'Come on.'

'Where are we going?' she asked, stepping in sync beside him. 'To find Cal and Kipp?'

'Soon, but not yet,' he told her. 'It's time you met the shadow-touched, Princess.'

# CHAPTER TWENTY-THREE

## THEA

Wilder led her into the depths of the Aveum mountains, and after a time, wordlessly handed her his cloak. She could barely feel the bite of the cold, but then, she hadn't known she'd been slowly freezing to death in those caves, so she took it gratefully, glad for its weight and warmth around her shoulders, glad for the scent of him that wrapped around her with it.

She didn't like that they'd left the others in the middle of a skirmish. After everything she, Cal and Kipp had been through, it didn't feel right that they weren't together. They had stood by her through everything, they had —

'They're safe with Torj,' Wilder told her gruffly.

Thea unclenched her jaw and relaxed her furrowed brow. She supposed her worry had been written all over her face, as usual. 'But the attack —'

'They had it in hand.'

'How can you be sure?

'The Bear Slayer just saved my life,' he replied. 'If he said he'll bring them to the meet point, that's exactly what he'll do.'

There was no room for argument after that.

As they trudged through the undergrowth, a sliver of moon appeared, the eclipse shifting at long last. Thea didn't know what it meant, that it had lasted so long, or that it was finally fading. She didn't ask.

In the returning moonlight she could see the furrow of Wilder's brow, the conflict across his face. He was at odds with himself; she'd seen that look many times before, often pertaining to her. But this time... This time guilt curdled in her gut. She didn't have the whole story, not yet, but she knew she'd been wrong about him, and that thought alone mortified her into silence. She had felt in her bones that it didn't add up, but she had hunted him across the midrealms anyway. She had cursed his existence and had him thrown in the ice dungeons. She had allowed hatred to make her bitter, to make her resent what they had once shared together. But here he was – stoic and sturdy as ever.

The tension between them grew tauter with each passing moment, and she knew he was processing his own feelings about it all as well. What could she say to undo even a little of the damage? What could she do to take away the pain she'd caused him? She didn't deserve his forgiveness.

The heated kiss they had shared in the Vios stables came back to her, as did the words he'd spoken to her there.

*'I'll never stop being yours.'*

Thea hardly knew what to feel about everything unfolding around her, but she knew that she'd been wrong, so deeply and utterly wrong. And that Wilder had paid the price for it.

Every time a question formed on her lips, she bit it back.

How long until they met up with the shadow-touched? What had become of the monster in the floating dome, and of all their friends? How would they face the realms now, knowing all that stood against them?

The silence from Wilder reminded her of their first journey together, when he had escorted her from Thezmarr to Harenth to petition the rulers to become a shieldbearer. That had been two years ago. Two years that felt like a lifetime with all they had endured between.

'Watch your —'

But it was too late – Thea slipped on the uneven terrain as they descended over a ridge. Wilder caught her, his warm hands closing around her waist, his long fingers spanning her ribs, the strength of him near-intoxicating. She couldn't help it; she breathed him in, relishing his familiar scent, the touch that seared through her clothes.

And just for a moment, his gaze dropped to her mouth, his eyes darkening.

But then the heated look was gone, and he cleared his throat, holding her until her feet were steady beneath her once again.

'Thanks.' She willed his touch to linger.

It didn't.

'Wilder...' she started, unable to bear the quiet any longer.

'It's just down here,' he said, cutting her off and moving ahead of her.

She followed, noting how twisted all the barren trees were in this part of Aveum, as though some force had swept through and tangled them. A particularly large naked trunk stood in the middle of the woods, its base surrounded by jagged boulders covered in a pale green moss that reminded Thea of fine lace.

With a grunt, Wilder put all his weight behind one of the giant rocks and pushed. The huge stone rolled to the side to reveal an opening just beyond.

'I thought we were going to a campsite...' Thea said tentatively.

'We are. Of sorts.'

'Where are we, then?'

'We're still in Aveum, just deep underground.'

'Is this where we're meeting Torj and the others?'

'Not yet. We'll meet them after. They won't be far from us.' He motioned to the gap. 'Princesses first.'

Out of habit, she shot him a look before she remembered herself.

At a crouch, Thea entered the dark space, placing her hands out before her face and finding that she couldn't see a single finger as she edged into what must have been some sort of tunnel. The crunch of rock sounded behind her, and she heard Wilder brushing his hands off as he followed her inside. There was a strike of flint, and a moment later the cavern was illuminated by torchlight.

'This way,' Wilder said, taking the lead once more, down into the depths of the underground.

'Is this place at all linked to the tunnels beneath the midrealms you mentioned?'

'It is,' he allowed, glancing at her as though he were surprised it had taken her this long to break the silence with one of her questions. 'As far as I'm aware, the network is modelled off a similar design in another realm beyond the Veil. But for our tunnels, it started with connections between five key points.'

'The five ruling kingdoms,' Thea guessed.

'A little more lowbrow than that... Remember I told you of the connected sister taverns?'

Thea pushed a loose strand of hair from her eyes. 'The Laughing Fox in Harenth, the Dancing Badger in Naarva, the... Stag in Delmira...' She trailed off, the rest of the names escaping her.

'The Flying Stag, yes. And the Blushing Bear in Tver, and the —'

'Singing Hare in Aveum. I should have remembered that one. Kipp has been harassing me for months to go there.'

Wilder huffed a gruff laugh at that. 'Why am I not surprised?'

Thea shrugged tentatively. 'Kipp is Kipp.'

Wilder continued down the path. 'In any case, those taverns were the starting point for the whole network. Originally it was to counter a particular prohibition law, then it was to avoid the kingdoms' various importation taxes. It's far more extensive than that now, but few know of these tunnels. And those who do, well... They were the people likely to frequent the original taverns in the first place. Riff-raff, so to speak.'

The Warsword grew quiet again after that, but as they moved deeper into the caverns, Thea could hear other sounds.

People. Crackling fires. Children.

At last, the tunnel opened up into a much larger cavern, which was filled with golden light from small campfires, torches and candles. Domed tents were set up all around the space in little circular hubs, just like a village or town might be structured. Judging from the parents chasing after their youngsters with laughter on their lips, this place was safe...

It was a community, a family. That was obvious, even to an outsider. Somewhere in the distance, a fiddle played, and Thea sucked in a breath.

'This isn't like...'

But she didn't finish her sentence. She'd never explicitly told Wilder about the visions of Anya she'd had. Of the Daughter of Darkness cutting her hair and stalking through the torture camps, screams echoing in her wake. There was no screaming here, no torture. In fact, it was the warmest place Thea had been to in a long while.

'Not like what?' Wilder asked, frowning at her.

Thea opened her mouth to tell him what she'd seen of her supposed sister —

As the name formed on her lips, the Daughter of Darkness in question came storming towards her through the small crowds mingling around the fires.

And that was what she was – a living storm. Embodying the very magic Thea herself had once had and lost. That hollow yawned wide inside her, searching for the kernel of power that was no longer there. The absence of it hurt, an ache deep within.

'Storm magic runs deep through the Delmirian line... It is just as powerful in each of us,' Anya had said to her. Now, Anya's eyes were bright with an unbroken tempest as she stopped abruptly right in front of Thea. She looked every bit the fearsome leader of an enemy force, with her shaved head, the lines of her face razor-sharp, and that savage scar that sliced from above her brow through her right eye and halfway down her cheek. It looked even more pronounced than Thea recalled.

'A shame we're not meeting under different

circumstances,' Anya said stiffly, surveying Thea from head to toe.

'We've met,' Thea reminded her. 'When you took my sister hostage in Notos.'

'Our sister,' Anya replied, her voice rough with emotion, her great wings flaring behind her. She looked even more fierce, even more vengeful.

Thea could only stare. The words Malik had once spoken to her came rushing to the forefront of her mind: *'Beware the fury of a patient Delmirian...'*

Anya was fury personified, alright, and it took all of Thea's backbone not to yield a step back.

'Our sister,' Anya repeated. 'I'm your family, whether you like it or not.'

'You didn't leave a great first impression.'

'At least you remembered me this time.'

The two women stared at one another. It wasn't just eye colour they shared, but their dark, strong brows as well, both currently fixed into scowls.

*Sister.* The word vibrated through Thea like a bell as she took in the proof of it before her eyes. 'Why did you not come forward and tell Wren and me who you were, rather than hiding in the shadows?'

If there were ever a time Thea thought her magic might come surging back to the surface, this was it. The mix of emotions that churned within her was like a foaming sea whipping into a whirlwind.

Anya gave a dark laugh. 'You think I was in any state to do such a thing? Let me show you, little sister. Let me show you what your precious guild and precious king did to me. To our family.'

Darkness unfurled, gathering around her and Anya, its

touch like a cool breeze. Thea shot an alarmed look towards Wilder, but the world around her was suddenly ripped away in a whirl of shadow.

She stumbled as cobblestones hit the soles of her feet and she found herself in an all-too-familiar place…

From the base of the ramparts, Thea looked onto the courtyard of Thezmarr's fortress. Dozens of shadow wraiths swarmed the space, shadows coiling and lashing at their will, the scent of burnt hair nearly overpowering.

Anya stood beside Thea, her expression grim as she pointed to the grate in the stone, from which a pair of green eyes gazed out. 'I was down there with you at first,' she said, her voice distant. 'All the children were. Audra told me to stay with you and Wren. But I was never very good at listening.'

Thea watched on in horror as Guardians of Thezmarr spilt from the fortress, falling to their knees as the monsters unleashed their own nightmares upon them.

*Where are the Warswords?* Thea scanned the chaos, watching as one warrior after another succumbed to the darkness, the gleam of Naarvian steel nowhere to be seen.

'It had already begun…'

Anya trailed off, watching as a supply cart flipped into the air, surrounded by a mass of shadow and tendrils that whipped out at bystanders. Soon, crimson seeped into the ground while the wheels of the cart still spun and mead flowed from broken barrels.

Dazed, Thea took in the scene around her. 'I've seen this before…'

'Not like this,' Anya said, pointing.

More shadow wraiths descended upon Thezmarr, clawing at the stone walls with their talons, lashing their cords of darkness upon the Guardians and shieldbearers brave enough to defend the fortress.

'There.' Anya pointed to the outskirts of the battle, where a little girl cowered against the stone wall. No older than six, clutching a necklace of dried flowers, the girl – Anya, Thea realised – made a dash for the servants' entry, wide-eyed and panicked.

'Come with me,' the older Anya said, tugging Thea's sleeve.

They crossed the stretch of carnage, following the child into a side passage of the fortress, away from the battle. Thea had walked this very hallway many times herself, but it had never felt like this. All the torches had been snuffed out except one at the far end.

She watched as young Anya saw what that lone flame illuminated, throwing herself into a small alcove just in time.

Thea stopped short, spotting two cloaked figures at the far end of the darkened hall. In the distance, she heard screaming, someone in a fit of rage being dragged away.

'Stop this! Stop this now —' someone shouted, but their words were cut off, only to be followed by a different kind of scream. One of fear. Panic.

Heart pounding, Thea moved closer to the end of the passageway, flicking a questioning gaze at her older sister as the outline of the two men became clearer. Anya simply watched on, impassive, while her younger self stayed hidden in the nook.

The men at the far end of the hall snapped their heads towards the sound of more screams, before turning back to one another, the tension palpable.

'You'll tell no one of this.' The voice was strangely familiar, as was the feel of his presence, though Thea couldn't place it. Instead, she watched on as he gestured to the weapon in his hand – a scythe, ribbons of shadow shimmering from its steel.

'Of course,' the other man replied – another recognisable baritone. 'I would never —'

The first figure raised a hand for silence and his gaze flicked down the hall, right to where young Anya was hidden in the alcove.

He surged forward, closing the distance in just a handful of steps.

The little girl cried out as his hand closed around her arm, hard enough to bruise, by the look of it.

'The answer to our problem, right under our noses...' the second man said, nodding to the scythe.

Thea's blood ran cold as she recognised that voice, clear as day now.

Osiris, the Guild Master of Thezmarr.

But the shock had no time to settle, for the first man shoved the scythe into little Anya's trembling hands, darkness still spilling from the blade. As he did, his hood fell from around his face.

Thea choked on a gasp as King Artos of Harenth hauled the child from the alcove and down the passageway, not away from the threat, but back towards the blood-soaked courtyard.

'What...' Thea breathed. This wasn't how she'd seen it happen before; this hadn't been what her visions had shown her —

King Artos, with Osiris at his heels, kicked the door open and thrust young Anya into the fray. 'We have found the culprit of this insanity,' he shouted above the violence and mayhem. 'It is as it was prophesied! The Daughter of

Darkness has wielded a blade and brought the end of days upon us!'

Little Anya tried to scramble away, but Artos kept the weapon in her tiny hand, darkness still leaking from its point.

Thunder clapped beyond the fortress walls.

'She is the one who was prophesied,' Osiris declared, pointing to the tendrils of magic that roiled through the air around them as lightning flashed in the night sky.

The little girl began to cry, trying to back away from the men, towards the shelter of the cart. The storm raged on, swallowing wisps of obsidian in its path, but it wasn't enough to save her.

Osiris made a dive for the scythe, making a show of knocking it from Anya's grasp. With a quiet cry, she dropped it, the steel singing as it hit the stone, as it fell amid the rivers of blood that trickled towards her slippered feet.

And as it did, the shadow wraiths and their darkness retreated from Thezmarr.

The timing, utterly perfect.

The next minute, Thea and older Anya stood in the Great Hall of the fortress, watching as the little girl was presented as an enemy of the midrealms.

Everyone had seen her with the Naarvian weapon.

Everyone had seen the darkness recede upon the blade being knocked from her hand.

Everyone who mattered.

Osiris' voice rang out like a bell. 'She is a daughter of darkness, a monster. She needs to be dealt with before she unleashes more madness upon us all. She has brought the truth of the prophecy to our very doorstep...'

*Lies... All lies...* A fist of panic gripped Thea's heart, but it wasn't over, not by a long shot.

'How did one little girl do all this?' someone shouted.

'You saw it for yourselves,' King Artos said from the dais. 'As did I. It was just as the prophecy predicted – a girl wielded a blade and brought darkness upon us all. Had Osiris not disarmed her, we would face a dawn of fire and blood.' He drew a trembling breath. 'Take her.'

Obsidian swirled around Thea and suddenly she was whisked away into the night, watching another scene unfold, this one more terrifying than the last.

There was a blur of movement as the same little girl was thrown into a deep pit somewhere in the woods on the outskirts of Thezmarr.

She let out a sob – and in the shadows, a chain rattled.

A scream died on Thea's lips as she watched a wraith stalk towards the girl, both its ankles in manacles, but its chain long enough to reach her.

The girl scrambled back, but she wasn't fast enough.

Lightning crackled around her, but she was too small, too young to wield it against such a monster.

Talons flashed through the air.

The girl screamed and screamed as the wraith reached into her heart.

Talons pierced flesh and bone, the wraith snarling and hissing as it battled an invisible force – the force of the girl herself, Thea realised.

*'The shadow-touched people are those who fight against the curse when a reaper attempts to turn them...'* Wilder had told her.

The poor girl's screams turned into a choked gurgling noise as her body thrashed beneath the attempts of the wraith who brutalised her.

With an incensed shriek, the monster cast her aside, discarding her as though she were worthless, before it shot into the sky, breaking its chains and leaving tendrils of shadow in its wake.

The girl lay bleeding in the dirt.

'They did that to you...' Thea breathed to her older sister, tears burning her eyes as she forced herself to watch the ragged rise and fall of the unconscious child's chest.

'Yes, they did that to me,' Anya said simply, her expression unreadable.

On the shores of the Broken Isles, Thea found herself at the mouth of a cave, the briny sea air tangling in her hair, with the older Anya at her side and the same little girl facing the hollow in the rocks. Beneath her skin, her veins had darkened, creating a network of black that seemed to shimmer.

'Some Warsword told me our parents were inside,' Anya said, watching as her former self took a step towards the jagged outcrop. 'I knew he was lying somehow, even then.'

Thea wasn't sure she was breathing. 'What did you find inside?'

'Not our parents, that's for sure.'

*Our parents.* The phrase sounded strange, even though Thea knew it to be true. The woman beside her and the girl before them – she was a part of Thea, a part of Wren, though she'd been absent all their lives.

'What then?' Thea pressed, not sure she wanted to know the answer.

And all at once, she was in her sister's shoes, experiencing the damp of the cave and the kiss of shadow in her body as though it were her own.

Anya walked into the cave, deeper and deeper, until she was alone. For a moment, the pitch-black swallowed her.

There was no swift and painless death waiting for her. There was no death at all.

A breath rattled from within – not her own.

But Anya was not afraid.

For she knew the darkness, and the darkness knew her. It was already inside her, coursing through her veins, wrapping around her heart.

And then it started.

The transition to becoming a half-wraith.

The little girl fell to her knees as brutal pain speared through her back, her fingertips, her chest. Everything was on fire and the agony was so great that her screams were silent.

On and on it went, the darkness demanding to be felt as it made its way through every part of her, battling her body into submission.

*In the shadow of a fallen kingdom, in the eye of the storm*
*A daughter of darkness will wield a blade in one hand*
*And rule death with the other*

Thea didn't know when she came back to herself, didn't know how long they stood there watching the torture unfold, unable to help the poor girl in the throes of agony. Little Anya writhed and begged, screamed and crawled across the floor. When talons sprang from her fingertips, she panicked, clawing at her skin, her face, her eyes.

At some point, older Anya touched her arm.

'It's over,' she said, her voice devoid of any emotion.

The younger version of her had passed out, membranous wings protruding from her back.

The present day came rushing back to Thea. The damp rocky walls of the cavern were all too close, the flickering light of the fires all too bright. Her heart was racing, sweat dampening her brow, as she tried to wrap her mind around all that she'd seen.

Anya watched her closely. '*That* was why I didn't try to find you and Wren,' she said quietly. '*That* was why I have stayed hidden in the shadows. Until now.'

Thea's hands were shaking at her sides, but she didn't know what to say. No words could undo what had been done to her sister.

'Now do you see?' Anya pressed. 'He's been setting us up, blaming us for the darkness all along. It's *him*. *King Artos* is the blight on these realms.'

'*Beware the fury of a patient Delmirian.*' Malik's words came back to Thea once more in a whispered rush.

The Delmirian in question was patient no longer. And Thea couldn't say that she blamed her.

She met Anya's gaze, a storm of desperation, sorrow and regret. It was like looking into a mirror.

'At last.' Anya exhaled. 'We are seeing eye to eye.' And with that final word, she walked off, her people parting for her as she made her way through the camp.

Thea watched her go, wondering if she should follow, unsure of what she could possibly say if she did.

'Could have been worse,' an unfamiliar voice drawled. 'Could have been better, too.'

Feeling sick, Thea looked to her right to find a winged man observing Anya, his arms crossed over his broad chest, his striking features lined with apprehension. Delicate shadows danced around him, as though moving with his thoughts. He looked to be around Wilder's age and was handsome in his own rugged way. At Thea's scrutiny, his bottle-green eyes slid to her.

'We haven't officially met,' he said in that same almost lazy drawl, as he offered her a wide hand. 'Dratos Castemont. Dratos the Dawnless, if you like.'

Thea reached for his hand, quietly stunned. She'd never seen one of his kind up close before. Whenever she'd been near Anya, she'd been too focused on everything else to even register her sister's wings. But Dratos... He looked like some sort of terrifying aerial warrior, ready to cleave through the skies.

'No one fucking calls you that,' Wilder interjected, rolling his eyes at the general.

Dratos shrugged and stuck a small pipe between his teeth, his shadows coiling around him. 'They will, my friend.'

'I'll believe it when I hear it,' Wilder said gruffly before looking at Thea and surveying the torn ballgown that left much of her exposed. 'We should get you something to wear.'

Dratos' eyes lit up. 'But she looks *ravishing*.'

Wilder was already pulling her away from the shadow-touched general. 'That wasn't in question,' he muttered.

Thea's stomach fluttered at that, and at the warmth of his hand as it grasped hers to lead her through the camp. The hour was late. Long gone were the laughing children and constant movement between the canvas structures, but the quiet that had settled over the cavern was comforting, nothing like the eeriness Thea had experienced on the road for the past year. Here there was warmth and life... and her actions had jeopardised that. How many times had she saved Artos' life now? Twice? Dread lurched low in her gut as she thought of poor Jasira. Did she know what her father was? What would this mean for her when it all came to light?

Wilder took her to a tent on the far side and opened the flap for her. Inside, it was large enough for even Wilder to stand upright, and from the weaponry and maps on the table, she guessed the tent was his and his alone.

He pointed to a rucksack on the floor. 'There's a spare shirt and pants in there. I'll find you something more suitable in the morning.' He turned to leave.

'You're going?' Thea said without thinking.

He tensed, his silver gaze like liquid heat as it met hers. Thea felt him in her blood, under her skin.

His muscular chest heaved, as though it was taking every ounce of his willpower to stay rooted to the spot. 'Whatever you're thinking... I don't think it's a good idea.'

Thea took matters into her own hands, closing the distance between them, resting her palms on his chest, feeling his heart hammer beneath her touch.

'Wilder...' She relished the heat of him against her, savouring his scent.

His hands cupped hers and drew them away. 'I... I don't think we're there.'

Thea's throat grew painfully tight and her lungs constricted as her arms dropped to her stomach, clutching the pressure there. 'But you said...'

She was mortified to hear her voice crack. She was not that girl. She had been that girl once before and vowed never to be so again.

'You didn't trust me with the truth,' she said instead, peering up at his face, willing the tears not to fall.

'You didn't trust me, full stop,' he countered, nostrils flaring.

'I could have, had you just told me.'

Wilder stared at her, his expression pained. 'I didn't know the truth myself. I wanted to make sure before I threw you into all this chaos.'

Thea raised her voice in desperation. 'Then that's what you should have told me. You should have told me that you didn't know.'

Wilder's brows shot up and he started to pace, exasperated. 'And what? Put your future at Thezmarr at risk? Liaising with the shadow-touched is treason! You wanted to be a Warsword more than anything —'

Thea drew a ragged breath. Still on the verge of tears, she grabbed him, forcing him to look at her. 'Not more than anything,' she said quietly. '*You* are what I wanted. More than anything. I know that now.'

Conflict warred in Wilder's eyes as he towered over her and lifted her chin with a single finger. 'Is that so?' The melodious depth of his voice made her toes curl. 'Prove it.'

Thea went rigid for a moment, before she grabbed a fistful of his shirt and slammed her mouth to his.

His lips were intoxicating. He tasted like fire and temptation, like home. His mouth moved over hers in a fervour, their kiss intensifying, out of control as his hands slid down her spine, curving over her backside and lifting her up. Impossibly fast, he had her on the table, maps cast aside in one swipe, her legs wrapped around him, the tattered remains of her dress riding up.

'Thea,' he groaned, voice ragged with need.

She arched up into him, pressing her breasts to him and rubbing against the hardness she could feel beneath his pants. Every nerve in her body came alive, fraying beneath the slightest friction. Gods, she wanted him – she wanted him with everything she had. She shoved his shirt up, raking her nails down the ridges of his carved abdomen, determined to mark him as hers, until he hauled the fabric over his head and cast it aside. Desperate for contact, she spread her hands across the breadth of his chest, revelling in the heat and hardness of him, passion coursing through her, dampening her core.

With a moan, Wilder slid his rough palms up her thighs, spreading her wide so he could grind against her, pinning her to the table as his mouth devoured her.

She sucked in a sharp breath as he bit her lower lip and dragged his teeth down the column of her throat, ripping the bodice of her dress down to expose her breasts.

'Furies save me,' he murmured at the sight before his mouth lowered to her nipple.

Thea cried out, her whole body becoming molten beneath his touch, beneath his tongue. Her hands went to his belt. She needed to touch him, needed to taste him, needed to feel him inside her after all this time.

He gasped as her hand slipped inside his pants and wrapped around the rock-hard length of him. She stroked him, imagining that first thrust inside her, imagining the force of him unleashed upon her —

With a muttered curse, he pulled back, removing her hand, panting slightly.

'What is it?' Thea said, pulling her dress up to cover herself.

He ran his fingers through his hair and snatched up his shirt from the ground. 'I... We're not there, Thea. So much has happened, I don't...'

Thea's heart seized. 'You don't feel that way about me anymore?'

'I didn't say that.' He buttoned his shirt with trembling fingers, the evidence of his arousal still bulging in his pants.

'Then stay,' Thea murmured, biting her lip and ignoring the sting of tears in her eyes.

'I could stay. I want to.' Wilder's gaze raked over her like a starved man's. 'But I won't. Not yet. Not when you're unsure.'

'I *am* sure —'

'You're sure about sex, about distraction. But not about me. About us. There's still a lot that needs to be said between us, and I won't fuck you again until you're certain. Until you know there's no coming back from this.' His eyes darkened as they drank her in once more before he opened the tent flap. 'Night, Thea.'

Thea stared after his muscular back as he disappeared outside, her blood still hot, still burning for him.

# CHAPTER TWENTY-FOUR

## WILDER

'Fuck,' Wilder muttered to himself as he stalked through the slumbering campsite, his cock still raging hard, straining uncomfortably against his pants.

Those hooded eyes, that *mouth*, that peaked nipple between his teeth...

'Fuck,' he said again, spearing his fingers through his hair as he looked for something to hit, something to release that pent-up —

'Rough night?' Dratos grinned from where he sat smoking his pipe against a wall stacked with supplies.

'Fuck off,' Wilder snapped.

Dratos only grinned wider. 'Sounds like you've got something on your mind, Warsword.'

'Nothing I'd share with you.'

'You don't need to. It's written all over your face.'

'Have I told you that I prefer you in writing? You're more bearable in your letters than in person.'

The winged ranger put a hand to his cheek in mock offence. 'You wound me.'

'I wish someone would.'

Dratos puffed away on his pipe. 'That's right. Get it all out, you moody bastard.'

Wilder shook his head in disbelief and sank against the wall, holding out his hand for the pipe.

Dratos handed it over with a look of delight.

'You're a fucking pain in the arse, you know that?' Wilder said, taking a drag before coughing hard and thrusting the pipe back at his friend, eyes watering. 'Fuck's sake, Dratos. That's not tobacco.'

Dratos frowned. 'Why would I smoke tobacco? Tastes like shit.' He took a hearty pull on the pipe, embers glowing in the bowl. 'This here is the finest Naarvian grass a smile like mine can buy.'

Wilder spat the bitter taste on the ground. 'You're getting high? Now?'

'Takes the edge off your vicious insults.'

'It'll take the edge off your fighting if we're attacked.'

'Nothing takes the edge off my fighting,' he replied, with a pointed look at the shadows coiling at his back.

Wilder surveyed them warily. It was something he still hadn't grown used to after all this time – that the darkness could wage war *for* them as well as against them.

'You saw what they're doing in that torture camp, then?' Dratos prompted, studying his face. 'You showed your feisty apprentice?'

Wilder nodded. 'I saw, and I did.'

'Good. She needs to know. Anya and Adrienne both say we need her and her magic onside for the war to come.'

'That's up to Thea.'

'No shit. But I imagine you've got something to do with that.'

'Maybe once... Not anymore.' Wilder sighed heavily. There had not been a whisper of Thea's magic, not in anger, not in desire. Nothing. It was as though it had been snuffed out, erased from the world itself. 'I think we need to adjust our plans accordingly.'

Dratos blew out a long stream of smoke. 'You think one storm wielder will be enough?'

'It'll have to be.'

'What of the other sister, the alchemist?'

Wilder raised a brow. 'You realise I'm not the official spokesperson for the Embervale family?'

Dratos shrugged. 'Coulda fooled me.' He kicked a satchel at his feet. 'Anya said to give you this.'

Wilder didn't recognise the bag, but rather the clothes and armour spilling out of it. It was what he'd been wearing before he'd been stripped and thrown in the ice cell. He couldn't say he'd missed the shoddy breastplate and pauldrons, but he was always in need of more shirts, and he'd be glad if his belt was there. It had been Malik's, once upon a time.

As he picked up the satchel, Kipp's yellow kerchief fell to the ground by his boot. Scooping it up and stuffing it in his breast pocket, he almost laughed. The Guardian had been right; he'd certainly needed it again, though he'd not had the chance to use it. He'd bled a lot since that encounter.

'That armour's a pile of shit,' Dratos declared, with a nod to the boiled leather peeking out of the bag.

'I've noticed.' Wilder rolled his eyes. 'Where are we at with the rest of the forces?'

His friend's expression changed. 'Adrienne's got the Naarvian rangers as prepared as they can be. Anya's spreading the word among the shadow-touched across the midrealms, but even with shadow magic, it's taking longer than expected to gather willing fighters. Not all of us have made our peace with this life.'

Wilder nodded. He remembered what Talemir had been like in the early days. He'd hated his new form so much he'd nearly poisoned himself seeking a cure.

'What of our resources? Steel and —'

'Steel is a problem, as always. The Naarvian forge is being watched, as you can imagine. Mining the iron ore at the source is another issue. It's not a quiet job.' Dratos cleared his throat. 'Our prince has the other efforts in hand.'

'He's your prince, not mine.'

Dratos waved him off. 'You and your grudges, Warsword.'

Wilder ignored him. 'When can we expect to make a stand?'

The ranger gave a hoarse laugh. 'You bringing anything to the table? Besides your mood swings and muscles, I mean?'

'I brought a soon-to-be Warsword.'

'Great, and I brought my cousin Gus,' Dratos replied drily. 'Anything else?'

Wilder followed Dratos' line of sight to the unruly mop of dark brown hair across the campsite. He started. He'd briefly met the boy in Naarva, when he and Talemir had been assigned a mission there years ago. Gus was not only Dratos' cousin, but the orphan Adrienne and her friend Drue had all but adopted as a little brother of their own. Along with several others, he'd been taken hostage by shadow wraiths. Tal and Wilder had helped rescue them.

Back then, Gus had barely been able to keep his balance

because of the new wings at his back. Now, the only thing that told Wilder the teenager across the way was Angus Castemont was the knitted jumper he was wearing. Dratos was always complaining about his knitting habit.

'Furies...' Wilder muttered. 'How old is he now?'

'Nearly nineteen,' Dratos said regretfully. 'He's a real prick most of the time.'

'Wonder where he gets it.'

'Fuck off.'

That forced a laugh out of Wilder at last before he returned to the conversation at hand. 'I've got a team meeting us in two days' time.'

'A team? How mysterious.'

'Gotta keep you on your toes.'

'I've got several women doing that already, Warsword. Maybe save it for your pretty apprentice.'

Wilder heard himself growl. 'Not another word about her, Dratos.'

Mischief danced in the ranger's bottle-green eyes. 'But you make it so much fun.'

Wilder gave him a half-hearted shove. 'Have another toke.'

'Oh, I fully intend to.'

Wilder left the winged ranger to his vices and wandered to the perimeter of the camp, starting a lap. He didn't trust himself to return to his tent, not with Thea there. He had made the right decision, cooling things between them, or so he told himself. It felt like there were far too many unspoken words, things that needed to be out in the open before they picked up where they had left off – if that was even possible at all, given what they'd been through. He knew he'd hurt her, but... she'd hurt him, too. He hadn't dared to say it aloud, but now, as he paced the outskirts of the shadow-touched camp, he finally admitted it to himself.

As he walked, he tied himself in knots – then grew frustrated that he wasn't in knots over the war to come, but over her.

# CHAPTER TWENTY-FIVE

## THEA

Someone cleared their throat from the entrance of the tent. Thea sat bolt upright from where she'd been half dozing, wondering if Wilder had changed his mind —

'I'd knock,' came Anya's voice, 'but canvas doesn't really allow for it...'

Trying to quell her disappointment, Thea palmed the sleep from her eyes. 'Come in.'

The fabric shifted and Anya ducked inside, looking around, her gait slightly awkward. Her wings weren't visible, and as she spoke with a note of self-consciousness, she looked more like Wren than Thea had realised. 'Wasn't sure you'd be alone... You've got that Warsword in pieces.'

'He's not here,' Thea said, watching as Anya paced across the width of the tent, running her hand over her shaved head, as restless as a storm out to sea.

Thea herself didn't know what to do with her hands, didn't know what to say. This stranger before her was her *sister*, bound to her by blood, and yet... she knew nothing about her beyond her shadows and wings.

Luckily, Anya spoke first. 'I'm sorry I walked off before.' She paused her pacing, only to trace a circle in the dirt with the tip of her boot. She looked as uncomfortable as Thea felt. What *was* the protocol for talking to a long-lost sister who'd been deemed an enemy for the better part of a year?

'It's alright,' Thea ventured. 'I can't imagine it was easy, watching all that again...'

Anya shrugged casually, still toeing the dirt. 'No worse than the nightmares I have every night.'

'I'm sorry you went through that. That you go through it still.'

Anya dipped her head. 'Thank you.'

Thea gestured to the table and chairs. 'Do you want to sit?' Wren would have offered the moment Anya had walked in.

Anya hesitated, those sharp features softened with uncertainty for the first time.

Thea dropped into a seat without ceremony. 'Third time's the charm,' she tried to joke.

Her shadow-touched sister gave a sheepish half-smile at that and sat down in the chair beside her. She rummaged through her pockets and produced a lump of something wrapped in cloth.

'Thought you might need something to eat,' she said. 'It's just bread. There'll be porridge in the morning.'

'Thanks.' Thea's fingers touched Anya's as she accepted the food, and a burst of electric current made her jump.

'Sorry,' Anya muttered. 'I usually have it well under control, but... it's been an emotional day.'

'It used to be like that for me too,' Thea admitted, unwrapping the bread and holding back a moan as she took a bite. It was fresh sourdough, still warm.

'Not anymore, huh?'

'Not anymore.'

Anya nodded to herself and leant back in her chair, unsheathing a dagger from her boot and twirling it between her fingers. 'So you don't remember me at all, do you?' she asked, voice soft, attention fixed on the blade.

Thea grimaced. 'Not clearly... but there are little things.'

Anya glanced up.

'Some things came to me when Wilder and I visited Delmira over a year ago. There were flowers... I remember braiding necklaces with someone... At first I thought it was Wren, but she would have been too young. It was you, wasn't it?'

Anya nodded. 'Our mother taught me. I used to make them for everyone. I did nothing else for two summers.'

'I don't remember her either,' Thea said. 'Or him – our father.'

'I feared that for the longest time – forgetting them,' Anya told her. 'Especially without you and Wren. Every now and then, there will come a day where I realise I don't remember the exact sound of Mama's laugh, or the way the sunlight caught in Pa's hair. But I remember the important things. That they were good and kind rulers. That they were good and kind parents.'

'We were told they were tyrants.'

Anya shook her head. 'There wasn't a bone like that in either of their bodies.'

'They left us on Thezmarr's doorstep...'

'To *protect* us.'

'They could have —' Thea cut herself off as she caught Anya studying her, head tilted. 'What?'

Anya hummed. 'It makes sense now.'

'What does?'

'That you so readily believed your Warsword had abandoned you too.'

Thea opened and closed her mouth, her skin suddenly tingling with discomfort. 'I never thought about —'

But Anya dimissed her with a wave. 'They were good people. You need to know that. Too trusting, but good.'

'Like you.' Thea pictured the little girl swept up in the corruption of Thezmarr.

'A lesson I needed to learn only once,' Anya said grimly.

Thea passed her the other half of the bread, noting that Anya herself looked a little on the thin side. Her sister took it without a word.

'What happened after the cave-in on the Broken Isles?' Thea asked.

Anya chewed on the bread thoughtfully. 'There was a creature there... Something like me. It kept me alive for a time. A new shadow-touched person is like a newborn foal. Clumsy. Clueless.'

'You were, what? Six? In the visions you look —'

'Tall?' Anya offered. 'I was for my age. But no, I was younger. You and I were only born ten months apart.'

Thea stared, thinking back to the thick tome she'd found in Wilder's cabin, *A Study of Royal Lineage Throughout the Midrealms*. No heirs had been listed in the Delmirian line, let alone the name days of the royal offspring. 'How do you know that? There were no records of our birth.'

'Not on the mainland. But when I was in Naarva —'

'You found archives?'

'Not quite... I found letters. Personal letters from our mother to Queen Yolena. They were friends.'

'But Delmira had already fallen before we were born.'

Anya shrugged. 'It seems they stayed in touch, even while our parents were in hiding.'

'Did you keep these letters?'

'I did. They're in my quarters at the University of Naarva. I'd like to show them to you someday. And Wren.'

'I'd like that... I'm sure she would too.'

The gratified glint in her sister's eyes brought a wave of heaviness down on Thea.

'You were so young...' she said quietly.

Anya gave a grim smile. 'I survived.'

'How?' Thea pressed.

'Naarva was shrouded in darkness, but there were a few places of refuge, underground. Some people were shadow-touched like me. Others were civilians who had fled the fighting... I learnt quickly to control my abilities, so it wasn't immediately obvious what I was. I kept my shadows to myself. The people of a fallen kingdom don't take kindly to the likes of me – not then, anyway.'

'And you were alone?'

'For a while.'

'I saw you,' Thea said carefully. 'In a vision. You cut your hair with a dagger... and then you walked out into a field. There were shadow-touched there. In pain. Being tortured...' She didn't mean it as a question, but she heard the inflection in her voice.

Anya did too. 'That was one of Artos' camps. We'd defeated a host of shadow wraiths. The people you think were being tortured were shadow-touched, transitioning for the first time. You watched the same thing happen to me in that cave. There was nothing to be done. They had to feel it. Accept it.' She took a deep breath. 'I didn't hurt them.'

Thea flushed. 'I know that now.'

'Do you?' Anya pressed, piercing her with what she now knew to be their mother's eyes.

'Yes,' Thea told her, lifting her chin. 'So while Wren and I were tucked away safe and sound at Themzarr, you were...'

'Rallying the shadow-touched, tracking the tears in the Veil, hunting monsters... There were more and more of them, and not just wraiths. I had a small force loyal to me when we heard the rumour about a colony. After a time, I met Dratos...' Anya heaved a sigh.

'I wish I could have been with you, fighting by your side,' Thea said.

A sad smile graced her sister's lips. 'I'm glad you weren't. I'm grateful that you were safe at the fortress. It helped, knowing you and Wren weren't in the same kind of danger, though I know your time there was less than perfect... I came back once, you know – back to Thezmarr. I was so desperate to see you and Wren. Dratos didn't want me to go, said it was too big a risk, but... I had to.'

'When was this?'

'I'm not sure... We weren't quite teenagers yet,' Anya told her. 'Audra and Farissa had everyone out playing on the Plains of Orax. Wren was practically glued to Farissa's side, but you... you had broken off from the group and were wandering on your own, a stick in hand. I think you were pretending it was a sword,' Anya said with a note of fondness. 'I used storm magic to get your attention, to coax you into the woods. You followed those little bolts of lightning so confidently, I was sure everything would be the same as it always had been. But when you were only a few feet away, I realised... the world I could offer was fraught with nothing but danger and darkness. Thezmarr was safe. Thezmarr, with its Guardians and Warswords, was light...

You and Wren deserved that, not the half-life I led in the shadows, hunted and hated.'

'So you didn't show yourself? You didn't speak to me?'

Anya shook her head. 'I left. It was the last time I saw Thezmarr.'

'And us.'

'And you,' Anya agreed.

'I don't remember it – following storm magic into the Bloodwoods.'

'I wouldn't expect you to. I don't think you even knew what you were following. It was subtle, not like the display you put on in Notos.'

The mention of Tver's capital made Thea's blood run cold, the brutal battle seared into her mind. 'Why did you try to take Wren?'

'I wanted to take you both. To get you out of their clutches and explain everything.'

'Funny way to go about it.'

'I'll admit, I could have thought it through in a bit more detail.'

'No shit,' Thea scoffed.

'But then Dratos went and got himself shot with an arrow, courtesy of your friend, I believe? And I knew if I took Wren without you, you'd never forgive me.'

'You've got your work cut out for you with Wren as it is.'

'Any advice?' Anya quipped.

Thea gave a laugh. 'Get her a massive bag of weird plants and potions.'

'Thanks.'

'Anytime.'

And in that brief exchange, Thea's heart ached for what might have been. Ached with loss for the years that Artos had stolen from her and her family, and with fury for what had been done to her sister.

Anya's pained expression mirrored her own.

'I'm sorry.' Thea's words came out as a whisper. 'I'm sorry for how it all happened. And I'm sorry we weren't there for you.'

'You're here now,' Anya replied.

'And Wren —'

'Will find us again.' Anya smiled then. 'Just as the fates intended.'

'You believe that?'

'I do.' Anya got to her feet, dusting the breadcrumbs from her lap. 'We don't know each other well... But I'd like to.'

'Me too,' Thea said.

Anya offered her hand. 'We storm wielders have to stick together.'

Thea shook her sister's hand, her palm as rough and calloused as Thea's own. 'I'm not a storm wielder anymore.'

Letting go, Anya simply raised a brow and lifted the tent flap, readying to leave. 'Aren't you?'

# CHAPTER TWENTY-SIX

## WILDER

M orning came sooner than Wilder would have liked, marked by the soft bell tolling from the heart of the camp. There was a quiet rhythm to the place that he appreciated, though. It reminded him of life at Thezmarr in his earlier days. When life had consisted of meals at set times, training sessions and scrapping with his friends and brother. Things had been simpler then.

He made his way to the centre of the cavern, where several tables had been set up and Adrienne was already poring over several pieces of parchment, a deep crease in her brow. Anya stood at her side, running her hands over her closely shaved head, looking impatient. Anya always looked impatient, though; she reminded him of Thea in that respect – always wanting to move, always needing to go forward, as though a storm bit at her very heels.

They looked up at his approach.

'If it isn't the fallen Warsword himself,' Anya said by way of greeting.

He shot her a warning look. She knew it hadn't been easy

for him to turn his back on the guild, even after seeing what Osiris had done to her. Even in jest, the comment still stung.

Adrienne slid a bowl of steaming porridge across the table to him. 'When's the last time you ate? Or slept? You look like shit.'

Wilder grunted. 'Aren't you both a delight to be around this morning.'

'We do our best,' Adrienne replied with a smirk.

Shaking his head in disdain, he picked up the bowl and lifted the spoon to his mouth – where it hung suspended as his eyes landed on Thea.

She was wearing his shirt.

And nothing else but her boots.

It was entirely possible his mouth was hanging open, but he couldn't help it as he drank in the sight of her long, bare legs and the hint of her perfect body underneath that almost threadbare fabric.

As she reached the table, she raised a brow at him in challenge. 'Your pants were too big.'

Adrienne's head dropped back as she snorted, knocking over her own breakfast, porridge splattering across the parchment.

'Charming,' Anya told her, flicking a clump from her own clothing back onto Adrienne. Wilder had half a mind to toss his own breakfast at the Naarvian ranger for her lack of subtlety, but then, that would be hypocritical, wouldn't it?

'Problem?' Thea asked, giving him a hard stare.

Wilder opened his mouth to make some sort of smart-arsed retort, but was saved by Adrienne, who got to her feet and looped her arm through Thea's.

'Come on,' she said. 'Let's get you some proper clothes before your Warsword over there pops that vein in his neck.'

Wilder hadn't realised how tense he was, that he was clutching the side of the table so hard the timber was splintering beneath his grip as he watched them go.

Anya followed his gaze with a bemused expression. 'Do you think they're comparing notes?' she quipped.

He shot her a filthy glare before seeking them out again. The thought hadn't even crossed his mind. The truth was, he didn't think of Adrienne like that at all, no matter what had happened between them all that time ago. She was his friend, nothing more, besides a pain in his arse. She and Dratos made a fine match in that respect.

And yet Anya's comment burrowed into his mind. Adrienne wouldn't say anything to Thea, would she? Not when things were so fragile…

'Thea and I… We spoke last night,' Anya said. 'Properly.'

Wilder didn't hide his surprise. Anya was notoriously guarded. He hadn't expected her to open up to Thea anytime soon, nor tell him about it, for that matter. 'And?'

'And it was hard.' As was Anya's voice, but he knew her well enough by now to understand that a lot of hurt and trauma lay beneath that granite exterior. 'Hard to know the extent of what was taken from us. Hard to tell her. Hard for her to hear it, no doubt. It was all hard.'

'Are you alright?' he asked.

'I've had years to come to terms with the truth. Thea's had a few hours…'

Wilder's chest caved. For all her rage and confusion, there would be a lot of grief for Thea now. He knew she'd be hurting, and no matter their issues, he couldn't stomach the thought of that.

'That's not an answer,' he said to Anya, not wanting her pain to be swept under the rug either.

'It's answer enough,' she replied coolly.

Wilder let it lie, let the silence settle for a time. There was a fine line between knowing when to push an Embervale sister, and when to stay quiet. So he ate his porridge, which was now cold. While he did, he continued to scan the camp for any sign of Thea and Adrienne, a kernel of discomfort unfurling in his gut as he let his mind drift to what they might be discussing.

Eventually, Anya made a noise of disgust at the back of her throat. 'Fuck's sake, Hawthorne. Go on, then. I'll plan the fucking rebellion by myself. You're no good to me like this anyway. Piss off.'

The supposed Daughter of Darkness practically chased him away from the table, and that was all the encouragement he needed to go striding across the campsite, scanning the rows of tents for the two women.

As he made his way towards his own tent, Adrienne emerged, pausing at the threshold to give his arm a squeeze. He frowned after her for a moment. What did that mean? Was it in support? Sympathy?

Wilder entered the tent to find Thea wearing pants and buttoning a fresh shirt, one that actually fit her. For a moment, all he could do was watch as she tucked her fate stone beneath the folds of fabric and belted Malik's dagger at her waist.

'It's rude to stare,' she commented, not looking up from her task.

'I liked my shirt on you better,' he said, voice low.

'Funny way of showing it.'

Wilder continued to watch her, noting the hesitation in her movements, her reluctance to speak more than five words to him. She was tense, on edge.

'Anya told me that you spoke...' he ventured.

'We did.'

'Did it not go well?'

'It went as well as a conversation between lost sisters raised as enemies can go. I... I think I like her.'

'Then what is it? Did Adrienne say something to you?' The words were out of his mouth before he could stop them.

Thea still didn't meet his gaze. 'She said several things.'

'Well, I'm talking about the one that made you look like that.'

It wasn't anger in Thea's eyes. It was sorrow on top of sorrow. He knew its look well, along with the regret that swept in in its wake.

Wilder went to her, her pain becoming his, feeling it deep in his chest. 'Whatever she said —'

'She said that long ago, she told her best friend about you...'

Wilder's stomach dropped. Had he misread the friendly rapport between himself and the Naarvian general? They had ended things amicably, hadn't they? Or had he hurt her without realising? His thoughts began to spiral. For Adrienne to speak to Drue about him —

Thea took a breath. 'She told her best friend that you would need a warrior fiercer than her to withstand the force of you. Then she told me that *I* am that warrior, that you found that strength in me. She told me not to let you down.'

Everything in Wilder softened. 'Thea...' he breathed.

Her eyes were brimming with tears as her gaze darted around the tent. 'But I *did* let you down. I was so stupid, refusing to question what was right in front of me, letting blind loyalty rule my actions, believing the worst of you when I know better. I put you in that dungeon. I put you in harm's way. And I almost —'

Wilder leant in, tucking her hair behind her ears and touching his forehead to hers. 'Look at me, Thea...' he said quietly. He had been so deeply hurt by her – hurt that his love hadn't been enough to earn her trust, her faith in him, but... he couldn't stand her pain. He couldn't bear it.

At last, she raised her head, meeting the intensity of his stare.

He cupped her face, his thumbs stroking the contour of her cheekbones. 'What do you need, Princess?'

Thea made a noise that could have been a whimper, her hands rising to rest on his forearms. Raw grief was written all over her face. He should have known that there would be a breaking point, that any one of the revelations Thea had experienced would be enough to overcome a regular person. Thea had taken each one in her stride, and now they had piled up, the weight becoming too great. Adrienne's words, however kindly meant, had been the final straw. He saw how her guilt compounded, lining her gaze with tears.

Wilder ran his fingers along the sharp line of her jaw. 'Tell me what you need,' he said again.

'You,' she told him. 'It's always been you.'

He felt himself cave. He could no longer deny her that.

There was no telling who moved first. They came together passionately, violently, in a tangle of limbs, their kiss hard enough to bruise.

Gods, her *mouth*. Wilder moaned against her lips as she opened for him and allowed his tongue to brush hers. That alone sent a frisson of need straight to his cock.

Thea melted into him and he into her as he grasped a handful of her hair and tipped her head back so he could worship her more thoroughly. She met every kiss with a demanding one of her own, the strokes of her wicked tongue matching his, deepening the longing unfurling between them, an attempt to wash all the hurt away.

'I want you,' Thea breathed, clawing at his clothes. 'I want you so badly.'

Wilder fused his mouth to hers, regretting nothing but the time he had spent not kissing her. For every moment he wasn't doing this was a moment wasted. He ran his fingers down her delicate throat, feeling her pulse fluttering beneath her skin, her softness so intoxicating he was drunk on her.

He was desperate to slide his cock inside her, desperate to feel her clamped around the length of him, but her muffled cries from their deep kisses alone made him want to draw this out. He wanted to make her beg, to sob with the need for him, to drive her so mad with desire that she'd never let him go again.

Thea's hands were all over him, raking down his back, tugging at his shirt, but he batted her attempts away and backed her up against the support post in the centre of the tent. He would have her his way first.

There, he slid his hand down the front of her pants. Thea's breathing hitched and Wilder broke their kiss to watch her face as he dragged a finger down her centre, through the wet heat he found there.

Thea's head tipped back, a flush spreading from her cheeks to the tops of her heaving breasts. Furies, he wanted her naked. He wanted to lick and suck every inch of her and then he wanted to fuck her so hard she couldn't walk straight. But now was not the time. Right now, it was about her and her alone.

A strangled cry escaped her as he circled her clit. In slow, luxurious strokes, he teased her until she was writhing beneath his hold. She reached for his belt, but he caught her by the wrist and trapped both her hands above her head while he continued his taunting touches. An echo of their first time together in the Bloodwoods.

She arched her hips towards him and he chose that moment to slide a finger inside her, biting back a moan of his own as with the motion he imagined burying himself in that tight heat.

'Holy Furies,' Thea panted, her eyes wide, her mouth open as he began to fuck her with his finger slow and hard, adding another and circling her clit again with his thumb.

She cried out loudly, spreading her legs wide for him.

Wilder had never been more aroused in his fucking life. His cock was nearly bursting from his pants, the tip damp with need, his balls aching.

'You're going to come for me, Thea,' he told her, his voice thick with lust, curling his fingers inside her until she was half sobbing. 'You're going to come *hard.*'

They were both still fully clothed, with just his hand down the front of her pants, but gods, it turned him feral. His control was slipping second by second, his own desire pulsing through him, a force of its own, only intensifying as Thea became wetter and tighter around his fingers.

'Thea...' he warned, about what, he wasn't sure anymore. He was lost in her.

'Wilder, I —'

Thea's whole body tensed, and her eyes locked on his as a moan broke free from her lips. She shuddered as her climax hit. Wilder took her over and over, dragging every wave of her orgasm from her with primal satisfaction until she was shaking beneath him.

He was playing with fire when it came to Thea. He'd known it from the moment he'd first seen her, but this...

Still watching her, he slid his fingers from her body, revelling in the raw hunger in her face as he brought those fingers to his mouth and sucked on them.

Her eyes grew wide as he groaned at the taste of her, his cock pulsing against his pants.

'You want to know what you taste like?' he growled.

Slowly, Thea nodded.

Wilder lunged for her, kissing her savagely before he pulled back, breathless. 'You taste like you belong to me. You always have.'

Thea was staring at him as though seeing him for the first time. Her eyes smouldered with longing, her hands breaking free from his grasp at last, pulling at his belt.

He stopped her, a smile tugging at his lips. 'I believe we have a war to plan... The others are waiting. Not so patiently by now, I imagine.'

Her eyes narrowed as she tugged him closer. 'We have unfinished business, you and I,' she told him, the very words he'd once spoken to her in the Bloodwoods of Thezmarr before everything had changed between them.

He kissed her again, lingering in her space, relishing the warmth of her and the intensity of what raged in her eyes. 'That we do,' he said.

Wilder gave her a moment to gather herself, hiding his amusement at the muscle that twitched in her jaw. He'd gotten under her skin, and that was exactly where he intended to stay.

When she was decent, he laced his fingers through hers, savouring the simple act of intimacy. 'To battle we go, Princess.'

# CHAPTER TWENTY-SEVEN

## THEA

Every nerve ending in Thea's body felt completely frayed as Wilder led her into the meeting. She could still feel the imprint of him in her body, on her soul, so much that she kept stealing glances at him, wondering if this was some Warsword magic she'd yet to uncover. Just glimpsing his handsome face, just the stroke of his thumb across the back of her hand set her alight again. She wasn't nearly finished with him.

A smile quirked the corner of his mouth, his dimple showing, and she knew he could see every thought written plainly across her face. She didn't care. She wanted him to know what he'd done to her, and *exactly* what awaited him when she finally got her hands on him.

As they entered the enormous tent, Thea spotted Anya first, at the end of the table. Her sister's wings were nowhere in sight, nor were her shadows. But she looked just as cutthroat without them, with her harsh features and shaved head, her sharp gaze piercing them all. The hesitancy and sadness from their conversation last night was gone.

'About time...' Anya said, her voice laced with innuendo and a note of amusement.

An unwelcome blush stained Thea's cheeks as she accepted the chair Wilder offered her, sitting down and surveying the rest of the strange group gathered around the table, noting the knowing smirks on their faces. Wilder was to her left, and Adrienne was sitting opposite them. A young man – a teenager, really – with a mop of unruly dark curls and a lumpy woollen jumper was knitting in the corner, glancing up every now and then with the same bottle-green eyes as Dratos. There were several rangers Thea didn't recognise, but she guessed they were from Naarva, as was most of the camp.

On the back of a chair was Terrence, the hawk who'd played the role of emissary between Wilder and the Naarvian forces for some time. He was perched regally, his yellow eyes boring into Thea as though he were annoyed, as though he had somewhere better to be.

Then there was Dratos, his wings tucked neatly behind his back, his shadows dancing close by. Thea couldn't help but flinch at the sight of them. For so long, she had seen both things as the epitome of evil, and yet here they were... as much a part of Dratos as the hand that raised a pipe to his lips.

He caught her staring. 'Something to say, would-be Warsword?'

Thea didn't shy away. Instead, she met his gaze. 'Can you hide them? If you want to? The shadows and wings, I mean?'

The green-eyed ranger blew a perfect 'O' of smoke from his lips. 'And why would I want to do that? I hide my true nature for no one's comfort.'

He seemed to wait for her to argue. But Thea simply shrugged. 'Fair enough.'

'Yes, yes.' Anya rolled her eyes. 'We all know how dark and mighty you are, "Dratos the Dawnless". Now if you don't mind, can we make some fucking plans for this war? There have been enough delays.' The last she said with a pointed glance at Wilder.

The corner of his mouth tugged upward again, and Thea elbowed him, sitting up straighter. But the mention of war had her mind churning. Had it only been a matter of days ago that she'd been honoured in the floating domes of Vios as a defender of the realm? Where she'd left Cal and Kipp in the middle of an arachne skirmish? Wilder had assured her they were safe with Torj, but that didn't make it right. So much had happened, so much that she needed to talk to them about. Everything had changed. Her world had been turned upside down, and she wanted them by her side.

Anya glanced at her, gaze full of understanding, as though she too couldn't quite believe it. She offered Thea a tentative smile.

Thea returned it. There was a lifetime of secrets and experiences to share, but they would not get the luxury of time together, not with the midrealms in tatters around them, not with the fate stone hidden beneath Thea's shirt. And yet, Thea wanted to know her sister. She hoped that showed in her smile now.

Anya nodded, seeming to gather herself before she turned to the group and banged her cup on the table three times, glaring around at them all until the chatter died down.

'Welcome, welcome, and all that shit,' she said gruffly,

waving her hands unceremoniously to them. 'I hereby bring this war council to order. There is much to discuss.'

A *war council*. That was what the shadow-touched were calling this.

It was official, Thea realised with a start. She was sitting in on a war council with the enemy, or those who had once been her enemy. What did that make them now? Allies?

Anya's gaze snapped to Dratos. 'What news from Vios? Where did we leave things with that arachne, for starters?'

'Dead,' Dratos said bluntly. 'The two Warswords took care of it. After a fashion.' He glanced at Thea. 'Your friends are unharmed. They got out with the Bear Slayer.'

Though he was merely confirming what Wilder had told her, Thea's relief was immeasurable. She gave Dratos a grateful nod.

'The children in the ice dungeons were rescued without incident thanks to the Warswords' help. They're being cared for now in one of our quieter camps.' He moved on quickly, however, and did not mince his next words. 'There was a royal fatality.'

Thea's initial relief transformed to dread, her mind instantly going to Princess Jasira. She shouldn't have left her; she should have seen her to safety —

'Who?' Wilder asked.

Dratos grimaced. 'The King of Aveum.'

Silence washed over the group.

'Gods,' Anya said at last, running her hands over her head. 'Do we know the details?'

'No... Only that in the skirmish in the ballroom he was injured, and he died later that night. Venom from the arachne, I'm told.' Dratos refilled his pipe from a pouch at his hip. 'It'll make it that much harder for us to ally with any royal force now.'

'It was always a long shot,' Adrienne offered.

'But to have a king die as a result of an attack like that...' Anya shook her head. 'Queen Reyna will see no reason now.'

Dratos lit his pipe. 'You don't know that.'

'Don't I?' Anya raised a brow. 'Was the rest of the capital affected? Were there further attacks beyond the domes?'

'Not that we know of. And we still don't know if the arachne was an intended strike or not. These monsters have a tendency to creep through the Veil unchecked. It could have been a misstep on Artos' part, or part of a bigger plan. Besides the exterior of the dome itself and the ballroom, the damage wasn't significant.' Dratos chewed on his pipe thoughtfully. 'Did you find out where the reapers' lair is?'

Thea's head whipped to Anya in surprise.

'That's what we were doing in Vios,' her sister explained. 'Someone besides Artos himself knows where the main host is. We had planned to find them and interrogate them. Once we know where the lair is, we can attack. To slay the reapers is to slay their wraith kin. Kill the sire, kill the swarm.'

'But you didn't find that person?'

'No.'

The realisation dawned coldly on Thea, dread yawning in the pit of her stomach. 'Because of me? Because I tried to stop you in the ballroom?'

'Because of a lot of things,' Anya said. 'It was a long shot, anyway. Artos' empath abilities are astounding. It was unlikely that we would have discovered the location of the reapers' lair in a single night.'

'So, what now?' Dratos asked.

'We do the only thing we can do,' Anya replied. 'We try again.'

'I have a question...' Thea ventured, resting her palms flat on the table to keep from fidgeting beneath the scrutiny she was greeted with. 'What have you heard about Wilder's escape? And the fact that I disappeared with him? There must be speculation...?'

Dratos nodded. 'Nothing solid. Some say you were taken hostage by the fallen Warsword, others say you had a change of heart after seeing your former mentor imprisoned. Others claim the Shadow of Death threw herself after the traitorous bastard to hunt him down all over again.'

The hair on Thea's nape stood up and a rush of goosebumps washed over her.

'Are the rulers leaning a particular way?' Wilder asked beside her.

'With the death of King Elkan, there hasn't been much news from the domes beyond funeral preparations.'

'Dratos,' Anya said. 'See to it that we start some whispers of our own. That the wraith slayer of Thezmarr is indeed on the hunt for the traitor.'

'Consider it done,' Dratos replied.

Adrienne cleared her throat and jutted her chin towards Terrence. 'Who's had word from the prince?'

'That would be me.' Dratos reached to ruffle Terrence's feathers before handing over a scroll. 'Everything is going to plan on his end – so far, at least.'

The youngster who was knitting what appeared to be a scarf looked up. 'Will the weapon be ready —'

A shadow shot out from Dratos and clipped the boy around the back of the head.

'Good gods, cousin, are you as thick as that fucking jumper?' Dratos pinched the bridge of his nose.

*Cousin*, Thea noted, watching the exchange with piqued interest.

'I was only asking,' the boy said, rubbing the back of his head.

'Well, don't. We've got new blood here and we don't know if she's trustworthy yet.'

A flush crept up Thea's neck. Strange, how the tides had turned and she was now the traitor in their midst.

The youngster frowned. 'I thought she was Anya's sister. She's family, right?'

Something twinged in Thea's chest at that. They had had only one real conversation, had exchanged a single smile... For all the blood they shared, Anya was a stranger to her. And Wren was farther away than ever.

Dratos rolled his eyes. 'Must be nice in the rosy, simple world of Gus, huh? Why don't you go knit your socks somewhere else?'

The boy called Gus calmly placed his knitting on the table and leant back in his chair, giving his cousin a challenging stare as shadows leaked from his torso, forming a threatening mass around him.

'Make me,' he said, nostrils flaring.

Dratos was on his feet in an instant. 'You little shit —'

'Enough,' Anya shouted. 'Fuck's sake. If you Castemonts want to measure your dicks, go do it elsewhere.'

A minute passed as shadows flickered around the tent, before both men seemed to simmer down.

'It's a fucking scarf, you prick,' Gus muttered, taking up his needles again.

Thea had to bite her knuckles to stop herself from

laughing. For all the darkness and evil in the world, this familial spat between cousins wasn't exactly what she'd imagined when it came to the shadow-touched kind.

Dratos threw himself back down in his chair and took up his pipe again with an irritated noise. 'Where were we?'

'Weapons and this prince of shadows you all talk of,' Thea supplied.

'Shadow Prince,' Dratos corrected her. 'And you'll find out soon enough, Thezmarrian... We just need to be sure about you first.'

'I vouch for her,' Wilder said.

Anya watched the exchange from the head of the table, her brow creasing in apprehension.

'Thing is, I was never sure about you either, Warsword,' Dratos quipped. 'Plus, you're hardly an unbiased perspective, judging from the noises coming from your —'

'Finish that sentence.' Wilder leant forward menacingly, elbows resting on the table. 'I dare you.'

Anya slammed her cup down on the table again. 'All the men, out. *Now*.'

'Anya,' Dratos drawled. 'We're just —'

'Wasting my fucking time, as usual,' she said. 'Get out.'

Dratos raised his hands in surrender. 'We'll behave.'

Cords of shadow unfurled from the Daughter of Darkness herself, coiling around the backs of the men's chairs and pulling them away from the table.

'I won't tell you again,' Anya told them, no compromise in her voice. 'You have exactly three seconds before you find out whose shadows are truly the biggest.'

Dratos, Wilder, Gus and a handful of other men scrambled, leaving the war council at once. A beat of silence followed as Anya's shadows retreated, dissipating into nothing.

Thea couldn't suppress her grin, nor the confirmation that she truly did like her sister.

Adrienne snorted and put her boots on the table. 'Thank fuck for that. Shall we get to work, ladies?'

'Thought you'd never ask,' Anya replied, shaking her head as the tent flap swung back into place.

For the first little while, Thea remained quiet but alert as the rebel women went over logistics and numbers, spreading a large map of the midrealms across the table, using wooden markers for the forces they had spread throughout the lands. Thea knew they were putting a great deal of trust in her by allowing her to stay for this, knew there were countless lives on the line should the information fall into the wrong hands.

Pride bloomed in Thea's chest at the sight of women running the war efforts, women making the hard decisions. Having grown up in Thezmarr, she had been held at length her entire life, relegated to the outskirts, and yet now…

Thea studied the map intensely, her gaze falling to markers in unexpected places. 'I thought Naarva was lost,' she heard herself say as Adrienne placed a marker on the second isle, where the university had once been.

Adrienne glanced at Anya, seeking permission.

Thea tried not to be offended. She'd given them every reason not to trust her. She hadn't questioned the things she should have; she'd seen one of their greatest champions locked away in an ice cell… She had saved King Artos' life not once, but twice, *and* she'd botched their attempt to obtain valuable information.

But to Thea's surprise, Anya nodded her approval without hesitation.

Adrienne beckoned Thea closer, and Thea didn't need telling twice. She came to stand alongside the Naarvian and gazed down at the map.

'Lost? Or hidden?' Adrienne asked, shifting the marker to give Thea a clearer look. 'Besides the Broken Isles, there are three main islands of Naarva. Here' – she pointed – 'is where the capital, the citadel of Ciraun and the famous forge of Naarva is located.'

Thea knew as much already, having longed for a Naarvian steel blade her entire life.

Adrienne continued. 'Then you have the southern island, closest to the Scarlet Tower. You know of it?'

Thea nodded.

'Good,' Adrienne said. 'So you know to stay the fuck away from it. Very close to there is where Hawthorne and his mentor helped us destroy a wraith lair a long time ago.'

Thea was desperate to hear more about it, but she clamped her mouth shut and told herself to listen.

Adrienne moved her finger to the third island. 'This is where the University of Naarva once was. A fine institution for agriculture and horticulture...' She took a measured breath. 'To the rest of the midrealms, Naarva ceased existing when it fell to the darkness years ago. But many of our people went underground. Many survived and kept surviving, despite the wraiths and reapers stalking the lands. It was here that many of our shadow-touched originated. It was here that we first started fighting back.'

'All this time?' Thea couldn't help her gaze lifting to Anya, who was busying herself at the far end of the table, clearly pretending she wasn't listening. Her sister had told her that she'd rallied the shadow-touched, but from

Adrienne's expression, it meant a great deal more to them than that.

'We took back the dark bit by bit,' Adrienne told her. 'The shadows we live in now are of our own people's making... There are still areas of the kingdom that are unsafe; there are still wraiths and reapers, and all manner of the cursed ilk you've seen so much of these past months wandering the lands, but Naarva is ours. And we've fought hard to ensure it survives.'

'How?' Thea asked, running her fingers across the lines on the map.

'When we destroyed that wraith lair all those years ago, we discovered something that could help us. More than steel, more than men. The one we call the Shadow Prince guards it – our most valuable asset against —'

'That's enough,' Anya said quietly.

Adrienne gave Thea a regretful look before countering her leader with: 'Surely you realise Hawthorne will just tell her everything?'

'Which is precisely why I didn't tell *him* everything.'

Adrienne considered this for a moment before she shrugged. 'As you wish, then.'

'I understand,' Thea said. 'I haven't earnt that level of trust yet...' She squared her shoulders and faced her sister fully. 'How do I earn it?' When Anya didn't respond right away, Thea insisted. 'What do you need from me?'

She let the implication hang between them. Anya knew she had no magic left, that the power she had once wielded had been snuffed out like a candle.

Anya poured herself some water from a jug and drank deeply before she spoke. 'Hawthorne has arranged for us to meet with some allies in a rather delicate but important location.'

'Alright...'

'We need you and him to go ahead of our party, and secure a discreet entrance for us. Hawthorne assures me that it won't be a problem, but he's a wanted man throughout the midrealms. And he hasn't exactly kept a low profile lately.'

Thea scoffed. 'And I have? You know there's some speculation now, given that he and I disappeared at the same time...?'

'We'll cross that bridge when we come to it.'

'We?' Thea echoed.

A hint of a smile tempted Anya's lips. 'That's what I said.'

Thea cocked her head. 'I thought you didn't trust me?'

'I don't trust anyone,' Anya countered. 'It's why I'm still alive.'

Adrienne cleared her throat. 'I'll pretend I didn't take offence to that.'

'Great.' Anya turned to Thea again. 'So, will you go ahead for us? Make sure it's safe for the likes of Dratos and Gus, who can't keep their shadows in their pants?'

Thea shrugged. 'Why not?'

'Good.' Anya threw her a pack that had been lying on the ground beside her and grinned. 'You leave now.'

# CHAPTER TWENTY-EIGHT

## WILDER

Wilder cursed Anya as he and Thea took to the passageways again, packs hoisted high on their backs, weapons strapped in place. He had been on the move for the better part of a year, barely staying in the same spot for more than a single night at a time. Now, he was on the road again, with more conflict on the immediate horizon.

'You're quiet,' Thea ventured as their boots crunched over wet gravel.

'I'm always quiet,' Wilder countered, picking up the pace.

'Horseshit. You were quiet when we first met because you were a grumpy bastard, but you warmed up after a time.'

'I'm still a grumpy bastard.'

'True,' Thea said with a sideways glance at him. 'What are you thinking?'

'Honestly?'

'Honestly.'

Wilder wanted to tell her that although they'd been intimate, although he'd held her hand, there was still an ache in his heart. He'd hurt her, but she'd hurt him too. And now that her hunt for him was over, that hurt lingered even as the dust settled. But it was too heavy a subject to unburden here and now. Instead, he sighed. 'I miss my fucking cabin.'

Thea's head snapped in his direction and she looked at him in utter disbelief. 'You can't be serious.'

'I'm deadly serious,' he replied flatly.

'We're on the brink of war. We're allying with shadow-wielding *teenagers*. Monsters with eight eyes and eight fucking legs are coming through the Veil, trying to kill us. And you miss your cabin?'

'I don't think you understand the gravity of the situation,' he told her. 'Can you imagine the state of my plants? I bet Malik hasn't watered a single fucking thing.'

Though it hurt to mention his brother, it was worth it when Thea looked at him as though he'd grown two heads, before a smile broke across her face and she tipped her head back, laughing.

There wasn't a more glorious sound.

Except for —

He promptly cut that thought off before it bloomed into something dangerous.

'Glad you find my misery amusing, Apprentice.'

'Am I really your apprentice anymore?' she asked, still smiling.

Gods, he could look at that smile all day.

'Tal called me his apprentice long after I passed the Great Rite,' he told her. 'Mainly just to piss me off.'

'Isn't that why you do it to me?'

'Maybe.'

For a moment it was as it had been before, before

everything had gone to shit. A little reprieve, a little reminder of how easy, how comfortable it could be. They hadn't been alone since he'd brought her to climax with his fingers in the tent. The very thought of it heated his blood even now. But time was not on their side, if it ever had been. They needed to keep moving, to secure a safe entry for Anya and the rest.

'Who are we meeting, anyway?' Thea asked, adjusting the straps of her pack and rolling her shoulders beneath its weight.

'Allies.'

'There's the cryptic Warsword I know and...' She trailed off. 'Will Cal and Kipp be there?'

'Yes, this is the meet point I told Torj about. They should be joining us there.'

The surge of relief was obvious on Thea's face. Wilder knew that while she trusted the Bear Slayer with her friends, a part of her wouldn't rest easy until she clapped eyes on them again herself. The sooner that happened, the better.

'Last I heard, Torj was trying to get Esyllt onside, and Audra,' he continued. 'I get the feeling she's been waiting for this for twenty years.'

'Audra's coming to... this meet point?'

Wilder shrugged. He didn't want to get Thea's hopes up, not about Audra or whoever else might show up. 'I guess we'll see.'

He'd asked Torj to put the word out discreetly, and to trusted friends of the guild only. It was time Thezmarr knew how deep its own corruption ran, and it was time for it to play its part in the war to come.

'No more questions?' he prompted.

Thea seemed to consider this before she spoke again. 'I have endless questions,' she told him slowly. 'But I feel as though I no longer have the right to ask them...'

He hated the tentativeness in her tone, but he appreciated the raw honesty of her words, because he felt the same.

'It's guilt, among other things,' he said quietly. 'I feel it too.'

'I don't... I don't know how to move past it.'

'Little by little,' he told her. 'Perhaps we start with a question each, and go from there... What do you think?'

Thea glanced at the seemingly endless tunnel ahead. 'I guess we have time.'

He huffed a laugh at that. 'I guess so. You first.'

Thea was quiet for a time, but he didn't press her.

At last, she looked at him and he saw that same sorrow in her eyes as before, the same regret beneath the surface. 'Do you think we can go back to how it was?'

'We're not starting out small, then...' he murmured.

She turned away, her gaze now trained ahead with militant focus.

'Thea,' he said, pulling her to a stop, waiting until those stormy eyes met his. 'I don't think we can go back...' he said slowly, trying to choose his words carefully.

'Then what —'

'I don't want to go back,' he said, more firmly this time. 'Not back to what we once were. But I want to go forward, to what we could be.'

The words hung between them, and Wilder had never felt so naked, so vulnerable in all his life. But he was done with half-truths and lies. He was done with wearing whatever mask suited the occasion. She had asked for honesty more than once, and so honesty was what he would give.

He felt her exhale before she nodded. 'And you? What's your question?'

There were a million things he wished to know, a million more he wished they could have spent the past year uncovering together, but in this moment, he needed to ask a question not for him, but for the fate of the midrealms.

He motioned for them to keep walking, holding the torch out before them, illuminating the rocky path ahead.

'Has there been any sign of your magic?'

Thea didn't break her stride, but he sensed her hesitation. 'That's your question?'

'That's my question.'

For a moment there was no sound but for the drip of moisture from the cave walls and their footsteps.

'The answer's no. No magic,' she said at last. 'Sorry to disappoint you.'

'You haven't,' Wilder replied.

But the sigh that escaped her told him that she didn't believe it.

'They were counting on having another storm wielder at their disposal, weren't they?' she asked.

'It was discussed.'

'At length, I'm sure,' she said, sounding resigned.

'So?' he challenged. 'Fuck them.'

She raised a brow. 'Fuck them? The rebel forces you've broken your vows and about a hundred laws to ally with?'

'I'm yet to make my peace with all that,' he admitted. 'But yes. That's how I feel. You're more than your magic, Thea. You're more than any one thing. And fuck anyone who says otherwise.'

A small smile tempted her lips, and Wilder had to take pride in that.

'Have they tried Wren? Although her last meeting with our dear older sister didn't go so well,' Thea ventured.

'I don't know. There are some things Anya won't share with the likes of me.'

'Because of me?'

'Something like that.'

'Sorry to keep you from the inner circle.'

Wilder shrugged. 'Sometimes it's nice not to be in the thick of all the bullshit.'

'I don't believe you for one moment, Warsword,' she quipped, sounding a little lighter. 'So, Dratos is something else...'

'Oh?' Wilder quirked a brow in her direction. 'He caught your eye, did he?'

'Jealous?'

'A lesser man might be.'

'But you're not a lesser man.'

'Not last time I checked, Princess.'

They rounded a corner, and the distinct scent of fermenting liquor hit Wilder's nostrils.

'We're nearly there,' he told Thea.

'Already?'

'We weren't going far. Just cross your fingers we can slip in unnoticed.'

'I don't know if you realise this about yourself, but you're not exactly the average citizen of Aveum. Isn't the entire military might of the midrealms out hunting for you as we speak?'

'Which is why you're going in first.' Wilder shoved the

torch into the nearby sconce and felt his way along the wall until he found the divot.

'Where are we?' Thea asked.

Wilder pushed the hidden door inward with his shoulder, the hinges rusted with disuse. Snatching up the torch again, he stepped inside, motioning for Thea to follow.

Her brow furrowed at the sight of various casks and shelves of dark bottles covered in dust. 'You've brought me to a cellar,' she said blankly.

Wilder couldn't help but grin. 'Not just any cellar.'

'No?' Thea scoffed. 'I'd hate for the rebel forces to meet in a less-than-average crawl space...'

Wilder laughed. 'It's far more than that. This is the cellar to one of the best taverns in the midrealms.'

He located the staircase leading up to a trapdoor, waiting for Thea at the top. And when she joined him, he lifted the door, light flooding the cellar.

'Welcome to the Singing Hare, Thea.'

Her eyes widened, and in an instant, she yanked the trapdoor back down, muting the noise of fiddles and chatter from above.

'Are you fucking mad?' she exclaimed. 'You want to just walk into a fucking pub, when —'

'No,' he said calmly. '*You're* going to walk into the fucking pub. I'm going to follow. At a distance, until we know it's safe. Then I'm going to buy you a drink.'

Thea glared at him. 'You're a Warsword of Thezmarr and that's the best plan you can come up with?'

'Got anything better, Apprentice?'

She made a noise of irritation. 'At least wait until it's less busy.'

'This *is* less busy.'

'Furies save me,' she muttered, readying herself. 'Fine. Here goes nothing.'

Without another word of warning, the hatch was opened again and Thea emerged from the cellar, moving gracefully and confidently, as though she had been to the Singing Hare a hundred times before. Wilder waited a few moments before he followed, drawing his hood up over his face and adjusting the fall of his cloak to hide the swords at his belt.

The Singing Hare was exactly as it had been the last time he'd visited – warm and raucous and welcoming. Somewhere in the next room, a pair of fiddles crafted a merry melody, while the crowd clapped and no doubt danced along.

He emerged from the back room, spotting Thea lingering by the bar. The place was rammed with patrons, so busy in fact that Wilder couldn't move an inch without brushing up against someone. He could feel Thea's gaze as he crossed the space, trained on him until he came to stand at her side.

'What's your poison, Princess?' Wilder asked, signalling to the bartender.

But he didn't get to hear Thea's drink order, because someone bumped into him from behind, knocking his hood back from his face. And the man behind the bar froze, dishrag in hand, eyes narrowing at the sight of Wilder.

'I know you,' the barkeep said, sliding the rag and empty tankard he was holding onto the counter. 'You're that fallen Warsword...'

The music stopped, the chatter ceased, and everyone was suddenly looking at Wilder.

He grimaced, particularly as he saw several burly men get to their feet, clearly thinking of being heroes for a night. Beside him, Thea was doing the same as he was – assessing their odds. There was no way they'd leave this place without killing countless people.

Silence throbbed through the tavern, and Wilder shifted on his feet, judging the distance to the exit, gauging just how close the quarters were and how to do the least amount of damage —

Someone cracked their knuckles. A chair screeched as it was pushed back across the stone floor. The distinct note of steel singing as it left its sheath rang out.

'Told you this was a bad idea,' Thea muttered, her hand drifting to the grip of her sword.

'What's that?' The barkeep's voice cut through the tense quiet. He was pointing at Wilder's chest.

Exchanging a baffled look with Thea, Wilder glanced down. 'What?'

To his surprise, the barman approached, leaning across the counter and tugging at something in his pocket.

Wilder baulked. 'What the fuck?'

'*I'm* asking the questions...' The man pointed again. 'What's that?'

Shaking his head in disbelief, Wilder spotted the faded yellow square of fabric sticking out of his breast pocket, recognising it as the piece of cloth Kipp had given him to wipe his bleeding nose weeks ago.

'What's it look like?' he snapped, balling his fists. 'It's a handkerchief, you fucking idiot.'

'Where'd you get it?' the man asked, glancing at the patrons who had closed in around them.

'A friend. What does it matter?' Wilder replied, growing even more irate as the man pulled the material completely from his shirt pocket and spread it across his dirty palm, staring at the embroidered fox in the corner in wonder.

*What the actual fuck?* Wilder thought, completely bewildered.

The barman waved the piece of fabric at him as though he would understand its significance. 'You're friends with the Son of the Fox?'

Wilder stared at him. Was this man even speaking the common tongue? 'What?'

The man waved the kerchief at him again. 'You're friends with Kipp Snowden?'

Thea was suddenly pushing his clenched fists back down to his sides, a broad smile on her face. 'Yes,' she told him. 'We are.'

'Is that so?' the barman replied thoughtfully. 'Because a friend of Kipp is a friend of mine. No questions asked.'

'We're definitely friends with Kipp,' Thea said.

'Prove it.'

Wilder gaped at Thea as she sized up the barman, folding her arms over her chest. 'He'll annoy you to tears. He's got a massive mouth, he's always eating, and he *never* pays for anything.'

The bartender stared at her. A moment passed, then two.

And then the man's expression changed entirely as he slapped the counter with the flat of his palm and burst into a rumbling belly laugh. 'So you *do* know him.' He reached across and clasped Wilder heartily on the shoulder. 'Why didn't you bloody well say so?'

As Wilder gawked, utterly speechless at the turn of events, the man tucked Kipp's kerchief back in Wilder's pocket and motioned for the patrons to go back to their business, for the music to continue. 'I'm Everard, owner of this fine establishment,' he declared, before he addressed a server. 'Bring out the boar. And the wine! And the tart! And the...'

He walked away shouting orders, gesturing flippantly with his hands.

Slowly, Wilder looked to Thea, stunned.

Her smile was radiant. And then she tipped her head back and laughed, deep and rich and melodic.

It was the most beautiful sound he'd ever heard.

# CHAPTER TWENTY-NINE

## THEA

Thea laughed, truly laughed, for the first time in what felt like forever. The weight that lifted from her shoulders as she did so was indescribable. She wiped away a tear and met Wilder's gaze.

His silver eyes were bright, his shoulders tense, as though he'd taken a breath and forgotten to exhale. He was looking at her in a way that made her stomach flutter, taking in her face as though she wasn't the apprentice he'd never wanted, or the lover who'd had no faith in him. He was looking at her as though he'd known her his entire life, as though she'd always been a part of him.

'What?' she asked, suddenly nervous, despite the tavern humming with noise and activity around them.

He gazed at her a moment more. 'I —'

'Your table awaits!' Everard barged between them enthusiastically, motioning for them to follow.

Thea hesitated, but Wilder simply followed the tavern owner, a small smile playing on his lips as they moved deeper into the Singing Hare.

Thea hadn't realised how enormous the place was. There were several sprawling rooms throughout, all filled with mismatched tables and chairs, a fire blazing in every hearth. Exposed weathered oak beams and doors embellished with wrought iron vines gave it an intimate feel despite its size, and the air was thick with the comforting aroma of spiced mead and roasted game. It was well lit, with flickering candlelight creating a warm glow that spilt onto the worn stone floor. With Everard guiding Thea and Wilder through, the patrons didn't look twice at the pair; they were much too enamoured with the host himself. In that respect, he reminded her of Kipp.

As it turned out, Kipp – or 'the Son of the Fox', as everyone in the Singing Hare referred to him – was incredibly well connected. Everard showed Thea and Wilder to a curtained booth with cushions covered in velvet and a pile of fur blankets to keep their laps warm.

Thea settled herself against the wall, drawing a plush throw across her lower half, realising that she liked the Singing Hare more and more with each passing moment.

'What will it be, then?' Everard said, clapping his hands together as though the prospect of feeding them gave him great joy. 'I have boar and an array of dishes on the way, but to drink? What's your poison, friends?'

Wilder went to reply, but Everard cut him off by clapping a palm to his forehead in sudden realisation.

'It all makes sense now!' he declared. 'Marise sent something —'

Without finishing his sentence, he was off.

'Are all the tavern owners like him?' Thea asked, watching him disappear into what she assumed was the kitchen.

'Well, you've met Albert at the Fox,' Wilder replied. 'He's certainly less... eccentric?'

Before Thea could answer, Everard was back, holding two glasses and a dark bottle of wine, a note attached around its neck with a piece of twine. The tavern owner pushed it across the table. 'I suspect this is for you?'

Wilder's brows knitted together as he read the messy scrawl. Then, a slow smile broke across his handsome face and he sat back in his seat with a huff of laughter.

'What does it say?' Thea asked.

Wilder handed her the note while Everard removed the cork from the bottle and poured them each a generous glass. Thanking him, Thea returned her attention to the note. The ink had splattered with every word across the parchment and Thea had to squint to make out the letters.

*You missed the Dead Red event. You'll be sorry.*

Thea frowned. 'Is he threatening you?'

Wilder barked a laugh. 'Threatening? No.' He looked up to Everard. 'Have a glass with us, friend. We have some logistics to discuss with you.'

Thea didn't think she'd ever seen a person look so thrilled to be invited to talk logistics. But she soon realised it wasn't the conversation that was the drawcard, but the wine.

'I warn you, it's entirely possible we'll need another,' Wilder told him, clinking his glass against Everard's.

'I warn you, that's never a problem in this tavern.'

Thea watched with quiet amusement as the men spoke about Marise's famous Dead Red event with great intensity before Wilder turned to the actual topic at hand.

'We have need of a discreet entrance and private meeting room tomorrow evening,' the Warsword began slowly, seeming to mull over his words carefully. 'The guests... Well, they're of a controversial nature.'

'Say no more,' Everard said. 'You're a friend of Kristopher's. When it comes to that lad, we have a *no questions asked* policy.'

'Surely, to protect your business you must —'

Everard waved him off. 'The sister taverns of the midrealms have withstood every terrible moment in history thus far. They are the safe havens for the drinkers and thinkers of our age. Kipp is one of the best of them. He's the reason this place is still standing.'

'What did he do?' Thea asked, curiosity piqued. How was it that her friend had garnered such a reputation across the lands when he'd spent much of his life at the fortress?

'Ah, that is top-secret information,' Everard replied with a wink. 'But his friends are our friends, and what you need, you get.'

Warmth bloomed in Thea's chest at the man's loyalty, at his faith in her friend, who was so often overlooked or deemed 'useless' by the commanders. It was a strange and wonderful world where Kipp Snowden was more legend than the legends of Thezmarr.

'Thank you,' she said earnestly.

Everard bowed his head. 'It's an honour to serve the midrealms. So, tell me what you need, then I'll see about this delay with the boar.'

Wilder still seemed a little stunned by the whole scenario, and he sat back with his wine as Thea took the reins. As succinctly as possible, she told Everard of their need for a private meeting room, with space enough for more than a dozen people by her count. That they would need to be able to arrive and leave unseen by other patrons.

And, where possible, there would be several overnight rooms required.

When she had finished, Everard simply nodded. 'Consider it done.' He walked away, promising their food would be with them shortly.

She felt Wilder's gaze on her again. 'Something to say, Warsword?' she asked, picking up her own wine and taking a sip. An explosion of red fruit met her tastebuds and she closed her eyes, savouring the flavour. It wasn't anything like the wine she had tried at the masquerade ball; it was more complicated, more layered somehow.

'Nothing to say, Princess,' Wilder told her, voice low. 'Not yet, anyway.'

Thea was about to press him, but the food arrived in a flourish more befitting of a royal family than two ragged travellers. Any concerns went out the window along with Thea's manners as the steaming plates were set down before them, the aroma of delicately spiced roast boar wafting through the air making her mouth water.

Suddenly, she was starving. Hot meals had been few and far between in the long winter months past, and so she decided to take a leaf out of Kipp's book and make the most of it. She wondered if he'd ask for her king's coin to pay for it all – not that she minded; she'd happily run King Artos' treasury into the ground at this point.

She and Wilder ate together, leaving the curtains of their booth open so they could watch the rest of the tavern, quietly observing all the goings-on.

'I like it here,' she said, watching a minstrel with a lute swagger through the crowd, and a rowdy group of women tossing back tankards of ale in the far corner.

'Thought you might.'

'Why's that?'

Wilder shrugged. 'You can be anyone you want here, and no one gives a fuck.'

Thea took another swig of her wine. 'Makes a nice change from the rest of the midrealms, doesn't it?'

'It does.'

'Who do you want to be, then?' she asked, pushing her plate away, unable to eat another morsel.

'Someone worthy,' Wilder replied, but before Thea could tell him that he certainly was someone worthy, his gaze strayed from her and landed on the billiards table on the other side of the room. 'Remember when we played?'

'Yes.'

A sultry heat burned in his gaze as it met hers again. 'Remember what happened after?'

Thea swallowed, her body going taut and a rush of arousal sweeping over her at the mere mention of that night. 'Yes,' she breathed. She had relived those hours many times, often against her will in the dark of her tent or beneath the stars.

The cushion beneath her shifted, and she realised she was sliding across the booth. Wilder dragged her towards him until she was flush against his side, his warmth instantly encompassing her.

When she tilted her head up, he was already looking at her, his silver eyes molten.

'You want to play billiards again?' she asked, biting her lower lip.

'No.'

Thea traced a finger up the muscular curve of his thigh. 'Then what do you want?'

Wilder was unbelievably still, but for a brief tremor that

betrayed the efforts of his restraint. Finally, he leant in, pressing the barest whisper of a kiss to her neck, but it was enough to set every nerve ending in Thea's body on fire.

'You know damn well what I want.' His deep voice vibrated against her skin, sending pulses of yearning rippling through her.

Thea tilted her chin up in challenge. 'So take it.'

Desire flared in Wilder's gaze and he crowded her body with his, ignoring the patrons beyond their booth.

Thea breathed him in, his mouth dangerously close to hers, arousal throbbing at her core. Gods, she wanted him. She wanted him with every fibre of her being.

He reached for her, running his thumb over her bottom lip before letting his fingers fall down the column of her throat, and trail between her breasts. The touch was light, barely a caress, but Thea felt it like a line of fire. Her legs parted involuntarily beneath the blanket across her lap and she arched into his touch, stifling a whimper.

Wilder ran his nose along her neck before he sank his teeth into the soft skin there, brushing his tongue over the tender spot. 'You don't get to make the rules, Princess,' he said.

A cry of fury half left her lips before Wilder stood abruptly, scooping her up and throwing her over his shoulder. Not breaking his stride, he swiped their key from the bar and made for the stairs in the far corner. She vaguely remembered him threatening to do exactly this to her, when they'd first met in the Bloodwoods...

*'Are you going to come to the fortress willingly? Or would you prefer to suffer the indignity of me throwing you over my shoulder and carrying you?'*

He hadn't asked this time.

The patrons of the Singing Hare whistled and cheered as Wilder wove through the crowd, Thea too shocked to do anything but hang over his broad shoulder. She stared out at their grinning faces and lewd gestures as Wilder's hands grasped the backs of her thighs firmly and he charged up the stairs. He moved fast, and soon, a door was being unlocked and kicked open, slamming shut behind them as he threw her down on a feather bed.

# CHAPTER THIRTY

## THEA

Thea waited for the weight of him to follow, but it didn't. Flushing with embarrassment and desire, she gazed up at him as he stalked the length of the room, running his hands through his hair and taking measured breaths.

'We need to talk,' he managed through gritted teeth.

'That wasn't what it seemed like you wanted to do,' Thea replied boldly, sitting up, a crease forming between her brows.

'Want and need are two different things,' he said.

'I'm not sure that's the case when it comes to us.'

The words had flown out of Thea's mouth before she could stop them, and now, they hung between the pair like grains of sand suspended in an hourglass.

Wilder looked at her then. 'I always knew you would be the end of me.'

Thea swallowed, hard. She didn't want to be the end of him, not anymore. She wanted to be the beginning. 'I...'

'I am not the first man to break a vow... Nor the first Warsword,' he ventured, his deep voice suddenly hoarse.

She surveyed him from across the room, not sure she trusted herself to move a step closer to him, not when the air between them crackled like fire, not when the words they'd long suppressed were at last being spoken aloud. He was magnificent, even in his travel-worn clothes, his dark hair messily tied back, his beard untrimmed. Every one of his movements seemed to disturb the energy around him, as though he were struggling to contain that Furies-given power.

He took a step towards her, an ocean of turmoil behind those silver eyes.

'I may have broken my oath to Thezmarr...' he said roughly, as though it hurt to say the words, his shoulders caving forward, like the weight of the burden was all too much. 'But I never broke a promise to you. Not one that mattered. I need you to know that.'

'Wilder...' Thea breathed.

'I told you I *loved* you. That meant something, *everything*, to me.'

'I know.' Thea's insides were twisting with regret.

Wilder straightened, very slowly, reaching to rub the spot beneath his shirt where the scar from her arrow must still have pained him. He stared at her without speaking. A tremor ran down the strong column of his throat as he swallowed. Still, he said nothing.

Thea could hardly fill her lungs with enough air. Another second and she'd lose her nerve.

The words spilt forth like a tide as she closed the distance between them. 'I'm sorry. I'm so sorry, for everything. I fucked up. I should have trusted you, I should have known that there was more to the story, that you'd never hurt me deliberately, that you had a reason —' Her voice broke. 'Forgive me. Please. Forgive me, Wilder.'

'I already have,' he murmured, lifting her chin with his index finger so her gaze met his. 'I understand your reaction. Trust doesn't come easy, given everything you've been through. I was trying to protect you, trying to safeguard your future in case what I suspected wasn't true. But that's no excuse. I shouldn't have kept secrets, not from you. Do you forgive me?'

Thea loosed a sharp breath at the contact. 'There's nothing to forgive,' she said.

She waited for one or both of them to pull away, but neither of them did. Not this time. Never again, if she had any say in the matter. They stared at one another, Thea's hand reaching for Wilder's, curling around his wrist. Each moment that passed was like a strike to an anvil, nailing the unstoppable force between them into place.

Her chest hitched, her fate stone warming against her sternum. 'I wish we could take back this past year. I robbed us of that time together.'

'You robbed us of nothing,' he murmured, eyes scanning her face desperately. 'I have only cared for you more with each passing day.'

Thea fought back a sob as the realisation hit her hard. 'But we could have had more…'

Wilder's eyes darkened, and Thea saw it all: heat, need and the thing they'd never been able to shed – love.

'If you only have a year left, then live it well, and live it with me at your side.'

He said it as though it were simple. Perhaps it was.

'Thea... What measure of time is enough to be life-changing?'

Before she could reply, he kissed her.

Wilder's lips claimed Thea's with an intensity that nearly shattered her. She kissed him back, matching every stroke of his tongue, every brush of his lips, wrapping her arms around his neck, spearing her fingers through his hair.

He groaned against her mouth, lifting her bodily from the ground, pressing her to him as though he meant for them to meld together. Thea writhed against him, every part of her singing out for his touch, his mouth, his cock.

Wilder didn't carry her to the bed like she expected. He took her to the wall. The sconces rattled as her back hit the cool surface hard and she wrapped her legs around him, savouring the friction at her core where his hard length pressed against her. In a tangle of tongues and teeth, she explored his mouth with hers, relishing every sensation he wrought upon her. She kissed him like he was her air, losing herself to him.

'Do you think you can die from this?' she gasped, as he lowered her until her feet hit the ground, freeing his hands to explore. 'The need? The wanting?'

'It'd be a good way to go.' His voice was husky as he skimmed her curves, its rich tone vibrating through her, fuelling the longing that raged so fiercely within. Her hands went to the buttons of his shirt, undoing each one with fingers that trembled in anticipation. Furies, she had missed this, missed *him*.

A column of golden, scar-flecked skin was revealed as his shirt came undone. She ran her palms across the impressive breadth of his chest, revelling in the heat of him, in the way his nipples hardened at her touch. As the shirt came away from him completely, she eyed the scar just above his pectoral. The first time she'd glimpsed it, it had been with anger and false hatred in her heart. Now, as her fingers trailed the smooth pink line, she wanted to worship it. She put her lips to the mark, kissing it, running her tongue along the raised tissue.

Wilder tensed, his hands stilling at her waist, as though he knew she needed to do this. She trailed kisses along his scar, along his collarbone, and finally, at his throat, where she could feel his pulse racing.

She pulled back slightly, just to look at him. He was beautiful. Hard and fierce, but beautiful.

He knew the power he had over her; she could tell. It tempted his lips into a wicked smile.

And then he slipped his hand down the front of her pants, into her undergarments.

Thea gasped as he slid his finger down her centre, tracing exactly where she wanted him. She was already slick for him, already panting.

'Gods, you're ready for me,' he growled against her neck.

She gripped his cock through his pants, squeezing the rock-hard length of him. 'And you're not?'

Wilder gave a low, rough laugh. 'It's been a fucking year, Princess. I'm always ready for you.'

Any final notions of restraint vanished as Wilder claimed her mouth in a dark frenzy and slid his finger deep inside her.

Thea moaned against him, her hands flying to his belt as he added a second finger, tempting that coil of intoxicating bliss from her body. His swords hit the floor while his pants fell to his knees and his cock sprang free.

Thea broke their feverish kiss to look at him. He was perfect.

She must have said it aloud, because he laughed.

The sound skittered along her bones, sending a delicious lick of pleasure down her spine. Thea couldn't bear it anymore. She removed Wilder's hand from her pants and dropped to her knees.

'Thea...' he warned.

She glided her tongue across the broad head of him and took him deep into her mouth, until he nudged the back of her throat.

'Furies – fuck!' he barked, his fingers threading through her hair.

She smiled around him and moved up and down his length, cupping his balls as she sucked his cock. He was hot and hard and silken in her mouth, and the sounds he was making were nearly the end of her.

He fisted her hair in a punishing grip, and she moaned, her knees spreading beneath her as her own arousal amplified at the way he quivered for her. She swallowed him down, coaxing another carnal groan from his lips.

He moved with her, thrusting into her mouth. 'I have thought about you every day since we've been apart,' he rasped. 'I've thought about your perfect mouth.' He thrust again.

'Your perfect breasts...' Thrust. 'How perfectly we fit.' He ground into her for emphasis before thrusting again. 'Every. Fucking. Day.'

His coarse words turned her body molten.

Wilder pulled her up from the floor, his cheeks tipped pink, his breath ragged. 'I'll be damned if I'm going to rush this.'

He stripped her naked, moaning at the sight of her, worshipping every inch of her skin with kisses and teasing touches, so that she was almost a mere puddle at his feet. His rough palms skimmed across her, as though he didn't know where he wanted to touch her first. Then he decided.

He cupped her breasts, squeezing until Thea's back was arching and she could feel her wet arousal pulsing between her legs.

'Wilder...' she panted, pushing his pants down the rest of his legs.

He kicked the fabric away and they stood there together, naked, drinking in the sight of each other.

Thea let out a whimper as he pinched her nipple and slipped his hand between her legs again.

'Let me taste you before I fuck you,' he said, a pleading note in his voice.

'Yes,' she breathed, her legs nearly turning liquid as he lowered himself, kneeling before her.

He hooked one of her legs over his huge shoulder, and spread her open, the cool air kissing the most intimate part of her. She saw the wetness that glistened there as Wilder dragged a single finger down her core with a moan.

'Gods,' he murmured. 'You were made for me, Thea.'

Then his tongue was on her, licking straight up her centre, sucking gently, just where she wanted him. Thea cried out at the sensation, at the million tingling sparks that burst through her body, starting from the base of her spine through to each fingertip.

Wilder devoured her. Every stroke of his wicked tongue against her clit chipped away at what little control she had left, fed the inferno that unfurled inside her. When one of his hands reached up and rolled her nipple between his deft fingers, her head tipped back against the wall and she moaned, loudly.

'Fuck...' Wilder muttered against her core, and she glanced down to see him grasping his cock with his other hand, the tip wet with his own need.

'Wilder...' Thea panted. 'I want —'

There was a flurry of movement as he stood and pinned her to the wall, kissing her savagely. 'I know,' he growled. 'I know exactly what you want.'

He reached between them, dragging the head of his cock through the wet heat of her, pressing it to her entrance, pausing there.

Warmth bloomed in Thea's chest as he gazed into her eyes.

'It's me and you now,' he told her. 'Always.'

Thea struggled to swallow the lump that had formed in her throat. She nodded. 'Always.'

And then he sheathed himself inside her.

Thea gave herself over to the force of him, seeing stars in her vision as she clenched around him. She cried out as he moved inside her, one powerful thrust after another, each one more intoxicating than the last. She let go, climbing higher and higher as her love for Wilder drugged her.

He moaned against her neck and she almost climaxed then and there. He reached between them and stroked her clit, nearly reducing her to a million pieces.

She looked down, past the contours of his muscled stomach, past the V of sinew that pointed to where they were joined with those hot, powerful thrusts. Every stroke rendered her mind useless. There was no thinking here, only the feel of him, the feel of them, together.

Over and over he sank into her, both of them trembling

at the very precipice of desire, an energy forming around them that sang out to Thea's soul. She felt it, felt *him*, in the fabric of her soul.

Her eyes locked with his, that dark silver smoulder like a brand.

'Come for me,' he commanded, circling her clit as he fucked her hard and deep.

Thea gave a half-sob as her body did as he demanded. She screamed his name as she came, her whole body shattering with the force of him, her climax unravelling at a blinding speed, wave after wave – a feeling so intense she wasn't sure she'd ever come back down to reality.

Wilder tensed, his breath hitching as he dragged out the last spirals of her orgasm before he cried out. Her Warsword shuddered against her, spilling himself inside her with a ragged gasp.

They were both shaking, clinging to one another as though they might be swept away.

Thea waited for the current coursing through her to ebb, to leave her feeling sated and dazed. But whatever hummed in her veins didn't leave her.

Wilder's sharp intake of breath forced her eyes open.

Thea nearly choked. For at her fingertips danced little bolts of lightning.

Power crackled through her, and that dormant beast within her awoke from its slumber. She stared at her magic.

Wilder's deep voice rumbled against her, warm and full of pride. 'There you are, Princess.'

# CHAPTER THIRTY-ONE

## THEA

There she was, storm magic coursing through the very essence of her. That kernel of power that had been missing for so long was there, blooming to life, begging to be unleashed upon the world.

Thea hardly dared to breathe as she watched the sparks of brilliant white dance across her skin, as much a part of her as the heart hammering in her chest. With her magic now surging in her blood, she realised just how big the gaping hole had been. Just how broken a part of her had been.

Wilder had been right: grief had pulled her apart.

And she'd fought to pull herself back together.

Now, she could feel the power at her fingertips, the ability to conjure and control lightning and thunder. She could feel the call of the storms beyond the Singing Hare, far away in the distance. For a moment, Thea lost herself in the song of storms, both within and without. Gods, she had missed it.

As the lightning sang in her veins, hope blossomed. Hope

for the war to come. The rebel forces had wanted another storm wielder, hadn't they? Now, she had that very power at her fingertips. Now, she had something beyond her blades and stubbornness to aid in the fight against the darkness.

And the Great Rite? She had her edge back, and she would take what was hers. Who was going to stop her now?

As the thoughts barrelled through her one by one, she looked up in shock at the man who watched her, the man who had seen her through it all.

They were still touching.

How was her lightning not hurting him? How was it possible that his hands still skimmed across her heated skin? That there was nothing but adoration and admiration etched on that handsome face of his?

'Do you regret it?' she asked quietly. 'Not asking the Furies for immortality?'

'Not once, not until I met you...' Wilder said. 'But then I wonder how my path may have differed, and if things had happened another way, whether we would have met at all. That is something I would regret more than missing a thousand endless lifetimes.'

'Even with...' She touched her fate stone, lightning sparking there too.

Wilder closed a hand over hers and she once again marvelled at how it didn't pain him, but seemed to answer his Furies-given strength in kind.

'I want you to ask them,' he told her. 'For you. Not for us. For everything you have worked for. You deserve more than the hand you've been dealt.'

His words felt far away as Thea watched her lightning dance not only across her skin, but his as well, as she felt the thunder roiling in her chest. Her magic... It knew him. She felt the recognition deep in her bones.

Wilder Hawthorne didn't flinch when she touched him with the might of a storm. He didn't baulk at her power.

He had asked her where she was, where the Althea Zoltaire he'd known had gone.

Now, she looked up at him and smiled. 'Here I am, Warsword.'

# CHAPTER THIRTY-TWO

## WILDER

The lightning at Thea's fingertips seemed to pulse to a rhythm Wilder couldn't hear, but with every flicker of that power, he felt her come back to herself, come back to him.

She was no longer the girl spying on Warswords or training in secret in the Bloodwoods. Gone was the shieldbearer desperate to make her mark. Gone was the Guardian who followed without question.

Here was a storm wielder, a Warsword-to-be.

And she was *his*.

Still standing there naked, Wilder watched Thea in awe as she took in her magic, magic that didn't harm him as it danced across his skin with her touch.

'It's beautiful,' he told her. 'Like you.'

She blinked at the bright bolts. 'How is this possible?' she murmured.

A smile tugged at his mouth. 'I must be a really good fuck.'

Her gaze snapped to his, amusement bright in her

celadon eyes. 'Is that so?'

A grin spread across Wilder's face as he tugged her close to him and kissed her soundly. 'Credit where credit's due, Princess.'

Thea laughed, and he wished he could bottle the sound. Instead, he scooped her up in his arms and carried her to the bed. He didn't care for the late hour, not when he'd waited a year to have her again. He intended to worship her thoroughly, for as long as he could.

On the bed, he laid her down, surveying her naked body with appreciation, his cock already stirring to attention again. He ran his hands down the sides of her thighs, marvelling at the softness of her skin, at how her body responded instantly to his touch, her legs falling open for him, making his mouth turn dry. He'd never have enough of her – would never stop wanting her, mind, body and soul.

The way she looked at him told him she felt the same, and he swore by the Furies that as insatiable as they were, he'd never stop trying to please her. Making her happy and keeping her that way would be his life's work.

Her eyes were hooded with lust, her hands caressing her breasts and teasing her nipples, tempting him.

'Lower,' he told her. 'Move your hands lower.'

Challenge gleamed in Thea's eyes, but she obeyed, her hands slowly trailing down her stomach, to the heat he knew so well between her legs.

'Spread yourself,' he said, taking his rock-hard cock in his grasp, stroking it slowly from base to tip. 'Wider. I want to see all of you.'

He heard her intake of breath as she used one hand to bare herself to him completely, exposing everything.

'Like this?' Her breathing grew faster.

'Exactly like that.' His cock pulsed in his hand at the sight and he leant in, blowing a stream of cool air directly onto her glistening core. 'Touch yourself, Thea,' he told her. 'You know I love to watch you.'

At his instruction, her fingers circled her clit and a moan escaped her that sent a bolt of pleasure straight to Wilder's balls. He didn't take his eyes off her, didn't stop stroking his cock either.

'You want to add a finger? Or would you prefer I take it from here?' he said, edging closer to her.

At his words, her back arched, her breasts lifting, her peaked nipples practically begging for his mouth.

'You...' she panted. 'I want you.'

That was all he needed to hear. He seated himself between her open thighs, rubbing his cock through the slickness he found there. Closing his lips around one of her nipples, he pushed inside her, just an inch. He bit down on her nipple and she cried out, before he flicked his tongue over the sensitive spot and sank into her another inch.

'Oh gods,' she panted beneath him.

'If you need to pray to them to get you through, go right ahead, Princess,' he said, before he thrust inside her fully.

Thea bucked beneath him, bowing off the bed with a gasp, raking her nails down his back, spurring him on. He pounded into her, each movement rougher than the last.

He fucked her as he loved her: fierce, hard, unrelenting.

She gave as good as she got, biting his lip until he hissed, just on the right side of pain. 'Do your worst, Warsword,' she said breathlessly, raising her hips to meet his.

A primal noise escaped him as she writhed beneath him.

He wanted this to last forever, wanted to map every inch of her body with his hands and his mouth.

'Fuck me from behind, Wilder,' she told him, already moving.

She was on all fours in an instant, giving him a glorious view of her small waist and sinful curves. Arching her back, Thea pressed against him, demanding more.

More he was all too willing to give her.

He pushed inside her again. 'Fuck...' he muttered as the new position allowed him deeper.

'Yes, Wilder...' Thea murmured, dropping to her elbows.

The sight of her nearly undid him. Gripping her hips, he drove into her again and again. He was shaking once more, shaking with the effort of holding back. Her cries of ecstasy had him right on the edge, and all he could think of was how much he loved her and how he hoped she felt it with every stroke of his cock.

Slowing his pace to a rhythm torturous enough to drive them both to the brink of madness, he reached around and played with her clit until she gave a strangled cry. She sat back against him, her spine to his chest, her hand coming up to clamp around the back of his neck.

'Will you come undone for me again, Thea?' he murmured, his other hand grasping her throat and squeezing gently.

He moved with her, drawing out their pleasure in long, lavish strokes, relishing the feel of their sweat-soaked bodies sliding together as one.

Her grip tightened on him and he knew she was close – and thank the Furies, because so was he. He'd been teetering on the edge with her.

He circled her clit again, once, twice, before gently pinching the sensitive spot.

Thea screamed, clamping around him and pushing down, hard.

Wilder lost control. His climax tore through him like a storm, washing over him with so much force it was a miracle he didn't collapse right on top of Thea. He came long and hard, spilling himself inside her with a shout.

'Holy Furies…' he croaked, still riding the last waves in a haze of pure bliss, still thrusting slowly into his storm wielder.

'You can pray to them if you like,' Thea murmured, pulling him down with her as she sank into the mattress. 'But they won't save you now.'

He gave a rough laugh and drew her close, pressing a kiss to her damp hair. 'Who the fuck would want saving from that?'

Wilder was wrapped around Thea, breathing in the heady scent of her. Still sleeping, she rubbed her backside against him, seeking him out even in the depths of slumber, and he hissed at the contact in anticipation. He was already hard for her, already running through the various ways he could wake her up, when someone pounded on the door.

'I know you had a long night and day, Warsword, but your party is arriving…' came Everard's voice.

Wilder groaned into the crook of Thea's neck.

She stirred with her own muffled noise of complaint. 'Tell me I imagined that racket?'

Wilder dropped a kiss to her bare shoulder, fighting every instinct to turn her over and seat himself between her legs again. 'I'm afraid not.'

'He said something about our party arriving? I thought they weren't getting here till sundown?'

Wilder grimaced as his gaze shot to the window. 'It is sundown.' They had fucked and slept their way through the day.

'Fuck,' Thea muttered.

Wilder was inclined to agree. Only years of discipline and training got him out of that warm bed, and he went about stoking the fire in the hearth to life and heating water over its flames for them to wash.

He felt Thea's gaze on him as he moved about the room naked, his hard cock bobbing in front of him. His eyes met hers. 'Don't get any ideas, Princess.'

She licked her lips. 'Wouldn't dream of it.'

He forced himself to look away, lest he start something they didn't have time to finish, but he couldn't help the smile that played on his lips as he went about locating the clothes they'd discarded the night before.

It was in the quiet moments as they washed themselves before the fire, smiling at each other and sharing heated glances, that the need to express himself hit Wilder. He wanted to say something, something powerful to capture everything that rushed through him as he looked upon her buttoning her shirt – such a simple act that seemed so familiar, so intimate now. It was in this suspended moment of time that he realised words were not enough, that his love for her demanded everything of him and he would gladly give it all.

Thea looked up from tucking her fate stone beneath the folds of her shirt, the sight of it tugging at Wilder's chest. He searched for something to say, anything to relieve the swelling pressure in his heart. He was in awe of her, of everything she had fought and won for herself, of the magic he could feel humming from her even now – of the fact that she had chosen *him*.

'You're staring,' Thea pointed out. 'And you're only half dressed.' The smile she gave him nearly broke him. 'Not that I'm complaining,' she added, dragging her fingertips across his bare chest. 'But we'd best get downstairs. Torj and the others saw enough of us in Harenth, remember? Don't fancy them barging in again.'

The memory jolted Wilder out of his trance and he chuckled, shrugging his shirt on and quietly revelling in Thea's lustful gaze as his bare skin disappeared beneath the fabric.

They strapped their weapons in place and faced the door.

'You ready?' Wilder asked her, wishing more than anything that they could remain tucked away in their room.

'I don't think either of us are ready,' Thea admitted. 'But we'll figure it out.'

Wilder offered his hand. 'Together, then?'

Warmth bloomed in his chest as she laced her fingers through his and reached for the door with her other hand. 'Together.'

# CHAPTER THIRTY-THREE

## THEA

With her magic simmering beneath her skin and Wilder's hand in hers, Thea felt more like herself than she had in a long time. Despite the festering state of the midrealms, for her, the missing pieces of the puzzle had slid into place and she felt as though she could breathe again – felt that whatever came next, she could face it as she'd always intended.

Lightning sang in her every nerve ending; Wilder had made sure of that last night. As they made their way into the tavern below, more than once, Thea had to check that there were no sparks dancing off her. It was liberating to be whole again, to feel the full force of her power at her fingertips once more. She hadn't realised how much she had become accustomed to it until it was gone.

Sensing Wilder's gaze on her as they wove through the chairs and tables, she glanced at him.

He was smiling.

Not a slight quirk to the corner of his mouth, nor the

arrogant smirk he sometimes offered to drive her mad. No, this was a true smile. The harsh lines of his fierce face softened, his dimple was deep, and his eyes were bright like pools of starlight rather than molten steel. Gods, he was beautiful. And he was hers.

'Easy there, Princess,' he murmured, his warm grip tightening around her hand.

Thea blinked at him. 'What?'

He licked his lips and smiled wider. 'I can feel the storm gathering in you...'

She nearly stopped in the middle of the tavern. 'You can feel it?'

Wilder rubbed the centre of his chest. 'Right here.'

'It doesn't scare you?' She had asked some version of this question once before, on the cliffs at Thezmarr, a lifetime ago. But so much had happened since then. Everything had changed, and there were so many challenges still to come...

'It never has.' He pressed his mouth to the back of her hand, kissing it, the sensation hot but brief on her skin.

Something in Thea eased, a coil of tension she hadn't even known was there. She gave her Warsword a quick smile before taking the lead and making her way through the last few rooms of the Singing Hare.

True to his word, Everard had cordoned off an entire private section of the tavern for their meeting. A crackling fire blazed in the hearth, and sitting at a large round oak table were Torj Elderbrock, Cal and Kipp.

Thea dropped Wilder's hand and braced herself as the latter two jumped to their feet at the sight of her and half tackled her in an overzealous embrace, grinning from ear to ear.

She squeezed her friends tight, relief rushing through

her. 'It's so good to see you both,' she said, not quite ready to let them go yet.

'And you, Thea,' Cal replied, though he was pulling away, having noted the towering Warsword at her back.

She bit down a laugh and revelled in the joy of seeing them. 'You're both well?'

'Never better,' Cal reassured her, still warily keeping his distance.

Kipp, however, flung an arm around her shoulders, still beaming, his gaze sliding to Wilder. 'The Shadow of Death and her faithful mentor, the infamous fallen Warsword... Together again at last. You're both looking... refreshed.'

Behind him, Torj groaned.

The sound only seemed to delight Kipp further, and at last he released her and held out his hand to the others. 'Cough up, gentlemen.'

To Thea's shock, both Torj and Cal scowled, reaching into their pockets for their coin pouches. Cal passed a handful of coins to Kipp with a grimace, while Torj threw his whole bag on the table.

'Un-fucking-believable,' he muttered.

Wilder's laugh sounded. 'What was the wager?'

'Oh, nothing important,' Kipp said, gleefully scooping up his winnings and wiggling his brows. 'Just a little bet between friends.'

'Oh, fuck off, Kipp.' Thea threw herself down into the closest chair, unable to suppress her smile.

'That's how you treat your dear friend whose countless connections saved your sorry arses?' He gave Wilder a knowing look. 'I said you'd need that handkerchief again, didn't I?'

Wilder took the chair beside Thea. 'That you did, and I'm grateful. I owe you a debt.'

'Always good to have a Warsword's favour,' Kipp replied with a grin. 'I'll collect in good time.'

Wilder chuckled. 'I don't doubt it.'

'When did this exchange of favours take place?' Thea asked, brows raised.

Kipp shrugged. 'That's for us to know, and for you to never find out.'

Finally wiping the frown off his face, Torj stood, reaching across the table and grasping Wilder's forearm in greeting. 'Glad you made it out of that gods-forsaken floating dome, both of you,' he said with a nod to Thea.

Wilder bowed his head. 'I'm in your debt too.'

But Torj gave a warm smile. 'There are no debts between Warswords.'

There was a moment's pause as the mutual respect settled between the great warriors.

'Now I sound like a prick,' Kipp blurted.

Cal scoffed. 'You *are* a prick.'

Thea held back her laughter as Torj gave a long-suffering sigh, rubbing his temples as he sat back down.

Kipp ignored him entirely, leaning across the warrior to speak to Thea again. 'So what else is new, Your Royal Highness? You've got your Warsword back, got yourself a new sister, you've discovered the delights of my second-favourite tavern...' He waited eagerly for her to fill in the rest.

Unable to help herself, Thea reached out and tapped Kipp's arm with her finger, sending a sharp zap of energy his way.

'Ouch!' He leapt up, dramatically clutching his arm to his chest before his eyes went wide as the realisation hit him. 'You don't say...'

He whirled around, thrusting his hand out to Cal and Torj again.

'Hand it over, my friends.'

Cal gave another groan and fished more coins from his pocket, his face flushing deeply.

Torj just stared at Kipp's hand. 'I already gave you everything I have.'

'Well, I hate to break it to you, but you shouldn't have bet outside your means then, should you? That's irresponsible gambling —'

Torj raised a single brow in challenge. 'How about I fight you for it?'

'How about we call it even?' Kipp said smoothly, sitting down with a joyful glint in his eyes.

'That's what I thought,' Torj muttered, shaking his head in disbelief before he addressed Wilder and Thea once again. 'You two are quite the talk of the midrealms at the moment.'

'Is that so?' Thea asked.

'Indeed,' Torj replied. 'Half the kingdoms think you've run off into the sunset together and are both traitors to us all. The other half think you're on the hunt for the fallen Warsword again, Thea, and that this time, you'll bring him back in pieces.'

'We've tried to encourage the latter idea where possible, of course,' Kipp added.

'For which we're grateful,' Wilder said.

Kipp leant in, his bulging coin purse rattling. 'How grateful?'

Torj pulled him back into his chair, shaking his head. 'Hawthorne, will you tell us who exactly we're meeting? Before I lose any more of my hard-earnt coin? Before I strangle this imbecile for his incessant chatter?'

Wilder barked a laugh at that, but Thea's magic prickled suddenly, as if in recognition. She shot to her feet as three hooded figures entered the room. When they each lowered the fabric from their faces, a little cry escaped her and she surged forward, arms outstretched.

'Wren!'

Within seconds, the sisters were in each other's arms. Audra, the Thezmarrian librarian, and Farissa, the fortress' Master of Alchemy, waited behind them.

'I can't believe you're here,' Thea blurted, pulling back to study Wren's face. Her sister looked older, stronger, and she hummed with magic of her own. 'I'm so happy to see you.'

Thea meant every word. So much had happened since she'd last seen her little sister; there was so much she wanted to share with Wren. Thea didn't know when things had changed from being vitriolic between them, but they had. She no longer saw Wren as a nagging – sometimes scheming – younger sister, but someone to be respected, and at times, feared. A teammate. She was proud to have a sister like that.

'And you, Althea Nine Lives...' Wren returned Thea's smile before her eyes flicked to Wilder with a look of apprehension. 'He's not in my special chains, I see.'

'Not anymore,' Thea said.

'She had her fun with those wretched things,' Wilder replied. 'Told her if she wanted me restrained, all she had to do was ask.'

Wren's nose wrinkled. 'I didn't need to know that.'

'Here I was thinking you needed to know everything,' Torj chimed in with a smirk.

'I do *not* need to know everything,' Wren muttered. Torj had clearly found his way under her skin again. 'But the essentials would be nice.'

The Bear Slayer only grinned.

Wren ignored him and instead waved to Cal and Kipp. 'Glad you're both still in one piece.'

'I'm sure you never doubted us for a second, oh royal one,' Kipp said with a flourish and a half-bow.

Torj rolled his eyes.

Thea drew her sister's attention back to her. 'We have much to talk about.'

'I'll say,' Wren agreed, with another pointed look at Wilder.

Thea laughed, giving Wren another squeeze, warmth blooming in her chest. 'He's the least of it.'

Out of the corner of her eye, Thea saw Audra and Farissa quietly take up places at the other side of the table. When Thea made to greet them, Audra motioned for her to remain where she was.

'Later,' the librarian said simply. Her hand brushed one of the ceremonial daggers at her hip. Suppressing a laugh, Thea recalled Wilder once referring to them as *letter openers*.

'Who else are we expecting?' Wren asked, taking the vacant seat on Thea's other side.

With perfect timing, three thin ribbons of shadow curled around the doorframe. Torj, Cal and Kipp leapt to their feet, steel singing as they unsheathed their weapons, ready for attack.

Beside Thea, Wilder groaned and pinched the bridge of his nose. 'For fuck's sake, Dratos.'

Thea held out a hand to their friends. 'It's alright.'

But her words did nothing to placate them, and she could hardly blame them, given how long it had taken her to come around to the idea of the shadow-touched folk. Torj and the two Guardians stared as the darkness dissipated and Dratos the Dawnless rounded the corner.

Thea felt rather than heard Wren's intake of breath beside her, but her sister remained calm. A glance across at the two Thezmarrian academics assured Thea that neither of the older women were panicking either. Thea remembered Wilder telling her that Farissa had tried to help Talemir Starling in his hour of need, so she knew about the shadow-touched, and clearly, so did Audra.

With a smirk on his face and his black-and-red wings tucked behind his back, Dratos strode into the room. 'You know I like to make an entrance, Hawthorne,' he drawled, his bottle-green eyes sparkling.

'What the fuck…' Cal breathed, brandishing his sword.

'It's okay, Cal,' Thea soothed, worried he might do something stupid. 'It'll make sense in a minute.'

Dratos seemed to be revelling in the attention as he made a point of inspecting which chair might best accommodate his membranous wings. The Bear Slayer and the two Guardians stared in disbelief as the shadow-touched ranger had the gall to look up at them.

'What?' Dratos demanded, before his eyes widened in recognition as he focused on Cal. 'You're the bastard who shot me with a flaming arrow.'

Wilder's hand flexed around hers and Thea knew that although he wouldn't admit it, he was nervous about the two worlds colliding.

Cal's face went bright pink and he looked to Thea for guidance. But Dratos gave a dismissive wave.

'Water under the bridge, Guardian. The ladies love the scar.'

Torj, Cal and Kipp exchanged baffled looks, but didn't sheathe their weapons.

It was so bizarre that Thea almost laughed, but the moment was interrupted by another newcomer, or several. Anya strode in, scythe at her belt, head freshly shaven, scarred gaze fixing immediately on the trio on the far side of the room – and then her attention slid to Wren.

Wren tensed, spearing Anya with a look of utter contempt. Thea should have tried to warn her in advance somehow. The last time the pair had met… it had been less than friendly. Anya had taken Wren hostage. Thea recalled Wren's screams like it was yesterday. The three sisters had been reunited in chaos, wrapped in shadow and storms, each at war with their own darkness.

'Elwren,' Anya greeted her, her voice soft and tentative for once. 'I —'

But Wren's head snapped to Thea. 'You're with her?' she hissed. The rage laced through her words was palpable.

Thea didn't miss how Anya's face fell before her mask of cool detachment slid back into place.

Thea rested a hand on Wren's arm. 'It's complicated…'

'So *uncomplicate* it, Thee.'

Suppressing the urge to squirm in her seat from the discomfort of it all, Thea glanced at Wilder, who seemed to be doing his best to give them some semblance of privacy.

'I felt the same as you,' she told her sister. 'But there's a reason —'

Wren scoffed. 'A reason she bound me in shadow and lured you out into the darkness?'

'Yes,' Thea insisted.

Still standing a few feet away, Anya watched their exchange, her jaw set in a hard line. Wren's expression was murderous as she surveyed their older sister, but Thea drew her attention away.

'I want you to listen...'

Wren gave a derisive snort. 'To her?'

'To everyone here today,' Thea said gently. 'Then I want you to speak to Anya in private. To hear her out. As I did.'

She gave Anya a fleeting glance, trying to convey that it would take time, that her existence and history was hard to process for anyone, let alone the sister she'd held hostage.

Wren's eyes narrowed. 'If you think I'm going anywhere alone with that monster —'

'Please, Wren. It's not like you to make a judgement without all the information.'

Guilt bloomed in Thea's gut as the words left her mouth. Wasn't that exactly what she'd done with Wilder? Her face flushed and she refocused on Wren. She could practically hear her sister's teeth grinding, but thankfully, Wren sat back with a stiff nod, folding her arms over her chest, her gaze flitting back to the door.

Thea sighed, the tension tight in her shoulders.

Adrienne and Gus entered next. Adrienne gave Thea and Wilder a wave of acknowledgement.

'Had your horses taken from Aveum and stabled next door,' she said by way of greeting.

'Thank you.' Thea smiled at the crease between Wilder's brows. She imagined he didn't much like the idea of someone else riding Biscuit, but he said nothing.

Nor did Gus as he moved past them into the room, his lumpy, oversized knitted jumper making him look younger than his nineteen years. Wilder made a noise of disapproval, clearly not liking that a youngster was to sit in on their war council.

Dratos' gaze cut to his. 'We had words about it,' the ranger said, jutting his chin towards his younger cousin, making it clear he didn't want Gus there.

'And the majority won,' Adrienne said firmly, throwing an arm around Gus and guiding him to a chair, ensuring there was adequate distance between the two family members.

Torj and Cal looked particularly unsettled as several shadows still danced around the room. But they looked to Wilder, who subtly raised his hand from the table. *Wait*, he signalled.

Thea had to stop herself from shaking her head in disbelief. It was more than surreal to see the shadow-touched alliance out in a public space like this, let alone sitting opposite Thezmarrians. It had been only a week or so since she'd been hunting Wilder through the hinterlands with vengeance in her heart. Her loyalty to the rulers of the midrealms had been unflinching, unquestioning. And yet now here she sat. The two worlds were colliding with a force that left her momentarily stunned. The strain between them all had her on edge. She was sure a fight would break out at any moment —

Wilder squeezed her thigh under the table, as though sensing the shift in her.

However, Thea wasn't the only one who was having the realisation. The various groups from all over the realms stared each other down, almost a challenge as to who would break first.

'Someone better explain who called this meeting,' Torj said, eyeing Dratos suspiciously.

'Don't look at me, Bear Slayer,' Dratos replied. 'I can think of a dozen things I'd rather be doing —'

'Is the fate of the realms so low on your list of priorities?' Adrienne snapped.

'In case you haven't noticed, the realms haven't exactly been fair to —'

'*Fair?*' Anya cut in. 'You want to talk about *fairness?*'

The scrape of a chair cleaved through the tempest brewing between them, and Audra, the librarian of Thezmarr, stood at the head of the table.

'I called this meeting,' she declared, peering over her spectacles to pin each of them with a discerning gaze. But when her attention landed on Anya, her expression softened. 'For whatever it's worth... I'm sorry for all you endured so young.'

Thea started with the realisation that Audra had *known* Anya as a child.

*'Audra told me to stay with you and Wren. But I was never very good at listening.'*

'I tried to save you from that fate,' Audra said now. 'But what was done cannot be undone. I thank you for answering my summons now, despite everything.'

Anya simply dipped her head.

Audra went on. 'Whether you believe in such things or not, the prophecy binds us together. We are in the end of days... and a dawn of fire and blood is upon us at last. For too long, those who oppose the same evil have fought against one another instead of the enemy. For too long we have been divided and weak, played against each other like pawns on a chessboard.' Her hands came to rest on the hilts of her daggers. 'It's time we were allies. It's time we faced the war ahead *together*.'

Silence fell as the different factions glanced around the room, Audra's words washing over them all.

It was Cal who eventually said, with incredible dryness, 'We're going to need more drinks.'

Kipp clapped him on the back. 'Best idea you've had yet.'

# CHAPTER THIRTY-FOUR

## WILDER

The tension ebbed away as the discussion of liquor took priority. That, at least, was something they all had in common. The conversation, however, was interrupted by the sound of a deep bark.

Suddenly a giant dog was upon Wilder, its tail wagging so hard it hurt when it hit.

He stared at the enormous mongrel, frozen in shock.

'Dax!' Thea exclaimed, showering the dog with ear scratches and belly rubs while the creature gazed at her with unadulterated adoration.

Wilder's chair scraped as he stood, looking to the door in disbelief.

Malik's huge figure took up the entire frame.

'Holy shit,' Torj's voice sounded from the fire.

But Wilder kept his eyes on his brother, speechless. He'd been more than surprised when Malik had travelled to Tver for the battle of Notos, but this? Change and travel had been hard for his brother since his injury – two trips of this magnitude...

And then the wave of guilt hit him. When he'd all but declared himself a traitor, Wilder had abandoned his brother. Clapping eyes upon him now, he realised it was the longest he'd gone without seeing Malik since he'd been injured all those years ago. He didn't even know for certain if his messages had been received at the fortress. It must have been a shock, and a huge adjustment. The shame yawned wide inside him, threatening to swallow him whole. He hadn't even said goodbye before he'd fled with the shadow-touched. He'd let a whole year pass —

Malik took two giant steps towards him and clasped him on the shoulder before folding Wilder into a huge bear hug. He didn't say anything, as usual, but the force of his embrace was enough to form a lump in Wilder's throat.

He broke away from his brother, watching as Malik took another step towards Thea, where he touched the top of her head fondly and took up a place behind her. Though Wilder could still see a tremor in his fingers, he seemed to move with more ease than he had done before. Had someone been helping him?

'Malik the Shieldbreaker,' Dratos said, bowing his head. 'An honour to see you again.'

Malik didn't respond, but his mouth twitched upward.

Wilder's brow furrowed at that and he turned to the ranger. 'You've met?'

'A long time ago,' Dratos replied. 'At a wedding you missed.'

Another regret-laced realisation hit Wilder like a blow to the gut. There was only one wedding that Malik would have attended after his injury, only one other person he'd cross the seas for, even if it meant facing a thousand shadow wraiths.

Wilder tilted his head in his brother's direction. 'You went to Naarva for Talemir's wedding? And didn't tell me?' He knew there was no hiding the hurt in his voice, and that it was of his own doing.

Malik just blinked down at him, his grip tightening on the back of Thea's chair.

Just as Wilder was about to say more, the door banged open again and in walked Marise, his arms full of bottles. 'I brought refreshments!' he declared.

'Excellent.' Kipp was already on his feet, moving to help the wine merchant with his wares. 'Good to see you again, Marise. I missed you at the eclipse. It's been too long.'

Wilder's eyes bulged, but beside him Thea shook her head and exchanged a long-suffering look with Cal. 'We should know better by now... Kipp knows everyone, apparently.'

'Well,' Kipp said, looking pleased, 'not everyone. Just the important people.'

'You mean the drunks and rebels?' Anya offered drily from where she sat watching all the exchanges unfold.

Kipp met her gaze, deadly serious. 'Like I said: the important people.'

To Wilder's disbelief, a grin broke out in place of Anya's usual cutthroat expression. 'You and I are going to get along just fine,' she said, the smile making her look almost unhinged.

Kipp only looked more interested. 'Any Zoltaire sister is a friend of mine.'

Anya's brow was lined with amusement. 'Only we're not Zoltaires, are we?'

She paused, as though waiting for the shock to erupt around the room. However, upon Wilder's surveying, he realised that every person within these walls had discovered the existence of the Delmirian heirs at one point or another.

Kipp merely confirmed this with a shrug, sliding the wine Marise had brought across the table. 'All the same,' he told Anya. 'Any sister of Thea's is a friend of mine.'

'Good to know, Fox boy,' Anya replied, her shadows flickering.

To Kipp's credit, he didn't so much as flinch. Instead, his priority was on the refreshments, as always. 'Brought the good stuff, Marise?' he said, filling glasses and handing them around.

Marise scoffed. 'Naturally. Can't have you drinking the piss Everard serves here.'

'I heard that,' came Everard's voice from just outside.

'I'd say it to your face,' Marise retorted, but then shook his head with a grimace at Kipp.

A huff of impatience came from Audra's end of the table.

Thea cleared her throat. 'Can we make a start, or what?'

Wilder bit back a smile. He couldn't quite believe who graced the back room of the Singing Hare. Shadow-touched rangers, a Naarvian guerilla general, lost heirs of Delmira, Warswords, Guardians, alchemists of Thezmarr, a tavern owner, a wine merchant... and Gus, who was knitting silently in the corner. It was a combination the likes of which Wilder had never seen. It was history in the making.

At long last, when everyone was settled around the table, reunions over, drinks in hand, the tone turned serious.

There was a loud scraping noise as Anya pushed her chair back and stood, surveying the strange mix of people before her, her expression back to its usual harsh lines and scowl. 'Some of you only know me as the supposed

Daughter of Darkness, prophesied to bring fire and blood upon the midrealms...'

A scoff sounded somewhere to Wilder's right, and he knew even before looking that it was Audra, as she could never keep her opinions to herself. Sure enough, the librarian was shaking her head. 'Ridiculous,' she muttered, while Farissa nodded her support beside her.

'Agreed,' Anya continued. 'But in fact, I am Anya Embervale, the true heir of the kingdom of Delmira, storm wielder, shadow-touched, and' – she paused to glance down the table – 'eldest sister to Althea and Elwren of Thezmarr.'

The silence was palpable, broken by a single clap.

Kipp's hands froze mid-clap in front of his chest. 'No?' He looked around, shocked. 'I thought that was the moment —'

Thankfully, Cal gave him a violent shove and he sank back into his seat.

Again, that glint of amusement sparked in Anya's eyes, but she brought them back to the introduction at hand. 'I was captured as a child and framed for the assault on Thezmarr many years ago. The midrealms were told that *I* was responsible for the death and destruction of so many, that it was *I* who brought a dawn of fire and blood upon the lands... But despite what you may have heard, I am no evil force spreading darkness across the midrealms. I am no mistress of monsters or tyrannical shadow-lover.'

She paused, scanning the faces before her.

'What I truly am is someone who wants to see the curses banished from these lands, for the truth of our history and our present to be revealed to those who might do something about it.'

'And what is this truth?' Wren's voice cut across the table, her glare like poison upon her eldest sister.

Anya didn't so much as flinch. 'That there is a race of shadow-touched people who bear no ill will to our kingdoms. That they are being targeted and blamed for the acts of another...' Faint shadows flickered at her back as emotion warred across her face. 'That it is King Artos who has had the midrealms under his control since the fall of Delmira long ago. That *he* was responsible for Delmira's demise, alongside that of Naarva, and more recently, the attack on Tver.'

'You have the proof we need?' Audra asked plainly.

'Beyond the word of the shadow-touched themselves? Only fragments,' Anya admitted.

Wilder turned to Audra. 'Thea and I saw a camp on the outskirts of Aveum just a few days past,' he told her. 'Wraiths ran loose, using their darkness to curse innocents into shells of their former selves, into mindless soldiers... At the head of it all was Artos' dungeon master from Harenth.'

'Ignoring the fact that the word of a fallen Warsword isn't a great improvement... He could be acting alone,' Audra pointed out, though her tone suggested she believed no such thing. The fact that *she* had been the one to call the meeting told Wilder she knew much more than she ever let on, and always had.

'It's possible,' Wilder allowed for the sake of argument. 'But we were also present in Harenth when Artos had two shadow-touched folk in his possession. They were tortured for information, even when it was clear they were more human than wraith. It wasn't right, what was happening there.'

'What became of the shadow-touched prisoners?' Gus asked, his needles still clicking together in front of him.

Wilder allowed himself to take a breath to gather his strength. 'I killed them,' he said.

The entire shadow-touched side of the table recoiled.

'It was a mercy,' Thea cut in, her hand covering his. 'One had already succumbed to the darkness. Whether he was cursed or something else, we don't know. But he was too far gone to save. And the other...'

'It's alright, Thea,' Wilder said gently.

'No,' she told him firmly. 'They need to know why.' She faced each shadow-touched at the table. 'The second of your kin was in so much agony, there was no end to it in sight. They meant to torture him to death. Wilder stepped in and offered him peace, an end to the pain. And he took it.'

Torj's voice sounded from the far end of the table. 'That's why you killed the one Cal and I shot from the sky...'

Wilder dipped his head in confirmation.

But Gus' eyes were wide with accusation. 'You're killing shadow-touched folk? You're —' His shadows burst to life around him.

'Easy, cousin,' Dratos warned.

'Easy? You want me to calm down when he's just admitted to murdering our kin —'

'It's not like that,' Thea argued.

But Gus was incensed, his shadows multiplying. Instantly, Cal and Kipp were on their feet, brandishing their swords.

'Stand down,' Cal ordered, his jaw set in determination, even as Gus' shadows whipped around the perimeter of the room.

'No! Not when you talk so casually of —'

'Gus!' Dratos shouted. 'There's an explanation.'

Darkness swelled in answer and a glass shattered.

The group erupted in anger – everyone suddenly on their feet and shouting at one another. Weapons were drawn, more glasses knocked over, shadows surging.

And then a crackling noise filled the air.

Bolts of lightning danced across the tabletop.

'Enough,' Thea commanded, bracing herself on the table's edge.

Some jumped back from the electrical current. Others froze in place, staring in awe.

'Enough,' she said again, her magic pulsing in emphasis.

Everyone's eyes were on her, Wilder's included.

She was formidable.

Slowly, Dratos reached for his younger cousin and pulled him back down into his chair. 'Hawthorne wrote to Anya and me. We knew of this,' he said gently. 'Hawthorne did what he could to end their suffering. I would want the same were I ever in their position. Do you understand?'

The tension ebbed away from the others gradually. Though Wilder's chest ached, he grounded himself with the weight of Thea's hand on his as everyone took a breath and sank back into their seats.

Gus gave his older cousin a hard look. 'We were in that position once. Don't think because I was young, I don't remember,' he said quietly. 'And it was another Warsword who sought to end our lives, too. Thought we weren't worth saving.'

'And he was wrong,' Adrienne retorted with a note of reprimand. 'And that Warsword has fought for us ever since – has defended us, protected us and sought to make the world a safer place. Has he not?'

'You're not shadow-touched,' Gus argued.

Anger flashed in Adrienne's eyes and the youngster had the good sense to baulk. 'You telling me I'm not family to you, Angus Castemont? Are you telling me that I haven't fought for you like I would my own blood?'

A flush of shame crept across his face. 'No,' he murmured.

'Then that's the fucking last we'll hear of that,' she said, shaking her head.

'So much for not cursing...' he had the balls to mutter.

Adrienne rounded on him. 'When you've been the general of a rebel force for several years and you still have to deal with a little shadow brat, then you can curse.'

There was a sigh of frustration as Dratos drained the rest of his cup. 'Told you not to bring him.'

'Don't *even* start me on you,' Adrienne snapped.

'Glad to know the rebels we're potentially allying with are such a happy family,' Torj said.

'Least what you see is what you get, Bear Slayer,' Dratos quipped before saluting Anya with a fresh cup of wine. 'As you were.'

To her credit, Anya didn't miss a beat; she continued her address as though there hadn't been a familial spat midway through. 'If you take our word and the word of your Warsword, and you believe that Artos is behind the poison running through the midrealms, then the next thing to question is: *what does he want?*'

'What he's always wanted,' Audra offered. 'To unite the kingdoms under a single banner – his. And rule over the festering leftovers.'

'Something like that,' Anya agreed. 'With the resources he's put into "saving" Tver and helping with the rebuild of the castle, he's already got it quite firmly in his grasp, whether King Leiko knows it or not. Aveum is clearly his next mark, judging from the camps we've seen in its underbelly. And now that Queen Reyna is in mourning, the kingdom is more vulnerable than ever.'

'Will your kind take responsibility for the arachne attack?' Torj asked, teeth gritted.

'It wasn't us,' Anya said coldly. 'We are not to blame for every evil that spills into these lands. It was a diversion, created by Artos and his lackeys. There was something he wanted beyond the domes... Wasn't there?'

Torj had the decency to flush. 'While Vios was in disarray, reapers sent a unit of wraiths and howlers to the Pools of Purity. They attacked.'

Gasps and murmurs broke out across the room.

'What are the Pools of Purity?' Gus asked, brow furrowed.

'They're the source of the healing Aveum springwater,' Wilder explained. 'The same water Warswords are gifted a vial of after they've passed the Great Rite.'

Gus' eyes widened.

'The damage?' Anya's voice was devoid of emotion.

'The Thezmarrian Guardians stationed there were able to defeat them, but the extent of the harm to the pools themselves is still unconfirmed,' Torj reported. 'There's no doubt in my mind that some will have certainly been tainted, and that the reapers will send reinforcements. It won't be the last time they attack.'

'Do we know *how* they were tainted? With what substance?' Wren's soft voice sounded out of place amid the harsh words of war, but her questions settled over the group like a blanket.

'We assumed some sort of shadow magic,' Torj replied with an apologetic grimace. 'The same poison they've been using to corrupt men into howlers, and infect other monsters with darkness. Why?'

Wren looked distant for a moment. 'So it could be a different poison entirely?'

Torj frowned. 'It could, but...'

Wren glanced across the table to Kipp, who seemed to be the only one whose mind was working in tandem with hers. He nodded in realisation.

'When a Guardian becomes a Warsword...' Wren ventured slowly, as though the ideas were still forming as she spoke. 'Each of the kingdoms bestows a gift, yes?'

'Yes,' Torj confirmed.

'Harenth's gift is poison, correct?'

The Bear Slayer gave a shrug. 'Yes, but that's hardly —'

'What does the poison do?' she cut him off.

Torj's brows shot up. His hand went to his pocket and he pulled out a small vial, placing it on the table before him with a perplexed expression. 'I don't actually know,' he murmured. 'I've never used it.' He looked to Wilder. 'Hawthorne?'

Wilder tensed. 'Lost mine when I was taken prisoner. I'd never used it either.'

'You both *never* used them?' Wren said, clearly baffled. 'Have you seen any other Warswords use them over the years?'

Torj's cheeks tipped pink then. 'No... Not now you mention it.'

'Why is that, do you think? Surely it would have come in handy at some point in history?' Wren pressed, raising a brow as though she had her suspicions.

'Uhh...'

*Don't say it, you fool.* But Wilder knew he couldn't save Torj from himself.

'I suppose there's a feeling among Warswords... Why use poison when you can end a man with your blade or your hammer or your fists? It's just that... Well, poison... It's a woman's weapon.'

Beside Wilder, Thea shook her head with disdain. 'Idiot,' she muttered, only loud enough for Wilder to hear.

Wren gave a derisive laugh. 'You're telling me that in all the years of Warswords fighting for the midrealms, none of you know what sort of poison Harenth gifts those blessed by the Furies?'

Torj looked as sheepish as Wilder felt when he answered: 'Uh... none of us here.'

'As much as I enjoy watching warriors squirm at the questioning of our alchemists,' Audra mused, 'perhaps you can get to the point, Elwren?'

Wren nodded. 'My point is that if we could link the poison gifted to the Warswords from Harenth to whatever is tainting the Pools of Purity, then you'd have your proof about Artos.'

'Or another Warsword,' Adrienne added. 'There's one of you who's not here, yes? The one with a reputation for cruelty and malice...'

Wilder groaned. 'Not this again. Vernich is a bastard, to be sure, but he's no fallen Warsword.'

Adrienne considered him. 'Then where is he? Why haven't you rallied him to our side? No doubt we could use someone called the Bloodletter.'

Raking his fingers through his hair, Wilder grimaced. 'Vernich has always been difficult. Unpredictable.'

'So you can't trust him?'

'I would hesitate to divulge the intricate plans of a rebellion to him, yes,' Wilder admitted. 'But he's not aligned with the reapers. That much I'm sure of.'

'If you say so.' Anya didn't look convinced. 'Which means we come back to Artos, then. He caused the diversion *and* had his lackeys infect the pools.'

Silence followed. Several people shifted in their seats, while Kipp nodded enthusiastically at the far end of the table.

'Why would they not just use shadows, then?' Dratos blurted, ribbons of darkness flickering at his back.

Anya sighed. 'I'm not sure. But Thea and Hawthorne said they felt empath magic at the prisoner camp... It seems unlikely to me that if Artos is behind it all, he'd leave everything in the control of others.'

'How do we find out what the poison is, then?' Cal asked.

Torj's chair groaned beneath him as he leant forward and slid the vial across to Wren. 'It's yours.'

Wilder noticed the slight shake of Wren's fingers as they closed around the vial.

'I may not be able to give it back when I'm done,' she said.

'I'm sure you can do whatever you put your mind to,' Torj replied. 'But if that's the case, so be it. Serves me right for not questioning it before.'

Audra took control of the meeting. 'So, it's settled. Elwren will investigate the poison and report back if it's anything we can use to prove Artos' part in all this.'

Wren looked to Farissa, her mentor, for approval before giving Audra a nod.

'Good,' the librarian said before motioning for Anya to continue.

Anya's gaze shifted from Wren to Dratos. 'You'll have one of our shadow-touched see if they can find out more at the source, yes?'

Dratos made to stand. 'I can go myself.'

But Anya stopped him with a subtle wave of her hand. 'You're needed here.'

He hesitated briefly, but sat back down with a nod.

Before the shocked quiet could sink into the room, Anya ploughed on. 'We know that Artos is slowly making his way across the midrealms, attempting to curse its people and devour its lands with darkness. We've all witnessed the fading daylight, the tears in the Veil and the barren forests. Reports from the other kingdoms share similar findings. Rivers are turning brown. Crops are wilting on the vines, buds are no longer blooming... The world festers with each passing day, with more monsters encroaching than ever before – many of them cursed with the same blight of the wraiths and reapers.'

'I'm assuming you have a broader proposal for us? A plan of attack?' Thea asked. Wilder noticed that she hadn't touched her wine; she had been watching the conversations unfold intently, her hand still covering his.

Anya nodded. 'Adrienne?'

Adrienne stood, wearing the same hardy expression Wilder had seen several times during his time in Naarva, whenever she spoke to her rangers.

'First,' she started, her voice clear and confident, 'the midrealms need to be made aware of what's happening. Artos can't hold the wool over their eyes forever, and they need to pick a side... Light or dark, men or monsters.'

Dratos made a noise at the back of his throat. 'I resent that.'

Adrienne rolled her eyes. 'You know what I mean. The remaining kingdoms need to be united against Artos and his host of reapers, wraiths and cursed creatures. Yes?'

'Yes,' several voices sounded.

'Good,' she said. 'Thezmarr also needs to be united against him. We need the Guardians, the shieldbearers, and most of all... we need your alchemists.'

*What?* Wilder twisted in his chair to look at Wren and Farissa. Both women sat with their shoulders back and their hands clasped neatly before them, completely calm. Wilder supposed he shouldn't be surprised, given what Thea had told him about her sister's talents – he'd seen them in action himself on occasion. But alchemy? To face an army of monsters?

'Audra told us we would be needed,' Farissa said, her voice smooth. 'We're listening.'

Adrienne bowed her head in respect. 'And we are grateful to you. We have reason to believe that your particular skillset will serve us well in Naarva —'

'Naarva?' Thea demanded. 'You want to send Wren to Naarva?'

'And the Alchemy Master, yes,' Adrienne replied patiently. 'We have been working on a substance over there that could turn the tides of a war against the reapers and their kin.'

'We have already created an alchemic gas to patch the Veil, though we've had very few chances to test it... What kind of substance do you speak of?' Wren's curiosity was clearly piqued.

'We do not talk of it outside of our safe houses, but know that it is heavily guarded and protected by the most powerful of our kind.'

Wren stared at Adrienne. 'So, you expect us to turn our backs on Thezmarr, become known traitors to the midrealms, and go with you willingly to a fallen kingdom to meddle with some substance we know nothing about?'

'Sounds like your dream come true,' Wilder heard Thea mutter to her sister, who shot her a disapproving look.

'I'll give you more specifics after this meeting,' Adrienne reassured them. 'But as for the rest of us, the tasks are clear. Anya and Dratos are to gather the shadow-touched folk into a unified fighting force. I will be gathering intel and doing what I can to free prisoners from the shadow camps we've mentioned. We need a party to go to Tver to speak with King Leiko; we need another to convince Queen Reyna of Artos' treachery. And we need more to cut out the rot at Thezmarr and install fair rule there.'

'Is that all?' Cal mumbled.

Adrienne ignored him. 'There's one more thing. Audra... you may have called this meeting, but there's something you're not sharing —'

The librarian looked up, leaning back in her chair and resting her hands on what she insisted were *ceremonial* daggers. 'What?'

'Word has it that you know someone who knows where the women Guardians of Thezmarr fled twenty years ago.'

'Don't know where you heard that.'

'I don't recall,' Adrienne said. 'However, were that possible, I'd encourage you to get in contact with that person, and seek them out.'

'I don't know what you're talking about,' Audra said coldly.

'Naturally,' Adrienne allowed. 'But all the same.'

Farissa raised her hand – which, from the look on Adrienne's face, she found both amusing and disconcerting.

'Yes?' the ranger asked.

'I was wondering what you propose regarding the Delmirian heirs?'

Wilder felt Thea tense beside him.

But Farissa ploughed ahead. 'One is currently apprenticed to me, another to a supposedly fallen Warsword of Thezmarr...' She eyed Wilder sardonically. 'And the other is a half-wraith, which is far from ideal, given the royal family's previous reputation. What is your plan of action?'

Thea jutted her chin at Anya. 'She's the oldest. She's the heir.'

But Wren interjected. 'She's a shadow wraith. No citizen of the midrealms will accept her as a ruler, even of a fallen kingdom.' She spoke harshly, several of the Naarvians flinching at her words.

'First,' Anya addressed her coolly, 'we prefer to be called shadow-touched. Second, I don't see how any royal announcements would impact our battle plans. No one is rallying to our cause based on the Embervale name, I assure you.'

'They might if they knew the truth,' Audra said, twirling one of her daggers between her fingers. 'That your mother and father weren't responsible for the darkness that descended upon Delmira.'

'And how do we prove that? All we have is my word,' Anya said bitterly. 'The word of a shadow wraith, as my dear little sister put it, works against us entirely. And our mere existence doesn't prove Artos' treachery. Storm-wielding heirs aside, as far as the midrealms know, the Embervale family brought about the destruction of their own kingdom.'

'What about the letters?' Thea asked. 'Between our mother and the Queen of Naarva?'

Anya shook her head. 'Anyone can forge a letter.'

'So, you find someone who knows the truth —'

'Anyone alive who knows such a thing will never come forward, not now. We have to find another way.'

'What does it matter?' Thea said.

Wren made a noise of agreement. 'Can Delmira even be saved? It's nothing but rubble and ruin.'

'It's been done before,' Torj murmured from across the table. 'I know of a kingdom like it that came back from destruction.'

Noting the conflicting emotions warring on the Embervale sisters' faces, Wilder cleared his throat. 'Perhaps we should prioritise the preservation of the kingdoms that are still standing first.'

It was Kipp, as always, who broke the tension. 'Judging from the location of today's meeting, I'll assume we still wish for a degree of discretion as we go about these important tasks?'

There was a murmur of agreement and several nods around the room.

'Then myself, Marise and Everard have means of passage, some of which you have uncovered, much of which you know nothing about.'

Thea leant close to Wilder. 'Is he some sort of cross-kingdom bootlegger as well?'

Wilder huffed a laugh. 'I think there's a high chance of that.'

The Son of the Fox motioned for Marise and Everard to join him. 'Once you know who is going where, come to us and we'll find you safe passage, under the noses of those who hunt you,' he told the rebels, the cheeky glint gone from his eyes.

Wilder gave Thea's hand a squeeze before he got to his feet, unable to stand the stillness any longer. 'Kipp makes a good point... Who decides on everyone's missions, should anyone here actually be willing?' he asked.

Adrienne smiled. 'That's the beauty of it,' she replied. 'You do. All of you.'

# CHAPTER THIRTY-FIVE

## THEA

Anya took over from Adrienne and informed them that they were to think on the tasks at hand and reconvene to assign missions come the dawn. But as heated chatter broke out around the room, a wave of dizziness washed over Thea. She was glad she was still seated, needing to steady herself against the edge of the table, needing to breathe through her nose as the odd sensation passed. Perhaps she shouldn't have called upon her power so suddenly earlier. She needed to get used to it again...

Wilder glanced at her, his brows knitted together in concern. He didn't miss a thing, it seemed. But she gave him a reassuring smile. It wasn't surprising she was a tad out of sorts, not when she'd had next to no sleep – thanks to him – and her magic was once more flickering in her veins. She hadn't had a moment to process its return, nor had she had the time to test its strength or her control over it. But even the thought of her power had it crackling within.

With magic on her mind, Thea looked to Wren, but her

sister's attention had fallen elsewhere: to scrutinising Anya from across the table, her lip curled slightly.

She leant close to Thea. 'Am I honestly meant to believe that we're all on the same side now?'

Thea sighed, that unsettling dizziness tugging at her again. 'She showed me, Wren... What she went through before she was taken from us for all these years. I'm sure she'll show you too —'

'I don't want to see anything. She held me hostage a year ago, Thee. You know how many nightmares I've had where I see her face? Where I feel her shadows pinning me in place?'

Thea rubbed her temples. While she was thrilled to see her sister, she hadn't had nearly enough sleep to deal with *two* of them at odds with one another. It was a strange place to be, for Thea was usually the one causing the trouble... The thought trailed off in her head as she realised Wren was staring at her.

'What?'

'You didn't tell me it had returned. Your magic...' Wren ventured.

Thea huffed a laugh. 'It's a very new development.'

'That was quite a display before.'

'Someone needed to shut them up,' Thea replied.

Wren scanned her from head to toe, and then paused, as though she were concentrating on the exact thread of power she sensed between them. 'It's stronger, Thea,' she said. 'At first I thought it was...' She jutted her chin towards Anya. 'But no. It's you, very distinctly *you*. I can feel you in the air around me, in my magic too...'

To Thea's despair, Anya chose that moment to approach them. 'If it isn't my long-lost sisters.' Her hands were held out as though she were about to embrace them, but she stopped short. 'Hello, Elwren.'

'You certainly haven't acted like a sister,' Wren replied, not yielding a step, not stepping forward either.

Sorrow lined Anya's face. 'I'm sorry for how we met. It was the only way at the time. I regret it —'

'Your regrets mean nothing to me.'

Thea winced at her harsh words, reminding her of her own recent failings. She had learned the price of making snap judgements and holding the wrong grudges. She didn't want Wren to make the same mistake.

And then, Thea saw it: fear. Wren had been terrified in those moments of shadow amid the battle of Notos, bound with ropes of darkness, not knowing what horrors were to come.

And Anya – her expression warred between desperation and anger, for she had never asked for the hand fate had dealt her. While Wren and Thea had grown up in the confines of Thezmarr, and had certainly not always been the best of friends, they'd always had each other. They had braided each other's hair and shared their secrets. Anya had grown up in the dark, with monsters for company.

'Wren,' Thea heard herself say, placing a gentle hand on her arm.

Wren's cheeks flushed and her eyes widened in surprise at Thea's interference.

'Please,' Thea said. 'Give her a chance.'

Anya stilled, and though her expression remained unreadable, Thea guessed she'd taken her by surprise as well.

The Daughter of Darkness softened momentarily as she met Wren's fiery gaze. 'Hear me out, please. We can talk somewhere quiet. And then you can keep hating me all you want if you wish.'

Wren sought Thea's gaze and Thea gave her a nod. As she watched them leave the main room, Anya glanced back, mouthing *thank you*.

With her sisters – it still felt strange to think it – working out their differences, Thea returned her attention to the bustling room. Cal and Kipp were in deep discussions with Marise and Everard. Several maps had been produced and spread across the end of the table, already covered in ringed wine stains, to no one's surprise. Dratos and Adrienne were leaning down and talking to a sulking Gus, whose knitting had been confiscated. Thea wondered what he'd meant when he'd broached the topic of a Warsword trying to kill them as Wilder had killed those prisoners.

Wilder himself had sought out his brother. The two giant warriors looked out of place standing next to the average-sized hearth and mantle. Dax was sitting stoically at Malik's feet as Wilder talked in a hushed voice to his brother, his expression strained. She could see the pain in his eyes, but Malik's expression remained distant.

'You seem well,' came a familiar voice.

'Audra,' Thea said before she'd fully turned around.

The librarian of Thezmarr looked as she always did: stern and rigid, with the piercing eyes of someone who knew a million things she shouldn't.

'An interesting year you've had, Althea,' Audra noted, looking around at the strange network that had gathered.

'That's one word for it.'

'And yet here you stand... I trust my words weren't wasted on you when we rode the Mourner's Trail together?'

Thea blinked at her, recalling that surreal journey she'd

taken with her once-warden. '*If you seek power in a world of men and monsters, there is nothing more powerful than knowledge...*' Thea trailed off.

'And the ability to wield it,' Audra finished.

'Do you have any knowledge for me to wield, then, Audra?' Thea asked boldly.

'More than my lifetime's worth,' the librarian told her cryptically. 'But there is only one thing I want you to take from me today...' She produced one of the daggers from her belt and handed it to Thea. 'It's a loan, of course,' she cautioned.

The dagger was tiny compared to her Naarvian steel blade from Malik, but the significance wasn't lost on her, not for a second. She tried to pass the weapon back. 'Audra, I can't take this —'

Audra refused it. 'But you will. There will come a time when you will need it, and we will need you.'

'I...' Thea didn't know why she was arguing; her whole life she'd been trying to argue with her warden to no avail.

She nearly staggered back at the sight of Audra *smiling*.

'Remember what I told you?' Audra prompted. 'That the smallest blade can make the biggest difference.' Then the older woman slipped away, leaving Thea staring after her, still holding the jewelled dagger.

'Is she still insisting they're for show?' Torj asked, nodding to the weapon gleaming in her grasp as he topped up her wine.

'I think the days of her holding up that pretence are long gone,' Thea murmured, still dazed.

Torj chuckled. 'No one ever believed her anyway.'

'Not that she cared.' Thea couldn't keep the note of

admiration from her voice. 'Do you think she'll find out where the former women warriors of the guild are?'

'Find out?' The Bear Slayer laughed. 'Thea... Audra's known exactly where they went since the day they left.'

'But...'

'But what? Osiris interrogated her? Threatened her? For years and years? Surely you know Audra's as tough as they come. She never broke. She never will, if you ask me —'

Torj tensed suddenly at her side, and Thea saw why.

Wren had reappeared in the doorway, her eyes red and puffy. Thea made an instant move towards her sister, but Torj's gentle hand on her shoulder stopped her.

'Allow me,' he said softly. Without waiting for her answer, he went to Wren, his huge frame enveloping her, leading her away from the commotion and out of sight.

Thea smiled to herself. *Funny, how things turn out.*

As the evening wore on, in the rare moments where she was not engaged in any conversation, Thea took in the scene around her. She watched the Daughter of Darkness salute the wine merchant, and the general of the Naarvian guerilla forces clap Cal on the back. She saw Dratos the Dawnless project ribbons of shadow across the room, and she saw Malik smile as Dax tried to catch them. Thea realised what she was truly seeing – the possibility of a world that she had never dared to imagine... The start of something fair, equal and unmistakably good.

The wine and talk flowed, and at some point Kipp declared that the great drinkers and thinkers of the midrealms had come together. Were it not for his drunken lean and the slight slur to his words, Thea might have agreed with him.

A warm, towering presence came to her side, wrapping her in the familiar scent of rosewood and leather, of home.

'Take me to bed,' Thea murmured to Wilder.

He leant down, close enough that his lips brushed the shell of her ear. 'The day I say no to that is the day I've lost my mind.'

'Then what are you waiting for, Warsword?'

They made no excuses and said no goodbyes as they slipped away from the raucous night that had unfolded around them. Thea glanced back, a smile on her lips. There would be several sore heads in the morning when they reconvened to solidify their plans, but... an ember of hope flared within her. It was certainly not the group of disciplined, ruthless warriors of Thezmarr she'd always imagined fighting alongside.

It was better.

As she and Wilder climbed the stairs to their room, she asked, 'Is there a particular task that you want to volunteer for tomorrow?'

He fitted the key to the lock on their door and ushered them both inside. As soon as the door was closed behind them, he had her up against it, his mouth hot and insistent on hers before he broke away, peering into her face.

'I don't give a fuck where I go, so long as it's with you.'

Thea loosed a breath.

'You good with that, Princess?' His eyes took on that dark smoulder that made her toes curl and his hand dropped from her nape, down to her chest, where he put his hand over her racing heart.

'I'm good with that,' she told him, covering his hand with hers. She stared at their fingers lacing through each other's, his large, calloused palm turning to greet her own small, scar-littered hand.

Then she shifted onto her tip-toes and kissed him, hard and wanting. A noise of pleasure escaped her as he opened his mouth to her and brushed his tongue against hers while his body crowded her against the door.

She wanted him everywhere.

And Wilder Hawthorne obliged her.

# CHAPTER THIRTY-SIX

## THEA

Wilder had wrought so much pleasure upon her that Thea thought she might die. There was a delicious wickedness to her Warsword when he was completely unleashed, uninhibited. The things he could do with his fingers, his mouth, his cock... Yet despite the countless climaxes he'd wrung from her trembling body, despite the steady rise and fall of his broad chest beside her, Thea couldn't sleep.

Whether it was the return of her magic or the thoughts of the war to come keeping her awake, she didn't know. But she felt restless, far more alert than she had any right to, and her skin was crawling, like she needed to move.

For a while, she watched Wilder sleep in the golden glow of the dying fire. She studied the lines of his beautiful naked body, the hard muscle sculpted by years of training and fighting, the scars he wore like badges of honour... His fierce expression was softened in sleep, a side of him she knew not many were lucky enough to witness.

When she had memorised every scar, every freckle, every

line that graced his sun-kissed skin, Thea slipped from the bed, unable to quell the unrest within, her feet practically itching to move.

She dressed in silence, congratulating herself that she was still stealthy enough to get ready without disturbing the mighty warrior in her bed. As she left the room, closing the door with a quiet click behind her, the restlessness in her body eased, ever so slightly.

*Nervous energy*, she told herself, making her way downstairs.

It must have been the very early hours of the morning. In the tavern, the chairs and stools were placed upside down on the tables, the notes of lutes and fiddles long gone. Folding her arms over her chest against the faint chill of the open space, Thea wove between the furniture, hearing the faint tinkle of glasses beyond.

In the heart of the tavern, a fire still crackled in the main hearth, and she found a smaller group gathered around the bar, talking softly with one another. Anya, Dratos and Marise sat on stools, while Everard stood behind the bar, drying tankards with a rag.

'Couldn't sleep?' Anya asked, pulling out a stool for her.

Thea shook her head. 'You?'

'Don't sleep much in general,' Anya replied.

Thea sat down, though she couldn't sit still completely, her knee bouncing beneath the bar.

Marise pushed three bottles towards her. 'What will it be?'

Thea passed a hand over her face. 'There isn't any tea, by chance?'

Everard laughed. 'I've never known someone to come to the Singing Hare and ask for tea...'

'First time for everything,' Dratos drawled.

Everard shrugged. 'Indeed.'

'I could use a cup myself,' Anya declared. 'Got any peppermint?'

Thea did a double take.

'What?' Anya asked with a frown.

Thea suppressed a smile, watching Everard go about setting the pot of water over the stove. 'Make it two, please,' she said.

Anya gave her a strange look, before her gaze dropped to the fate stone that had slipped from the folds of Thea's shirt.

'You gonna ask me about it?' Thea prompted her, taking the piece of jade between her fingers and rubbing her thumb along its edges.

'I don't think I want to... Those things never did anyone any good.' Anya turned back to Dratos. 'When are you gonna ease up on Gus, eh?'

Glad for the change of subject, Thea tucked her fate stone away and wrung her hands, still feeling that creeping sensation along her skin, her stomach fluttering strangely.

Dratos gave a groan. 'When are you gonna ease up on *me?*' he griped. 'I've been watching over that kid since he was trying to eat mud. And after what he said to Adrienne... He deserves a fucking hiding.'

'She still upset?' Anya asked, her voice softening.

'She'll be fine.'

'Not what I asked.'

Dratos rolled his eyes and gave Thea a pitying look. 'You'll never be free of this shit now.'

Thea stopped her hand from going to her fate stone again. Her limited time left in the midrealms flashed before her, each day, each month passing by like a grain through an hourglass.

She said none of that. Instead, she told the shadow-touched ranger, 'It doesn't seem so bad. A bunch of people caring about one another.'

He scoffed. 'You'll be singing a different tune after a few more weeks with this lot.'

Thea laughed, and gratefully accepted the steaming mug of peppermint tea Everard set down before her. 'What happened to Cal and Kipp?' she asked Marise and the tavern owner, whom she'd last seen with her friends.

'Drunk and Drunker? Ah, they left our party a while after midnight in search of finer company,' Marise told her. 'I believe one had more luck than the other, if you catch my meaning.'

Thea snorted. 'Kipp does seem to have a surprising effect on women.'

Everard snorted. 'Not him, the other. The Flaming Arrow, or so their countless toasts called him.'

Thea blinked. 'Cal?'

'That's the one. The archer. Saw him sneaking off with a lass a few hours ago.'

A laugh bubbled out of Thea, and she wished she could have seen the look on Kipp's face as Cal at long last won the girl. She shook her head with a grin. 'Good for him.'

'He had the right idea,' Dratos complained. 'I made the mistake of choosing to drink with you sorry lot.'

Anya made a choking noise, tea slopping over the side of her cup. 'Like that was a choice. I didn't see any women lining up to —'

Dratos spread his wings in a flash of red. 'Didn't think

you wanted me to show the good people of the Singing Hare
these beauties.'

'When's that ever stopped you?'

Thea sipped her tea, watching the verbal sparring match
with amusement. But no matter how entertained she felt, the
strange sensation within was still bothering her, her feet still
kicking beneath the stool. Was she so unfamiliar with her
own magic now that it made her want to crawl out of her
own skin?

Thea didn't know how many minutes or hours she
passed sitting at the bar. She must have retreated into herself
for a moment, because when she refocused on her
companions, they were in a heated debate about who should
escort the alchemists to Naarva, should they agree to it.

'How did your talk with Wren go?' Thea asked Anya,
suddenly remembering her younger sister's red-rimmed
eyes and how the Bear Slayer had swept her away.

Anya stiffened. 'As well as could be expected.'

'You upset her,' Thea ventured.

'My *life* upset her,' Anya corrected. 'It was no easy thing
to see, as you know. No less an easy thing to show.'

Thea bowed her head, recalling the horrifying details the
Daughter of Darkness had shared with her only days ago.
'She needs time...'

'Time we do not have,' Anya said. 'But I spoke with the
Master Alchemist... She helped one of our own long ago, or
tried to, in any case. She knows a lot about the Veil, about its
make-up, its strengths and weaknesses. She might see
reason.'

'And if she doesn't?'

Dratos looked as though he were about to say something

brash, but his eyes widened at someone's approach and he shut his mouth.

A warm, muscular arm banded around Thea's chest from behind, a familiar scent engulfing her senses.

'Don't like waking up with you not in my bed,' Wilder's gruff voice rumbled against her hair.

Thea twisted in her seat, finding him deliciously dishevelled, his dark hair ruffled, his shirt only half buttoned, as though he'd felt her absence and come searching without fully waking.

But then his mouth closed over hers, capturing her lips in a deep, decadent kiss. He kissed her slowly, thoroughly, in front of everyone.

Someone whistled loudly. 'Wasn't long ago you were trying to kill the bastard,' Dratos said as they broke apart. 'My, how the tides of fate have turned...'

Anya cleared her throat on the stool beside Thea. 'The tides of fate are as they always intended,' she said quietly. 'I'm going to wake the others. It's nearly dawn.'

Dratos groaned and rested his head on the counter, covering his eyes, while Marise and Everard topped up their glasses with an amber liquid and toasted to the drinkers and thinkers of the midrealms for the fiftieth time. Thea didn't know how the pair were still standing. They could certainly give Kipp a run for his coin.

With his arm still around her, Wilder reached for her mug, taking a sip of the lukewarm tea and making a face. 'Don't know how you drink this grass water.'

Thea frowned. 'What are you talking about? You drink it all the time.'

Wilder huffed a laugh. 'Never.'

'But you always have it in your saddlebag. You had it at the cabin.'

He rested his chin on her shoulder and pushed the mug away. 'Who'd you think it was for?' He kissed her neck gently. 'You told me on our first journey together that it was your favourite. I only had it for medicinal purposes. I kept getting it because of you. I hate the stuff.'

Warmth bloomed in Thea at the thought of her burly Warsword buying peppermint tea for her and her alone.

The sweet, quiet moment was interrupted all too soon with the arrival of almost everyone from the meeting last night, all of them looking slightly worse for wear. Though Thea noted that Cal wore a sheepishly pleased expression on his tired face.

The noise was instant, and suddenly they were surrounded by everyone helping themselves to drinks over the bar. Apparently after Thea and Wilder had left, a serve-yourself mentality had been adopted by the group.

'We should have stayed in bed,' Wilder grumbled, reluctantly releasing her and finding his own stool to perch on. Thea was surprised the seat could accommodate the sheer size of him.

'Should we move to the private room?' Adrienne's voice sounded from the other side of the bar. She was tying her thick blonde hair up and out of her face, dark circles shadowing her eyes.

Everard waved her off. 'No need. The Singing Hare doesn't open to the public until noon.'

'Is there food?' Kipp said, stumbling in, his auburn hair like a bird's nest atop his head.

'There is if you cook it,' Everard replied, his brows raised in apprehension.

Torj strode into the room with an armful of firewood and fed it to the flickering flames. 'This might be the last hot meal a lot of us have for a while. Let's not fuck it up by getting Kipp or Cal to make it. Show me where the kitchen is, Ev.'

At this, Dratos snorted. 'I've had meals cooked by Warswords, and I'm not sure the rest of us have the same love for salt. I'll supervise.'

The main part of the tavern became a hive of bustling activity. Breakfast was being cooked by the unlikely duo of a Warsword and a shadow-touched Naarvian ranger, while chairs and tables were set up by Cal, Kipp and Gus, who'd managed to part with his knitting temporarily.

Thea and Wilder helped Marise and Everard fetch more firewood from the storehouse outside. The icy wind churned that restlessness back up inside her; it had been temporarily quelled by the busyness of the tavern. She breathed in the crisp winter air and longed to take a step towards the woods, despite the kindling bundled in her arms.

'Thea?' Wilder said from the door.

Her gaze snapped back to him. He looked every bit the warrior with a cloak of grey furs around his shoulders, his eyes as sharp as steel.

'Coming,' she told him, with a final glance at the whispering frost-kissed woods.

At last, the unusual party settled around a long table, several trays of steaming food laid out before them, Kipp already digging a big spoon into a pile of scrambled eggs. As hungry as she knew she should be, Thea felt nothing but the insistent nagging sensation that she needed to move.

*Fucking magic,* she cursed silently.

As everyone served themselves and started eating, Anya stood at the head of the table. To Thea's surprise, Wren sat beside her.

'Today's the day we make hard choices,' Anya told them. 'By the end of this meal, I want everyone to know exactly what they're doing and where they're going. Remember the missions we discussed last night – if you can,' she added with a pointed glance at Kipp, Marise and Everard. 'Think about your strengths and where you might be best suited to serve the midrealms. Talk to each other. Discuss your options. Then we'll finalise the details.'

Chatter broke out once more across the table and Thea couldn't help but admire the command her long-lost sister had not only over those she knew, but those who had been strangers, adversaries even, only a night ago.

*Beware the fury of a patient Delmirian.*

As the words came back to her this time, Thea looked across at Malik, who was staring into the fire. He had known, even all those years ago, who Anya was, and what she was capable of.

'You're not eating,' Wilder murmured, glancing at her untouched plate.

Thea pushed around a strip of bacon with her fork, her toes tapping the floor. 'I can't.'

Wilder gave her a pointed look and she sighed, shovelling food into her mouth.

'You're insufferable,' she mumbled.

That earnt her a hint of a smile.

As the meal continued, Thea listened to the various conversations at play about who should go where and why. Kipp, as usual, was at the centre of all things strategy, and she felt reassured by his cool head, in spite of his hungover appearance.

Torj was insisting that he take the alchemists to Naarva, but Kipp was shaking his head. 'We need someone we trust at Thezmarr. Who better than a Warsword to shed light on the truth of what we've learnt here? We need the fortress onside. It's a stronghold we cannot afford to lose, particularly with its proximity to the Veil.'

'Esyllt remains at Thezmarr. If he can be convinced, he can be trusted,' Torj countered. 'If the alchemists are as vital as Anya says —'

'They are,' Anya chimed in.

'Then they'll need a worthy protector,' Torj argued.

'And they shall have one,' Dratos replied. 'I'll escort them. I'm a seasoned warrior, and I know Naarva like the back of my own hand.'

'But —'

Thea turned to Wilder. 'What makes the most sense for us?'

'You don't want to tell me?' he said, amused.

'My first instinct was to go to the rulers,' she told him slowly. 'But I'm not sure they'll take kindly to your presence after the lies they've been fed.'

'Alternative?' he prompted.

She thought aloud. 'Rally the Guardians dispersed across the midrealms into a unified force?'

'Might encounter the same problem...'

Thea sighed. 'Perhaps the search for proof of Artos' treachery? At least we could do that in the shadows.'

Wilder glanced at Anya, who was in deep conversation with Audra, Wren listening intently as well. 'I don't think we'll be keeping to the shadows this time, Princess.'

Suddenly, Thea was on her feet, unable to remember making the decision to stand. Her chair scraped across the floor as she left the table, the room falling silent around her.

Wilder was at her side instantly, cupping her face in his large hands. 'What is it?'

'I have to leave,' she insisted. The restlessness that had been simmering since the night before had grown all too much, utterly unbearable if she remained still. She surged for the door.

Wilder blocked it. 'What's happening, Thea?' he asked, voice calm, but silver eyes aflame.

She paced erratically. 'My magic,' she murmured. 'I'm not used to it. It's tugging at me from inside, making me feel...'

Wilder's hands came down on her shoulders this time, stilling her body but only fuelling her desire to move.

'Tell me exactly what you feel,' he commanded, his voice resonant with authority as he lifted her chin, forcing her gaze to meet his. 'Look at me, Thea. Tell me.'

Thea took a trembling breath. 'It feels like I'm in the wrong place. It feels like something is pulling me away from here, like I should be somewhere else. Outside, somewhere.' She looked at him, not bothering to hide her fear, her panic. 'My magic... It's out of control, isn't it?'

For a moment she couldn't understand the expression that passed over her Warsword's face. Pain and pride, longing and fear, all in one beautiful, intense stare. He rested his forehead against hers for a moment.

'That's magic, alright,' he said at last. 'But it's not yours.'

He took a deep breath of his own, as though he were steeling himself for what was to come.

'It's the magic of the Furies. What you're feeling, Thea, is the call to the Great Rite.'

# CHAPTER THIRTY-SEVEN

## WILDER

Complete and utter silence descended on the tavern and Wilder watched Thea's face change as the piece of the puzzle fell into place.

'The Great Rite,' she murmured, a note of disbelief lingering in her voice.

'Yes,' he told her, fighting to keep his own voice steady, to keep his terror at bay.

Wide-eyed, she looked to the table of rebels behind him. 'This can't be happening now. The war, the —'

'It's happening.' Wilder remembered the feeling vividly, noting the shock, the fear and, slowly, the determination wash over his apprentice. 'A storm-wielding Warsword is exactly what this fight needs.'

He looked to Anya in challenge, expecting her to object, to argue that a storm-wielding Guardian was better than a dead would-be Warsword. But to his surprise, she dipped her head in agreement.

'Thea's path is clear.' The Daughter of Darkness touched

three fingers to her left shoulder, as many did to show respect to a Warsword.

'Then so is mine,' Wilder said.

Thea's attention snapped back to him. 'You can't —'

'I'll escort you there, wherever it opens for you. As my mentor did for me,' he told her, no ounce of compromise in his voice, which he was still struggling to keep calm and even. But she need not know that.

'Fuck...' Kipp managed as he got to his feet, shaking his head in shock before squeezing between Wilder and Thea, wrapping his long arms around his friend. 'Always knew you'd be first.'

'Did you?' Thea murmured.

Kipp looked pale to Wilder, and for that, Wilder couldn't blame him, but the Guardian made a good show of plastering on his usual grin. 'Course I did. You're basically a Warsword already, Shadow of Death.'

Thea broke away from Kipp and Cal swooped in next.

'You've got this, Thea,' he told her.

'Thanks,' she said, a flush blossoming across her cheeks.

Wilder watched as Adrienne stood up and approached Thea, her expression hard, determined. She grasped Thea's hand in hers, holding onto it as she spoke. 'My friend and I have parted many times over the years to face unimaginable perils... and we always survive, always find our way back to each other. So, I'll say to you now, Althea Embervale, luck be with you, but you don't need it. You're the warrior I knew was coming all along.'

Wilder watched in awe as Thea's face transformed into a wicked grin. 'Thank you.'

It was Audra who came next, placing a firm hand on

Thea's shoulder. 'Go get your things. Weapons, armour and such. You won't need much else.'

Clearly numb, Thea nodded and disappeared up the stairs.

Wilder made to follow her, but the Bear Slayer blocked his path, pulling him aside. Wilder wished for nothing more than to make sure she was alright, that she had everything she could possibly need.

'Another dose of wisdom to share, is it, Elderbrock?' he said flatly, making to push past his fellow Warsword. 'Been in this position before, have you?'

Torj wore a pained expression. 'Not exactly.'

'Then why are you blocking my way?'

'Just listen to me for a second.'

Agitation vibrated in Wilder's chest. 'I've given you more than a second.'

Torj pinned him with a stare. 'The closer you get to true happiness, the more you fear it,' he said. 'It's a fear that slips quietly through the cracks, that lies in wait for those weaker moments before it pounces. It's the *what ifs* while you wait in the dark... *What if* it all goes wrong? *What if* you lose it all?'

Wilder went rigid where he stood, his worst fears coming to life in Torj's words.

The Bear Slayer gripped his shoulder, hard, bringing him back to the present. 'But my brother, those are not the questions you need to ask. Not today, not now. Instead, ask yourself: *what if you got everything you ever wanted?*'

'She's about to partake in the Great Rite, Torj,' he heard himself say, his voice on the verge of cracking.

'As she has wanted to do since she could walk,' Torj reminded him. 'Be strong for her.'

Wilder swallowed the rock in his throat. 'I am not as

fearless as I once was,' he admitted. 'Not now I have something to lose.'

'Is that not what it means to be a Warsword? To face the fear anyway?'

Torj's words hit Wilder like an axe to the chest, and he was momentarily rooted to the spot as the truth of what his friend had said sank deep into his being. And by the time he'd gathered himself and turned towards the stairs, Thea was descending them.

The sight of her took his breath away.

Clad in the armour he'd had altered for her, her bronze hair rebraided in the style of the foreign warrior women from beyond the Veil. Her sword was strapped to her back, both Malik and Audra's daggers belted at her waist. She wore a heavy fur cloak around her shoulders, and her eyes, once wide and worried, were now clear and fierce.

Torj had been right to stop him. She had needed that moment alone.

Steeling himself, he left Thea to her farewells so he could gather his own things from their room. He made it quick, knowing that the call of the Rite would only be growing stronger for Thea, as it had for him, and those who came before.

He strapped his scabbards to his back. Sheathed every dagger he owned on his person. Scanned the room for anything she might need on the journey to wherever they were going. He looked for practical tasks to quieten the raging fear coursing through him, but nothing could stop the force of it. Wilder wanted to protect her from everything she was about to face, but that was not who she was and he knew it. Thea would face the Great Rite alone, as she had always intended, as she was always meant to.

Wilder splashed water on his face, and when he rejoined the group downstairs, Thea was waiting for him in the doorway, the wind and snow howling outside like a cyren's song luring her across the ancient deep. He took his place at her side, marvelling in the strength of her, the determined set of her jaw as she surveyed their companions who'd gathered around.

Wren rushed forward, flinging her arms around her sister before whispering something only Thea and Wilder could catch.

'Remember what you are, Althea Nine Lives.'

'Let's hope that name serves me well,' Thea replied, attempting to release her sister.

But Wren held on a moment longer. '*What* you are, Thea...' she repeated.

Thea pulled back, meeting her gaze. Something Wilder didn't understand passed between them.

'I am the storm...' Thea murmured.

Wren smiled and let go. 'That you are.'

Out of the corner of his eye, Wilder caught Anya lingered on the outskirts, shifting from foot to foot, discomfort written all over her face, as though she didn't know her place.

Thea spotted her and drew her into a firm hug. 'I'll be seeing you, sister.'

Wilder felt a stab of empathy as relief washed over Anya's expression, quickly hidden by a mask of calm sliding into place. 'I'm counting on it.'

Thea nodded, drawing herself up, pushing her shoulders back before she addressed the whole group. 'Furies give you strength for the battles ahead,' she told them, resting her hands on the grips of her daggers. 'But by gods, don't start the war without me.'

Each and every one of them held three fingers to their shoulder in salute, tears lining several pairs of eyes.

And the remaining Embervale sisters stood shoulder-to-shoulder, united.

Wilder motioned for Thea to start walking, and together, they left the Singing Hare, trudging out into the blistering cold to retrieve their horses. 'It's just you and me, apprentice,' he said.

'Not your apprentice much longer, Warsword.'

'No, you won't be.'

The journey through the Aveum hinterlands was both excruciatingly slow and terrifyingly fast. The daylight hours were fleeting, the climate was brutal, and the snow showed no sign of relenting, carrying with it the biting cold that gnawed at Wilder's bones. His dread mounted with each step Biscuit took. It was more than knowing the fate that awaited Thea, more than knowing that the trials she would face were perilous at best, fatal at worst... It wasn't long before he realised why a different terror had him so firmly in its clutches.

The Great Rite was calling Thea to the same place he had entered it all those years ago, at the foot of one of the Aveum Ranges' looming mountains.

As they trekked through the thick snow and braced themselves against the stinging winds, Wilder tried to recall what Talemir, the Prince of Hearts, had shared with him on the way to his own Great Rite. But that time was a blur to him. He merely remembered the single-minded focus that had seen him cross a kingdom to meet the Furies, the same focus that drove Thea through the frozen lands now.

He was glad for that focus, that her determination eclipsed any shadow of doubt that threatened to consume them both. He believed in her, with every fibre of his being, but the thought of what she was about to endure was a burden almost too much to bear. His heart was already aching for her.

Wilder told her none of this as they rode through the icy expanse of the outer reaches of Aveum. He could tell by her grip on the reins and the set of her shoulders beneath her furs that she was already mentally preparing herself, that she had been doing so from the moment she'd slain that first *rheguld reaper* in the Bloodwoods.

As they ventured deeper into the forests, towards the dark, jagged mountains in the distance, the dread Wilder tasted on his tongue thickened in the air around him too, a palpable force that threatened to swallow him whole. The land itself seemed to conspire against their progress. Every step the horses took was battered back by howling winds, the terrain uneven and rife with hidden perils beneath their hooves. But they pushed on, as they always had in the face of danger and challenge.

Wilder was the one to insist they stop to rest every few hours, which was a constant war with Thea's single-minded focus and the power of the Furies themselves.

'You need to be rested when you reach the starting point, Thea,' he told her gently. 'There's no point in running yourself ragged to get there. You need to be strong, energised.'

She grumbled, but acquiesced eventually. However

stubborn she was, his apprentice knew there was no arguing with that logic.

It was during one of those brief respites, where the silence around them seemed deafening, that Wilder felt the weight of another presence. The hair stood up on the nape of his neck, a prickle running down the length of his spine.

'We're not alone,' he murmured, sliding his swords from their sheaths with expert quiet.

Thea did the same with a wary glance at him. 'Is this it? Has it started?'

Wilder scanned the horizon, shadows dancing in the periphery of his vision, darting in and out of view like phantoms in the night. 'No,' he told Thea. 'This is something else entirely.'

But to his surprise, Thea gave a wicked grin. 'Good. I need something to take the edge off.'

'Well, in that case...' Wilder raised his blades as movement blurred beyond the trees again.

The air crackled around them and he glimpsed the storm in Thea's eyes.

'Not now,' he cautioned. 'You'll need all that power for the Great Rite.'

For once, his apprentice heeded his warning. He noted her grip on her sword tightening as she unsheathed Malik's dagger from her belt and gave him a single nod.

Side by side they stood, as three arachnes crept into their space from beyond the trees.

They were smaller than the one in Vios, but just as cursed with darkness. A strange clicking noise permeated the air as they approached, their forms grotesque: a twisted fusion of spider and human and hatred, their multiple eyes gleaming with a sinister hunger.

'Good odds,' Thea quipped, twirling her steel in invitation.

Wilder baulked. 'How d'you figure that?'

Thea shrugged. 'Last time you were fighting with broken chair legs.'

Then, his apprentice lunged.

Wilder followed, his blades glinting in the weak sunlight and reflection of the snow. He moved with the grace of the Furies, each strike to the lashes of darkness swift and precise as he fought his way to the largest monster's layers of chitinous exoskeleton.

'Mind your left!' Thea shouted, and he dodged just in time to miss a thick net of webbing flying at him. The arachne snapped its pincer-like fangs, dripping venom as it surged towards him on its eight freakish legs.

Wilder somersaulted, feeling the icy kiss of snow on his back as he rolled beneath the monster and cleaved his blades through the lower half of its limbs.

The screech that followed shook icicles from the nearby trees, but Wilder was already on his feet, seeing Thea as a blur of movement in his periphery as he launched himself onto the arachne's back and plunged his blades through its thorax from behind.

The monster staggered on its severed legs, black blood pouring from its wounds onto the snow as it collapsed.

Wilder leapt from the falling creature, not wasting a moment as he sought Thea. She was wielding her sword and dagger against the two lesser arachnes, her face lined with determination, her footwork as flawless as ever, even in the snow.

Twirling his blades, Wilder came to her side.

'Don't know if you realise, but I'm in a bit of a hurry,' she muttered.

'Thought you'd have these two little ones handled,' Wilder retorted, knowing that Thea often responded to a challenge.

A wicked smile curved her lips. 'Well then, stand back and watch how it's done, Warsword.'

Thea threw herself at the remaining monsters, her sword and dagger carving through darkness and sinewy flesh, eliciting shrieks from both creatures, black gore spattering onto the pristine snow around them. Wilder guarded her back, but allowed her free rein on the attack, knowing she needed this. She needed her blood hot and her body warmed up for the trials ahead. She needed the confidence in her abilities.

The cursed forms of the two remaining arachnes faltered with every swipe of her blades, unable to withstand the ferocity of Thea's assault. She embedded a dagger in one of their human-like skulls and flung an array of silver throwing stars at the other's many eyes.

'I was right, all that time ago...' Wilder mused, watching her carve up the monsters.

'About what?' she managed between blows.

'You're even more beautiful with steel in your hands, and the blood of your enemies splattered across your face.'

He saw a flash of a smile before, in a final manoeuvre, Thea jumped, avoiding a slash of darkness, her body twisting in mid-air only to come back down in perfect form, her sword slicing through the thick neck of the final monster, severing its head completely.

The head rolled across the snow with a dull thud as Thea landed deftly beside the falling carcass.

'Not bad, Apprentice,' Wilder murmured. 'Not bad at all.'

But Thea's eyes were fixated between the trees, where a naked branch bounced, disturbing settled flakes of ice. 'Someone's there.'

Wilder charged towards the bush, instantly finding the tracks that led away from the muddied slush. He scanned the surrounding forest, but there was nothing but white snow and barren trees. Whoever had watched the battle had fled.

And that someone had likely set the arachne upon them.

A drip sounded, and another.

Wilder searched the snow at his boots, spotting a tiny patch of red, so stark against the white. Blood. Human blood.

*His*, he realised.

The sleeve of his shirt was wet with it. Turning his back to Thea, who was still in the clearing with the monster corpses, he looked down at his forearm. There, beneath the tattered leather of his vambrace and the torn fabric of his shirt, was a thin, bloody slash through his skin.

The cut wasn't deep. Wilder couldn't even feel it, but what caused him to falter was the translucent film of something else around its edges.

*Venom.*

'What's the hold-up?' Thea called. 'Did you see anything?'

Wilder wrenched his sleeve back down and wiped away the smear of blood. 'There was someone watching,' he told her, returning to the clearing. 'But they're long gone.'

'Spies?' Thea asked, frowning into the forest.

'Perhaps,' he replied. 'They're not our concern now, though.'

Thea sheathed her blades. 'Onwards, then?'

Wilder whistled for Biscuit, who came trotting through the trees, Thea's mare close behind. 'Onwards.'

~

The towering mountains of Aveum loomed close now, bearing down on them in the fading light just as the weight of the impending Great Rite did.

Wilder could feel the faint edge of the venom in his system, but he shoved the thought aside. His priority was Thea and getting her to where she needed to be. He could deal with the consequences of the arachne scratch later.

He and his apprentice wove through the barren trees, the incline perilously steep through snow and ice. The air was getting colder by the second, clouding before their faces, and Wilder was beginning to lose feeling in his fingertips.

'Wilder?' Thea's voice cut through the quiet.

'What is it?'

'We're nearly there.'

He had felt it too. He noted the familiarity as they approached the foot of the mountains, his heart lurching, threatening to come up into his throat. Torj's words echoed in his mind.

*Be strong for her.*

So he simply nodded. 'Good.'

All too soon, the trees around them thinned, revealing the foot of a formidable mountain. The towering behemoth reached skyward, crowned by a jagged peak, wreathed in a swirling tempest of fog and snow.

The very air they breathed sang with an otherworldly chill, biting at their lungs as they inhaled. To the left of the rocky base was one of the roads to Tver... The road Wilder and Talemir had taken after he'd emerged from his Great Rite ordeal, to claim his Tverrian stallion. To the right, the road was swallowed by more forest, a sea of ancient pines burdened with the weight of endless winter.

Thea drew them to a stop and dismounted, staring up at the mountain before her, taking in its sharp rocks and the eerie trees, their gnarled branches like bony fingers grasping for something they'd never have.

'It's calling me,' she murmured in wonder, her hands falling from her mare's bridle.

Wilder followed her gaze, his chest aching, his more primal instincts warring inside him. Part of him wanted to snatch Thea up and whisk her away from this place, but he beat those feelings back.

'I go no further,' he told her instead.

The mountain had its own presence, etched by history and time, harbouring secrets that would never come to light. Even now, it whispered to him as though it knew him, recognised him from long ago and had known he would return. So many fates had been determined in the depths of its valleys, in its dark crevices, atop its razor-edged peak.

But it was the fate of only one that mattered most to him now.

Those celadon eyes locked with his.

Only decades of training kept him breathing as he took in her fire, her beauty and her determination. He struggled to find his voice, but when he did, it came out hoarse and full of unchecked emotion.

'When I stand against the gods at the end of my days,' he told her fiercely, 'I will regret nothing. Not the lies I've told, nor the lives I've claimed or the rivers of blood I've spilt. I do not regret a single moment, because every one of them led me to you.'

Thea's chest heaved. 'Wilder...' she breathed, closing the gap between them.

His mouth was on hers in an instant, as though with a kiss he could stop the force of the Furies themselves. The dark frenzy that had always connected them took hold and they became a tangle of limbs and a tempest of longing. He threaded his fingers through her hair, deepening the kiss, trying to put everything he felt for her into every brush of his lips, every stroke of his tongue, desire burning white-hot from the inside out.

He wanted to tell her he couldn't, and wouldn't, live without her. That, should the Furies wish to take her from him, he'd tear their fucking mountain down to get her back.

But it was Thea who broke away, panting. 'I want you to know... If I come out of this unrecognisable, if I leave this Rite a different person... I want you to know that I have felt for you what I have felt for no one else. That I —'

'Don't.' Wilder's mouth crashed to hers again, an outlet for the rising tide of panic within. 'We don't say those words again until we're on the other side. Until we can say them Warsword to Warsword.'

Understanding filled those stormy eyes, and slowly, Thea nodded, her fisted grip on his cloak loosening.

They broke apart and the cold swept in, more brutal than before. Mist swirled at the base of the mountain, beckoning her with smoke-like tendrils.

'Warsword to Warsword, then,' she said, her shoulders rising and falling as she steeled herself.

Wilder stood with the horses as she checked her weapons and left the rest of her belongings in her saddlebags. He had told her she could take nothing more with her into the Great Rite.

His heart hammered mercilessly as his apprentice, his love, gave him one final look. He lifted three fingers in salute, in deference to her, before she turned to face the mountain, squaring her shoulders.

A hundred moments flashed before Wilder's eyes, but he didn't dare blink as Thea took a breath and walked into the swirling mist.

In seconds, her form was obscured. A moment later, it was gone.

Wilder stared after her, at the fog that danced in her wake.

He thought he had known terror before, known it intimately. But this was a different kind entirely. The kind that saw a man glimpse what he'd always wanted, only to watch her walk into the clutches of fate itself, knowing that for the first time, he could not follow.

# CHAPTER THIRTY-EIGHT

## THEA

The mist devoured her, and suddenly Wilder was gone. When Thea looked back the way she'd come, she could see nothing but swirling white fog that seemed to push at her back, to coax her forward.

*This is it,* she told herself as she stepped onto the sacred grounds of the Great Rite. She had dreamt of this her whole life, and now... now she was about to face the deadly trials crafted by the Furies themselves, challenges that would push the limits of her mortal resilience.

*Let them try,* Thea thought as she started up the incline of the mountain.

The terrain was uneven and steep, with icy rocks concealed beneath the frost-kissed leaf litter. All around her, the air was damp and prickly, bearing down on her along with the closed-in feeling of the woods. She could barely see the glimpses of sky beyond the barren canopy, but it didn't matter. By the magic of the Furies, she knew the way: *up.*

The mist danced around her ankles as she trekked on, her calves burning as the gradient became even more arduous. She was quietly grateful that she bore no pack across her shoulders. But with every step, her trepidation grew. Her heart was racing in anticipation for the first trial to be sprung upon her. At any moment, she expected to be thrown into a pit of chaos.

She wasn't.

*Strong of mind, strong of body, strong of heart,* she chanted to herself with every foot placed in front of the other. Thea knew that the imminent prospect of danger could be almost as trying as the danger itself, and so she steeled her mind, trying to lose herself in the physical task of climbing the formidable mountain. When the trial began, she'd know it.

Time became an expanse of nothing. There were no markers to signify the hours passing, only the sweat on Thea's brow and the thirst that dried her tongue and throat. It didn't take her long to realise that she needed to hydrate if she meant to continue. Thankfully, there was no shortage of narrow streams carving their way down the mountain, and Thea dropped to her knees beside one now, cupping her hands beneath the icy water. She brought it to her lips and drank deeply. Closing her eyes as the crisp taste hit her lips and soothed her parched mouth, she drank her fill.

When she opened her eyes, she was no longer by a stream.

She was inside the mountain itself, staring at a wall of mirrors.

Torches illuminated the cavernous space, their flames reflected in the shiny surfaces before her. Thea saw her startled expression in her own reflection, her confusion winding tighter as she walked the length of mirrors. As she did, they shifted, creating a strange optical illusion that followed her with every step.

The nape of her neck prickled as two of the reflective sheets swung inward.

Inside was a mirrored passageway. Beyond that, more mirrors.

*A maze*, she realised.

Silence echoed louder than a shout down that glimmering path, the eeriness of its call almost palpable. Thea stood at the threshold, gathering her wits, knowing that whatever awaited her within those walls would test her mental resolve beyond anything she'd ever experienced.

*I have to get to the heart.*

The thought came to her out of nowhere, a distant voice of reason, and she knew in her bones that was what she must do. Something was waiting for her at the centre.

Resting her hands on the grips of each of her daggers, she took a breath, and stepped inside.

Instantly, the mirrored doors swung shut behind her, leaving her standing at the start of the long path. Lanterns hung from the ceiling, their flames lighting up the sea of stalactites hanging down like daggers above. But Thea knew that being impaled by a falling mineral formation was the least of her concerns. There was danger here – she could feel it crawling along her skin, waiting to sink its teeth into her... and more dangerous still was whatever waited for her beyond the winding paths.

Slowly, she started the march, trying not to jump every time a mirror shifted and showed her reflection at a new angle. It was all a trick of illusion and light, all designed to keep her tense, anticipating the first strike.

With every step into the labyrinth, Thea's chest grew tighter, the pressure sitting right over her heart growing heavier by the moment. There was no way of knowing the way to the heart of the maze, no discernable markings or clues. The twisting corridors offered more of the same: her own visage unnervingly multiplied.

Then, there was a whisper.

Her own voice called out to her, only she couldn't understand the words.

Thea picked up her pace. The sooner she got to the centre of this place and dealt with the challenge there, the better.

*Time works differently in the Great Rite*, Wilder had shared with her in the Bloodwoods. She knew that hours within the ritual could be mere moments in the midrealms beyond, and vice versa; it was part of the Rite's legend. It only made her all the more eager to hurry things along.

But as she increased her speed, something flickered in her reflections. Thea's blood ran cold as they stopped following her actions.

Now, when she moved, they did not.

Dozens of Theas stared back at her. They did not step when she stepped. They did not wave when she waved. They did not blink when she blinked.

Instead, they mirrored the rot inside her.

A strangled gasp tore from Thea's mouth as she saw what lurked beneath the surface of her.

Selfishness. Greed. Hatred.

A version of herself she hardly recognised, one that would see all those she cared for chained and broken before she gave up what she wanted. But there was a whisper of truth there, too... Her reflections twisted and danced in triumph as that kernel settled in the chasm of Thea's aching chest.

She gripped her daggers hard enough to make her

knuckles burn, and it was this pain that grounded her enough to keep moving.

*Get to the heart,* she told herself. *Get to the heart and slay whatever monster lies in wait.*

Whispers filled the air, haunting murmurs in her own voice that trailed over her skin like oil. Promises of power, if only she would give up a sliver of herself – *the parts that don't matter anyway,* her voice echoed in her mind.

Dull pain throbbed at her temples whenever she looked away from the mirrors, as though she'd had too much wine or was looking at direct sunlight. Her gaze was forced back to the glass, where she was broken apart for all to witness: her streak of cruelty, her self-obsession, her pig-headedness and her disregard for others.

Yes, she had regressed and sunk into every one of those traits and more to stand where she now did, where she now looked upon herself in all her ugly glory.

Thea fought to get enough air into her lungs, one hand flying from her dagger to her chest, as though she might alleviate some of the pressure there. But without the rough grip of the dagger against her palm, she became more untethered. For the heartbeat she sought to feel beneath her skin wasn't there. There was nothing but hollowness, and the kiss of malice against her soul. Not that of monsters and evil tyrants, but her own. It tasted of her. It knew her.

Thea staggered under the force of it, but managed to take the next turn. She was greeted with more reflections, every one of them a more twisted version of herself, clawing at her psyche, gnawing at her beliefs.

*Yield,* she heard herself whisper in the distance. *Yield to what you are.*

'No,' she rasped aloud. The sound of her true voice gave

her a momentary reprieve from the onslaught of madness that was nearly consuming her.

On some level, she knew that the maze of mirrors had been designed to unleash chaos in her mind, to fragment her beliefs, her memories, her perception of herself. But that knowledge did nothing in the face of her identity, for with each new facet she saw, the ability to discern illusion and warped perception from reality frayed.

'Don't go mad,' she told herself. 'Keep walking, keep walking,' she chanted, feeling her feet move beneath her but unable to process the distance covered. She didn't know if she was closer to or further away from the centre of the maze, but she couldn't stand there and watch the nightmare versions of herself unfold.

Everything was distorted. Her regrets, her fears, everything she thought she knew about Althea Zoltaire, Guardian of Thezmarr.

A soft crackling sounded.

At first, Thea thought it might be her magic, and wondered if she could sweep herself away in a storm of lightning and thunder.

But no storm whispered at her fingertips.

Instead, she saw frost form on the edges of the mirrors, ice crystallising out of nowhere around her many reflections.

Like a sailor to a cyren's song, in a trance she was lured closer to the glass, staring at what unfolded there.

It was the scene Anya had shown her: they were children, hiding in the cellar with Audra and Farissa at the helm, keeping them safe from whatever darkness consumed Thezmarr's courtyard above. Only this time, Thea was whispering to Anya.

'I dare you,' she said softly, her eyes eager and bright. 'I dare you to see what's happening outside.'

Anya fidgeted. 'Audra said we needed —'

Even at just four years old, Thea's smile was smug. 'I knew you wouldn't.'

Anya's eyes flashed. 'Fine!'

Thea's expression was pure triumph. 'Get as close as you can. You want to see everything.'

Wren was too little to play with, but Thea was a keen adventurer, brave and always getting into trouble. Even at such a young age, she knew it irked her older sister to be left behind, which made Anya all the more determined to solidify her place as the trailblazer of the orphaned Zoltaire girls.

'Hurry or you'll miss it,' little Thea taunted.

'I'm going!' Anya hissed.

Thea watched her sister go, watched as she skirted Audra's hawk eyes and ducked past Farissa, who was distracted with one of the infants.

It was only when Thea heard the screams from above that she realised what she'd done.

Thea staggered back from the mirror with a gasp. 'It's not true,' she wheezed, pressing her hand to her chest, where the weight was nearly unbearable. 'I didn't... I couldn't have...'

*Illusion or reality?* That was the game at play here. *Illusion, illusion,* Thea told herself.

But her reflection answered her horror with a cruel twist of her lips.

With a cry, Thea staggered down another winding path of mirrors, boneless beneath the weight of the events she'd set in motion for her older sister. The scars she bore, the eye she'd lost, the shadows that had nearly devoured her. It was all Thea's fault.

The Daughter of Darkness had been her creation after all.

Letting out a scream of anguish, Thea lurched into a sprint, ignoring the movement of her mirror selves, slamming mental walls down around her against the shouts of her own voice echoing through the maze.

It was Anya's words from the Singing Hare that she clung to, words she knew without a shadow of a doubt her sister had truly spoken.

*'The tides of fate are as they always intended...'*

Anya had been at her side, with Dratos, Marise and Everard... and Wilder.

*Wilder...* His name crashed through her like a wave over fire, and in the distance, she heard glass shattering.

*'We don't say those words again until we're on the other side. Until we can say them Warsword to Warsword.'*

She realised that amid everything they'd been through together, and of all the times before where they *had* uttered those unutterable words to one another, she had never been the one to say it first. It had always been him. He had always taken the leap for them. He had always risked his heart first. For her.

*If I ever get out of here, I'll say it first,* she vowed. *I'll be the one to take the leap for him.*

More glass shattered, sounding closer this time.

Not knowing why, she ran towards it, only to find that the mirrors behind her had started to crack as frost crept across their faces.

Suddenly there was a surge, and the ear-piercing sound of a thousand mirrors shattering into a million pieces. It grew louder and louder, closer and closer. All the while, Thea raced through the maze, twisting and turning at every bend, her reflections either chasing her or fleeing the flood of glass. She didn't know which, nor did she care; she just had to get to the centre, had to —

Her heart seized and she skidded to a stop, her boots sliding across the damp ground, her arms flailing to keep her balance.

The space opened up.

Before her stood a colossal mirror. The largest she had ever seen.

She was shown a hundred different versions of herself, distorted and ugly, broken and hollow, raging and vengeful. Thea drew a ragged breath as she saw each angle of herself with clarity, saw the kernel of truth in each of them, along with the falsehoods.

At long last, she locked eyes with herself.

There, she saw every horrible thing she'd ever suspected about herself. Saw the darkest, most rotten parts of the girl she'd been, and the woman she'd become.

Althea Zoltaire faced her shadow side.

'I...' she croaked. 'A Warsword must accept themselves... especially the darkest parts...' She gulped for air. 'I accept me. All of me.'

Thea met her own gaze, recognising that every broken part could be reforged into something stronger, something that did not yield in the face of adversity.

Beyond the flawless shine of the glass, beneath the layers of poison she'd been doused in, Thea watched as her reflection at long last cast something back towards her that she understood.

It was her determination.

She watched in awe as it crumbled like ash around her, only to be reborn in the crucible of the maze of mirrors.

As it did, the final expanse of glass cracked in two.

The sheets of mirror fell, crashing to the ground and splintering into millions of tiny pieces of silver.

Only to reveal two elaborately carved doors.

Still trying to catch her breath, Thea wiped the sweat from her brow and pushed the loose strands of hair from her eyes, steeling herself once more.

Both doors swung inward.

A strangled noise escaped her as she realised what they revealed.

Two futures.

One choice.

'You cannot be both a storm wielder and a Warsword.' Audra's words echoed through the cavernous chamber. 'You have to choose, Thea...'

Thea's stomach lurched and a bitter taste spread across her tongue. She hadn't believed Audra. She had thought... What had she thought? That she was above the laws of the midrealms? That the Furies would make an exception just for her?

Her throat went dry as she surveyed the futures before her.

The first showed her in a field of heather, her very presence singing with storm magic, the magic she'd come to love. Lightning crackled at her fingertips and thunder rolled through the sky. Her power was more than she had ever imagined. From the mirror doorway, she could feel it vibrating through the world – it was hers for the taking, a force so strong she would never again question her place in the midrealms, her worthiness.

The second showed her amid the ashes of an achingly familiar place, wielding a blade of Naarvian steel. Not Malik's dagger, nor Wilder's swords... But a blade of her own. A Warsword blade. She was fighting shadow wraiths, cleaving through darkness in a blur of silver. A Warsword totem displayed proudly on her right arm over her armour.

But there was no magic. No storm within her.

*'You have to choose, Thea...'* Those words echoed once more.

As if in answer, her magic surged. Its current coursed through her, from her chest to her fingertips and toes, demanding to be felt, acknowledged.

She had come to love that part of herself, had accepted it wholeheartedly into her life, into her identity.

And now?

Thea kept the panic at bay. She cast aside the versions of herself that she'd been shown – those that terrified her, those that made her heart ache.

She wanted so much more than she'd ever realised. But if there was a price to be paid, she would pay it.

Shaking, she crossed the threshold, towards her Warsword self.

A scream tore from her throat.

Eyes streaming, she could only watch as her lightning ruptured all around her, as it was violently severed from the very fabric of her existence. In an unimaginable blaze of pain, her power was ripped from her. It left her body in forceful waves, as though someone were physically wrenching it out of her blood, her bones, her soul.

The agony went beyond the pain itself.

As the final forks of lightning left her skin, Thea watched a piece of herself go with them.

And when at last the torture was done, she was hollow, on her hands and knees, panting in the dirt. Trembling and exhausted, she wiped a trickle of blood from her nose and hauled herself to her feet.

A portal materialised before her and she staggered towards it.

How many hours had she endured so far? How long had she battled with herself amid the maze of mirrors? Thea squared her shoulders. It was far from over.

*Strong of mind, strong of body, strong of heart*, she chanted to herself again, as she stepped from one ring of fire into the next – into the second trial of the Great Rite, without her storm magic.

# CHAPTER THIRTY-NINE

## THEA

Thea had danced with death her whole life, believing that the piece of jade around her neck somehow held her ultimate demise at bay. But as she craned her neck, staring up at what was now in front of her, she wondered if she'd been wrong all along.

Perhaps this would be the moment death claimed her after all.

She was on the outside of the mountain again, a wall of utterly vertical ice before her, reaching up into the swirling mist, so high she couldn't see the top, so high that looking up at it was dizzying.

Its surface shimmered in the pale moonlight, and Thea abstractly noted that night had fallen. What night, she had no idea; she had no concept of how long she'd taken trekking up the mountainside, no idea how long she'd been trapped in the maze of mirrors. She felt the faint pang of hunger low in her gut, and the distant craving for water, but neither meant anything. The sensations, the light... There was no telling what was real and what had been manufactured by the gods themselves.

Thea took a breath and studied the frozen titan before her, the way it seemed to defy gravity and any semblance of mortal courage. It was a testament to the unforgiving nature of the Furies, a vertical deathtrap that shot skyward, an endless barrier, stretching out of sight on either side.

Towards the top, there was a shadow beneath the ice as well... It looked like a great chain trapped beneath the freeze, its presence stark against the pristine surface.

Everything else was white and glasslike, except for a small pile of items at the foot of the wall. With the frigid air biting at her skin, Thea crouched to examine what had been left for her.

Ice axes. Spikes.

The challenge was clear.

They meant for her to climb the wall.

Heart slamming against her ribs, Thea picked up the spikes, hardly feeling their weight in her already numb hands. How was she meant to scale a wall if she couldn't feel her limbs at the base?

Gods, it hardly ever snowed in Thezmarr... Now here she was, facing the most perilous wintry ascent imaginable. As she fitted the spikes over her boots, she cursed herself for not training harder throughout her travels. She had always known there would be some test of her bodily strength during the Great Rite – how had she not prepared herself better? It didn't matter how many monsters she had slayed if she couldn't lift her own fucking body weight.

*Monsters...* The thought roiled through Thea suddenly, and her attention went back to the line of shadow that cut through the white. She had fought reapers, wraiths, reef dwellers, arachnes and howlers, but this was deep beneath the ice... and there were human-made contraptions just as terrifying as monsters. She had heard of a device employed around the walls of Aveum that, when released, shaved an entire layer from the facade, raining chaos and carnage down on anyone who might be bold enough to attempt the climb.

Dread curdled in Thea's gut. Whatever it was, it didn't matter. There was only one way through this trial and it was up the icy obstruction before her.

She finished lacing the spikes to her boots, testing their sturdiness with a few kicks to the snow. They felt clumsy on her feet, but there was no doubt she'd be glad for them soon enough. Next, she took the ice axes in her hands. Small and simple, the blades gleamed sharp in the pale moonlight.

Trying to shake the nervousness from her body, Thea went to the foot of the cliff face and looked up, her breath whistling between her teeth as she did.

*The Glacier's Embrace...* The words came to her as though she'd spoken them aloud, but she knew she hadn't opened her mouth. It was a whisper from the Furies, along with the icy gust of wind that swept along the wall's face. A warning.

Though every instinct within her screamed to run away, to not swing that first blade into the ice, there was nothing for it.

This was the Great Rite.

There was no going back.

Thea swung her axe above her head. The first sound of steel piercing ice echoed across the strange, desolate space like a battle cry.

She kicked her spiked toe into the wall, testing her purchase there before allowing the tools to bear her whole weight.

'Here goes nothing,' she muttered to herself, swinging her second axe into the ice.

With several more pitches of her blades and kicks of her spikes, Thea was suspended several feet above the ground, the bitter cold of the wall pressing into her front, soaking through the layers of her clothing. She would have to move fast if she wanted to avoid the heart-stopping effect exposure to such conditions could have.

Steeling herself against the increasing drop below, and the stiffening of her joints in the face of the freeze, Thea threw her blade upward, pulling herself up while digging her spikes into the vertical surface, again and again. Her breath clouded before her face, and for once she was grateful, as it distracted her from looking at the distance yawning between her and the unforgiving ground below.

At what felt like an agonisingly slow pace, Thea climbed.

Her teeth chattered, enough to rattle her brain inside her skull, but she pressed skyward, losing herself in the rhythm of her axes and spikes, testing her purchase with each push up into the mist. Her muscles ached and then burned in protest with each movement, but she held fast, knowing that a single misstep could send her plummeting to what now looked like an abyss below.

With every ounce of momentum, her heart raced, and she didn't dare to look down at how much of the wall she'd covered. She breathed in through her nose, the frigid air hitting her lungs hard enough to make her gasp, her grip faltering on her axe.

She pressed herself to the wall with all her strength, screwing her eyes shut in a moment of panic.

*'I will regret nothing. Not the lies I've told, nor the lives I've claimed or the rivers of blood I've spilt. I do not regret a single moment, because every one of them led me to you.'*

Wilder's words came back to her like a flicker of flame in a long, dark night, and Thea gritted her teeth, spearing her axe into the unbroken surface of ice above her, hauling her body along with it.

She clung to those words as she clung to her axes: for dear life. She let them hold her together as Wilder himself had held her through many nights before.

The pale light of the moon was fading, darkness kissing the ice, the temperature around Thea dropping even more. The wall groaned. The heart-stopping sound of cracking filled the air as the ancient ice shifted in the gale that picked up at Thea's back.

Hours passed. Thea's limbs burned with every movement. On the horizon, the first golden rays of dawn had started to spill into the world. She clutched her axes hard enough that her knuckles split beneath her gloves and the warm trickle of blood graced her chilled skin.

Thea didn't know how far up the wall she'd managed to get, only that the howling wind now threatened to rip her clean off its surface. As though it had claws, the blast tugged painfully at her cloak, her braid, and Thea's whole body trembled with the effort it took to cling to the vertical face of the glacier.

*Althea Nine Lives*, she reminded herself. That was who she was. Those lives would see her through this ordeal, they would —

The ice groaned again.

And jagged crevices split its surface into a treacherous web of frozen veins. It was another labyrinth – an echo of the maze of mirrors over which she'd just triumphed.

With a cry, Thea flung her axe into the ice above, only for it to crumble – too close to a fault she could not see.

A scream of terror ripped from her throat.

Her loose hand went flying out into mid-air, and for a split second, she thought she was falling.

But all those countless hours of training snapped into place, and she managed to maintain her grip on her axe and swing it with all her might back into another patch of ice.

Panting, she tested it with her weight.

It held.

A half-sob of relief escaped Thea as she resumed her climb, a drop of sweat sliding down between her shoulder blades despite the frigid conditions. It was a fierce reminder not to become complacent, not to lose herself too deeply in the rhythm of the ascent, for the icy facade was getting more treacherous, offering only fleeting holds. Perilous crevasses lurked beneath its exterior, hungry for the slightest of missteps or an ill-placed axe.

Ignoring the tremor in her muscles and the ache in her hands and feet, Thea kept climbing. She had known that the Furies meant to test her in every way they knew how, and she had been more than willing to fling herself at their feet, at their mercy. She tightened her grip on her axe, wincing as her aching toes found purchase in the glasslike exterior. Scaling the monolith was meant to test her strength, her endurance, and by the gods, she'd show them everything she had.

One swing of an axe and then the next, one foothold and then the next, she worked her way up the sheer vertical wall, somehow sensing the presence of those who had come before, their fear, their triumphs and their failures all etched into the ice itself.

Pure will fuelled her where her physical energy was flagging, and she panted through every motion, every near-miss of a fault in the surface or a deceiving crevasse that nearly claimed her.

She was completely surrounded by dancing mist now, unable to see the abyss below even if she wished. It meant she was getting close to the top. She had to be.

But it was as this thought dared to enter her wrung-out mind that the wall shuddered beneath her.

A ripple of movement further down, out of sight, but enough to dislodge one of her boots from the facade, her foot slipping —

With a ragged gasp, Thea clung on to her axes and clawed at the ice with her foot, her spikes having destroyed any immediate area to gain traction or purchase. She struggled to find any sort of hold, the spikes sliding over the slick surface, making a painful scraping noise.

The wall shuddered again.

Like the structure itself was inhaling a deep breath before —

Thea's head snapped to her left, where an entire frozen sheet dislodged from the wall with an almighty crack.

A panicked cry escaped her as she grappled with her axes to plough ahead.

One of her spikes fell from her boot; the previous struggle had loosened its laces around her foot. With a silent scream of horror, she watched it fall – only to see, as more of the wall tumbled in a deadly cascade, that it was no human-made trap beneath the freeze, no chain of destruction.

It was a scaled tail, a vicious translucent barb on its end.

Both were cleaving through the ice, barrelling towards her.

Everything in the tail's path was obliterated, showering ice and rock and snow down into the chasm below.

Thea choked on the shout caught in her throat. There was no way she was going to make it, no way out of the path of destruction. She couldn't climb fast enough, not even if she had the spike she'd just lost.

Numb with shock, she took in the frozen domain as the unknown monster's tail carved towards her from above, shaving off the ancient surface as though it were a fine film.

Time slowed as the pale blue scales drew closer and closer. Thea tried to channel her inner Kipp, to assess rather than act out of panic. She tried to gauge the distance between where she was and the top of the wall, tried to calculate the speed at which the tail was cutting through the ice, and whether or not the creature was poised to strike from the ledge. Judging the rest of the sheer vertical climb, she came to the same conclusion she already had: it was impossible. And she wouldn't survive.

Thea could feel the force of the monstrous tail in the wind around her, whipping through her braid and stinging her face.

Only when she could taste the kiss of death in the air did she act.

Not to make a final scramble upward, but to let go.

Thea loosened her axes and leapt from the wall —

She fell.

Wind lashing at her, tearing at her clothes and skin.

Until she reached out, her numb hands fumbling for the thick tail itself as it swung across the face of the wall, ice raining down on her as she scraped along the jagged surface.

Thea let it take her, let it swing her down the formidable vertical face, ignoring the pain as sharp as blades ripping at her flesh. The momentum of the tail took her up, up and up the wall.

When she could see the blush of daylight above the mist, she let go once more.

Pulse pounding in her ears, Thea leapt into the crisp air, axes flung outward as she fell through the clouds.

Her blades sank into ice, sliding down that formidable vertical drop again. But Thea rammed her remaining spike into the wall below. Pain blazed at her ankle as that one joint took her whole weight suddenly. It jarred and she let out a wild scream. But she did not let go, did not falter as she clawed her way up.

Axe, axe, spike. Axe, axe, spike. Three motions again and again, her teeth clenched so hard her jaw burned. She could taste blood on her tongue. She could feel the fire of multiple lacerations to her body, and she could see the smear of her blood across the frozen wall where the tail had nearly crushed her.

Axe, axe, spike. Axe, axe, spike.

On the next swing of her blade, Thea met no resistance, nothing for her axe to sink into.

With a rattling breath, she reached up with her fingers...

There, she found the edge of the wall.

There, she found her salvation.

With every ounce of strength she had left, Thea climbed to that ledge and hauled herself over the top of the wall.

A sudden ear-splitting roar nearly sent her sprawling back over the edge to her doom. And then she looked up.

A broken cry of terror bubbled from her lips as she gazed upon a monster not of this world. Crystalline scales gleamed like tears of the gods themselves, and piercing sapphire eyes left ice in their wake.

Thea scrambled back, careful not to look directly into its stare, lest it freeze her completely.

For it was an ice basilisk.

An ancient creature, an embodiment of winter's wrath.

Its roar sounded again, ending on a high-pitched note that threatened to bring down the mountains around them.

Instinctively, Thea reached for her power —

Only to find it gone.

No magic would save her now.

She grasped her dagger with a trembling hand. The basilisk's body writhed in the mess of snow and icy shards around it, as though it had just woken from a great slumber beneath the ice. Its scales shimmered in shades of glacial blue and silver, and it tried to pierce her with those deadly eyes, twin orbs of frosted fire desperate to freeze her in her tracks.

Its massive form coiled, ready to strike.

But magic or not, Thea had never been one to wait.

With a silent cry on her lips, she lunged with her dagger, aiming for the softer underbelly of the monster.

But the basilisk was fast. Much faster than a creature of its size had any right to be.

It lashed out at Thea with its barbed tail, and now, she could see the poison that tipped its sharp point.

She leapt from its path, grateful for a lifetime of Dancing Alchemists, grateful for all the shadows she'd fought that had made her nimble. Avoiding another strike of that horrific barb, she managed to drag her blade across the softer scales, spilling its blood across the snow.

But scales were tough, and her blade hadn't stuck in deep enough.

Her efforts only served to enrage the creature further.

A blast of ice nearly hit her. She threw herself out of its path. A shriek pierced the air and she ducked, rolling through the bloodied snow to avoid the vicious slash of two fangs now sinking into the ground.

Panicked and exhausted, Thea felt the loss of her magic profoundly. She wanted nothing more than to reach within and find that surge of power to blast the fucking basilisk off the mountain. But all was silent within. No crackle of lightning answered her call. No rumble of thunder in the distance...

Instead, the ground beneath her shook with so much force she couldn't stand, and that deadly barb pierced the snow mere inches from her side.

Thea scrambled up, brandishing her dagger in her aching hand, swaying on her feet. She dodged another strike, and another, but her energy reserves were empty, her movements sluggish. Desperate, she tried to use her magic again —

A blur of movement momentarily blinded her, and she was pummelled into the snow, the wind knocked out of her completely.

A searing pain pierced her shoulder.

The scream that left her lips was garbled.

Warm blood gushed from the wound, the sensation shockingly hot against her chilled skin.

Thea gagged as she saw the source of the pain... where one of the basilisk's fangs was still embedded, torn from the monster's mouth.

With a cry of agony, she wrenched the fang from her flesh as the monster struck again, ice shooting past her.

But Thea was airborne.

She threw herself at the creature, wrapping her legs around its scaled neck and plunging its fang into one of its sapphire eyes.

The basilisk thrashed and roared, flinging Thea from its body, blood pouring from its eye, where the fang still protruded gruesomely. More blood rained down as its whole body spasmed in pain, jerking and flailing, until its tail slipped over the edge of the cliff.

Thea gasped for air desperately, clambering back as a final shriek nearly deafened her. The basilisk had no hold in the snow as gravity did the rest, dragging its upper body towards the deadly fall.

A mad laugh of disbelief died on Thea's lips.

With its own fang still embedded in its eye, the monster was hauled by its own weight over the edge of the cliff face.

It fell.

Several moments later, a crash echoed from below.

Thea blinked, shock wrapping around her like a vice. Half sobbing, she forced herself to crawl, to put as much distance between that ledge and the beast below as possible.

At last, her hands and knees met solid ground beneath the snow, and she worshipped it with tears and blood, bringing her lips to the frosted flakes with a broken cry.

Only when she stopped heaving for ragged breaths, only when her tears were spent and the bleeding had slowed to a trickle that cut through the soft white beneath her, did she look up.

A frozen wasteland stretched before her.

And time ground to an ominous halt.

# CHAPTER FORTY

## WILDER

Time was a circle without Thea: no beginning and no end. Wilder had no notion of the hours and then days that had passed, but for the vague awareness of the rise and fall of the sun somewhere beyond the pines.

He kept himself as busy as a man stranded in the middle of a frozen nowhere could: tending to the horses, gathering firewood, building a makeshift shelter, hunting. A simple existence punctuated by bodily needs and the changing colour of the sky.

At some point, he was wrenched from the haze of his days by a throbbing sensation across his forearm. It was the wound from the skirmish with the arachne. And the venom that had coated the cut.

'... *a fifty-fifty chance it'll kill you. It's slow to activate, so you won't know right away... But basically, avoid it at all costs. It'll fuck you up either way,*' Torj had told the apprentices in Aveum, the same words Talemir had once shared with them as Guardians.

Glad for the distraction, Wilder settled against the trunk

of the tree he favoured, right by the road and right in front of the swirling mist of the mountain. There, he removed his vambrace and grimaced as he worked the fabric of his shirt away from the sticky slash.

A bitter tang hit his nostrils.

'Not good,' he muttered to himself. He'd taken to doing that a lot since Thea had crossed the threshold into the Great Rite. Besides the horses, his voice was the only sound across the expanse, and it temporarily relieved him of the torture of being trapped in his own head.

He stared at the wound. It was on the verge of festering; that was his first mistake. The second was that he *knew* arachne venom was slow-moving, that its effects could sometimes lie dormant for days...

'Fuck.' The last thing he wanted when Thea emerged from the Great Rite was for her to find his frozen corpse.

The sensation at the edge of his senses was oddly familiar, and it was only after he'd cleaned and dressed his wound that he realised what it was. The manacles. They had been treated with some sort of strange alchemy that suppressed his strength. The site of the cut had the same weight to it, as did his whole arm.

He gave a rough laugh, loud enough to startle the horses. Wren had used arachne venom in her experiments; it was the very same thing. He didn't know why he found it so funny, but he laughed again, shaking his head in disbelief. He had probably reached a level of delirium.

Over the last few days, Wilder had tried to keep his mind from wandering to what might be happening within the mountain. Tried and failed. When he wasn't performing a task, his imagination took him on a vivid tour of all the horrors he'd faced himself at the demand of the Furies. He had seen the Great Rites of other Warswords too, in the memory orb. The only comfort he had was that Thea had seen them too, and that he had prepared her for every scenario the gods had concocted in the past.

As another night fell around him, Wilder saw to the horses and fetched the whetstone from Thea's saddlebag before settling into the makeshift shelter he'd built around the fire. There, he removed his weapons from his person and laid them out before him, beginning the methodical task of cleaning and sharpening each one. His blades were in near-perfect condition, but the job gave him something to focus on, something to steady the tremor that had begun in his hands.

As he expertly dragged the whetstone across the steel, he was taken back to teaching Thea how to do exactly that for the first time during their travels to and from Delmira. He had been so fearful of the thing between them back then that he hadn't taken her hands in his and guided them like he'd wanted to, but he'd guided her hands many times since then. As the flames of the small fire danced and crackled, he lost himself in the quiet scrape of metal on stone for a time, the motions of the task second nature to him after all these years.

Outside the shelter, the wind whispered through the ancient trees while dappled moonlight streamed through the broken canopy, casting an almost ethereal glow on the dark and icy surroundings.

Wilder's hand stilled on the whetstone, his scalp prickling as he heard a faint rustling nearby. Soundlessly, he gripped both of his Naarvian steel swords and rose to his feet, creeping out of the shelter, willing the snow not to crunch beneath his boots. Abstractly, he wondered if the spy from the arachne skirmish had decided to make a reappearance. He could certainly use the distraction; in fact, he would welcome a swordfight, or even a brawl if it meant getting his mind off the Great Rite, even for a few moments.

Looking to the horses and finding them calm, Wilder scanned the treeline, noting that the weight of his sword tugged insistently at the gash in his arm. He didn't dare think too hard about it, but he had the sneaking suspicion that the venom was affecting him more than he would have liked.

Twirling his great swords, he stalked the perimeter of the camp, his impatience finally getting the better of him.

'Show yourself,' he demanded, his voice hoarse.

Silence followed, stretching out long into the dark night.

But then Wilder's gaze snapped up – where he heard the distinct beat of wings.

Not membranous as he'd come to recognise them, but feathered. And sure enough, when he scanned the branches above, one sprung up and down beneath the weight of a great hawk.

'Terrence,' Wilder murmured. 'What the fuck are you doing here?'

The bird stared at him with those unforgiving yellow eyes, stretching out his wings before tucking them neatly away with a dignified squawk.

Something else rustled in the bushes and Wilder pivoted, blades still raised, ready to strike.

Snow shifted beneath a considerable weight and Wilder found himself staring at the huge mass that was Dax, his brother's dog. The mongrel gave a soft bark and ran up to Wilder, nuzzling his legs and licking his hands, which had fallen in relief to his sides.

He eyed both creatures with a huff of amusement. 'Sent to keep an eye on me, were you?' he murmured, scratching Dax behind the ears and starting back towards his shelter, feeling the gust of wind by his shoulder as Terrence soared closer to camp.

Feeling light-headed, Wilder settled back in by the fire, and at long last drifted into a fitful sleep.

~

He dreamt of Thea. Of her bronze hair trailing across his chest as she kissed her way down his torso. Of her stormy eyes as she argued with him, the scent of sea salt and bergamot toying with his senses. He dreamt of her swinging her blade and spilling cursed blood. He dreamt of the hot springs and of burying himself inside her. He dreamt of her whispering his name.

When Wilder woke, there was something wrong.

Dax was nosing his bad arm, which he'd been sleeping on. As he came to, the pain and fever hit. Gods, had there really been that much venom in the wound? He'd thought he might get away with a few days of queasiness, but what he was feeling right now – it went beyond that.

With a pained groan, Wilder hauled himself upright, his head spinning with the sudden movement. Half of all arachne victims died. That was the statistic. He didn't want to be one of them, but it wasn't looking good.

Dax sniffed the wound and growled.

'I know, I know,' Wilder told him, fighting the wave of nausea that hit him. He shouldn't have laid down; the horizontal position overnight had given the venom free rein to spread throughout his body. Scanning the place where he'd slept, he only hoped his head had been elevated, lest the poison get to his brain.

Dax's ears pricked up and Terrence let out a warning call overhead.

Wilder lurched to his feet, staggering to the edge of the forest to peer down the long, winding road to Tver. There was a cloud of dust on the horizon, a telltale sign of a force on the move.

Wilder cursed, unable to make out the banners or colours from a distance. He stumbled back to the horses, where he knew Thea had a spyglass somewhere. He damn near emptied the contents of her entire pack to find it, but once he had it in his grasp he went to the road again, sweat beading at his brow with the effort.

He put the small cylinder to his eye and adjusted the focus, lengthening the contraption to cover the greater distance.

Dax was already growling at his heels, and when Wilder saw the colours and banners, his knees nearly buckled.

For King Artos rode right towards him, an entire army at his back.

'Fuck...' he breathed, his mind struggling against the haze of poison coursing through him.

He had to act fast.

With a final surge of energy, Wilder moved. He dismantled his shelter and hid the evidence of any form of comfort. Every task was like a hot lance to the wound in his arm, causing him to dry-retch with the pain of it. He realised with each action that for the first time in his life, he couldn't fight. Not against one man, let alone an army.

And so he made a decision.

Wilder turned the horses loose, discarding their

saddlebags at the foot of the mountain, where hopefully no soldier would enter the swirling mist.

He only took one thing.

The manacles Wren had made with the same foul venom that coursed through him now.

Holding the hefty weight of them in his hands as the drumbeat of the army's march drew nearer, Wilder turned to Dax. 'Make yourself scarce,' he told the dog. 'I don't want Artos connecting anything about this with Malik.'

Daz gave a low bark and remained rooted to the spot.

'Go!' Wilder ordered, lacing his voice with authority, taking some of the much-needed strength he barely had. 'Get out of here.' He shooed Dax away, praying that he returned to his brother at the Singing Hare.

With a whimper, the mongrel retreated into the trees, and Wilder nearly collapsed with relief. He'd seen Mal lose too much for him to lose his canine companion as well.

His vision blurred, and for a moment, a wave of irrational anger washed over him. How had he gotten this far, only for it all to end here? For him to be so close to seeing Thea emerge from the Great Rite, only to be felled by a fucking scratch?

But he shoved those thoughts aside, urgency spurring him on.

He fell towards the tree where he'd left a coil of rope from his shelter. With a ragged gasp, he collapsed into the snow and worked the rope around himself and the trunk, his entire right side burning now.

When he could barely move, he twisted with his back against the bark to scratch something there with the tip of his dagger. A symbol, a calling card.

His dagger hit the snow, and he felt distant regret for all

the care he'd taken with it only to leave it to rust in the wet. But the thought was fleeting as his breath turned shallow.

*Just one more task*, he told himself. *One more thing and you can close your eyes.*

He placed his wrists in the manacles, another wave of discomfort washing over him, and then he locked them in place.

'What do we have here?' came a deeply smug voice.

Wilder took a moment to rally his strength, to inhale a lungful of crisp mountain air, to be grateful that no one he cared for was here to witness his demise. He looked up into the handsome face of King Artos Fairmoore, his will no longer enough to keep the force of the venom at bay.

He met his enemy's green-eyed stare without hesitation, without fear. 'You need not have brought your whole army, Artos.'

'A king of the midrealms is dead because of you,' Artos declared. 'An army to hunt you down and see you in chains is more than justified. But I see someone has saved us the trouble. It appears the rumours were true. I presume we have Althea Zoltaire to thank for your capture?'

'She makes a formidable enemy,' Wilder rasped.

The last thing he saw was Terrence's yellow eyes, and the flap of his great wings against a bright blue sky.

'I regret nothing,' he murmured, picturing stormy celadon eyes.

Then, darkness swallowed him whole.

# CHAPTER FORTY-ONE

## THEA

Dawn spilt like blood across the vast and ancient glassy surface. Thea had been here before. It was the Great Lake of Aveum, or another of its likeness, situated amid the desolate expanse of an endless winter.

Thea stood at its edge, her heart trapped in her throat, her body and mind at the precipice of all they could endure. And yet the final trial awaited her, here on the frost-kissed shores, across the unfathomable sheet of ice before her. It groaned under the weight of an eternal frozen wilderness, and beneath it, blue hues shimmered like the spirits of broken souls.

'A game of fate? Or a game of choice?' came a quiet voice beside her.

Thea startled, spinning on her heel to see a familiar figure.

Anya, as a child, exactly as she had been on the night darkness had descended upon Thezmarr. A shiver raked down Thea's spine.

'What...?' she murmured, dazed to find the girl not in

some strange ethereal form, but living and breathing beside her, solid beneath her touch as she gripped Anya's small shoulder.

'A game of fate, or a game of choice,' Anya replied, the foreboding words eerie in her child's voice. 'That is the trial at play. Will you decide your own hand?'

It was a strange turn of phrase, but not so strange as the scene unfolding before Thea.

'So many choices,' Anya continued, in almost a singsong voice. 'Or have you already made them? Alchemist. Althea Nine Lives. Althea Zoltaire. Althea Embervale. Wraith Slayer. Guardian of Thezmarr. Shadow of Death.'

'What is this place?' Thea breathed as thick mist roiled on the perimeter of the lake and figures on the other side began to take form. She squinted, trying to make out their shapes – their faces – amid the fog, beyond the glare of the ice beneath the rising sun.

A garbled sound escaped her when she saw who stood there.

'No,' she whispered.

'The Furies will it so,' Anya told her, following her gaze across the glassy surface. 'And so it is.'

Kipp. Cal. Malik. Wren. Wilder...

'How the fuck did we get here?' Cal stammered, squirming against the shadows binding him. 'What the fuck is happening?'

He twisted in the otherworldly restraints, imploring the others.

But they were all equally shocked.

And all of them in the clutches of *rheguld reapers*.

A reaper for each person Thea loved, the monsters' talons poised over each of their hearts, shadows swirling around them, dancing at their mouths as though they meant to invade.

Even from a distance, Thea could see the fear etched on each of their faces. Fear and defiance and love. As though they had already seen the horrors about to happen come to pass. As though they had seen themselves, and her, lying broken on the ice; as though their fate was to join the souls beneath it.

Five reapers. An endless expanse of frozen lake before her.

'I can't save them all,' she murmured, her gaze flitting from one loved one to the next, panic, like the cold, latching deep into her bones.

'No,' Anya agreed, her voice so mild it was cruel. 'The real question is... Can you save *any* of them?'

Thea gaped, her heart stuttering, her knees buckling as she opened her mouth to protest, to scream, to curse the Furies themselves. 'How —'

But younger Anya raised a small finger, pointing to three chasms of darkness that spanned the width of the great lake, punctuating the path to Thea's family. 'Those craters there are portals.'

Thea shifted from foot to foot as the mist seemed to encroach onto the lake's would-be shallows. Across the sheet of ice, the shadows around her friends, her family, her everything, were multiplying. 'Portals to what?'

Little Anya shrugged. 'They're created for those who oppose the Great Rite, so that they might enter whenever they wish and challenge warriors who seek their Warsword totems and Naarvian steel.'

'They let monsters in?'

'And others out,' Anya told her. 'They can take you

elsewhere. Out of the Great Rite. To Death's doorstep, to another plane, to nowhere. Only one way to find out.'

'I don't want to find out.'

'So don't cross the threshold.'

Flinching at an echoing faraway cry from Wren, Thea unsheathed her sword and Malik's dagger, before placing one foot on the creaking stretch of ice before her and addressing her sister once more.

'How? How can this be?' she asked, unable to keep the tremor from her voice.

The maze of mirrors had frayed her mind with its illusions webbed together with truth. The Glacier's Embrace had battered her body. But what of the people she loved in the clutches of the reapers? It couldn't be real... Could it? Wilder was waiting for her at the foot of this gods-forsaken mountain of terrors. The others were back at the Singing Hare. Weren't they?

But Anya smiled, the expression far too old, far too knowing for her young features. 'After everything you have seen, did you think the Furies wouldn't test you to the full extent of their abilities?' She eyed the wound clotting at Thea's shoulder, the slight lean in her gait as she favoured her injured ankle. 'Do you doubt the danger of the Great Rite? Those reapers have been summoned through the portals of darkness to test your mettle, your sacrifice. They are as real as the blood you taste on your tongue, as real as the frostbite you can no longer feel at your blackened fingertips...'

Another shiver scraped down Thea's spine like the tip of a reaper's talon. She swallowed the lump in her throat.

'So be it,' she said, and stepped out onto the ice.

The surface of the lake creaked beneath her weight, and

the thin layer of frost across it seemed to shiver in anticipation. She focused on placing one foot in front of the other, mindful of any fractures, any hidden crevices... She had learnt that lesson from the glacier. In the distance, she could see Kipp, Cal, Malik, Wren and Wilder... Each bound in chains and struggling in the clutches of a reaper whose razor-sharp talons teased the flesh above their heart, whose shadows wrapped tighter around them with each passing moment.

'I'm coming,' Thea murmured.

Kipp's shout was cut off by a whip of shadow across his mouth. His eyes bulged in terror.

'I'm coming,' Thea vowed, her heart seizing for him, for all of them.

The ice groaned as she approached the first chasm, but instead of water, she found a moving form of darkness – the strange glimmering crater that young Anya had called a portal. If she ran, she might be able to leap over it, depending on the slip factor, but...

But Thea didn't need to come up with an alternative, because from the eerie portal, a wraith emerged, hissing and spitting, the scent of burnt hair suddenly overwhelming her senses.

She turned her sword and palmed her dagger. The wraith was every bit as hideous and grotesque as the countless others she had slain. She'd carve out the heart of this one as she had all the rest. The screams and shouts from the other side of the lake spurred her on.

Thea lunged, not accounting for the slip of melting ice beneath her boots. Her arms flailed as she fought to remain upright and away from the edge of the rippling chasm.

Heart pounding, she steadied herself and eyed the monster.

*I'll have to make this fast, then*, she told herself.

A blur of silver followed as Thea flung her throwing stars with needlepoint precision, hitting the wraith in its clouded blue eyes, sending it staggering along the ice, on the precipice of the portal.

With a slice of her sword, she opened its throat, black gore oozing from its wound, a screech filling the air loud enough to shake the surrounding mountains.

She leapt upon its body, setting her dagger to its chest and sawing into the rotten flesh, sinew and bone, until she reached its heart. A final scream left the monster's mouth as she carved out the organ in a matter of expert slices, sending the still-pulsing mass flying back into the shadow from which it came.

It was only after she'd discarded its heart that she realised the corpse was sliding back into the strange substance, into the portal of unknown fates – and that its dead hand was still clamped around her ankle in a vice-like grip.

With a shout, Thea slid across the ice, dragged along with the wraith body as its lower half slowly disappeared into the shadow chasm. In a single, powerful slice, she cleaved through the monster's arm, severing it entirely from its body, just as the rest of it vanished into the darkness.

Panting, Thea scrambled back from the portal, prising the dead talon-tipped hand off her ankle and pitching it back into the shimmering substance with a ragged gasp.

'Fuck,' she muttered, her heart nearly leaping out of her chest in the aftermath of the close call. Blood trickled from her ankle where the wraith had clawed her, but she wiped it away and got to her feet at once, eyeing up the breadth of the shadow fissure she would have to leap across —

'Thea!' Cal screamed.

She looked up in time to see a cord of shadow forcing its way into Malik's mouth, his huge figure thrashing against the onyx bonds wrapped around him, the reaper hissing at her in invitation.

Thea tasted bile. She looked around desperately for a way to cross the chasm of darkness. For the briefest of seconds, she was brought back to her shieldbearer initiation test, where she, Cal and Kipp had made it to the Chained Islands from the mainland using nothing but sticks to launch themselves across... But there were no sticks to be found here, and time was running out.

'Hold on, Malik,' she called. Though from his fitting body, her words were lost to him. Panic tried to latch onto her; she could feel it in the air around her, fuelled by the malice of the reapers at the other end. They would take her family one by one, in the most agonising way.

She wasn't going to let that happen. She would save them all. And Furies help those reapers when she got there, because she was going to tear them apart with her bare fucking hands for all the pain they'd inflicted.

Thea took a deep breath and sheathed her weapons for the run-up. She didn't need them throwing her off balance. Taking several steps back, she measured the distance as best she could... and then she threw herself into a sprint.

Thea charged towards the pit at full pelt, ignoring the slip of her boots across the ice, allowing it to add to her momentum.

And then she was airborne, shooting across the dark

void, legs kicking beneath her as the other side of the portal came into view.

She landed hard, slipping on the wet surface, twisting her knee and rolling across the ice with a cry.

Despite the pain and jarring of her body, she loosed a shaky sigh of relief. She hadn't slipped across the breadth of the safe zone at least. She was on solid enough ground, and she could hold her own here.

Squaring her shoulders, Thea faced what came next. There were still two more gates to cross, and five reapers to face at the end. If she could free Wilder and Cal first, then they could help her with the reapers, she reasoned, trying to block out the sounds of their screams and the violent lash of onyx power she could see in the distance. There was no sign of more Naarvian steel, but she had her dagger. Her dagger would have to do.

But Thea's breath was stolen from her as someone emerged from the shadow portal before her.

*Wilder.*

# CHAPTER FORTY-TWO

## THEA

Gods, he was more beautiful than she had ever realised, more fierce, more *hers* than she'd ever allowed herself to dream.

Confusion flooded her, as she looked behind his broad shoulders to find that his form was now missing from the clutches of the reaper. The king of wraiths had released him, and now her Warsword was here with her.

Half mad with exhaustion, her body in pieces, Thea peered upon the face she knew so well, the face she had loved for what felt like a lifetime.

'Thea...' he said, his melodic voice pained as he watched her scrutinise the reapers, their shadows and their captives. 'It's nearly over,' he told her.

Just hearing his voice aloud made her knees buckle and coaxed a cry of anguish from her lips. What she'd seen, what she'd done during the past two trials – she wanted to tell him everything. He would be the balm to her wounded soul. Everything would be alright, now that he was here.

The scent of rosewood and leather wrapped around her senses. Wilder was *here.*

She wanted to cry. She wanted to give in to the weariness that clung to her bones and fall into his arms at last. He would catch her. He always did.

'I know,' he told her gently, reaching for her. 'We can get out of here, you and me...'

As the warmth of his hand closed over her shredded, blood-matted glove, his words almost didn't register. Almost.

But they made Thea flinch, and look up at him with a frown, her fingers clutched in his.

'I can't leave the others,' she said, her words drawing her attention back to where her friends and sister were being tortured on the frozen banks. She couldn't stand it. She had to move, had to get to them —

'You can't save them.'

Thea took a step back, dread curdling in her gut. '*We* could save them.'

Wilder shook his head. 'No. There's too many. And it's too dangerous to fight near the chasm.' He closed the gap between them again and touched the side of her face, tucking her loose, matted hair behind her ear, his silver eyes kind and understanding.

How she longed to lean into that touch, that comfort.

'But we can save ourselves,' he told her hurriedly. 'You can be done with all this madness. You can be free, with me.'

Thea tasted bitterness on her tongue. She took a step back. 'You would never ask that of me. You would never leave your brother.'

'I would if it meant saving you.'

'No.' Trembling, Thea drew her sword and her dagger. 'Let me pass.'

'I can't do that, Thea.'

'Yes, you can. Step aside.'

But Wilder shook his head, and out of nowhere, his own blade appeared. 'You're making a mistake.'

Though it fractured her barely healed heart anew, Thea knew that the Warsword before her was not the same man she knew. Be it an illusion of the Furies, or the dark magic of the shimmering portal, she would not be fooled, not with this.

'I'm sorry,' she murmured, and then she lunged.

Steel met steel and sparks flared at the contact as false Warsword and apprentice danced across the ice. The imposter's expression changed into one of cruelty and malice, and Thea knew she had made the right decision. He swung his blade not to injure, but to kill, and Thea, already weakened from the trials before, buckled beneath his Furies-given strength.

But whoever this creature was who wore the face of her love, he still fought like Wilder, and Thea knew every move, for Wilder himself had taught her and taught her well.

Across the slippery surface of the ice, Thea battled the imposter, meeting every blow with a strike of her own, her teeth singing with every impact, her bones aching. And yet she did not yield. Blood splattered as he sliced deep into her forearm, but she barely felt it, only registered the warm trickle of red across her skin.

The screams from the shores became one constant song now. *I'll save them, even if I die trying, but I have to get through this first,* Thea told herself.

They circled one another, Thea wary of the shadow

portals on either side of the ice. She could hear whispers from both of their dark depths, words to lure her to the edge, promises of victory and power. She could feel the surge of the broken souls beneath the ice as well, beckoning her to join them, down in the quiet depths.

She cried out as the imposter's sword rained down on her, only just managing to block a vicious blow to her face. The force of it sent her sprawling across the ice, knocking the wind from her lungs. Panting, she staggered to her feet, devastation caving her inward as she saw Wilder's handsome face curled into a snarl. He meant to kill her, to peel her apart bit by bit until there was nothing left.

Struggling to get enough air down her throat, Thea took stock of her resources and reserves. There were three throwing stars left in her boot; she still had the dagger she was holding, the dagger Audra had given her, and her sword. If she could just —

The false Wilder charged, the frozen lake beneath them shaking with the force of his power.

Fast as lightning, Thea slid beneath him, cleaving her dagger and sword across the backs of his knees like she'd seen the Warsword himself do to immobilise wraiths. Tendons and nerves ruined with the swipe of a blade.

He let out a roar that shook the mountains.

Black blood seeped onto the ice.

No, this was not her Wilder.

The creature before her was a monster of the underworld, born of the shadow portals that called out to her even now.

Thea let out a scream as she threw herself at the imposter, rage turning molten, fuelling her every move. How dare they take his face? How dare they take his body and turn it against her?

*'There you are...'*

An echo of words once spoken with love.

She leapt upon her opponent and twisted her body around his, a body she knew intimately, in spite of whatever powered it from within.

With a ragged sob, she ploughed her dagger of Naarvian steel low into his gut, through the flesh and wall of muscle, right into the soft vital organ beneath.

She wrenched the blade free once more, before plunging it right into his dark heart.

His eyes went wide, and the splinters of Thea's heart that remained crumbled into dust as those silver irises she had stared into countless times sought hers with the rise and fall of his final breath.

Darkness exploded, ripping across the ice like a tidal wave.

Thea yanked her blades from the body withering beneath her just in time to dig them into the ice like axes, clinging on against the force of the gale that tore across the surface, the lake groaning beneath her.

It was not over.

Thea lurched to her feet, bleeding, her chest aching, and took in the sight of the shadow chasm. She had slain two of its guardians thus far, and she had no doubt that she'd face another after she crossed this one.

She allowed herself a moment to breathe, to rest her hands on her knees and suck in the crisp air over and over. Her strength was fading, both inside and out. She didn't dare take stock of her injuries, for though she could barely feel anything, she knew they'd be far worse than she realised.

And her mind... Her mind felt as though it were in pieces, like the shattered fragments of the mirrors in the maze she'd faced, like the whispers of darkness that were all that was left of the imposter wearing her Warsword's face.

Who had she ever been to think that she could do this? That she was worthy of the Furies, of the Great Rite?

As the thoughts became louder in her mind, she noticed the swirl of shadow at her ankles, leaking from the shimmering gate between her and the next.

'No,' she whispered, straightening. 'This is not how it ends.'

Wiping the blood from the corner of her mouth, Thea spotted the sword of the fallen imposter lying in the snow. She limped towards it, picking it up with a wince. It was no Naarvian steel, that was for sure, but it wasn't entirely useless.

Gritting her teeth, she sheathed her own weapons once more and took up her position. She didn't hesitate, didn't falter, didn't let the biting pain of her wounds stop her.

Thea ran for the crater, springing up into the air at the last moment as her foot neared its edge. And then she was soaring once more, using the imposter's blade to ground herself on the ice on the other side, pinning herself to the solid ground rather than skidding out of control into the next pool of darkness.

The first thing she noticed was the silence.

The screaming had stopped.

Her gaze snapped to the shore, where her sister and her friends were almost entirely obscured by darkness, just their boots twitching beneath the power of the reapers.

A ragged sob escaped Thea, but she remained upright. The lake creaked ominously beneath her, but she stood tall, using every ounce of willpower to keep her terror and panic at bay as she scanned the shadow portal for its dark warden. Only this time, there was none.

Instead, all around the edge of the chasm was something else.

Vines.

Not getting too close, Thea crouched to get a better look. They were the colour of dark seaweed, gnarled and twisted along the ice.

As the icy gale danced around her, Thea's nostrils were filled with a putrid stench.

'A vine blight,' she muttered to herself, recognising it as the same thing she and Wilder had once investigated on the clifftops of Thezmarr.

As if in answer, the thing writhed, ice cracking beneath its grasp.

Thea shuddered. She could only see the tendrils of its limbs at the edge of the ice, but she knew that somewhere deep beneath the darkness, the monster was feeding off a host. More vines wriggled out towards her, the stench intensifying.

*Those vines are poisonous. A mere brush against your skin will cause immeasurable pain. It can get into your brain, too – with the right point of entry, it can render you a husk of the person you were...'*

Wilder's warning came back to her, eliciting another shudder.

But the monster wasn't attacking. Instead, it seemed to guard the border of the chasm, twisting over itself slowly, as though its mere presence could deter her.

Across the wavering lines of the portal, the reapers

withdrew their shadows, enough to show her the damage they'd done to her loved ones.

Wilder was back, his skin and clothes bloody as he fought against the talons holding him in place. That was the Wilder she knew.

Wren's eyes were wide, her brow damp with perspiration and her complexion pallid. Cal and Kipp fared no better; each of them bore the marks of struggle, while Malik seemed frozen in place, terror rolling off him in waves, so potent Thea could almost taste it.

'I'm coming,' she told them, though she wasn't sure if they could hear her.

She took an extra long run-up this time, to avoid the vine blight covering the perimeter of the gate. Once she was across, she could free Wilder. Together, they could take on the reapers and free the others. They had faced worse odds before.

Thea threw herself into action, sprinting hard and flinging herself over the final chasm, hurtling towards the solid ice on the other side.

Her breath shuddered when she landed, the surface slippery but hard beneath her boots. The scent of burnt hair was nearly strong enough to make her gag as the first reaper set its evil gaze upon her.

But Thea was done. She was done with the Great Rite, done with the obstacles, done with the threats to her and those she loved. She palmed Malik's dagger of Naarvian steel, and braced herself.

Thea approached the reaper that held Wilder captive, putting on a show of bravado, as though she might allow the monster a taste of the very thing it lusted after above all else, the very thing she no longer had.

'Take it, if you dare,' Thea taunted the creature, flicking her blades in invitation, praying to the Furies that it couldn't sense her power's absence. *Let it come. Let it find out the hard way that I'm just as deadly without magic.*

A screech erupted from the reaper, and it threw itself at her.

Thea ducked and wove between the swipes of its talons and the lashes of its shadows. She had been dancing with darkness long enough to know its rhythm now. Like a shadow herself, she fought back, no matter the ice beneath her boots, or the wounds littering her body. Determination blazing through her, she felt empowered, even as the other reapers sniffed the air and came towards her.

Five reapers.

One would-be Warsword.

She liked those odds.

Fighting through the onslaught of onyx whips and jagged claws, Thea couldn't get to Wilder to free him. She could barely see the others through the wisps of darkness, through the nightmares the reapers conjured all around her.

But everything she saw, she had seen before, had already faced it in the maze of mirrors and had emerged victorious. They couldn't break her. Not anymore.

She slayed the first reaper by leaping onto its chest and carving out its heart where it stood.

She killed the next by pinning its leathery foot to the ice with the might of her throwing stars and cleaving through its chest with her dagger.

The thud of their two cursed hearts hitting the ice was like the beat of a war drum that spurred her on.

When she looked upon the three remaining reapers, her own heart nearly stopped. For they were poised back at the plinths to which her family were chained. Dark shadows swirled around them, choking the life out of her loved ones, forcing their way down their throats.

'No!' Thea shouted, surging forward —

Blinding pain blazed at her wrist, unlike anything she had ever experienced before. White-hot and ice-cold all at once, it seared through her skin, flesh and bone, agony in its purest form.

Tears streaming from her eyes, Thea whipped around – to see the vine blight tighten its grip around her.

*A mere brush against your skin will cause immeasurable pain.*

Thea screamed as the torture intensified.

Spittle formed at the corners of her mouth as she fell to her knees with a broken sob. 'Make it stop,' she cried, her voice raw as layers of her flesh were burned away.

Somewhere in the distance, someone screamed.

Or was it her?

All she could think of was the agony that tore at her wrist, that inched up her arm, that was destined for her mind, too.

More screaming.

Thea blinked through her tears, through the swirling shadows, to see a reaper reaching into Wren's chest with its razor-sharp talons. And another doing the same to Wilder, and to —

The vine blight twisted its grasp and Thea's vision blackened.

A strangled noise escaped her and she forced her eyes open, forced strength into her one free hand. She groped for her sword, for her dagger, for anything —

Her fingertips brushed Malik's dagger and she lunged for it with all her might, her fingers closing over the hilt. With a strangled noise, she plunged it into the arm of the vine blight, the horrendous scent of it spilling out in force.

But the monster only twisted her wrist harder, forcing a garbled scream from her throat. She retched, the pain making her long for death itself. She couldn't cleave into it; its tendrils were too hard, practically impenetrable as she clawed at it with broken sobs.

It was the screams of the others that stopped her from plunging the dagger into her own chest. She fought with what little strength she had against the grip of the monster, which was dragging her towards the abyss. The agony was nauseating, threatening to consume her to her very core. Fierce pain lanced from where the creature gripped her, all through her body like a hot blade, followed by a wave of wildfire, sinking into her muscles, her bones.

Madness overcame her and she flailed in the blight's grip, jabbing her knife ineffectively at its wiry limbs. It was no use. There was no stopping it, no weakening its hold on her – there was no way but one.

With another shout, hoarse with the chaos that seemed to overcome her, Thea palmed her weapon. And with a swift, precise motion, she carved not through the vine blight, but through her own arm.

The scream that tore from her was more animal than human.

She felt every inch of the blade as it passed through skin, tissue, bone.

Her breathing changed. Short, shallow gasps that refused to pump the frigid air into her lungs.

Red blood spurted from the gaping wound. Thea nearly fell with the momentum as the blade cleaved through the last remaining layers of flesh.

The pain was like fire, blazing at the end of her wrist, and Thea's remaining hand shook so badly that she dropped her dagger as she scrambled back from the shadow chasm, dragging herself through her own blood.

The vine blight hissed and sputtered, coiling around itself, her severed hand still in its writhing tendrils.

Tasting bitter bile at the back of her throat, Thea nearly slipped in a puddle of crimson as she stood, swaying as she clutched the bloodied stump of her wrist to her chest. The warmth of her own blood seeped through her clothes as she panted through the pain and fought the urge to retch again. Spots swam in her vision, but she stayed upright.

She had made one unimaginable choice after the other. Storm wielder or Warsword. Her lover or her friends. Her hand or her life... And now she stared at several more.

Wilder or Wren or Cal or Kipp or Malik.

Her magic was gone. Her sword was gone. Malik's dagger was gone. All that she had left was Audra's jewelled ceremonial dagger, a letter opener against the monsters before her.

Pain was a constant now, so prominent that she could hardly tell where one wound ended and another began. Her clothes were in tatters, crusted with blood, her braid half undone and equally matted. Her ankle threatened to give out beneath her, while blood still pulsed from the stump of her wrist.

Althea Embervale was in pieces, and yet... And yet she stood, clutching the tiny blade in her one remaining hand.

A spark of energy teased her fingertips, a whisper of what once was.

It should have been impossible, but there was no denying

that sputter of power from within. She knew its song better than she knew herself.

Tilting her head to the sky, she embraced it all. The love, the pain, the reforging of herself amid the chaos. And there, barely able to stand, blood still flowing from her wounds, Thea decided that she would sacrifice no more.

She would not choose. She had been made to choose her whole life. No longer.

She had proven to within an inch of her life that she was strong of body, strong of mind, and at long last, strong of heart.

Thea gripped the dagger and raised her chin in defiance, ready to meet her fate.

'Even the smallest blade can make a difference,' she murmured.

She tasted rain in the wind. And then, the air crackled.

Thea breathed her first easy breath, recognising the call of the storm, recognising the surge as her own power, of which she had barely scratched the surface.

Until now.

*I am the storm.* The words echoed in her mind like a mantra.

Thea took hold of that kernel of magic inside and let it bloom, let it unfurl into something fierce and unforgiving.

Searing agony lanced through her as lightning cauterised her wounds, her flesh burning into newly formed scars. Thea let out a warrior cry as her magic charged through her, through the frozen lake beneath her. Brilliant white bolts danced across her skin and erupted into the air around her.

Ready to unleash herself upon the world, Thea drew upon her magic and used it as the extension of herself that it was, calling bolts of lightning into being and taking aim at the remaining reapers.

Their shrieks became the melody of her storm, only serving to enrapture her thunder and lightning further, the snow swirling around her, around the entire lake just as she commanded.

Her lightning cleaved the chains holding her friends apart, and she let the storm rage on, refusing to contain it or herself for anyone or anything. She forged the chaos in the sky and the thundersnow that now swarmed, engulfing the frozen lake.

With one hand, Thea summoned the might of ancient storms, everything around her crackling and churning with dark clouds, swelling with unimaginable energy, energy that she alone could master. Bolts of blue-white lightning exploded in countless forks, spearing the ground below, illuminating the frozen wasteland and banishing the shadow portals across the lake's surface in a near-blinding blaze.

'I am the storm.'

Finally, she speared the screaming reapers with her lightning, burning their hearts with storm magic from the inside out.

*One. Two. Three.*

She conjured and wielded the storm, chasing the wisps of darkness with a torrent of snow and lightning, brilliant flakes careening across the land in a deadly gale.

Thea stood at the heart of it all, splitting the sky open, inviting the blizzard to dance with her storm, charging each flake of snow with her magic, causing them to glow with a vibrant iridescence, before drawing them together in a halo of brilliant lightning. The force of it swallowed everything, an electrifying crown of her own making.

Thea's thundersnow wiped away the final traces of darkness, of blood, of pain, and shook the very foundations of the mountain upon which she stood.

For she was back where this had all begun, back on the Furies' mountain.

And she was alone.

Wilder, Wren, Cal, Kipp and Malik were gone.

Thea was resolute in her fortress of ice and power, channelling the very essence of the storm raging above her. She let her magic rage and clash, leaving a trail of frozen devastation in its wake.

She was unwavering, immovable – even as three cloaked figures emerged from the blizzard before her.

Thea gave the storm pause as each woman lowered her hood.

She knew them in her heart.

The original Warswords themselves.

The Furies.

# CHAPTER FORTY-THREE

## THEA

'You carry yourself like a queen, Althea Embervale,' the first Fury said, her expression unreadable.

The three goddesses were fierce and radiant before Thea, eyes ablaze like molten gold. The eternal guardians of the Great Rite, of the midrealms themselves.

It was only in their ethereal presence that Thea remembered that their names weren't known – that after all the legends told across the ages, their names had not lived on. They had not been honoured in title or individual esteem. Rather, the force of them had been reduced to a woman's anger, a woman's rage.

The Furies.

And yet together, they formed a triarchy unlike anything the realms had ever seen. They stood in front of Thea now, unwavering against the advancing tides of chaos, determining the fate of men, and now Thea herself.

'Did you not hear me, Althea Embervale?' the Fury spoke again. 'I said you carry yourself like a queen.'

*Embervale...* Pain throbbed everywhere, and Thea's voice

was hoarse, but she lifted her chin when she addressed the great gods before her. 'No,' she told them. 'I carry myself like a Warsword.'

A slow grin spread across each beautiful face before her.

'A new Warsword stands before us, then, sisters... One who can command storms as well as blades, it seems.'

'How?' Thea managed to croak. 'I thought I had to choose.'

'And you did,' the Fury replied.

'But...'

'But you were not born to wield steel and steel alone. We have never seen such fortitude of mind, body and heart before... It takes something more to reconjure magic that has been stripped away.'

Thea was a trembling mess, shock settling into her bones. 'Does this mean... Does it mean that I can be both? Both Warsword and storm wielder?'

A knowing smile tempted the Fury's lips. 'Who's going to stop you?' she said.

Those words washed over Thea like a distant dream, and she found that she could only stare, the remnants of her thundersnow fading quietly around them, until there was only an endless expanse of white. Slowly, the pain she had felt so intensely only moments before ebbed away.

Looking down, she realised that although she was still drenched in blood, she had *both* hands.

A soft cry escaped her as she turned them over before her, examining each and every finger and the lines of her palms. Thea wasn't ready to tear her gaze away from the hand she thought she'd lost. She could move it freely, every finger bending to her will, her clenched fist as strong as it had always been.

'It happened,' the second Fury told her, watching her with fascination. 'In a way. Lift your sleeve.'

Unable to find her words, Thea pushed the ragged, stained material up. Around her wrist was a horrific scar, thick and ugly, mangled as though the torn flesh had been melded back together with little skill.

The third Fury addressed her. 'You will feel it for the rest of your life.'

'And my sister? My friends? My...' The word caught in Thea's throat.

'Alive.'

Relief barrelled through Thea, and it was only then that she tried to swallow the rock in her throat and look up, taking in the sight of the gods before her, the gods that had created every nightmare she'd just endured.

The three Furies stood side by side, emanating glory and immortality, power and wisdom. They were alike in so many ways, and unlike in so many others. Untouchable and yet everywhere all at once. From their beauty and grace alone, they could have been sisters.

The thought was fleeting as Thea met their assessing gazes with one of her own. There was something otherworldly about them, but Thea couldn't pinpoint what made them so. It was not the flecks of golden ferocity in their eyes, nor the intricate, shimmering armour they wore over long skirts...

Her vision blurred and it took every last shred of willpower to keep herself upright. 'I passed,' was all she managed.

'You did,' the first Fury allowed. 'It was quite a Rite...'

She watched Thea as though she were a specimen to be studied, her gaze flicking to the jewelled dagger Thea couldn't remember sheathing at her belt. Her fingertips tingled with power as she touched its pommel.

'It's a beautiful weapon,' the Fury said, her expression unreadable.

'It belongs to a fellow woman warrior,' Thea heard herself say, wishing Audra was here to witness the moment.

'Yes, it does,' the Fury replied, before tearing her gaze from the blade.

With a wave of her hand, Malik's dagger of Naarvian steel materialised at Thea's belt once more, leaving Thea lost for words but for the hoarse *Thank you* that managed to pass her lips.

'Your efforts were valiant. There are few who can face themselves as well as their nightmares and emerge whole on the other side.'

Thea felt anything but whole. She doubted she'd feel like that until she saw Wren, Cal, Kipp and Malik for herself. She doubted she'd feel anything until Wilder wrapped his strong arms around her and they could speak those words they'd held back to one another... Warsword to Warsword. But Thea kept those thoughts to herself.

The second Fury spoke next. 'You will be honoured with all that a Warsword of the midrealms is owed.'

Thea let out a breath, but didn't dare speak. Not yet.

'The rulers will bestow their gifts upon you when you return to their lands. But there is one piece we present you with here and now...' The third Fury stepped forward, her empty hands outstretched before her.

A great sword materialised there.

Its blade gleamed, honed to perfection, its sharp edge tapering elegantly into a lethal point. It had been crafted masterfully, exuding an aura of both beauty and power. Thea could barely breathe. For how long had she dreamt of this moment? For how long had she imagined a blade of her own?

'Are you ready to take your Warsword vows?' the first Fury said.

Dazed, Thea nodded. 'Yes.'

Light danced on the flat of the blade as the Fury spoke her next words. 'Hold the sword and you will hear the words. Make your oath now.'

Heart pounding, Thea reached for the blade, wrapping her hand around the hilt covered in supple leather. At the contact, an ancient magic swept over her, words forming in her mind just as the Fury had promised.

She found herself speaking. 'I, Althea Zoltaire —'

'But *that* is not your name, storm wielder...' the Fury offered in gentle reprimand.

Thea faltered, adjusting her grip on the blade. Her magic hummed in response to that foreign power, stirring within. She listened again.

Her voice was stronger this time. 'I, Althea Embervale, pledge my sword and my life to the protection of the midrealms.'

She felt the depth of that promise in her bones, and the rest of the words fell from her tongue in a steady stream.

'In the light of the Furies, I swear my allegiance, my loyalty, to casting the evil from these lands. I will hunt. I will punish. I will kill. Any and all who threaten these kingdoms. My blood, my steel, are yours. I vow that in the end of days, I will answer the call.'

As her oath left her lips, Thea gripped the sword fully in her hands, the rest of the strange world fading away as she gauged the weight of it. She'd never seen a more beautiful blade, had never held something that fitted her so perfectly.

The sword sang in her grasp, and she felt the whisper of its magic, its origin.

'Naarvian steel,' she breathed before she could stop herself.

'Yes, storm wielder. Naarvian steel. The last of it, mined straight from the source. You are a Warsword now.'

The Fury touched the tip of her finger to the sharp point of the blade, and suddenly Thea could see it unfolding... The star shower with which the Furies themselves had struck the kingdom, a blur of bright, brilliant streaks across the night sky. The crater forming deep in the earth below, singing with their power, their magic.

Now, Thea held it in her hands. At long last, she'd found the missing piece of herself... and it had been forged with blood and steel.

She bowed her head. 'Thank you.'

'And yet, this is not all you ask of us,' the third Fury said. 'Not all you had hoped for in the Great Rite.'

'No...' Thea whispered.

'Then ask what you must,' the Fury told her. 'You have one question.'

Thea lowered her new sword to her side, her body still singing with the weight of it in her palm. She met each Fury's gaze, pushing her shoulders back. They could grant her time, a life to share with Wilder, with the family she had made along the dark and stormy road. This was the moment she had waited for all her life, the opportunity to take fate into her own hands and master her own destiny.

And so she took it.

'What are your names?' she asked, her voice quiet yet firm.

Their expressions mirrored one another, and told Thea it wasn't often that the great Furies themselves were surprised.

'That is not the question you came here with.'

'No,' Thea admitted. 'It's not. But it is my question all the same.'

'No man who came before you asked such a thing.'

'I'm not a man.'

A long, lingering silence followed.

'Why do you ask it now?' the first Fury asked her at last.

Each of her own titles surged through her. *Thea. Althea Nine Lives. Althea Zoltaire. Althea Embervale. Shieldbearer. Guardian. Wraith Slayer. Shadow of Death. Warsword. Heir.*

'Because there is power in names,' Thea replied. 'And women whose might is etched in history deserve to have their names carved there too.'

The Furies exchanged looks with one another, a silent conversation taking place between them before the third stepped forward. 'This is all you ask?'

'It's all I ask.'

The goddess nodded. 'Then I am Iseldra.'

The second came forward next. 'And I am Morwynn.'

The first Fury, the one who had addressed her as the Rite had faded around her, smiled now. 'And I am Valdara.'

*Iseldra, Morwynn and Valdara...*

'It's an honour to meet you.' Thea bowed low. She wondered if it would be the only bow she ever made of her own free will to those who had earnt it, rather than out of obligation.

'The honour is ours,' Valdara said.

The trio of goddesses watched her intensely and silence pulsed in the gulf that opened up between her and the

Furies. Thea's fingertips tingled, with her magic or theirs, she didn't know.

At long last, she turned to leave, to put the Great Rite behind her.

'Althea,' Morwynn called her back. 'Regarding the other question you had.'

Iseldra gave Thea a knowing look. 'Immortality.'

'We are glad you didn't ask it,' Valdara said, clasping her hands in front of her. 'For we would not have granted it to you.'

Stunned, Thea could only stare at the goddesses before her. She didn't know how much more her heart could take.

'You will do more than enough in the time you have left,' Valdara continued, her voice laced with kindness.

But Iseldra gave Thea a far sterner look. 'There is too much love in your heart for you to be an immortal.'

Thea's stomach bottomed out. 'I —'

Morwynn raised a hand, silencing her. 'You cannot live forever without love...'

Valdara came forward again, fitting her palm over the fate stone that rested beneath Thea's shirt. 'And you will love no other.'

The piece of jade warmed against Thea's skin under the Fury's touch, and she stared at the gods. There was more to the words leaving their lips, she was sure of it, but...

'Go now, Althea Embervale, Warsword and storm wielder of the midrealms. There is much to do.'

Thea's grip on her Naarvian steel sword tightened, and despite the ache in her heart, she knew there no convincing them.

*You will love no other.*

'Thank you,' she told them, bowing her head. 'I will aim to be worthy of the honours you have bestowed here.'

As the words left her lips, thick white mist swept in, obscuring the Furies from her view, lifting her into the air in a whirl of snow and light. Moments from the trials flashed before her as her body was pulled through time and space, the frost-kissed wind tangling her hair, stinging her cheeks.

Then she felt the ground beneath her boots.

Not the slippery glass surface of the lake, but real, solid earth packed with snow. When she moved, she felt it – the Furies-given strength, speed and agility – click into place. It was surreal, to suddenly have such power behind every movement, as though her body were too fast and strong for her surroundings all of a sudden. She marvelled at it for a moment. She had been strong before, fitter and faster than she had ever been in her life. But now? Now she was unstoppable.

As she took another step forward, she felt something close around her arm.

She glanced down and gasped.

Her Warsword totem.

Made of perfect steel, it shone bright in the ethereal afterglow of the Furies: two crossed swords, with a third cutting down the middle.

Thea ran her thumb over it, almost not daring to believe that at long last, she had one of her own.

But hers was different to those she had studied so intensely before. Her totem had an addition she'd never seen.

Behind the three blades were streaks of lightning.

'What the...' she muttered, dropping her hand to her side, her wrist twinging slightly with the movement.

*I'll deal with that later*, she decided. The only thing she wanted to do now was to see Wilder, to throw herself into his arms and rejoice in her victory, in *their* victory. She knew she would never regret her question, her choice; the Furies themselves had told her as much. Thea knew in her heart that whatever fate awaited her, she would rather live a single year with Wilder Hawthorne than face a thousand lifetimes without him.

Slowly but surely, the swirling mist receded, revealing a crisp snowy day beyond.

But Wilder wasn't there.

In his place was an army.

Harenth's army, to be precise, with King Artos at its head.

Thea tasted iron on her tongue as she marched towards the king, her hand resting on her Naarvian steel blade, her Warsword totem gleaming in the winter sun. In that moment, she forgot everything. Who she was meant to be, who Wilder was to the crown. She forgot the politics at play and all that mattered in the world kissed by darkness around her.

Only one thing, one man, mattered.

'Where is he?' she demanded, the thunderstorm brewing within. 'Where is my —'

'Prisoner?' Torj Elderbrock finished for her.

Out of nowhere, the Bear Slayer stepped between Thea and King Artos smoothly, clasping her hands in his, squeezing them hard in warning. 'Congratulations, Warsword Zoltaire,' he said. 'On both the Rite and your triumph here. We know we have you to thank for the traitor Wilder Hawthorne being apprehended once more. The midrealms owes you a great debt.'

# CHAPTER FORTY-FOUR

## THEA

Thea's heart threatened to burst from her chest. Whatever was happening was wrong, incredibly wrong. Why was Artos' army camped on the outskirts of these forests? Why was Torj calling Wilder a traitor again? Where was he?

But she found herself nodding, her instincts kicking in. 'Thank you,' she murmured.

King Artos pushed Torj aside and pulled her into a long, hard embrace like a long-lost daughter. 'My dear Althea. How you have triumphed time and time again! I am so proud.'

Thea remembered a distant time where those words would have warmed her heart, the same way in which Artos' empath ability attempted to breach her exterior now in a bloom of heat.

But Thea was a Warsword now. And she knew him for the treasonous bastard he truly was.

Twice she had saved his wretched life, and the damage he'd done with those chances was reprehensible.

A lesson from long ago came back to her then. *'The first lesson of being a warrior of Thezmarr,'* Wilder had told her, *'is this: know that your actions have consequences. Some more than others. And you will carry those with you for the rest of your life. Do you understand me?'*

She understood, alright. Artos Fairmoore had taken her gifts of life and spat in the face of all she had once believed. Thea knew she did not have long left in the world, but she would end him before her time was done.

Still, she pasted a smile on her face. 'All by the grace of your faith in me, sire,' she said calmly.

Behind Artos, she saw Torj relax. *Later,* he mouthed.

Artos clapped her on the back before pulling away to look at her again. 'Jasira is going to be thrilled. You have made history, Althea. Your name will live on throughout the ages – the first woman Warsword since the original Furies themselves.'

'A victory for the women of the midrealms, Your Majesty,' Thea told him, pressing a hand over her heart and bowing. 'Let us hope Thezmarr allows any girl of the three kingdoms to take up arms as a shieldbearer from now on.'

'Indeed, indeed,' he said, though his attention seemed to be drawn elsewhere.

'Forgive me, sire – time is not the same within the Great Rite. Might you tell me... How long since you arrived?'

The king's face pulled with sympathy. 'I can only imagine the terrors you faced, my dear. It has been five days since we set up camp here.'

It took all of Thea's training and willpower to remain impassive. 'Thank you.'

'Of course.'

Her stomach churned at the sickly-sweet note in his

voice. 'And what of my prisoner? Has the date for his trial been set?'

King Artos looked surprised. 'Trial?' he asked. 'My dear, after the horrifying events at the Moonfire Eclipse, the rulers decided there will be no trial.'

Thea fought the urge to double over as the wind was knocked out of her. 'No trial?' she managed.

'Absolutely not. He was sent to the Scarlet Tower as soon as we found him.'

Thea did stumble then, her whole body crumbling under the weight of her enemy's words.

*'What do you know of the Scarlet Tower?'*

*'Enough... Enough to know that I, too, would have chosen death.'*

It had been one of the earlier conversations she'd shared with Wilder, where he'd been all thorns and arrogance. To think of him there —

'Sire, might I suggest we allow Warsword Zoltaire to retire?' Torj interjected, his stoic presence grounding Thea, reminding her to keep it together. 'The Great Rite... It asks much of its contenders. She will need to recover —'

'Of course, of course.' King Artos waved him off before addressing Thea directly. 'You have our deepest gratitude, Althea. The traitor is where he belongs, thanks to you.'

Thea tensed. 'You have my word as a Warsword, sire: justice will be served.'

'Oh, I have no doubt.' King Artos beamed. 'You will find appropriate accommodations —'

'I'm afraid I cannot stay, Your Majesty,' she cut him off, steeling herself from within.

The king blinked at her. 'But you must rest! Elderbrock here —'

'I was advised to make haste to Tver, sire, to capture a stallion. I will need one for the war to come.'

The king looked as though he wanted to argue, but something stopped him. 'If that is the will of the Furies, then I cannot fault it.'

'It is, Your Majesty.' Thea bowed her head.

'Very well, Althea. Take one of our finest geldings. I insist. Do send word once you have secured your warhorse. The midrealms will have need of you yet.'

'Of course, sire. I am here to serve.' Thea dipped her head a final time before leaving the dark king of the midrealms in her wake, silent promises of vengeance on her lips.

First, she found a gelding, saddled and ready. Then, Thea sought Torj.

'Warsword Elderbrock, perhaps you might tell me the lay of the land for the Tverrian herds?'

Torj nodded, taking her lead and walking well away from the war camp, back to the side of the road, her gelding in tow.

'What the fuck happened?' she demanded as soon as they were out of earshot.

'He was injured —'

'Injured? He was whole when I left him.'

'Arachne venom. Rendered him completely incapacitated by the end.'

Thea could hardly breathe. 'But he's alive?'

'He's alive...' Torj replied slowly, but the pain on his face told her enough of the fate that awaited her Warsword. 'By the time Dax came and got me, Artos already had him.'

'Dax?'

'He's how we've been communicating between the

different groups, and Terrence too. Dax brought me here. But as I said, it was already too late.'

*'That place is every imaginable horror incarnate,'* Wilder had told her and the others aboard *The Furies' Will* in another lifetime. *'A sane man would wish for death before he set foot on that island.'*

*'Has anyone ever returned from there?'* Kipp had asked.

*'No,'* Wilder had answered.

Thea couldn't quell the hammering in her chest, nor the urge to call a storm down on them all as she looked upon the Bear Slayer. 'You were the one to find him here?'

Torj shook his head. 'They had already taken him.' He moved a couple paces before pointing to a wide oak trunk. 'He'd chained himself there. Must have seen them coming. Made it look like you'd captured him before the Great Rite.'

Thea fought against the sob that rose up in her throat as she crouched before the oak, noting the scuff of bootprints in the dirt. But something else caught her eye.

She shifted closer to the tree, her heart catching at what she saw there, carved into the trunk.

A message just for her.

A lightning bolt.

Grasping the grips of her new sword and Malik's dagger, the subtle hum of Naarvian steel the only comfort the Furies could offer her, Thea got to her feet. She clung to the thunder rumbling in her chest and the storm magic rushing through her veins as she turned to Torj.

'Well?' she prompted, her voice hard as iron.

Torj handed her a pack of supplies and pointed to the road. 'If you follow this trail till tomorrow's dawn, you'll come to a fork in the road. The first path will take you to

Tver. There you'll come upon the valleys where the stallions rule.'

'And the second path?'

'It'll take you west, far west, until you meet the seas.'

Thea nodded. 'Thank you.'

'I can accompany you —'

Thea shook her head, her course crystal-clear before her. 'If not at Thezmarr, your place is by the dark king's side. We need to keep someone close. We will need your intel when the time comes.'

'And what will you do?' Torj asked, something wary in his gaze.

'I'll do my duty to the midrealms,' Thea replied, fitting her boot to the stirrup and mounting her horse.

'Then I wish you well, Warsword.'

'And you, Bear Slayer,' she replied, squeezing her gelding's sides with her heels.

Leaving a spray of snow in her wake, Thea didn't look back as her horse surged into a canter. She pressed her body close to the gelding's mane, holding on tight as the icy wind whipped around them. She kept her eyes on the road ahead, eager for tomorrow's dawn.

As Althea Embervale rode across the midrealms, the passing lands a mere blur, she felt the Furies-given strength in her body and in her heart. She felt the ever-present crackle of storm magic too, simmering just beneath the surface, waiting to be unleashed upon her enemies.

She rode relentlessly through ice and snow. The hours meant nothing to her, only that they were hours that Wilder

Hawthorne might be suffering. She tried to keep such thoughts at bay, but there was no stopping them.

The only distraction was the occasional flap of wings from above, where the hawk, Terrence, had appeared, soaring in the moonlight. Thea found a small sense of comfort in his silent presence.

Not soon enough, it seemed, dawn arrived.

A blood-red orb rose on the horizon, spilling wildfire hues across the sky as Thea reached the fork in the road.

A lifetime ago, she had ridden through the valleys of Tver with Wilder at her side.

*'When you pass the Great Rite, you come here immediately... You come to claim your stallion straight away. The horses will sense the Rite on you. They will feel the call of the Furies. Remember that.'*

His words reverberated through her like an echo, and she could almost scent him on the wind. She looked to the first fork in the road, where in the distance, the golden hills of Tver and a Warsword stallion of her own awaited her. Thea took a breath.

*There are times in life to listen to your mentor*, she thought, before turning to the second fork. *And there are times to forge your own path.*

But as she started down the road that led west to the seas, and beyond that, the isles that housed the Scarlet Tower, a beat of wings sounded.

Thea whirled around, seeing nothing.

The wings sounded again, and this time she realised they were not those of the hawk.

Something much larger blocked out the rising sun.

Shadows and darkness, and a pair of great membranous wings.

The ground shook violently as something – someone – landed before her.

Thea drew her sword, her gelding rearing up in fright. She managed to stay on, to control the horse with the Furies-given strength of her legs as the shadows faded and a towering figure emerged from the obsidian mist, twin swords of Naarvian steel swinging at his hips, red-and-black wings outstretched at his back.

Thea didn't lower her sword, but instead, narrowed her eyes as she studied the shadow-touched warrior before her. His dark hair, streaked with silver, was tied up in a knot at the back of his head. Olive skin peeked out from beneath his black armour – Delmirian, if she wasn't mistaken.

'Who are you?' she demanded, noting the wisps of shadows still dancing behind him.

'Someone who cares for Wilder as much as you do.' A determined gleam shone in the stranger's hazel eyes.

Thea twirled her blade, her gaze narrowing in suspicion. 'Is that so?'

'I'm the one they call the Shadow Prince,' he told her, his dark power thrumming in emphasis.

Thea blanched. *This* was who her friends had spoken of? *This* was the man who was meant to be guarding the most valuable asset in Naarva?

Thea dropped down from her horse and took a dazed step towards the huge man before her.

'What are you doing on these roads?' he asked, yet to draw his weapon, but poised for battle nonetheless.

'I'm going to the Scarlet Tower. I'm going to save Wilder,' Thea replied evenly. 'And no one's going to stop me.'

'Are you sure you're up for that?' the shadow-touched prince challenged.

For the first time in her life, Thea let the leash she held on herself fall away, her magic surging forth. She embraced it with her whole heart. Lightning danced across her skin and travelled the length of her sword, sparking brilliant white bolts to life. Above her, ominous clouds rolled in, and the crack of thunder echoed across the lands.

She levelled the stranger with a stare. 'What do you think?'

The winged man gave a wicked smile at the sight of her gathered power. 'Good,' he said. 'Because I want to save my apprentice, and I can't do it alone.'

Thea blinked, again noting the dual swords and a Warsword totem strapped to his muscular right arm...

He offered her his calloused palm and a roguish grin. 'Talemir Starling at your service, Warsword Zoltaire.'

Thea looked from his roughened, dirt-lined skin to his square jaw and clear eyes. The dual wielding champion. The Prince of Hearts. The legend of Thezmarr.

She came back to herself, letting her magic dissipate as she took his hand and shook it firmly. 'You're truly here to help me break Wilder out of the Scarlet Tower?'

'As I said, I can't do it alone. And nor can you.'

Thea dropped his hand and, sheathing her sword, met his hazel eyes with a determined gaze of her own. 'So be it.'

'So be it.' Talemir's wings flared at his back, onyx ribbons of power multiplying around them, bleeding across the golden rays of dawn. 'It's time to take a walk on the dark side.'

Thea watched as obsidian swallowed the world around her, the light growing fainter, the gust of wind from his beating wings coaxing her forward, her storm magic answering in kind. In the near distance, the crack of thunder echoed across the midrealms as a bolt of lightning split the world in two.

For all the uncertainty and danger that lay ahead, Thea knew three things.

First: that she loved Wilder Hawthorne with every fibre of her being.

Second: she would do whatever it took to get him back.

And third…

No one, neither man nor monster, was going to stop her.

'I am the storm,' she vowed.

And so, freshly forged with blood and steel, Warsword Althea Embervale, the Shadow of Death, stepped into the darkness to rescue her love.

# ACKNOWLEGEMENTS

Every time I settle in to write the acknowledgements of a new book, I'm hit with the enormity of the task at hand. I've said this before, but I'll say it again: while a novel is written in solitude, it finds its final form slowly with the help of so many others along the way, and it is those people I want to express my gratitude to now...

First, thank you to my incredible partner in crime, Gary, for your unwavering support and enthusiasm, and for reminding me to truly appreciate the highs and celebrate the wins.

To Sacha Black: voice memo bestie, work wife and life coach, thank you for everything.

Thank you to Anne Sengstock, for always having my back, for your typo-hunting skills, and for being such an invaluable part of my team.

To my mum, Bronwyn, thank you for your proofing skills and support. Much love and many thanks to the rest of the Scheuerer clan back in Sydney as well.

A huge thank you to my street teams, past and present, who have helped spread the word about this series far and wide. I love having you in the Laughing Fox! Your beautiful photos, your reels and memes, and your passion for these characters have meant the world to me. Another thank you to the talented Instagrammers, TikTokkers and reviewers who have championed these books. Special mentions to Ash, Sam, Paris, Lili, Nicki and Sav.

And a special thank you to my lovely patron, Tonia Aymond, for helping with the title of this book.

As always, Claire Bradshaw, thank you not only for your incredible edits, but for the many years of friendship as well.

Thank you to my wonderful friends who continue to show their support in numerous ways: Meg, Angelina, Eva, Lisy, Aleesha, Ben, Hannah, Natalia, Fay, Erin, Danielle, Phoebe, Maria, Podge, Joe, Bethany, Annie, Chloe and Nattie.

And of course, last, but never least... Thank you, dear reader. I'm so grateful that you're here. I can't wait to share the epic conclusion to this story with you all.

# ABOUT THE AUTHOR

Helen Scheuerer is the bestselling fantasy author of the series: *The Oremere Chronicles, Curse of the Cyren Queen* and *The Legends of Thezmarr*. Her work has been highly praised for its strong, flawed female characters and its action-packed plots.

Helen's love of writing and books led her to pursue a creative writing degree and a Masters of Publishing. She has been a full-time author since 2018 and now lives amidst the mountains in New Zealand where she is constantly dreaming up new stories.

www.helenscheuerer.com

ALSO BY HELEN SCHEUERER

The Oremere Chronicles:

*Heart of Mist*

*Reign of Mist*

*War of Mist*

*Dawn of Mist*

Curse of the Cyren Queen:

*A Lair of Bones*

*With Dagger and Song*

*The Fabric of Chaos*

*To Wield a Crown*

The Legends of Thezmarr:

*Blood & Steel*

*Vows & Ruins*

*Fate & Furies*

Standalones:

*Slaying the Shadow Prince*

Printed in the USA
CPSIA information can be obtained
at www.ICGtesting.com
LVHW090725011224
798034LV00023B/270

* 9 7 8 1 9 2 2 9 0 3 1 5 0 *